Lynne Graham wa[s]
has been a keen rom[ance]
is very happily marr[ied]
who has learned to c[ook]
Her five children ke[ep]
very large dog who l[ikes]
small terrier who barks a lot and two cats. When time
allows, Lynne is a keen gardener.

Carol Marinelli recently filled in a form asking
for her job title. Thrilled to be able to put down her
answer, she put 'writer'. Then it asked what Carol did
for relaxation and she put down the truth—'writing'.
The third question asked for her hobbies. Well, not
wanting to look obsessed, she crossed her fingers and
answered 'swimming'—but, given that the chlorine
in the pool does terrible things to her highlights, I'm
sure you can guess the real answer!

THE ITALIAN'S INHERITED MISTRESS

LYNNE GRAHAM

THE BILLIONAIRE'S CHRISTMAS CINDERELLA

CAROL MARINELLI

MILLS & BOON

First Published in Great Britain 2018
by Mills & Boon, an imprint of HarperCollins*Publishers*
1 London Bridge Street, London, SE1 9GF

The Italian's Inherited Mistress © 2018 by Lynne Graham

The Billionaire's Christmas Cinderella © 2018 by Carol Marinelli

ISBN: 978-0-263-93558-5

MIX
Paper from
responsible sources
FSC® C007454

This book is produced from independently certified FSC™ paper
to ensure responsible forest management.
For more information visit www.harpercollins.co.uk/green.

Printed and bound in Spain
by CPI, Barcelona

THE ITALIAN'S INHERITED MISTRESS

LYNNE GRAHAM

CHAPTER ONE

'THAT'S IMPOSSIBLE... I don't believe it!' Alissandru Rossetti erupted from his chair in the midst of the reading of his brother's will, rigid with outraged disbelief. 'Why the hell would Paulu leave that little slut anything?' he demanded of the room at large.

Fortunately, his mother, Constantia, and the family lawyer, Marco Morelli, were the only parties present because all attempts to contact the *main* beneficiary of the will had proved fruitless. Disconcerted by that revealing word, 'main', Alissandru had merely frowned, thinking it would be just like his late brother Paulu to have left his worldly goods to some do-good favourite charity. After all, he and his wife Tania had died together and their marriage had been childless and Alissandru, his twin, had no need of any inheritance, being not only the elder twin and owner of the family estate in Sicily but also a billionaire in his own right.

'Take a deep breath, Alissandru,' Constantia urged, well acquainted with her surviving son's sizzling temper. 'Paulu had the right to leave his estate where he wished and we do not know that Tania's sister is deserving of so unpleasant a label.'

Alissandru was pacing the small legal office, a form of behaviour that was distinctly intimidating in a confined space because he was several inches over six feet tall, a lean, powerful figure, dressed in one of the elegant tailored black suits he favoured. That funereal colour had earned him the nickname 'The Raven' in the City of London, where his aggressive and hugely successful business instincts were famous, as befitted a renowned entrepreneur in the new technology field. Pacing that office, he reminded the family lawyer of a prowling tiger penned up in a cage.

Not deserving? Alissandru thought in outrage, recalling that little red-headed teenager, Isla Stewart, at his brother's wedding six long years before. At barely sixteen years old, she had been rocking a sexually provocative outfit, parading her nubile curves and shapely legs in a clear sexual offer to the highest bidder, he reflected in disgust. Later that day too, he had seen her emerging from one of the bedrooms in a dishevelled state, only moments before one of his cousins left the same room, straightening his cuffs and tidying his hair. Obviously Isla was just like her sister, Tania, who had been brazen, wanton and dishonest.

'I was not aware that Paulu was in any form of contact with Tania's sister,' Alissandru admitted curtly. 'No doubt she pulled the wool over his trusting eyes as easily as her sister did and wheedled her way into his soft heart.'

Very real grief fractured Alissandru's hard driven

drawl as he spoke because he had loved his twin a great deal and could still, even six weeks after the helicopter crash that had claimed the lives of both Paulu and Tania, not quite believe that he would never ever speak to him again. Even worse, Alissandru could not shake the guilt of knowing that he had been powerless to *protect* his brother from that designing harpy, Tania Stewart. Sadly, Paulu's last years had been deeply unhappy, but he had refused to divorce the sleazy underwear model he had married in such haste, believing that she was pregnant…only, surprise, surprise, Alissandru recalled cynically, *that* had proved to be a false alarm.

Tania had gone on to destroy his brother's life with her wild extravagance, her shrewish tantrums and, finally, her infidelity. Yet throughout those excesses, Paulu had steadily continued to adore Tania as though she were a goddess amongst women. But then, unhappily for him, Paulu had been a gentle soul, very caring, loyal and committed. *As unlike Alissandru in every way as day was to night.* Yet Alissandru had treasured those stark differences and had trusted Paulu in a way he had trusted no other living person. And although he was enraged at his conviction that yet another Stewart woman had somehow contrived to mislead and manipulate his brother into drawing up such a will, there was yet another part of him which, sadly, felt *betrayed* by his sibling.

After all, Paulu had known how much the family estate meant to Alissandru and yet he had left his home on the Sicilian estate and all his money to Tania's sister. A lottery win for the sister, a slap in the face for

Alissandru even though he knew his brother would have sooner cut off his hand than hurt him. Paulu, being Paulu, however, could never have dreamt that so tragic an accident might take both his and his wife's lives together, clearing the way for Paulu's sister-in-law to inherit what should never ever have become hers.

'Paulu visited Isla a few times in London during that period that…er…' Contantia hesitated, choosing her words with particular tact '…that he and Tania were separated. He was fond of the girl.'

'He never mentioned it to me!' Alissandru bit out explosively, his dark eyes flashing and his lean, darkly handsome features clenching hard at the image of yet *another* Stewart woman having woven her seductive, cloying charm over his impressionable brother in pursuit of profit. Paulu had always been a soft touch for a sob story, Alissandru conceded grimly.

Speaking for himself, however, Alissandru had never been that foolish. He liked women but women *loved* him, hunting him like a rare breed because he was rich and single. In his younger days he had heard every sob story going and once or twice, in his inexperience, had even fallen for such ploys, but it had been years since he had been that naive or imprudent. These days he chose his lovers from his own stratum in society. Women with their own wealth or very demanding careers were a safer bet for the kind of casual light affair in which Alissandru specialised. They understood that he wasn't ready to settle down and practised the same discretion that he did.

'Knowing how you felt about Tania, Paulu wouldn't

have mentioned it,' his mother pointed out gently. 'What will you do?'

'Buy Paulu's house back from her...what else?' Alissandru pronounced with an angry shrug at the infuriating prospect of having to enrich a Stewart woman yet again. How many times had he paid Tania's debts to protect his brother and shield him from her insatiable demands? But what else could he do in the present? Tania was dead and buried and her sister had not even bothered to attend the funeral, all attempts to contact her directly at her last-known address having failed. That fact alone really said it all about the weak bond between the sisters, didn't it?

'We'll have to track Tania's little sister down,' Alissandru breathed in a raw driven undertone of menace.

Isla blew on her frozen fingers, the gathering wind chilling her face below her woolly bobble hat as she fed the hens in haste and gathered the eggs. She would have to bake to use them up, she thought cheerfully, and then she immediately felt guilty for having a happy thought when her only sister and her brother-in-law were dead.

And even worse, she wouldn't even have *known* that it had happened, had not a kind neighbour driven over a week earlier to break that tragic news in person. Her aunt and uncle, who owned the Highland croft in Scotland where Isla was staying, but who were currently visiting her aunt's family in New Zealand, had read on the Internet about the news of Paulu and Tania's death in a helicopter crash. They had immediately contacted their neighbour and had then phoned to ask if Isla wanted them to come home so that she could travel out to Italy.

But what would have been the point in that trip when she had already missed the funerals? Isla asked herself heavily. It was the great sadness of her life that she had never got to know her only sibling. Of course, they had grown up apart and Tania had been ten years older, and Isla was the daughter who was an unplanned and not very welcome late arrival following their father's premature death. Their mother, Morag, already struggling to survive, had headed down to London with Tania to find work while accepting her own mother's offer to take care of her new baby until such time as the little family of mother and daughters could be reunited.

Only unfortunately that reunion had never happened. Isla had grown up in the same Highland croft as her mother had with grandparents who were effectively her parents. Morag had made occasional visits at Christmas, gifting Isla with vague memories of a soft-faced woman with red curly hair like her own and a much taller, leggy, blonde sister, who even as an adolescent had blossomed into a classic beauty. Tania had left home at a very young age to become a model, and not long afterwards Isla's mother had passed away from the kidney complaint she had long suffered from. Indeed, the first time Isla had communicated directly with her sister had been when Tania phoned the croft to invite Isla to her wedding in Sicily.

Isla had been embarrassed that her grandparents

were not also being invited but the elderly couple had insisted that she go alone because Tania was generously offering to pay for her kid sister's travel costs. Being fair-minded people, her grandparents had also pointed out that Tania had never had the opportunity to get to know *any* of them and that they were all next door to being strangers even if they were bound by blood.

Isla still cringed at the memory of how out of her depth she had felt attending that opulent wedding with all its important moneyed guests and of the unpleasant experience she had suffered when cornered by a predatory older man. But, worst of all, the longed-for connection with her only sibling had signally failed to materialise from her visit. Indeed, Tania's attitude to life in general had shocked Isla.

'No, you can thank Paulu for your invite,' Tania had breezed. 'He said I had to have *some* family member present and I decided a teenager was a far better bet than the boring old fossils in the croft Ma used to rattle on about. I'm moving *up* in life with this marriage. I don't want poverty-stricken relatives with a thick Scottish brogue reducing my status in our guests' eyes!'

Tania had merely been outspoken, Isla had decided forgivingly, the product of a liberal and far less old-fashioned upbringing.

'That girl ran wild,' her grandma had once insisted. 'Your mother couldn't control her or give her enough of what she wanted.'

'But what *did* Tania want?' Isla had asked in her

disappointment after her sister's wedding when there had been no mention of the sisters ever meeting again.

'Och, the only dream that one ever had was to be rich and famous.' Her grandma had chuckled. 'And by the sound of the wedding you described, that pretty face of hers got her exactly what she always wanted.'

Only that hadn't been true either, Isla reasoned wryly, recalling her next meeting with her sister several years later, after she too had moved down to London. Her grandparents had died within weeks of each other and her uncle had taken over the croft. Her uncle had urged her to stay with them but, after months of having helped her grandmother nurse her grandfather while he was dying and still sad over the loss of them both, Isla had believed that she needed to move out of her comfort zone at the croft and seek independence.

'Paulu misrepresented himself,' Tania had insisted with scorn after announcing that she had left her husband and the marital home. 'He can't give me what he promised. He can't *afford* to!'

And shortly after that, Paulu had come to visit Isla in her humble bedsit to seek advice about her volatile sister. A lovely, lovely man, she thought sadly, so much in love with Tania and so desperate to do whatever it might take to win her back. Her eyes stung as she thought that at least Paulu *had* got the love of his life back before their deaths, *had* reclaimed that happiness before fate had cut their respective lives brutally short. She had liked Paulu, had actually got to know him much better than she had ever got to know her sister.

Had Paulu followed Isla's feisty advice on how to

recapture Tania's interest? She supposed she would never know now.

In the snug croft kitchen, she fed the turf fire and shed her outdoor layers with relief. She loved being at the croft, but she missed her city social life with friends. Living where she had grown up meant that even a cinema trip to Oban required extensive planning and a very long drive. In another few weeks, though, she would be heading south again, her promise to her relatives fulfilled. Her aunt and uncle were lovely people; however, they were childless and had nobody but Isla to rely on if they wanted to leave home. It was over twenty years since her aunt had last visited New Zealand and Isla had been happy to help to make that dream come true, especially when that request had come at a time when the café where she had long worked as a waitress was closing and the rent had gone sky-high on her bedsit.

Her uncle's sheep and hens couldn't be left to take care of themselves, especially not in winter or when bad weather was expected, she reflected, casting a nervous glance out at the grey laden sky: heavy snow had been forecast.

She still smiled while watching her dog, Puggle, daringly nestle his tiny body in beside her uncle's elderly and increasingly deaf dog, Shep, the collie who herded the sheep. Puggle adored heat but the little dog was Isla's most impractical acquisition ever. Abandoned on a road somewhere near the croft, he had turned up shivering and starving the week Isla had arrived and she didn't know how on earth she was going to keep him when she returned to London, but his perky little wagging tail, enormous eyes and ridiculously huge ears had sneaked into her heart before she'd known what was happening. He was a very mixed breed with perhaps a dash of chihuahua and poodle because, besides the ears, he had a very curly coat but he also had very short legs and odd spotty black-and-white colouring. Regrettably, it seemed nobody was searching for him because she had notified the relevant authorities and had heard nothing back from any source.

The noisy sound of a helicopter overhead made her frown because the sheep hated loud noises, but she already knew, having checked, that the herd was safely nestled in the big shelter in their pasture, their reading of the temperature as good as any forecaster's. Minutes later, when she was brewing a cup of tea, she was startled when Puggle began barking seconds before two loud knocks thundered on the sturdy wooden front door.

Assuming it was her uncle's nearest neighbour, who had kindly been keeping an eye on her in the isolated croft, Isla sped to the door and yanked it straight open, only to fall back in shock.

It was him... Alissandru—Paulu's brother—the insanely *hot* and gorgeous twin who had knocked Isla for six the first time she'd seen him when she was a naive teenager. There Alissandru was, inconceivably, on the croft's doorstep, jet-black hair ruffling in the wind, dark eyes set below level ebony brows, flawless classic features bronzed by a warmer climate. A strikingly beautiful male, Isla had thought at that wedding while he stalked about the place like a brooding volcano, emanating the most extraordinary intensity of emotion. But Tania had *hated* Alissandru, she reminded herself ruefully, blaming Alissandru for everything that went wrong in her marriage to his brother.

Alissandru focussed on his quarry, Isla, dressed unexpectedly in a long tatty sweater and gym pants, not even shoes on her tiny feet. A woman down on her luck, he decided instantly. Why else would she be back in the family home in the back end of nowhere? An explosion of red curls tumbled down to her slight shoulders, eyes the same purplish blue as violets huge against the porcelain perfection of her skin, her full plump pink lips slightly agape. Another beauty like her evil sister, Alissandru reasoned, refusing to react in any way to the sudden surge of desire. He was a man with all a man's physical weaknesses and responding to a lovely face and beautiful hair was simply proof of a healthy libido, nothing to beat himself up about.

'Er… *Alissandru*?' she questioned incredulously, doubting her recognition because his arrival was so very surprising. They might have been linked by their siblings' marriage but she had never actually spoken to Alissandru before because he had regally ignored her at that long-ago wedding.

'May I come in?' Alissandru demanded imperiously, stifling the urge to shiver even in the black cashmere overcoat he wore over his suit.

Isla remembered her manners and stepped back, muttering, 'Of course…of course. It's freezing, isn't it?'

Alissandru scanned the humble interior, unimpressed at the sight of the one large cluttered room that acted as kitchen, dining and living area. Yes, definitely down on her luck when she was living in such a dump. Some man had probably got wise to her and thrown her out, he thought without hesitation. He was quite sure that the news of her inheritance would make her day and it galled him to be the one forced to make that revelation.

'Er… I was just making tea. Would you like a cup?' she asked hesitantly.

Alissandru flung his handsome dark head back, leaving her uneasily aware of how tall he was below the low ceiling above. His seemingly dark eyes flared to a vivid gold that was stunning below the lights she had on to combat the winter darkness that folded in so early in the day this far north. Unable to stifle the need, she stared, transfixed by those amazing eyes, gloriously fringed and accentuated with spiky inky lashes. Hurriedly, she turned her attention to making a pot of tea, every brain cell scrambled by his appearance into sheer stupidity as she grasped what she should have been saying first.

'I'm so sorry about your loss,' Isla muttered uncomfortably. 'Paulu was a very special person and I liked him a great deal.'

'Did you indeed?' Alissandru flared back at her, eyes sparking bright as the sun in his darkly handsome features, an oddity in his stance and intonation that struck a wrong note. 'Tell me, when did you start sleeping with him?'

In total shock at that offensive question, Isla froze. 'I beg your pardon?' she mumbled as she made the tea with her back turned to him, thinking she must have misheard him.

'I asked you when you began sleeping with my brother. I'm genuinely curious because guilt would explain a lot,' Alissandru admitted grittily, wishing she would turn back round again because he wanted to see her face.

'Guilt?' Still very much at sea as to what could possibly have brought Alissandru Rossetti to her door to abuse her with such horrifying enquiries, Isla gave up on the tea-making and flipped round. 'What on earth are you talking about? That was a disgusting question to ask me about the man who was married to my only sister!' she snapped back at him, colour flushing her triangular face, the colour of both anger and embarrassment.

Alissandru shrugged a broad shoulder as he took off his heavy coat and draped it over the back of a chair at the kitchen table. 'It was an honest question. Naturally, I'm curious and I can't ask Paulu.'

A slight quiver in his accented drawl attracted Isla's attention to the reality that Alissandru had been hit very hard by the loss of his twin, much harder than she had been hit by the loss of a sister she had only met on a handful of occasions. Alissandru Rossetti was grieving, and her anger dwindled a little in response to that awareness.

'I don't know why you would even think to ask me a question like that,' Isla admitted more levelly while watching him as though he were an unexploded firework still fizzing dangerously.

Paulu had once told her despairingly that Alissandru could not comprehend the love that Paulu had for Tania because he had never been in love and lacked the emotional depth to even fall in love, but Isla, at only her second look at Alissandru, thoroughly disagreed with that belief. In Alissandru, Isla saw a highly volatile male who literally *seethed* with emotion, every flashing tautening of his features, every spark of brightness in his extraordinary eyes telegraphing that reality.

He stood poised there below the stark light above him, blue-black hair gleaming with the gloss of expensive silk, the smooth hard planes of his flawless face the colour of bronze and doing nothing to hide the strength of his grim jaw line or the angle of his arrogant aristocratic nose, while the faint shadowing of stubble growth darkening the skin round his mouth only highlighted the sensuality of his chiselled lips. Heat mushroomed inside Isla, increasing her discomfiture.

So, she genuinely *didn't* know about the will? Did he look that stupid?

Alissandru tensed, hating the role forced on him by circumstance, wide shoulders straightening, long, powerful legs bracing with instinctive distaste. 'I asked that question because in his will Paulu left everything he possessed in this world to *you*.'

Isla's lips fell open in disbelief and she stared back

at him in silence for several seconds before stumbling into speech again. 'No…no, he couldn't have done that…for goodness' sake, *why* would he have done that? That would be crazy!'

Alissandru hitched an unimpressed ebony brow. 'And you're still trying to say you didn't have sex with him? Not even when he was getting friendly with you while he and Tania were separated? I'm sure only a purist would condemn you for loosening the knicker elastic at that point when he was legally *almost* a free man…'

Isla finally unfroze with those deeply offensive and aggressive words still echoing in her incredulous ears. She marched over to the door and dragged it wide, ushering in a blast of icy air that made Alissandru Rossetti shiver. 'Get out!' she told him fiercely. 'Get out and never come near me again!'

Impervious to the command, Alissandru merely laughed. 'Yes, let's take the gloves off, *cara*. Let me see the *real* Isla Stewart!'

Puggle was growling soft and low and circling Alissandru's feet while being ignored.

'Out!' Isla said again with biting emphasis, blue eyes purple with fury.

Still as a granite pillar, Alissandru surveyed her with cynical amusement, much as though he were watching an entertaining play. Maddened by that lack of reaction, Isla grabbed up his fancy overcoat and pitched it out of the door onto the frozen ground outside. *'Leave!'* she repeated doggedly.

Alissandru shrugged again with blatant unconcern.

'I have nowhere to go until the helicopter comes back to pick me up in an hour's time,' he told her.

'Then you should work at being a politer visitor. I've had enough of you for one day!' Isla replied with spirit. 'You're the most hateful man and I'm finally seeing why my sister loathed you.'

'Do we have to bring that whore into the conversation?' Alissandru asked so smoothly she almost missed the word.

And Isla just lost it at that point. Her sister was dead and she deeply regretted that fact because it meant that she could no longer hope to attain the relationship she had longed to have with Tania. His lack of respect for the departed was too much to be borne and she rushed at him, attempting to slap him, getting caught up instead by two powerful arms that held her back.

'You bastard…you absolute bastard!' she shouted at him in tears. 'How dare you call Tania that when she's gone?'

'I said it to her face as well. The married man she deserted Paulu for was neither the first lover she took nor the last during their marriage,' Alissandru informed her smoothly, and then he released her again, pressing her firmly back from him as though even being that close to her was distasteful. 'Tania slept more often with other men than she did with her husband. You can't expect me to sanctify her memory now that she's gone.'

Isla lost every scrap of colour at those words and backed away in haste from her visitor. *Was it true?* How could she know? Tania had always done what she *wanted* to do, regardless of morality or loyalty. Isla had recognised that disturbing trait in her sibling and had refused to dwell on it, telling herself that it was none of her business because she had been keener to see similarity rather than a vast gulf of understanding stretching between herself and her sister.

'Paulu would've told me,' Isla muttered in desperation.

'Paulu didn't know everything that she got up to but *I did*. I saw no reason to humiliate him with the truth,' Alissandru confessed harshly. 'He suffered enough at her hands without me piling on the agony.'

And the wild defensive rage drained from Isla in that moment. What on earth were they doing? Fighting over a troubled marriage when both parties had since passed away? It was insanity. Alissandru was grieving, she reminded herself reluctantly, bitter as hell about his twin's need for Tania when clearly he himself—in his brother's shoes—would have dumped Tania the first chance he got. He was not a forgiving man, not a man capable of overlooking moral frailties in others.

'Oh, go and fetch your coat back in, for goodness' sake!' Isla urged him impatiently. 'We'll have tea but if you want to stay under this roof you will not insult my late sister again…*is that clear?* You have your view of her but I have my own and I will not have you sullying the few memories I have of her.'

Alissandru studied her set face. It was heart-shaped, full of determination and unconcealed exasperation. In all his life no woman had ever looked at Alissandru

Rossetti as Isla did at that moment. As if she was thoroughly fed up with him and being the bigger person in her self-control and practicality. Her bright eyes challenged his, her head at a defiant angle as she awaited his response. Alissandru retrieved his coat. *Per Dio*, even inside the house he was cold!

An odd little creature, he reasoned as he scooped up his coat with a frown. No glamour, no grooming, no flirtation or fawning either. He didn't *drink* tea! He was Sicilian. He drank the best coffee and the purest grappa. It was, however, possible that in a temper he had been ruder than was wise in the circumstances, he conceded grudgingly. He had a very bad temper. He knew that; everyone knew that about him and made allowances. She didn't, though—she had talked down to him as though he were an angry, uncontrollable child. He was enraged by that little speech she had made; Alissandru's lean dark features froze into icy proud immobility and he stepped back indoors to head straight for the smoking fire. On his passage there, however, something bit at his ankle and he bent down with a Sicilian curse to smack away the little animal with the sharp teeth set into his leg.

'*No!*' Isla thundered at him, charging across the room to scoop up the weird little dog but only after slipping a finger into its mouth to detach its resolute teeth from Alissandru's silk sock and the bruised flesh beneath. 'Puggle's only a puppy. He doesn't know any better.'

'He *bit* me!' Alissandru snarled.

'You *deserved* to be bitten and bitten *hard*!' Isla

told him roundly, cradling the strange little animal to her chest as if it were a baby. 'Stay away from him.'

'I don't like dogs,' Alissandru informed her drily.

Isla dealt him an irritated glance. 'Tell me something that surprises me,' she suggested just as drily.

Huge ears set wide above his curly head, Puggle rested big round dark eyes on his victim from the safety of Isla's arms and if a dog could be said to smile, Puggle the puppy was smiling.

CHAPTER TWO

CLAD IN HIS COAT, Alissandru lowered himself reluctantly into a chair by the kitchen table. The silence was uncomfortable, but he refused to break it. It didn't help that he had never been so cold in his life or that Isla was still running around in bare feet and clearly much hardier in such temperatures than he was. His body wanted to shiver but, macho to his very fingertips, he rigorously suppressed the urge.

Watching Isla's quick steps round the small kitchen area that encompassed a good half of the claustrophobic low-ceilinged room, he absently and then more deliberately found himself taking note of the surprisingly full curves that rounded out the unflattering clothing she wore. Her sister Tania had been tall and model-thin but, being both small in height and curvy at hip and breast, Isla had a very different shape. The sort of shape Alissandru much preferred in women, he acknowledged grudgingly, momentarily becoming rigid as his body found something other than the intense cold to respond to while he struggled to curb that male weakness.

Even so, his response didn't surprise him because Isla was beautiful, even if she was rather less flashy and far more of a natural beauty than he was accustomed to meeting. She wasn't ever going to stop the traffic, he reasoned with determination, but somehow she constantly drew a man's attention back to the delicate bones of her face, the vivacity in her eyes and the sultry fullness of lips that would inspire any man with erotic images. *Any* man, Alissandru told himself insistently, noting the fine scattering of freckles across her fine cheekbones, even more naturally wondering if she had any anywhere else.

His mobile phone rang, uncannily loud in the silence.

'My goodness, you get reception here!' Isla exclaimed in surprise. 'You're lucky. I have to drive a mile down the road to use my mobile.'

The call was a welcome interruption, however, throwing Alissandru out of a rare moment of introspection and thoughts that thoroughly irritated him. He leapt upright and pulled out his phone with the oddest sense of relief at that sense of being connected with *his* world again. But, unfortunately, the call brought bad news and sent Alissandru straight to the window to stare out broodingly at the big fluffy snowflakes already falling and drifting as the wind caught hold of them.

'The helicopter can't pick me up until tomorrow,' he breathed grittily, annoyance and impatience gripping him. 'Blizzard conditions will hit this evening.'

'So, you're stuck here,' Isla concluded, wondering

where on earth she was supposed to put him because there was only one bedroom and one bed and no sofa or anything else to offer as a handy substitute. Usually when she stayed her uncle and aunt borrowed an ancient sofa bed from their neighbour and set it up downstairs for her use but in their absence she had been sleeping in their bed.

'Is there a hotel or anything of that nature around here?' Alissandru enquired thinly.

'I'm afraid not,' Isla told him ruefully, setting his tea down by his abandoned chair. 'We'd have to drive for miles and we could easily get trapped in the car somewhere. We don't go out unless we have to in weather like this.'

Alissandru expelled his breath in a hiss and raked agitated long brown fingers through his luxuriant black hair. 'It's my own fault,' he ground out grimly as he swung back to her, his lean, strong face grim. 'The pilot warned me before we took off about the weather and the risk and I didn't listen.'

With admirable tact, Isla compressed her lips on the temptation to remark that she wasn't surprised. Alissandru Rossetti had a very powerful personality and she imagined he rarely listened to the advice of others when it ran contrary to his wishes. Evidently, he had wanted to see her today and no other day and waiting for better flying conditions hadn't been an option he was prepared to contemplate. Now his impatience had rebounded on him.

'You can stay here,' Isla announced wryly. 'And I'm sure we're *both* absolutely thrilled by the prospect.'

An unexpected glimmer of amusement flared in his eyes, lighting them up with pure gold enticement. Isla wondered why nature had bothered to bless him with such beautiful eyes when most of the time they were hard and cold with sharpness and suspicion. She shook away that bizarre thought and instead tried to concentrate on what she could defrost from the freezer to feed him.

Alissandru sat back down and manfully lifted the mug of tea, his mother's training in good manners finally kicking in. But even as he did so he was wondering if he should simply have asked for coffee because he had never before been in a situation, aside of his brother's marital problems, where he was forced to make the best of things that were bad. He supposed he was very spoilt when it came to the luxury of choice because the Rossetti family had always been rich. It was true that Alissandru's business acumen had made his nearest and dearest considerably wealthier, but he still had to look back several generations to find an ancestor who had not been able to afford the indulgent extras of life. The tea proved not to be as horrible as he had expected and at least it warmed him up a little.

'Where will I sleep?' Alissandru enquired politely.

Isla rose in haste. 'Come on, I'll show you,' she said uncomfortably, leading the way up the small twisting staircase.

Alissandru's gaze flickered over the three doors opening off a landing the size of a postage stamp. 'That's the bathroom,' she told him, opening up one of the doors. 'And this is where you'll have to sleep,' she added tautly, opening up a room that was rather larger than he had expected and furnished with a double bed, old-fashioned furniture and a fireplace.

'Where do you sleep?' he asked.

'This is the only bedroom,' Isla admitted, sidestepping the question. 'There used to be two but my uncle knocked them into one after he found out that they couldn't have children. He felt the empty bedroom next door was a constant reminder they didn't need.'

The arctic chill in the air cooled Alissandru's face. 'There's no heating up here,' he remarked abstractedly, wondering how on earth anyone could live with such a privation in the depth of winter.

'No,' she conceded. 'But I can light the fire for you,' she offered, biting her lip when she saw him struggle to kill a shiver and recalling the heat of the Sicilian climate, as foreign to her as extreme cold appeared to be to him.

'I would be very grateful if you did,' Alissandru said with unusual humility.

Isla thought ruefully of all the to-ing and fro-ing up the stairs carting logs and coal and stiffened her flagging resolve. He was a guest and she had been brought up to believe that, if it was possible, guests should be pampered.

'I'll go for a shower…if there's hot water?' Alissandru studied her enquiringly, recognising that there was nothing he could take for granted in such a poor household.

'Lots of hot water,' Isla assured him more cheerfully. 'But you have no luggage so let me see if there's something of my uncle's that you could borrow,' she added, heading for the chest of drawers by the window.

'That won't be necessary,' Alissandru asserted, his nostrils flaring with distaste at the thought of wearing another man's clothing.

'My uncle wouldn't mind and he's tall like you,' Isla argued, misinterpreting his response and assuming that he had sufficient manners not to want to be a nuisance. She rifled through several drawers and produced a pair of worn jeans and a husky sweater that looked as though it had seen better days before the last world war, settling both items on the bed. 'You'll be more comfortable in these than in that suit. I'll go downstairs and sort out something for dinner.'

'Thank you…' Alissandru forced out the words. 'Considering what I said when I arrived, you've been surprisingly kind.'

A delicate coppery brow raised as she spun back to look at him. 'I don't think you consider what you say very often,' she admitted with a sudden spontaneous smile of amusement that lit up her heart-shaped face like a glorious sunrise. 'And you're completely out of your depth in this environment, which makes me more forgiving. I was just as ill at ease in your home in Sicily.'

'*Dio mio*… I thought we made you welcome.'

A tide of colour rose up beneath her fair skin, making Alissandru study her in fascination and move several steps closer to stare down at her.

'Oh, my goodness, of course you did. I stayed in a wonderful bedroom and the food and everything was incredible,' Isla babbled, belatedly conscious that she might have sounded rude and unappreciative of his hospitality and alarmingly aware of his proximity because he was so very tall and powerfully built. 'But it wasn't my world and I was a fish out of water there. I'd never even been abroad before, never seen a house like yours except on television…you know, everything in your home was unfamiliar…and rather unnerving, to be honest.'

Alissandru scanned the tiny pulse flickering wildly just above her delicate collarbone and he wanted to put his mouth there. He was convinced that her heart was hammering out the same fast nervous beat because naturally she recognised the heightened sexual awareness that laced the atmosphere between them. *Of course*, she did, he told himself cynically. She was twenty-two, no longer a teenager, precocious or otherwise, and an adult woman in every sense of the word. With that thought driving him, he lifted a hand to tilt up her chin, gazing down into startled dark blue eyes and the surge of pink suddenly brightening her cheeks. She blushed. When had he last met a woman who blushed? It was simply that fair skin of hers, doubtless telegraphing the existence of the same erotic thoughts that were currently controlling him.

Would she, wouldn't she? Alissandru asked himself but he rather thought the answer to the suggestion of sex would be yes. He always got the answer yes from women, couldn't remember when he had last been rejected, and the chemistry between him and Isla Stewart was indisputable. He didn't like it, indeed he despised it, but the same powerful drive that had hardened him to steel with arousal was what kept the human race alive and it was appallingly hard to resist for a man unaccustomed to having to deny such a normal urge. He pictured her spread across the bed with its ugly patchwork duvet set…pale and lush and pink and *freckled*? Sex would be one useful way of keeping warm and it would provide entertainment into the bargain, Alissandru rationalised with ease.

Alissandru slowly lowered his handsome dark head, giving her time to retreat. But Isla was frozen into immobility, disturbingly preoccupied by the tightening of her nipples and the low pulse of heat thrumming at the centre of her body. Once or twice before she had experienced such glimmerings of awareness with other men but the attraction had always vanished the moment they actually touched her, convincing her that the fertile scope of a woman's imagination had to explain a lot of encounters that were later regretted. Yet now, when her every cautious instinct with his sex urged her to back away from Alissandru, sheer curiosity kept her where she stood because she wanted, inexplicably *needed*, to know if it would be the same with him.

And he kissed her cheek and her temples and brushed his mouth with astonishing gentleness across hers in an exploratory sortie. 'Tell me now if you want me to stop.'

Isla quivered inside her skin, entrapped by feelings she had never felt before, her body alight from those fleeting caresses, the sudden heat in her pelvis making her squirm. And the *scent* of him that close… Oh, dear heaven, how did she describe that faint evocative scent of cologne and musky masculinity that made her positively quiver with powerful awareness?

'Do it,' she heard herself urge wantonly, and the breathless sound of her own voice shook her.

With a smothered laugh, Alissandru crushed her parted lips beneath his own and sensual shock engulfed her because with one passionate kiss he inflamed her, and her hands lifted to curve round his neck to steady legs that had turned bendy as straws. He scooped her up against him with a strength that initially disconcerted and then, ultimately, thrilled her. His tongue darted into her mouth, flicked, dallied, twinned with hers and extraordinary sensation exploded throughout her body, switching it onto an altogether higher plane of response. A choked little sound escaped low in her throat, and he set her down and stepped back from her, so aroused by that hoarse little noise she had made in the back of her throat that he had to call a halt.

'I need that shower. I've been travelling all day, *gioia mia*,' Alissandru intoned thickly, hot golden eyes locked to her flushed and embarrassed face. 'Now I look forward to the evening ahead with anticipation.'

And with that unanswerable assumption that Isla knew full well that she had encouraged, he vanished into the bathroom. Her bare feet slapped down the stairs in a hasty retreat and she caught a glimpse of herself in the mirror at the foot, hair a messy bonfire of curls, her face hot enough to fry eggs on.

Why *had* she encouraged him? A foolish thing to do when he had to stay the night and was the kind of man accustomed to easy, casual sex. At the wedding, Tania had gossiped about Alissandru's many affairs and even though Isla knew she shouldn't have listened, she had because at the age of sixteen she had been mesmerised by his looks and commanding charismatic presence. But she was twenty-two now, she reminded herself ruefully, and supposed to be beyond such silliness. Even so, she couldn't lie to herself. When the opportunity had presented itself, she had grabbed at it and him, desperate to know what it would feel like when a man of his smooth sophistication and high-voltage sensuality kissed her. And now she knew and she also knew it would've been better had she not found out.

He knew how to kiss—he really, *really* knew how to kiss—but of course they weren't going to take it any further. She was related to Tania and he had hated her sister, it seemed, as much as her sister had hated him. No, nothing more would happen, she told herself, striving to feel relief at that conviction instead of shamelessly disappointed. As Tania had once said, her kid sister needed to get out there and find a life, but Tania had been so much more confident and experienced, freely admitting that she much preferred the company of men to women.

Isla, however, had been raised with Victorian values that tripped her up when she tried to fit into the real world. Most of the men she had met or dated had expected sex the first night, and those that hadn't demanded sex as though it was a right hadn't appealed enough to her for her to experiment. And then there had been her off-putting *first* experience of male sexual urges, she conceded, recalling in disgust the older man who had followed her up to Tania's bedroom and cornered her at that Sicilian wedding. Ill equipped to deal with such an incident back then, she had been frightened and revolted when he'd tried to touch her where he shouldn't have and that episode had, for years, made her very wary of being alone with men.

She had stayed a virgin more from lack of temptation than for any other reason, however, hoping and trusting that eventually the right guy would come along. But her brain knew very well that Alissandru Rossetti would *never* be that guy. He had hated her sister and was clearly predisposed to be prejudiced against Isla as well. Alissandru would be the last man alive likely to offer Tania's kid sister a relationship.

Apart from anything else, Alissandru didn't *have* relationships with women. He wasn't looking for one special woman or commitment. He wasn't interested in settling down. Catching herself up on that revealing thought train with a mortified wince, Isla crept reluctantly out into the teeth of a gale and driving snow with the coal bucket while scoffing at her own foolishness. Alissandru kissed her once and *she* started fretting about their lack of a future as a couple. How ridiculous! He would run like the wind if he knew! Her grandma had raised a young woman out of step with the modern world, imprinting her with a belief pattern that others had long since abandoned.

And Alissandru would be the worst possible man for her to experiment with, she told herself impatiently. No, she would light a fire in the bedroom for him, cook him a hot meal and keep her distance by dozing in an armchair overnight. If she had roused his expectations of something more than a kiss, and she was convinced that she had, she would make it clear that nothing was going to happen. And with the options a man as gorgeous as Alissandru had in his life, that disappointment was hardly going to break his heart. In fact, it was much more likely that Alissandru had only come on to her in the first place because she was the *only* woman available. Her nose wrinkled. His apparent attraction to her suddenly no longer seemed flattering.

Isla trundled kindling, coal and logs upstairs and lit the bedroom fire while listening to the water running in the bathroom. There would be no hot water left for her use: he must've emptied the tank. The back burner in the fire was efficient at heating the water but Isla was trained to spend no more than ten minutes under the shower.

Warm for the first time since arriving in the frozen north of Scotland, Alissandru dried himself vigorously with a towel and stepped out onto the icy landing in his boxers, passing on through into the bedroom at speed where the flickering hot flames of a very welcome fire greeted him. In his eagerness to reach the warmth of the fire, he forgot to lower his head to avoid the rafters above and reaped a stunning blow to his skull. He groaned, teetered sickly where he stood for a second or two and then dropped like a falling tree to the wooden floor.

Isla heard the crash of something heavy falling overhead and stilled for an instant. Alissandru must've dropped something or knocked something flying. She rolled her eyes and got on with chopping the vegetables for the stew she was preparing, thinking that at least Alissandru had finally dragged himself out of the shower. The quicker she got the casserole into the oven, the sooner they could eat.

What had Alissandru knocked over? Her brow indented because there was very little clutter in that room and nothing that would make a noise of that magnitude when it fell, unless it was the wardrobe or the chest of drawers. Suddenly anxious, Isla called his name up the stairs and waited but no answer came. Compressing her lips, she went up and through the ajar door saw Alissandru lying in the middle of the floor on his back. He was naked apart from a pair of black cotton boxers. With a stricken exclamation, she sped over to him, horrified to register that he was unconscious. What on earth had he done to himself?

She touched a bare brown shoulder, noting how cold he was, and she jumped to her feet to drag the duvet off the bed and wrap it round him. That small step accomplished, she carefully smoothed her fingers through his hair and felt the smooth stickiness of blood as well as a rising bump. She released her breath in a short hiss and raced back downstairs to lift the phone and call the local doctor.

Unfortunately, the doctor was out attending a home delivery but the doctor's wife, a friendly, practical woman whom Isla had known since childhood, was able to tell her exactly how to treat a patient with concussion and warn her what to expect. Out of breath, she hurried back to Alissandru's side, relieved to see the flicker of his eyelids and the slight movements that signified his return to consciousness.

'Alissandru...?' she murmured.

His outrageously long black eyelashes lifted and he stared at her with a dazed frowning look. 'What happened?'

'You fell. I think you bashed your head on something.'

'Hellish headache,' he conceded, lifting his hand and trying to touch his head. He was noticeably disorientated and clumsy and she grasped his hand before he could touch the swelling.

'Lie still for a moment until you get your bearings,' she urged. 'I'll bring you painkillers when it's safe to leave you.'

Alissandru stared up at her, the blur of her face slowly filling in on detail. He blinked because her hair looked as if it were on fire in the light cast by the flickering flames. Her mop of curls glinted in sugar-maple colours that encompassed every shade from red to tawny to gold. Her blue eyes were full of anxiety and he immediately wanted to soothe her. 'I'm fine,' he told her, instinctively lying. 'Why am I on the floor?'

'You *fell*,' she reminded him again, worried by his confused state of mind. 'Can you move your legs and arms? We want to check that nothing's broken before we try to get you up.'

'Who's *we*?'

'You and me as a team,' Isla rephrased. 'Don't nitpick, Alissandru. What a fright you gave me when I saw you lying here!'

'Legs and arms fine,' Alissandru confirmed, shifting his lean, powerful body with a groan. 'But my head's killing me.'

'Do you think you could get up? You would be more comfortable in the bed,' she pointed out.

'Of course I can get up,' Alissandru assured her, but it wasn't as easy as he assumed and Isla hoped because the instant Alissandru began to get up, he was overtaken by a bout of dizziness, and Isla struggled to steady him when he swayed.

But he was too heavy for her to hold and he slumped back against the bed for support, shaking his head as though trying to clear it and muttering something in Sicilian that she suspected was a curse. 'I feel like I'm very drunk,' he acknowledged blearily, bracing himself on the mattress to stay upright.

'You'll feel better when you're lying flat again,' Isla declared, hoping she was right while her brain spent an inordinate amount of time struggling to process his near nudity at the same time as guilt that she had noticed that reality attacked her conscience.

But there it was, a near-naked Alissandru was a shockingly eye-catching sight, particularly when Isla had never seen a flesh-and-blood man in that state close up. Of course, she had seen men in trunks at the swimming pool but had never found her gaze tempted to wander or linger on those men, but when it came to Alissandru, dragging her attention from the corrugated expanse of his muscular abs and powerful biceps was a disconcerting challenge. Was it because she knew him? Simple feminine curiosity? Her face burning, she moved forward to help him turn around on unsteady feet and climb into the bed.

But what looked easy turned out to be anything but and in her fear of his falling again she got pinned between him and the bed and safely manoeuvring him down onto the mattress involved a considerable amount of physical contact that drenched her in perspiration and embarrassment. Finally, she managed to get Alissandru lying flat but by that stage she was painfully aware of the tented arousal beneath his boxers that all that sliding against his near-naked bronzed body had provoked. She pounced on the duvet still lying on the floor and flung it back over him with relief.

'No, you lie there and don't move. Don't touch your head either,' she instructed. 'I'm going downstairs to get painkillers for you and the first-aid box.'

Alissandru gave her a dazed half-smile. 'Bossy, aren't you?'

'I'm good in a crisis and this is a crisis because if it hadn't been for Dr McKinney's wife I wouldn't have known what to do with you,' Isla admitted guiltily. 'First chance I get, I'm going to do one of those emergency-first-aid courses that are so popular now.'

'I'll be fine,' Alissandru asserted, unwillingly impressed by her genuine concern for his well-being.

Tania would have kicked him while he was down and taken advantage of his vulnerability any way she could but Isla's only goal was to take care of him to the best of her ability. He rested his aching head on the pillows with a stifled groan, feeling trapped, knowing in frustration that he didn't dare even stand up when his balance was so out of sync. His vision was blurred as well, only slowly achieving normal focus. He should have told her that he had done four years at medical school before his father's death had made his dropping out of university inevitable. Neither his brother nor his mother had been up to the demands of taking control of his father's business enterprises. Alissandru had had to step in and take charge and if, at the time, he had loathed the necessity of giving up his dream of becoming a doctor, he had since learned to love the cut and thrust of the business world and revel in the siren call of new technology worthy of his investment.

Isla returned with a glass of water and a couple of pills. 'Don't know if they'll help,' she said ruefully, trying to prop pillows behind him to help him sit up.

'Might take the edge off it.' Alissandru drained the glass and slumped back down again. 'I want to sleep but I know I shouldn't sleep for long.'

'I didn't know that until the doctor's wife told me that I had to keep checking on you, waking you up if necessary to work out whether you were getting worse. But if the helicopter couldn't pick you up this evening, I'm not sure how the emergency medics could get through either,' she told him ruefully. 'Lift your head.'

Isla knelt beside him, skimming cautious fingers through his luxuriant silky hair and swabbing away the blood, finally spotting the cut and tracing the swelling beneath. 'It doesn't look like it needs stitches but it's still bleeding a little. You could have a fractured skull,' she warned him. 'Try to stay still. I'm going to get dinner into the oven and then I'll come back up.'

'Could you put the light out?' Alissandru asked. 'It's hurting my eyes.'

Isla switched off the bedside lamp and fed the fire to keep it burning. Before she left the room she glanced back at him where he lay in the bed, his dark eyes reflecting the golden heat of the firelight at her. He didn't look right to her lying so still and quiet, his innate restless volatility suppressed.

She finished the casserole and put it on to cook before laying a tray. That achieved, she went up to check on Alissandru. He was awake and watching the fire.

'I'm supposed to ask you stupid questions now like what day it is and who the British Prime Minister is,' she confided.

Alissandru responded straight away with the answers. 'There's nothing wrong with my brain. It's just working slower than usual,' he told her lazily and he stretched out an arm and patted the vacant side of the bed. 'Come and sit down and keep me company. Tell me about you and Paulu.'

Isla went stiff and stayed where she was, belatedly recalling the inheritance he had mentioned and feeling very uncomfortable at the thought of her late brother-in-law having left her anything. 'We were friends. While he and Tania were separated he came to see me several times to talk about her, not that I could tell him much because I didn't know her that well,' she pointed out tautly. 'I liked your brother a lot...but I assure you that there was nothing sexual between us.'

Lifting his tousled head several inches off the pillows, Alissandru shrugged a bare brown shoulder in fluid dismissal. 'It would've explained a great deal if there had been,' he commented.

'There *wasn't*,' Isla emphasised flatly.

'I'm not going to apologise,' Alissandru warned her. 'It was a natural suspicion.'

Isla gritted her teeth, swallowing back a rude remark about his lack of faith in standards of family behaviour and the kind of people he must know to harbour such a sleazy suspicion. He was a hard, distrustful man and she wasn't going to change that reality by arguing with him. 'Paulu would never have been unfaithful to my sister.'

Alissandru compressed his wide sensual mouth. 'More's the pity.'

'I'll bring dinner up when it's ready,' she said stiltedly, burrowing into the hot press on the landing to find fresh clothing for herself and heading into the bathroom for a shower.

She found it *so* hard not to rise to Alissandru's every pointed comment, but she was determined not to lose her temper with him again. It had scared her when she'd lost her temper to the extent she had earlier because she had flown at him like a shrew and tried to slap him. He had brought out a side of her she didn't like. Being that out of control was frightening.

She dried herself on a very damp towel and pulled on her fleece lounging set, which also doubled as pyjamas on the coldest nights. Coloured grey, the set was sexless and unrevealing. In any case, she was convinced that Alissandru's accident had banished any raunchy expectations she might have awakened by succumbing to that kiss. Thankfully they had moved way beyond that level now, she reasoned, scolding herself for the tiny pang of disappointment that made her heart heavy.

She had only once envied her sister, Tania, and that had been when she'd recognised how much Paulu *loved* Tania, regardless of her capriciousness. Always popular with men, however, Tania had simply accepted her husband's devotion as her due.

But nobody had *ever* loved Isla the way Tania had been loved.

Tania had been the apple of their mother's eye but Isla had barely known the woman and their father had died before she was born. Her grandparents had been both kind and loving but she had always been conscious that she was an extra burden and expense to two pensioners, who had worked hard throughout their lives with very little material reward.

Alissandru's momentary interest had sent Isla's imagination rocketing and made her body fizz with new energy because that kiss had been just about the most exciting thing that had *ever* happened to her. And wasn't *that* in itself a pathetic truth? she told herself with self-loathing.

CHAPTER THREE

WHILE ISLA WAS keeping busy in the kitchen and setting a tray, Alissandru lay back bored in bed and wondered why Isla had yet to ask him *what* she had inherited from his brother. Was that a deliberate avoidance tactic calculated to impress him with her lack of avarice? But why would she want to impress him? After all, regardless of Alissandru's feelings, she *would* receive that inheritance. Her attitude, however, was an anomaly and Alissandru didn't like anomalies. He flatly refused to accept that Tania could have a sister who wasn't greedy. His sister-in-law had craved money the way a dying man would crave water or air.

And moving on from his inflexible conviction that Isla had to be a gold-digger like so many other women he had met, he thought about that kiss and wondered what insanity had possessed him. Tania's sister, *so* inappropriate a choice. But she tasted like strawberries and cream, all the evocative flavours of a summer day and sunlight. Alissandru frowned darkly, forced to recognise afresh that his brain had yet to recover its normal function. That blow to the head had done more damage than he appreciated when his sharp-as-a-tack logic was failing to filter out such a fanciful comparison. Isla was curiously sexy and that was it, no need to be thinking about tastes and flavours, he told himself irritably.

Stupendously sexy, he adjusted, the ready stirring at his groin provoking him to greater honesty. He didn't understand why, he simply recognised that the minute she touched him, or indeed got anywhere near him, he reacted with an almost juvenile instant surge of excitement. A woman had never heated him up so fast or with such ease and it bothered him, because no way was he in the market for an affair with Tania's sister.

Isla brought in the tray, watching as Alissandru dragged himself up against the pillows to accept it. His bronzed skin gleamed in the firelight, accentuating a honed and very muscular physique straight out of a woman's fantasy. Her face burned and she wondered if she should be searching for a pair of her uncle's pyjamas to offer him. But wouldn't that make her look like a prude? It was her bet that Alissandru routinely wore little in bed.

'What on earth are you wearing?' Alissandru enquired as he accepted the tray, his brows drawing together as he studied the furry fabric top and loose bottoms to match.

'It's warm.'

'Where's your meal?' he asked.

'Downstairs,' she admitted stiffly.

'*Per carita*, Isla!' Alissandru exclaimed. 'It's boring up here alone.'

The tip of her tongue slid out to moisten her dry lower lip, discomfiture gripping her. 'I'll bring mine up,' she finally said, feeling a little foolish over her determination to avoid him simply because he made her feel uncomfortable.

She sank down on the side of the bed beside him, both flustered and harassed by the amused glance he flung her as she slowly lifted her legs up after her to balance the tray on her knees. So, it was a *bed*, no need to make a silly fuss about that when there was no chair available, she instructed herself in exasperation.

'You still haven't fully explained your connection with Paulu,' Alissandru remarked softly.

Isla gritted her teeth on her fork. 'We became friends…he was upset about his marriage breaking down and I tried to advise him on how to get Tania back.'

'Good to know who I have to thank for that final mistake,' Alissandru commented drily.

'You need a filter button before you speak,' Isla told him tartly.

'Share with me the advice you gave him,' Alissandru urged.

She turned her head to look at him and, unexpectedly, her heart softened. She recognised the glow of curiosity in his eyes for what it was: a kind of hunger to know and understand *anything* about his twin that he had been excluded from, and naturally Paulu had not shared his eagerness to reclaim his estranged wife with a brother who had probably cheered at her departure.

'Paulu was behaving like a stalker. He was sending Tania emails, texts and showering her with invitations and it wasn't getting him anywhere. Tania was annoyed he had followed her back to London,' Isla admitted ruefully. 'She told me the marriage was over.'

'So, what changed?'

'I don't know for sure because, apart from a text from Paulu telling me they were giving their marriage another go, I didn't get to see either of them again,' Isla confided ruefully. 'But I had warned Paulu to stop chasing her and to back off and give her some space. She took him for granted…you see.'

'*Sì,*' Alissandru agreed grimly.

'But at the same time, Paulu was Tania's security blanket, her safe place, and I suspect that if he did show a little backbone and she started to fear that she truly was losing him for ever, she might think again.'

'It's the eighth wonder of the world that Paulu and I shared the same womb,' Alissandru intoned. 'We barely had a thought in common.'

'You were twins.'

'Fraternal. I inherited more of my father's traits but Paulu didn't have an aggressive bone in his body.'

'He had much more important gifts,' Isla cut in. 'He was kind and loving and generous.'

'*Sì, very* generous,' Alissandru sliced in darkly, setting his tray down and welding his broad shoulders to the headboard in physical emphasis of his exasperated sarcasm. 'If he hadn't almost bankrupted himself *treating* Tania to her every wish before he married her, he wouldn't have got himself into so much financial trouble afterwards.'

Isla set down her tray as well, her heart-shaped face troubled. 'Is that what you always do? Take the gloomy view?'

'The truth can hurt and I don't avoid it,' Alissandru assured her.

'But what you're refusing to see is how *happy* Tania made your brother. You may not have liked her, but *he* adored her and I'm so grateful they got back together before they died,' Isla confessed emotively. 'How happy was he the last time you saw him?'

Unimpressed by her sentimental outlook, Alissandru thought back to his last meeting with his twin. Ironically, only days before the helicopter crash, Paulu had been full of the joys of spring, striding into Alissandru's office to cheerfully announce that Tania was willing to try for a baby. Alissandru had been taken aback by the unashamed depth of his brother's desire to have a child of his own because it was not an aspiration that had ever entered Alissandru's head. No, for Alissandru, having a family featured only in some far distant future and it was not something he felt any need to consider before he even reached his thirtieth birthday.

'He *was* happy,' Alissandru admitted grudgingly, and even as he uttered those words he felt some of the weight of his grief slip free and lighten his heart. Suddenly he realised what a comfort it was to look back and recognise that his twin's last months had been joyful because he had reunited with the love of his life and together they had been planning a more settled future.

Isla turned to study him, her wide blue eyes full of understanding and compassion. 'And doesn't that make *you* feel better? I know it makes me feel better.'

That truth was so simple it positively shrieked at Alissandru but he had not seen that truth for himself and in a sudden movement he snaked an arm round her and pulled her close.

'*Grazie*...thank you,' he breathed in a hoarse tone of relief, his eyes hot liquid gold with naked emotion.

He had such beautiful eyes, she found herself thinking again, and the spiky black lashes surrounding them only boosted their appeal. And as she gazed up at him he lowered his dark head and crushed her soft mouth under his, sending a wave of such hopeless longing snaking through Isla that she shivered with the effect of it.

'You're cold,' Alissandru assumed, lifting her onto his lap to throw back the duvet and then shift her beneath it and back into his strong arms.

Spontaneous laughter shook Alissandru's body as he held her. 'You feel furry like a teddy bear,' he confided unevenly. 'Is there really a woman underneath the fur?'

Taken aback by both his boldness and his amusement, Isla winced. 'I didn't want to be wearing anything provocative around you.'

'It's definitely not provocative,' Alissandru assured her, long fingers smoothing her soft curls back from her face. 'But then I only need to look at you to want you, *mia bella*.'

Sentenced to stillness by that startling admission,

Isla gazed up at him, barely crediting that she was in his arms in a bed. Could it be true that she attracted him to that extent? Even though he had despised her sister and had revealed, with his accusation about Paulu, a worrying bias against her likely character as well?

'Stop thinking so hard,' Alissandru urged her, a fingertip smoothing the frown line forming between her delicate brows.

The heat of his big powerful body filtering through her lounging pyjamas made her feel warm and secure. He actually wanted her. Alissandru Rossetti *wanted* her and somehow that made Isla feel less alone. But then, at the age of twenty-two she had lost every living person who had ever mattered to her and she often felt alone. Her uncle and aunt were one of those couples so content to *be* a couple that they rarely invited visitors and, although they always assured her that she was welcome, Isla was not comfortable inviting herself.

'Are you warm enough now?' Alissandru enquired silkily, a hand sliding beneath her top to splay across her midriff.

Her breath snarled up in her throat at the feel of his big hand against her skin. She couldn't think straight and an instant of panic claimed her because she had never been in such an intimate situation with a man. Her brain whirred at a frantic pace because she knew that Alissandru would expect sex. And why not? another little voice chimed in the back of her head. Why not? *Why shouldn't she?* She was finally with a man who made her heart beat so fast she felt breathless.

And shouldn't that be celebrated rather than denied or suppressed?

'Yes…you're as effective as an electric blanket,' she told him awkwardly.

Alissandru dealt her an incredulous look from glittering dark eyes and then his wide sensual mouth curved and he laughed again. 'Never heard that one before.'

And Isla knew it was the moment where she should mention her lack of experience because he obviously hadn't a clue, but pride silenced her. He would think she was a freak still being so innocent at her age and she didn't want him thinking *that* of her, much preferring that he should assume that she was as casual about sex as she had been told he was.

'I feel at peace for the first time in weeks,' Alissandru admitted reflectively. 'What you said about Paulu being happy…it helped.'

'I'm glad,' she whispered, lifting a hand to trace her fingers down over his stubbled jaw line, appreciating the masculine roughness of his skin and the dark shadowing that accentuated his beautifully shaped mouth.

'*Maledizione…ti voglio…* I want you,' Alissandru breathed in a raw, driven undertone, his body hot and taut from even that glancing caress.

His sensual mouth ravished hers, sending a shower of sparks flaring low in her belly, and he shifted against her, letting her feel the hard thrust of his readiness in the cradle of her thighs. The pressure of him at the junction of her thighs electrified her, making her almost painfully aware that that was where she really needed to be touched. He leant back from her to lift her top up over her head and she gasped in surprise, only just resisting the urge to cover her exposed breasts.

The cold air pinched her nipples, and she flushed all over as he gazed down at her hungrily.

'It's a sin to cover those,' Alissandru growled, curving a reverent hand to a lush breast crowned with a pouting pink nipple and dipping his head to savour that peak with his mouth.

Her brain in a wild whirl, Isla felt her back arch of its own volition and her pelvis tilt up as heat surged between her legs. He toyed with her other breast, tugging at the sensitive crest until her head fell back, her neck extending as the storm of her response grew stronger. She had never felt anything so powerful before, had not known her body had the ability to feel anything that intense. And then before she could even catch her breath, Alissandru was divesting her of her pants and prying her thighs apart to bury his wicked mouth there instead.

Shock consumed Isla and she parted dry lips to protest. Of course, she knew what he was doing but it was not something she had ever thought would appeal to her, at least until Alissandru applied his tongue to the most sensitive spot on her entire body and a spectacular wave of sensation engulfed her. And the tide of sensation built and built as he entered her with his fingers until she was writhing in response, agonised gasps torn from her parted lips, and for a split second as that explosive peak of pleasure gripped her she saw stars, jerking and out of control, blissful cries wrenched from her lips.

Alissandru grinned down at her with outrageous satisfaction. 'I love a passionate woman,' he told her thickly. 'You match me every step of the way.'

Isla was in a daze of shattered satiation as he shifted lithely over her and lifted her legs to increase his access to her still-thrumming body. She was reeling with disconcertion at what he had done and what she had felt and even then she was questioning what they were doing when he was supposed to have concussion.

'Do you feel all right?' she asked abruptly.

'In a few minutes I will feel one hell of a lot better,' Alissandru asserted with unquenchable certainty, and she felt the powerful surge of him against her swollen entrance.

There wasn't time for her to tense because he sank into her with raw energy and suddenly he was where she had never felt anyone before and he was thrusting deep and hard. She flung her head back and squeezed her eyes tightly shut as discomfort mutated into a sharp stab of pain but not a whisper of sound escaped her. The instant she registered that the worst was over, her body made her more aware of other sensations, stretching to accommodate his invasion and the deeply satisfying burn of him where she ached for more. And once he set up a fluid rhythm, deep down inside her muscles began to clench and tiny ripples of growing need assailed her.

'You are so tight and hot,' Alissandru growled thickly, dark eyes sheer gold enticement in the firelight casting flickering shadows across the walls and the bed.

Her hips rose to meet his because finally she was part of something, fully involved and sentient and wanting, *wanting* so much she could hardly contain it. The driving need to reach the same plateau again consumed her as he speeded up, his every lithe invasion feeding her hunger while her heart raced insanely fast. The tension inside her knotted and knotted ever tighter until he sent her flying again and the wild excitement and hot, sweet pleasure rolled over her again in wave after wave, leaving her limp and weak as he shuddered over her with his own release.

'That was spectacular,' Alissandru muttered raggedly in the aftermath, rolling off her but carrying her with him and keeping both arms wrapped around her so that she sprawled on top of him, drenched in the hot, already familiar scent of him.

And she had no regrets, Isla recognised in a stark instant of clarity as she pressed her lips sleepily to a broad brown shoulder. Alissandru had made her feel truly *alive* for the first time in months and she felt gloriously relaxed and warm and safe. More troubled thoughts tried to nudge at her but she was far too sleepy to let them in. There would be time enough in the morning to consider what she had done but, just at that moment, she didn't want to torment herself with what she couldn't change.

He was attracted to her but he would never love her. Well, that was life, she told herself drowsily, giving with one hand, taking with the other. It still struck her as better than what she had had before.

* * *

She woke up very early and slid out of bed, flinching at the tenderness of her body. She tugged out the case below the bed with care, careful not to make too much noise as she extracted warm clothes to take into the bathroom with her. But she didn't leave the room until she had taken her fill of looking at Alissandru while he slept. His face was roughened with dark stubble, his black hair very dark against the bedding while the long golden sweep of his muscular back was a masculine work of art. Carelessly sprawled across the bed, he looked utterly gorgeous and impossibly sexy. He was out of her league, *totally* out of her league, she told herself as she washed and dressed in the bathroom, hurrying downstairs to let out the dogs and feed the hens.

She would also have to take some hay out to the sheep in their shelter because the snow was probably too deep for them to forage. Wrapped up against the cold, she took care of the livestock first, trudging through the snow to the barn for the hay and driving the old tractor as close to the pasture as she could get so that she could heft the hay into the sheep shelter with greater ease.

By the time she finished her chores, however, her shoulders and back were aching and she was breathing heavily and hoping the snow wouldn't last long because snow made everything twice as much work.

When she walked back indoors, it was an intense relief to shed her outdoor clothing and let her face and hands defrost close to the fire she had banked up the night before, and which she now revived. Steps overhead and the creak of the stairs warned her that Alissandru was about to join her, and she turned her head with a shy smile, not quite sure how to greet him in the light of day and reality. Like a lover? Like a friend? Like a relative? There was no etiquette rule that covered what had taken place between them the night before.

'Isla…' Alissandru came to a halt at the foot of the stairs and studied her, his lean, strong face clenching hard. 'We have to talk.'

'I'll make breakfast,' Isla proffered readily, keen to make herself busy and pretty much unnerved by the grim brooding expression tautening his dark devastating features. He had put his suit back on and, even unshaven, he looked like a super-sleek businessman again, expensive and detached.

'Thank you, but I haven't got time for breakfast… perhaps a coffee?' Alissandru suggested smoothly. 'The helicopter is picking me up in about fifteen minutes. Where were you?'

'Feeding the sheep and the hens,' she explained, putting on the kettle, shaken that he was leaving so immediately while anxiously wondering what he planned to talk about. Puggle was showing a worrying tendency to prowl around Alissandru's feet while growling threateningly and she shooed him away.

Having ignored the dog's ridiculous moves entirely—for how intimidating did something barely six inches tall think it could be—Alissandru withdrew a folded document from the pocket of his suit jacket, straightened it out and settled it down on the table.

'The details of your inheritance. All you need to do is contact the solicitor and give him your current address and you will receive your bequest. Paulu, I should warn you, also left you his house in Sicily on the family estate...if you are agreeable, I would like to *buy* that back from you as it should stay with my family.'

Isla studied him in dismay, disconcerted that he had plunged straight into the impersonal matter of his brother's will. 'I'll think about that,' she murmured, playing for time, barely able to comprehend the concept of becoming the owner of a property abroad when she had never owned a house before. But she did receive his strong hint that he didn't want her using that house on the Rossetti estate and that made her feel uncomfortable and distinctly rejected.

With hands that shook a little with nerves, she prepared coffee for them both. She had shared a bed with Alissandru last night and that was no big deal in the modern world, she reminded herself firmly. She needed to wise up and expect less. Alissandru only had a few minutes before he had to leave and naturally he would be keen to get the business aspect of Paulu's bequest dealt with first.

'Do you want to discuss the sale of the house now?' Alissandru asked quietly, watching her like a hawk, hopeful she would grab at that option and agree an immediate deal.

For someone dressed like a homeless waif, she contrived to look astonishingly pretty, he acknowledged reluctantly. The cold had forced colour into her cheeks and blown her vibrant hair into a wild curly mop. She fiddled with a stray curl nervously and her sparkling dark blue eyes clung to him. Alissandru studied his coffee instead, keen to move on fast and without fanfare from his monumental error of judgement the night before. He had made a mistake, well, in truth, *several* mistakes, but there was no need to dwell on that unwelcome reality.

'No, let's leave the house aside for the moment,' Isla suggested unevenly, sitting down opposite him. 'I'm sure all that can be dealt with at some more convenient time.'

'Isla…?' Alissandru hesitated. 'Last night was a blunder on my part.'

'A…blunder?' she framed and then paled. 'You mean, a mistake?'

Alissandru lifted his chin in acknowledgement. 'I wasn't playing with a full deck. The concussion and the discussion we had about my brother put me in a weird frame of mind.'

Isla stiffened. 'You kissed me *before* you bashed your head. Are you saying I took advantage of you when you were vulnerable?' she asked in angry mortification.

Dark colour edged Alissandru's high cheekbones and he flung her an incredulous glance. 'Of course not. I'm saying that I was confused and unable to think clearly. Bearing in mind your sister's history with my family, it was very unwise for us to blur those lines with sex.'

Isla was frozen to her chair, feeling very much as though he had punched her in the stomach without warning. He was pairing her with Tania, who was, sadly, dead and buried but also Tania, whom Alissandru had loathed. In fact, he was backtracking so fast from their intimacy it was a wonder he wasn't succumbing to whiplash.

With as much dignity as she could contrive, Isla shifted an offhand shoulder.

'Whatever,' she said as if his about-face meant absolutely nothing to her. 'Do we really need to talk about this?'

Alissandru's lean dark features shadowed and hardened. 'I'm afraid that we do because I didn't take precautions with you. That's what I meant when I said I was…er…confused. That is an oversight I have never made before and, although I'm quite sure you are on the pill and safe from any risk of pregnancy, I want to assure you that I'm regularly tested and clean,' he completed with icy precision.

Isla could feel the colour draining from her face because the danger of conception or indeed infection had not crossed her mind even once, which seemed to underline how very stupid she had been to impulsively succumb to temptation. The man she had given her virginity to hadn't even noticed her lack of experience and now he chose to simply assume that she was taking contraceptive precautions to facilitate her non-existent sex life with other men. She didn't want to disabuse him on that score because the idea of him worrying that she *could* conceive struck her as even *more* humiliating. And just at that moment, she felt almost overwhelmed by the crushing hurt and humiliation Alissandru was already inflicting on her.

Alissandru was conscious as he watched her turn the colour of the ash scattered on the hearth that he had used all the wrong words because he still couldn't concentrate, couldn't find the words that usually came so easily and smoothly to his lips with a woman. Something about Isla was different and he was different with her too, and that acknowledgement freaked him out.

'I shouldn't think there's much risk of conception from one sexual encounter,' Alissandru asserted confidently, while wondering why she wasn't reassuring him that she was fully protected from such a danger.

'I shouldn't think so,' she mumbled in careful agreement, burning her tongue on the hot gulp of coffee she forced down her clenched throat.

Overhead, the noise of a helicopter intruded, and Alissandru sprang upright with alacrity while Puggle bounced and barked. Alissandru couldn't *wait* to get away from her, Isla interpreted, a sinking sensation of shame over her own conduct gripping her tummy.

'I'll leave my card in case of any…complications,' Alissandru said as he shrugged into his cashmere overcoat at speed and slapped a business card down on the table. 'And the offer for the house will be made in due course. Naturally, it will be a most generous offer.'

Naturally, Isla echoed dizzily inside her head. Only there was nothing natural about anything that had happened between them, she reflected painfully. She didn't believe that waitresses and billionaires regularly got together in the same bed but then what did she know? What did she know about *anything*? she asked herself in sudden anguish, realising that ignorance was anything but bliss when naivety could leave her open to such dreadful humiliation.

'I wish you well in the future,' Alissandru murmured coolly on the doorstep.

And she wanted to bury him deep in a snowdrift, but not before she punched him hard for rejecting her in every way that a woman could be rejected. He had hammered nails of fire into her self-esteem, puncturing her pride on every possible level. But then he wanted to be sure that there was no misunderstanding, wanted to be sure that she would not use his phone number for anything other than the direst emergency.

Alissandru didn't want to *see* her again, didn't want to *talk* to her again, really didn't want *anything* more to do with her at all. Only he had clumsily contrived to put those facts across as politely as he could.

And Isla had no plans to disappoint him, assuring herself that she would sooner be publicly whipped than even glance in his disdainful direction again.

CHAPTER FOUR

ISLA LIFTED THE wand to check it with an unsteady hand. And there it was, what she had most feared to see: the positive pregnancy result that confirmed that she had conceived a child with Alissandru Rossetti. Perspiration beaded her brow and her tummy muscles winced in dismay.

He wouldn't like that news, he wouldn't like that at all, wouldn't be expecting it either if she went by the tone of their final conversation. Of course, he had assumed that she was taking birth-control pills and that the risk of pregnancy would therefore be minimal. Well, he had been wrong and did it really matter how *he* felt about this particular development?

A couple of months ago, following that night they had spent together at the croft, such a discovery would have filled her with sheer panic, Isla acknowledged ruefully, but her life had changed out of all recognition since then. How? Well, first and foremost Paulu Rossetti had left her a very generous amount of money. She was already making plans to sign up at a further education college to remedy the lack of qualifications that restricted her in the job market. She had been forced to drop out of school as a teenager to help care for her grandfather because her grandma hadn't been able to nurse him alone. She had always hoped to go back to school some day to pass the exams she had missed. However, the revelation that she was expecting a child altered everything because even though she could still study while pregnant or as a single mum, her head spun at the amount of organisation it would require and she baulked at the prospect of putting her baby into someone else's care.

After all, Isla very much wanted her baby. In fact, a warm glow spread inside her at the mere thought of the precious burden she carried. Her baby would give her a family again, and wouldn't that be wonderful? Not to be alone any more? To have her child to focus on and look after, to have a seriously good reason for everything she did in the future? And that she could warmly accept its accidental conception was solely down to Paulu Rossetti's generosity and thoughtfulness. Had her sister even known what was in her husband's will? She didn't think it would ever have occurred to Tania to leave her kid sister anything if she passed away first. Of course, Tania had never had much of her own and what she had had she'd spent on designer clothes and the like.

A week after that snowbound night, when Isla had still been feeling very depressed about having slept with Alissandru, her uncle and aunt had returned from New Zealand. After spending a fortnight on the rickety old sofa bed her relatives had borrowed for her use, and catching a bad bout of flu, Isla had been ready to leave. Although she had missed a period by that stage, she had not been unduly concerned because the flu had left her run-down. Only when her menstrual cycle had failed a second time had Isla realised that she needed to buy a pregnancy test, and by then she had flown back to London, encouraged by the fact that her inheritance had given her options. Instead of worrying about where she would stay or how she would afford to stay anywhere without an income, thanks to Paulu she had the luxury of choice. Her friend Lindsay had announced that Isla and Puggle could stay in her flat with her for a while because her flatmate was away on a training course.

Paulu's bequest had included far more money than Isla had ever dreamt of receiving, and no sooner had Isla asked her Scottish solicitor to contact the Rossetti family's solicitor than a ridiculously generous offer had come through to buy Paulu's house back from her. But Isla was, as yet, in no hurry to sell the house and the discovery that Alissandru had got her pregnant had only complicated the situation.

Isla wanted to *see* the house where Paulu and her sister had been living. She wanted to go through Tania's possessions and keep a few sentimental objects to remember her sibling by. And the knowledge that her baby would be a Rossetti had also made her reluctant to immediately sell the house on the family estate. Not that Alissandru would want her there or even visiting, she conceded uncomfortably, but her baby would have rights too, she reasoned, and might well appreciate that connection to his or her Sicilian heritage. No, selling the house, totally breaking that connection, wasn't a decision to be made in haste, she reasoned ruefully…regardless of how Alissandru felt about her owning part of his precious family estate.

So, now what did she do about Alissandru? She would *have* to tell him that she was pregnant because he had the right to know, but she wasn't looking forward to breaking that news because she was convinced that it would be a deeply unwelcome announcement. Alissandru didn't want anything more to do with her, so the news that they would be linked for ever by a child could only infuriate him. But there was nothing she could do about that, so Alissandru would just *have* to deal with it.

Before she could lose her nerve, Isla pulled out her phone and called the number he had given her.

'Alissandru?' she queried the instant she heard his dark deep drawl answer with an impatient edge. 'It's Isla Stewart. I'm sorry to have to bother you but I have something to tell you.'

At the other end of the line, Alissandru had tensed. 'You want more money for the house?' he assumed, stepping away from the conference table he had been seated at, jerking his head in dismissal at his staff as he stalked into his office next door, tension stamped in every angular line and hollow of his darkly handsome features.

'It's nothing to do with the house,' Isla admitted. 'I haven't made a decision about that yet.'

'Why not?' Alissandru cut in edgily.

'Because I've just found out that I'm pregnant and right now that is all I can think about,' Isla confided reluctantly.

A freezing little silence fell at the other end of the line. Alissandru was reeling in silent shock because he had not once considered that possibility and when it came at him out of nowhere, he froze, stunned by her announcement. How *could* she be pregnant? Was it even his? What were the odds?

'I don't understand how this has happened,' Alissandru murmured flatly.

'Well, I've done my duty by telling you and for the moment we can leave it there,' Isla told him, eager to conclude the call. 'We've got nothing to discuss.'

'If what you claim is true we have a great deal to discuss,' Alissandru contradicted harshly.

'Why on earth would I lie about being pregnant?' Isla snapped.

'I don't know, but your sister *did*,' Alissandru told her with ruthless emphasis. 'But be assured that even if you turn out to be having triplets, I'm unlikely to offer a wedding ring.'

Isla sucked in a deep steadying breath. 'Since I'm well aware of your habit of saying exactly what enters your mind and because I have better manners than you have, I will just ignore those comments,' she responded tartly. 'But allow me to assure you that I *am* pregnant, you *are* the father and I wouldn't marry you if you were the last man alive!'

'I will arrange for you to see a doctor first and we will move on from there.'

'I'm ready to move on past you *right now*, Alissandru!' Isla flashed back, so angry she could barely vocalise.

'I will call you back once I've made arrangements,' Alissandru countered grimly and finished the call.

Isla was pregnant? How could that be? Why hadn't the contraceptive pill worked? And why would she have waited weeks to tell him? It seemed like a long time since that night they had spent together. In a rage, Alissandru slammed his phone down on his desk. What an idiot he had been that night to fall into the trap of having unprotected sex! He had run an insane risk and incredibly he had done it with Tania Stewart's sister. Of all the worst possible women to have got entangled with, why had he succumbed to her?

Over the past two months, Alissandru had repeatedly relived that night. Waking or sleeping, he just couldn't seem to shake free of those memories of Isla. The sex had been phenomenal. That was why he couldn't get that night with *her* out of his head. Clearly, he was more driven by his libido than he had ever appreciated and the knowledge that he was guilty of that fatal flaw, that demeaning weakness, had turned him off casual sex and other women. He had not been with a woman since that night, which was probably even unhealthier, he reasoned rawly.

Pregnant! Was it possible? Of course it was possible, but it was equally possible after several weeks that even if Isla *was* pregnant the child would ultimately turn out not to be *his* child. Dragging in a shudder-

ing breath of restraint, Alissandru called his lawyer
to ask for advice and only after that enlightening discussion, and in a much cooler frame of mind, did he
organise a medical appointment. He requested Isla's
address by text and informed her that he would pick
her up the next morning at nine and accompany her
to the examination.

Isla gritted her teeth and told him that he would be
waiting outside the door if there was to be any medical examination. She gave him the address, though,
reasoning that once he was satisfied that she was telling him the truth they could move on and she would
need to have nothing more to do with him. After all,
she didn't need his financial help, did she? Paulu had
left her comfortably off, giving her the means to raise
a child as a single parent. While she was pregnant, she
would attend classes and study, she decided, making
the most of that time before she sought employment
again. Many women were successful working mothers and so would she be.

Another worry now clawed at her, though. Was it
true that Tania had claimed to be pregnant at some
stage of her relationship with Paulu? Was that, in fact,
why she and Paulu had married as Alissandru seemed
to think? And even if it was true and Tania had made
an understandable mistake in assuming that she was
pregnant when she was not, why was Isla's word now
being doubted and why was she expected to hang her
head in shame for her sibling's error?

Suddenly, Isla knew exactly what she would be saying to Alissandru in the morning and none of it would

be polite, she thought furiously. How could she have slept with a man like that? He was horribly suspicious and distrustful of women. Not to mention unreasonably biased against Isla because of the blood in her veins. She would be the mother of Alissandru's child. How the heck could they ever establish a civilised relationship as parents on that basis? The guy was a living nightmare! Nobody halfway normal could handle him! Her poor sister was dead and he was *still* holding Tania's past actions against her.

Lindsay, a pretty blonde with tough views on men, had an entirely different take on Isla's situation. 'Of course, you need Alissandru's financial help.'

'I don't,' Isla protested.

'Paulu left you a lovely nest egg but it's not going to keep you or a child for the rest of your days. Not unless you flog that house in Sicily as well and invest the proceeds,' Lindsay pronounced. 'And the child is his child, as well…why shouldn't he pay towards his child's upkeep? That's his duty.'

'He assumed I was on the pill.'

'But he didn't ask you if you *were*, did he? You both took the risk and it didn't pay off, so you're not any more responsible for this development than *he* is,' Lindsay completed roundly. 'Stop beating yourself up about it.'

But Isla was tormenting herself because she felt very guilty that on a secret level she was *pleased* to be pregnant and already excitedly looking forward to becoming a first-time mum. Family was what she cared about most and finally she was going to have a family again. At the same time, even the sound of Alissandru's voice on the phone had warned her that *he* was angry, bitter and unhappy about the prospect of her being pregnant with his child. How could she feel anything other than guilty in the circumstances? Another woman might have been willing to consider a termination or adoption but Isla wasn't prepared to consider either of those options.

In the morning, she got up early, ate a good breakfast and donned a winter-weight jersey dress, teaming it with knee-high boots, items recently purchased with her newly affluent bank account. She questioned why she was making that much effort for Alissandru and decided that pure pride was motivating her, because Alissandru had rejected her on every possible level after the night they had spent together. She needed the comfort of knowing she looked her best in Alissandru's radius.

The bell buzzed through the empty flat, Lindsay having long since left for work. Isla used the peephole and undid the chain, standing back as she opened the door. Alissandru stood there, six-feet-plus inches of volatile brooding male.

'Will you come in for a moment?' Isla asked politely.

'The traffic's bad and we don't want to be late.'

'If you want me to go anywhere with you, you have to come in first,' Isla delivered without hesitation, wondering how he could look so gorgeous early in the morning and yet be a total irredeemable toad beneath the surface sophistication.

Wide sensual mouth flattening with annoyance, Alissandru skimmed grim dark golden eyes over the flushed triangle of her face. *Sì*, he reasoned angrily, *already* he could feel the dangerous pull of sexual attraction. The dress cupped the full swell of her magnificent breasts to perfection and hinted at her gloriously curvaceous hips while the boots accentuated legs that were surprisingly long despite her diminutive height. Isla could cover herself from head to toe and screen every atom of bare flesh and still look like a total temptress with her pink sultry mouth, sexy curves and sparkling violet-blue eyes. She didn't look remotely pregnant to him but then she wouldn't be showing yet, would she? Alissandru knew virtually nothing about pregnancy and at that moment, his ignorance galled him.

'Why do you want me to come in?'

'I want your full attention and I don't want to stage an argument with you while you're trying to drive,' she confided.

'I have a driver,' Alissandru slotted in icily. 'And I do not see what we have to argue about.'

Isla raised a dubious coppery brow. 'Your attitude? It *stinks*. I'm not my sister. I don't look like her and I don't think I behave like her but you can't seem to see that. Getting pregnant after a one-night stand is worrying enough without me feeling that I'm constantly up against your irrational prejudice against me.'

'I do not suffer from irrational prejudice,' Alissandru declared in a stubborn tone of denial.

'Sorry to be the one to tell you but you *do*,' Isla replied quietly. 'I can accept that you didn't like my sister and that it's too late now for you to change your mind about her, but you *have* to accept that I'm a different person. Stop comparing us and being suspicious of my every move because this baby I'm carrying doesn't need that tension in the air between us.'

'Mr Welch will tell us if you *are* carrying a baby but we won't know if it's mine until the child is born. DNA testing can be done while you are pregnant but it *could* compromise your pregnancy, so I'm prepared to wait for that confirmation until after the birth,' Alissandru informed her, looking very much as if he was expecting a lofty round of applause for that consideration. 'May we leave now?'

'You didn't listen to a word I said, did you?' Isla exclaimed angrily. 'Well, maybe you didn't listen but you can sit down and think about your prejudice later, can't you? I'm tired of dealing with it.'

'The car's waiting,' Alissandru murmured, standing back for her to precede him, careful to be courteous as advised by his lawyer. Arguing with Isla, who was potentially the mother of his child, would be unwise. He needed a plan and then he would deal with the whole situation. *Irrational prejudice?* What was she talking about? She was Tania's sister and naturally he distrusted her. That was *not* unreasonable, he told himself squarely.

The limousine impressed Isla to death but she refused to reveal the fact, sinking into the opulent cream padded upholstery and looking out at the traffic as if she travelled in such style every day. Not a word passed either of their lips until they entered an elegant waiting room to await the appointment he had arranged. When Isla's name was called, an argument broke out when Alissandru stood up, as well.

'No, you can't come in with me. This is private. You can speak to the doctor afterwards with my permission, but you are *not* coming in with me!' Isla warned him furiously, her cheeks infusing with hot colour as the other couple waiting across the room stared at them as though they had escaped from a zoo.

Impervious to such self-consciousness, Alissandru settled glittering dark golden eyes on her. 'I wish to accompany you.'

'I said no, Alissandru, and *no* means *no*!' Isla bit out angrily as she stalked off and left him behind.

Fizzing with pent-up energy and frustration, Alissandru paced the floor. Of course, her pregnancy would be confirmed. He wasn't expecting to discover that she had lied about that, but the real question was whether or not it was *his* child she carried and he wouldn't have the answer to that question for months to come.

Isla found Mr Welch friendly and professional. He confirmed that she was pregnant and seemed a little surprised that she had not experienced any textbook signs of pregnancy like dizziness or nausea. 'Of course, it's very early days,' he added comfortably. 'Now that you know for sure, you'll probably start feeling small effects very soon.'

It was a little embarrassing having to ask the doctor to speak to Alissandru separately, but Isla kept a smile on her face and did so, returning to the waiting room just as Alissandru was called. He was gone for longer than she expected and returned, looking taut and serious, to usher her back out to the limousine.

'So, not a false alarm,' he remarked as the limo moved back into the traffic.

'I'm to come back for a scan in a couple of weeks,' Isla told him brightly, determined not to be affected by Alissandru's mood.

'Do you have any idea why the pills you were on failed?' he asked flatly.

'I wasn't taking any pills,' Isla admitted baldly, keen to get that misunderstanding out of the way. 'You assumed that I was, but I wasn't.'

Alissandru shot her a startled glance. 'In other words, we were entirely unprotected that night.'

Isla nodded stiffly. 'Yes, and I'm as much to blame as you are for not appreciating the risk that we were taking.'

Faint dark colour edged Alissandru's sculpted cheekbones, accentuating the bronzed hollows beneath and the perfect bone structure that gave his face such masculine strength. He was a twin but he and Paulu had not looked much alike, Isla acknowledged. Paulu had been slighter in build and much more boyish in his looks.

'Why weren't you taking any contraceptive precautions?' Alissandru prompted, his wide sensual mouth taking on a sardonic slant.

'I wasn't having sex so there was no need for me to consider precautions,' Isla revealed, lifting her chin, refusing to succumb to her embarrassment. She had had sex with Alissandru, she reminded herself in exasperation. There was no excuse for such prudishness now that she had conceived.

A frown line indented his brow. 'You *weren't*?'

Isla jerked a slight shoulder in a dismissive shrug. 'You were the first…and you didn't notice, but that's all right. To be fair, at the time I didn't want to draw your attention to my lack of experience.'

Alissandru had lost colour below his Mediterranean tan and his stunning dark eyes had narrowed, his black lacelike lashes almost tangling. 'You're telling me that you were a virgin?' he pressed in disbelief.

'Yes, and the sooner you accept that and that this child can *only* be yours, the happier we will both be,' Isla responded doggedly. 'Telling yourself that this child may be someone else's is simply wishful thinking—'

'I refuse to accept that you were a virgin,' Alissandru interrupted in a raw undertone.

Tranquil in that moment as a garden pond, Isla gazed steadily back at him. 'I expected that reaction. You learn everything the hard way. However, I've done what I had to do. I've told you. But I *can't* change the way you think. You can drop me home now and we can talk again after the baby's born.'

Her tone of careless dismissal set Alissandru's perfect teeth on edge. 'Whether the child is mine or not, I will be much more involved before the birth than you seem to expect.'

'I don't think so…not without my agreement. And you won't be getting that. I don't need the aggravation. I want to make plans and look forward to my baby.'

'*Look forward?*' Alissandru incised thunderously.

Isla gave him a sunny smile, refusing to conceal her feelings. 'Yes, I'm very excited about this baby and I won't pretend otherwise.'

Mindful of his temper, Alissandru breathed in deep and slow. She was delighted to be pregnant, openly admitting it. Was she one of those women he had read about who just decided to have a child and went out and picked a man to do the deed? He gritted his even white teeth. Even if she was, what could he do about it? He was in a situation in which he couldn't win. An unwed pregnant mother held all the aces. He would be damned if he did help her because the child might not be his, and damned if he didn't because if he didn't help her now, he could be denied access after the child was born because his child's mother would hate him.

The child. He remembered how much Paulu had longed for a child, and his heart clenched painfully. Paulu would've celebrated such news and their mother would've been ecstatic at the prospect of a grandchild. Alissandru didn't know how he felt beyond shocked, frustrated and bewildered. He studied Isla from below his lashes, recalling that night in astonishing detail for a person claiming concussion as an excuse for mental confusion. A virgin? He had never been with one. It was true that she had done nothing that implied a higher level of sexual skill. It was also true that he had had to utilise more power than usual to gain access to her squirming little body.

Feeling strangely breathless and hot, Alissandru dragged his smouldering gaze from her and focussed on a leather-clad leg instead. *He had parted those knees.* Hard as a rock and uncomfortable, he shifted position, angling his long, lean, powerful body back into a corner. Yes, it was possible she had been a virgin. Tania's sister a virgin at twenty-two years of age? Surprising but not impossible, he reasoned doggedly, battling his arousal with all his strength.

Isla watched Alissandru, wondering what he was thinking about, wondering if she should even *want* to know. She was on edge in his radius, unable to relax while recalling everything she had worked hard at trying to forget. His touch, the feel of him over her, inside her, the seething, storming excitement of his every movement. He had made her ignite in a blaze of elation and pleasure that still haunted her at weak moments. An ache stirred at the heart of her, warning her that even remembering that night was dangerous. But there he sprawled, effortlessly elegant and infuriating and still breathtakingly beautiful, from the blue-black fall of hair he wore rather longer than was fashionable to the broad shoulders and powerful muscular torso that even the fanciest suit couldn't conceal.

'We could talk over an early lunch at my town house,' Alissandru suggested, startling her out of her reverie.

'I don't think we have anything to talk about at present,' Isla said in surprise.

'That's where you're wrong,' Alissandru asserted without hesitation.

'I wish I could say that that declaration surprises me…but I can't,' Isla said ruefully. 'You always think you're right.'

CHAPTER FIVE

ALISSANDRU'S TOWN HOUSE lay off a quiet, elegant Georgian square. It was a family-sized house, not at all the ritzy single-man accommodation Isla would have expected him to inhabit and, when she commented, he confided that he needed a spacious property because his family stayed with him when they were visiting London.

'My mother likes London for shopping and so do my cousins. She usually brings company with her.'

An inner shudder of recoil assailed Isla as she recalled Alissandru's cousin Fantino, who had cornered her in that bedroom in Sicily and assaulted her. Not that she had recognised it as an actual assault at the time, being young and ignorant of such labels. Tania, after all, had dismissed the incident as a misunderstanding and had angrily warned a distraught Isla not to kick up a fuss over what had happened and spoil her wedding day. Did Fantino come to London? Was Alissandru close to him? The men were about the same age. Suppressing her wandering thoughts, she pushed the matter and that unfortunate connection back out of her mind again.

Alissandru showed her into a contemporary dining room decorated in fashionable shades of soft grey and tucked her into a comfortable chair. 'Would you like a drink?' he enquired.

'No, thanks. Alcohol is off my menu for the immediate future—better safe than sorry,' she quipped.

'I didn't know. In fact, I don't know anything about pregnant women apart from the fact that they put on weight and get very tired,' Alissandru admitted wryly. 'And I only picked up that from listening to my cousins' complaints.'

His honesty disconcerted her. She watched as an older woman brought in a tray and set plates out for them. It was a light meal, exactly what she preferred at present because, although she had yet to feel sick, her appetite had dwindled and she had lost a little weight.

'You said that we had to talk,' she reminded him as she sipped at her water. 'What about?'

'About me getting involved in all this,' Alissandru specified. 'You're behaving as if you want me to step back and stay out of things until after the birth.'

Isla glanced up, her violet eyes troubled. 'That *is* what I want.'

'That won't work for me,' Alissandru countered bluntly. 'I'm opening a bank account for you to take care of your expenses. Who are you living with at present?'

Isla flung back her shoulders. 'A friend, but it's only a temporary arrangement. I'll need to find my own place. Alissandru... I really don't need your financial help, not when I have what Paulu gave me.'

'I *have* to contribute,' Alissandru spelt out resolutely.

'Even though you're not convinced that this is your child?' Isla snapped in exasperation.

'Even though,' Alissandru confirmed without hesitation. 'I also intend to cover all your medical expenses and, with your agreement, accompany you to any important procedures…such as the scan Mr Welch mentioned was coming up. You can't ask me to stand back and act like this has nothing to do with me. If this is my child I need to take an interest and take responsibility, as well.'

Isla swallowed hard on the flood of disagreement rising to her lips. Alissandru was very much a man of action and she could hardly fault him for stepping up to demand a share of the responsibility. He didn't want to be excluded. He didn't want to stand on the sidelines hearing stuff third-hand from her. But his wish to get involved contravened her earnest need to shut him out. Not very charitable, she scolded herself, not very fair. He had rejected her but he was not rejecting the possibility of their child. He was trying to do the right thing and if she denied him, it would only increase his distrust.

Playing for time, Isla toyed with her food. 'I understand what you're saying but I don't need your money.'

'Allow me to contribute towards your expenses. I want you to have the very best medical care and decent accommodation. I don't want you worrying about the future.' Brilliant dark golden eyes rested on her. 'I *must* help. That's not negotiable. I need to be supportive. I won't interfere in your life, but I will be there in the background.'

Somewhat soothed by that reference to his staying in the background, Isla sighed. 'I suppose I can hardly say no. I will keep you informed but I don't want anything else to do with you. I don't think that you can expect any warmer welcome from me after the way we parted in Scotland.'

'I don't want to upset you in any way,' Alissandru told her. 'But I do need to be part of this situation.'

Travelling back to the office, having dropped Isla home, Alissandru took stock at a more leisurely and reflective pace than was usual for him. He was imbued with the energetic conviction that he had plans to make, a *lot* of plans. First and foremost, he needed to find somewhere comfortable and with good security for Isla to live because at present she wasn't staying in one of the safest areas of the city. Where she lived was a priority, he reasoned. And Mr Welch had impressed on him that she also needed a healthy diet so he would organise some sort of food service or delivery, as well.

A baby. If it was a little boy, it might be a little like Paulu, he reasoned, startling himself with that thought. Or why not a little girl with Paulu's sweet nature? He didn't care either way and his mother would be ecstatic with either possibility, for Constantia Rossetti was still struggling to cope with the loss of her son. A baby would be something positive to focus on and ultimately a comfort to them all.

As long as it was *his* child…

But why would Isla lie on that score? He had warned her that he wouldn't marry her because naturally he couldn't forget the disaster of his twin's hasty marriage with Tania. Tania had wanted a rich husband much more than she had ever wanted a child. Isla, on the other hand, needed persuasion before she would even accept Alissandru's involvement and financial support during her pregnancy. She hadn't snatched at his offer for Paulu's house, either.

Maybe she was playing a long game and trying to impress him, although it was hard to see what she could gain from denying her legal right to have his support. Maybe he *was* too jaded after Paulu's experience to see the wood for the trees, he conceded uneasily, frowning at the mere suspicion that he could deserve Isla's accusation of irrational prejudice. Regardless, however, he was already beginning to see a much more positive angle to the baby scenario.

His interest had been caught, and was that thanks to Paulu, as well?

'What's it all for?' his twin had demanded that day in Alissandru's office when he'd admitted his own desire for a child. 'Who have you built this empire for? You already have more than you could spend in a lifetime. Wouldn't you like a son or daughter to leave it all to?'

And Alissandru had laughed, deeming that a question for the future, not the present, only now everything had changed and it was amazing how priorities could rearrange themselves in the aftermath of loss. Paulu was gone and there was nothing he could do about that, but a child would give him a fresh focus. A child would need teaching and guidance and love. Alissandru suddenly smiled at the prospect. A baby just might be exactly what he needed...

Two days later, Isla lay in bed mulling over her final conversation with the father of her child. It wasn't so much that Alissandru wanted to be part of the situation, more like he wanted to *take over*. He had already sent her details of three London properties he owned, inviting her to move into any one of them at his expense but, although it was a very lavish offer, Isla didn't want to become Alissandru Rossetti's kept woman. At the same time she only had a week to find somewhere of her own to live because Lindsay's flatmate would be returning soon. It would be easier to accept Alissandru's offer but the easy way wasn't always the wisest way, Isla acknowledged uneasily.

But she *knew* that the child she was carrying was *his* child even if he did not and it would not be as though she would be taking advantage of his generosity. He had also organised an early scan for her with Mr Welch and she had wanted to turn down that offer too, but she was too eager to see her baby for the first time, even if it was only the size of a pea. Alissandru also knew how to tempt a woman, she conceded ruefully, but could she face a scan at which he would undoubtedly expect to be present, as well? she asked herself. She would only be baring her stomach...

In the early hours of the following morning, Isla wakened to a cramping pain that made her wince. She sat up in bed, a sensation of dampness between her thighs stirring anxiety. When she realised that she was bleeding she started to panic. Was she losing her baby? What had she done wrong? Hadn't she looked after herself well enough?

Lindsay calmed her down and rang the emergency helpline, herding Isla into clothes and then into a taxi to take her to hospital. Her friend told her all sorts of soothing stories about false alarms and minor complications and Isla managed to hold herself together while they sat for hours waiting their turn in the hospital waiting room, surrounded by a mass of other anxious people.

In the end it took very little time for her to be dealt with. A doctor told her gently that if she was suffering a miscarriage nothing could be done to stop it happening and that such an experience was much more common than she realised in early pregnancy. Isla sat frozen to her seat as if a sudden movement might provoke a more serious crisis. Ushered into another room, she was prepared for a scan by a radiographer. Suddenly the kind of scan she had earlier been so much looking forward to receiving harboured a more menacing vibe.

The wand moved smoothly over her still-flat tummy, and Isla was barely breathing as she strained without success to see something recognisable as a baby on the screen. When the woman stopped and reached for her hand, Isla knew what was coming because the radiographer looked so sad for her.

'I'm so sorry. There's no heartbeat. It's not a viable pregnancy,' she said quietly.

A junior doctor saw her next. Isla was in shock: her baby was dead. Her wonderful beautiful baby was gone as if it had never been. Her surroundings suddenly seemed to be stretching away from her and she couldn't concentrate on what was being said. The doctor pressed medication into Isla's limp hand while Lindsay sat beside her not even trying to hide her tears, but Isla couldn't cry. Her eyes stayed dry while a great gulping sob of anguish seemed to be trapped somewhere in her throat, making it a challenge to breathe or speak.

'I'm so sorry,' Lindsay whispered in the taxi on the way back to the flat. 'This has happened to a couple of my friends at work. It's why some women won't tell anyone that they're pregnant until they're past the first trimester. That's the danger period…'

Isla nodded vigorously, striving to be strong and stoic, reluctant to subject her friends to the tears penned up inside her. 'It could have been the flu I had,' she mumbled.

'It could have been any of a dozen things.' Lindsay sighed. 'Do you want to talk about it?'

But, suddenly, Isla felt that there was nothing left to talk about. Talking wasn't going to bring her baby back and she had already kept Lindsay out of bed for half the night, she reflected guiltily. Her poor friend still had to go into work in the morning and she was already exhausted. Assuring Lindsay that all she wanted to do was sleep, she went back into the bedroom. Her first real thought was that she would have to tell Alissandru and that he would be pleased. Not that he would dare to *say* it, she assumed bitterly, but he had seen their baby as an undesirable complication and now that their baby was no longer on the way, he could only be relieved.

Unfortunately, Isla wasn't relieved because the whole cosy future she had envisaged around that precious baby had suddenly been cruelly taken from her and she didn't know what to do next. That was scary when she had felt so confident about managing everything after she first realised that she was pregnant. Now the floor of her world had suddenly vanished and she was fighting just to stay afloat.

The next morning, she agonised at length over the need to contact Alissandru. She couldn't face phoning him, saying those wounding words out loud about her baby and, midmorning, she sent him a text bluntly telling him that she had had a miscarriage.

In receipt of that unexpected message, Alissandru stared at his phone and felt sick. A *miscarriage*? How had that happened? Suddenly he was full of anxious questions.

'Something wrong?' one of his directors asked, and Alissandru glanced up, only then registering that his companions were regarding him expectantly.

'I've had bad news,' Alissandru admitted soberly. 'If you will excuse me…'

Isla's news had blindsided him even more than the announcement that she was pregnant. One minute they were having a baby, the next…? It was dead. He stared out of his office window, fighting the feelings engulfing him just as he had fought them when he'd learned that Paulu had died. He had to be strong, he *always* had to be strong because other people relied on him to be that way. When it had been Paulu, his mother had needed him, but now Isla needed him more because Isla had *wanted* that baby. *Their* baby, he adjusted, reluctant to credit any other option in that moment. He remembered Isla's glorious smile as she'd admitted how much she was looking forward to becoming a mother and he lost colour, his eyes prickling. She *had* to be devastated. He rang her immediately.

'Isla, it's Alissandru.'

'I've got nothing to say to you,' she framed woodenly.

'I got your text and obviously I want to see you and talk to you. I'm very sorry.'

'Are you?' she questioned doubtfully.

Anger flared in Alissandru's dark golden gaze. 'Of course I am! I'd like to come round and talk to you.'

'No, thanks,' she cut in immediately. 'I don't want to see you.'

'Have you had proper medical treatment?' Alissandru asked worriedly.

'Yes. I'll be fine,' she told him stiffly.

'Obviously, it wasn't meant to be,' Alissandru said heavily, raking long fingers through his tousled black hair in a gesture of frustration because he honestly didn't know what else to say to her. Words were empty. Words wouldn't change anything. He didn't want to mutter meaningless platitudes the way people did when they were faced with a difficult situation, nor did he feel that he could dare admit that he was upset, as well. Because she would *never* believe him, never believe that he too was full of regret for what was not to be.

He had warmed up to the idea of the baby just a little *too* late, he acknowledged grimly. The baby had been a surprise and he wasn't good with surprises. He had never liked the natural order and routine of his life being changed or threatened. Predictably the advent of a baby would have altered many things and he had resisted that prospect to the best of his ability, until he'd defrosted enough to concede that a baby could just be the best thing that had ever happened to him.

It wasn't meant to be... Isla flinched from that crass and demoralising assurance that cut to the quick. No, in Alissandru's rarefied world, billionaires did not have babies with former waitresses. Now, mercifully for him, if not for her, the real world had intervened, and no such baby would be born and the status quo would be preserved. Of course, he was relieved and fatalistic about her miscarriage. He hadn't wanted their baby in the first place, could hardly be expected to cry crocodile tears now that there was no longer a baby to worry about. Unlike her he hadn't learned to love their child, hadn't even begun to accept that the baby she carried *was* his child.

A bitterness as cutting as a knife slashed painfully through Isla and she finished the call. Without even thinking about it, she blocked Alissandru's number on her phone because she didn't want to be forced to speak to him again, *ever* again. That connection was finished for ever, severed by fate. She would never have to see him again, never have to speak to him again, never be hurt by him again. Eyes wet, she discovered that that was no comfort whatsoever.

The following morning, Lindsay got a call from her parents and grimaced through the conversation while offering repeated apologies for being unable to change her own plans.

'What's wrong?' Isla prompted.

Lindsay grimaced. 'My parents' friends are going on a round-the-world trip and they had a house-sitter organised to look after their pets. Now the house-sitter has cancelled and Mum and Dad are trying to put together a group of us to look after their house and their animals. I feel awful for saying no but I'm not prepared to use up my leave sitting in the back of beyond looking after dogs and cats,' she confided guiltily.

Isla, petting Puggle, who was turning into a lapdog, given to sleeping across her feet and nestling in her lap at every given opportunity, looked thoughtful. 'Could *I* do it? The house-sitting, I mean?'

'You?' Lindsay queried in surprise.

'Well, if I could bring Puggle with me, I'd be glad to get away for a while. I mean, I have to find somewhere to live anyway and the change, a little breathing space, would do me good while I decide what to do next.'

Lindsay frowned thoughtfully and warned Isla that her parents' friends lived in a converted farmhouse down a long track in Somerset and that it was a very quiet area. After a few minutes, however, she called her parents back and before Isla could even catch her breath it was all arranged and she was agreeing to travel to Somerset at the end of the week to meet the Wetherby family and receive their instructions before they departed. Isla breathed easier at the pros-

pect of leaving London and Alissandru far behind her.
A change of scene and the time and space to make
practical plans were exactly what she needed, she told
herself urgently.

It wasn't meant to be... His words haunted her but
where Alissandru was concerned there were no sad
thoughts of what might've been in Isla's troubled mind.
His rejection had been brutal and blunt. She had been
a mistake, a mistake he regretted, and the miscarriage
and his reaction to it had drawn a final line under that
reality.

And yet she had been drawn to Alissandru Rossetti
in a way she had been drawn to no other man. That
bothered her, seriously bothered her. Admittedly he
was gorgeous but she had been aware of his prejudice
from the outset and should've protected herself better, holding back instead of surrendering to the fierce
attraction between them. She had believed that she
could be totally adult and blasé about sleeping with
him and she had been devastatingly wrong in that assumption because Alissandru had ultimately hurt her
more deeply than anyone had ever hurt her. She was
not as tough as she had believed and was now even
more painfully aware that she had to get tougher.

When Alissandru turned up that evening, Lindsay
tried to head him off, but when he became icily impe-
rious with her unfortunate friend, Isla gave up listening behind her bedroom door and emerged, bitterly
conscious that she looked a mess.

'Alissandru...' she said flatly.

He had never seen her so pale, her freckles stark

across her porcelain skin, her violet eyes dull and haunted. He had to tighten his hands into fists not to reach for her, not to try to offer the physical comfort that he knew would be offensive to her. 'I don't want to crowd you, but I thought you might want to talk,' he reasoned quietly.

Bitterness flashed through Isla, sharp and painful and unfamiliar, for such bitterness did not come naturally to her. 'We have nothing left to talk about,' she told him curtly.

Alissandru looked amazing...*of course* he did, breathtakingly elegant in a dark designer suit that was exquisitely tailored to his lean, muscular physique. He emanated energy and authority in vibrant waves, the smooth planes of his high cheekbones taut below his incredibly expressive dark golden eyes. Such stunning eyes, now telegraphing the kind of guilt that was unwanted because she knew as well as he knew that he hadn't wanted their baby and that any offer of sympathy was sheer hypocrisy on his part. Yet the sheer pulsing zing of his dark, sizzling, sensual allure still filtered through that awareness, mocking her failing self-discipline as every skin cell in her body fired with wanton renewed energy.

'Why don't we have dinner and discuss that?' Alissandru murmured hoarsely, his tension increasing as she stood there, her delicate face colouring with much-needed warmth, lighting up her sad eyes and accentuating her fragility.

'I'm leaving London in a couple of days, so there'd be no point,' she declared. 'I'll let you know what I decide to do about Paulu's house once I've thought stuff over.'

Alissandru was startled by the truth that he had genuinely forgotten about the house. 'I'm not such a bastard that I'd trouble you with that matter *now*,' he argued in a vehement undertone. 'Where are you going to stay?' he pressed curtly.

'That's my business,' Isla assured him, half closing the door. 'Goodnight, Alissandru.'

Where the hell was she going? Would she be safe there? Would someone be looking out for her? Looking after her? She looked like hell! With difficulty, Alissandru suppressed his concern, acknowledging that it was time for him to move on. He could hardly force Isla to talk to him or to listen to him. He had walked away from her in Scotland and now he had to do it again. He could not understand the wrenching sense of loss attacking him or the sensation that something in his world was very wrong. 'I'll stay in touch,' he breathed in a driven conclusion.

Good luck with that, Isla thought wryly, knowing she was not about to unblock his number on her phone. Alissandru Rossetti was in the past now and only wounding memories would result from any further contact from him. She had to find a new focus in life, she told herself urgently, and embrace her future alone.

CHAPTER SIX

ISLA EXPERIENCED JOY for the first time in many weeks when she first saw the glorious cherry trees that lined the imposing private road that led up to the Palazzo Leonardo. Great foaming swathes of white blossom hung low above her hire car, making her feel as though she were driving through a tunnel of bridal lace.

It was a hot day, hotter than she had naively expected in spring, and she recognised familiar sights in every direction she looked on Rossetti land. Her visit at the age of sixteen had filled her with more memories than she had ever cared to recall. Although it had been her only trip abroad, Fantino's assault had distressed her and made her reluctant to dwell on her recollections of her visit to Sicily.

The Rossetti family lived in a very grand home but the place where their ancestors had chosen to build was quite simply magnificent. A lush green grove of natural woodland covered the hills behind the ancient *palazzo*, which presided over a wonderful patchwork carpet of lemon and orange groves, olive trees and vines. It was still very much a working agricultural estate, and Paulu had run the estate for his brother.

Stiff with considerable nervous tension, Isla parked on the gravel fronting the sprawling property. She had to call at the *palazzo* to pick up keys and directions for Paulu and Tania's house but it would only be polite to greet Paulu's mother first and offer her her condolences and some explanation for her arrival. Constantia Rossetti had been very kind to Isla when she had attended her son's wedding and, since Isla was planning to live in Paulu and Tania's home for at least a few weeks, she wanted to be on good terms with the older woman.

As far as Isla had been able to establish, Alissandru was still in London. The fact that she had lost Alissandru's child or that they had ever got close enough to even conceive a child was a secret, she thought gratefully, a secret known only to the two of them. Not that Alissandru had been grieving, she conceded ruefully. An Internet search of his recent activities had shown him attending a charity function with a beautiful but severely underdressed blonde on his arm. Was that sort of woman the type he went for? Skinny as a twig and showing off all of her flat chest?

Clutching a wriggling Puggle tightly beneath one arm, for Isla did not dare to leave him unattended in the hire car when he was still so disposed towards chewing anything within reach, Isla hit the modern doorbell. The bell was somewhat comically overshadowed by the giant wooded metal-studded double front doors that provided the main access to the *palazzo*.

A manservant greeted her and without hesitation showed her through the echoing main hall out into the delightfully feminine orangery, which was decorated in classic pale colours. The entire wall of glass, which overlooked a courtyard garden, had been pushed back to allow the fresh air and sunshine from outside to percolate indoors. The single occupant, a tall dignified woman with greying hair swept up in a chignon, stood up with a quiet smile.

'Isla… I can hardly believe that you're here with us again,' she remarked warmly.

'I'm so sorry that it's taken me this long to visit,' Isla murmured, offering her condolences and a brief explanation for her failure to attend the funerals. 'But I wanted to see the house.'

'Of course, you did,' Constantia commented sympathetically. 'I haven't been back since…er, the crash, although I have ensured that the house was kept clean. Nothing has been touched or changed. I want you to know that. Everything is exactly as it was when they left that morning.'

'I'll go through my sister's stuff,' Isla proffered hurriedly. 'And perhaps Alissandru would like to take care of his brother's things when I've left again?'

'Is this only a flying visit?' the older woman asked as a tray of tea was brought into the orangery, and in response to her inviting gesture Isla took the seat beside hers, feeling ridiculously like a schoolgirl in the older woman's dignified presence.

'I'm afraid I don't know. I haven't made up my mind about what I'm going to do next,' Isla told her, her cheeks warming a little with self-consciousness as she thought of the short-lived secret interlude she had had with Alissandru.

'Oh, what a dear little dog!' Constantia carolled, stroking Puggle beneath his chin and urging Isla to let him down to explore while she explained that her pug had died the previous winter and she had not yet had the heart to replace him.

The older woman was friendly and welcoming, although tears were visible in her eyes more than once as she reminisced about her son, finally squeezing Isla's hand and apologising for her emotionalism by saying, 'It's such a treat to talk about him to someone.'

'But don't you and Alissandru talk?' Isla had asked before she could think better of that personal question.

'Alissandru doesn't like to discuss such things,' his mother admitted wryly.

Puggle scrambled up onto Constantia's lap with the insouciance of a dog who knew how important humans were to his comfort. Fed crumbs of chocolate cake, he quite naturally refused to get down again, and when the older woman offered to look after him for Isla, to let her get established at the house and do some shopping, Isla didn't have the heart to take him away again when she could see that Puggle's easy affection was a comfort to her hostess.

An estate worker called Giovanni was summoned to guide her to the house, which Paulu had extended and modernised to please her sister, who had initially described the property as a 'horrible, dark, dank, cobwebby hole of a place'. There wasn't even a hint of darkness about the building slumbering in the warmth of midmorning, brilliant sunlight reflecting off the sparkling windows and accentuating the cheerful yel-

low shutters and the plant pots that sat around the front
door. It looked so peaceful that it made Isla's heart ache
when she reflected that the house's previous owners
would never live there again.

Scolding herself for that sad thought, she let herself
into the hall and then froze in the porch doorway at the
sight of a little stool covered with leopard-print fur fabric and dripping with cerise crystal beads. It was outré,
ridiculous, very, very much to her flamboyant sister's
taste, and she knew she would never part with it yet it
was so out of keeping with Paulu's murderously tidy
and conservatively furnished and decorated study. Two
very different people, Isla acknowledged, and yet in the
end they had made their relationship work with both
of them making compromises to achieve a better fit.

Tania must've loved him, Isla decided, seeing no
other reason for her sister to agree to live in a quiet
country house far from the more sophisticated amuse-
ments she enjoyed. Her eyes wet with tears, she walked
through the house, peering into cupboards and standing feeling like an intruder in doorways. Everywhere
she spotted flashes of her extrovert sister's personality.
It was there in the bright colours, the marital bedroom
awash in cerise pink and white lace like the ultra-fem-
inine lair of some cartoon princess. She closed the
door on that room, telling herself that she would start
going through stuff in the morning while choosing a
guest room for her own occupation. The room was
still furnished with antiques and it had plain white-
washed walls. It had always been the estate manager's
house, Paulu had once told her, and presumably that

was one good reason why Alissandru wanted it back again. Obviously he had to have a property to offer to his twin's replacement.

She supposed her only real option was to sell the house back to Alissandru. If she hoped to buy a house in England she would have to sell, and maintaining a second home abroad would be far too expensive. Even so, that didn't mean she couldn't first enjoy a few weeks vacationing in Sicily on a beautiful private estate. Alissandru wouldn't like her being here in *his* brother's house on *Rossetti* land, though…well, what was that to her now and why should she care that she was an unwelcome visitor?

Her thoughts were interrupted by the arrival of one of the *palazzo* staff laden with food to fill her empty fridge, and they even prepared a meal for the evening, sparing her the pressure of having to go on an immediate shopping trip. Isla smiled, charmed by Constantia's welcoming kindness. At least she didn't have to worry about how Alissandru's mother felt about her arrival.

Almost two months spent mostly alone in a comfortable old farmhouse had gone a long way towards restoring Isla's peace of mind. Walking dogs and feeding kittens had kept her fully occupied. She would never forget the baby she had lost, but that first punishing weight of grief had eased. Worrying about what to cook for her next meal had been the summit of her problems in Somerset, but even there she had become disturbingly aware that she still harboured a great deal of anger and bitterness towards Alissandru. That was *why* she couldn't forget him, that was why she had regularly scoured the Internet for references to him, gleaning facts and figures and a list of glittering business triumphs, all of which had utterly failed to shade in the nuances of his complex and volatile character.

After an early evening meal, she ran a bath for herself and borrowed a silk robe from Tania's wardrobe because she had neglected to pack one. After she had bathed she would drive back up to the *palazzo* to collect Puggle, who would surely have worn out his welcome by then or eaten his way out of house and home. Always hungry, he was a greedy little monster of a dog for all his small size, she acknowledged ruefully as she settled into the deliciously warm water.

She was drifting close to falling asleep in the cooling water when she heard the loud knocking on the front door, and with a groan she sat up, water sloshing noisily around her. Who on earth could it be? Had Constantia sent someone down with Puggle? Roughly towelling her dripping body only semi-dry, she grabbed up the robe and threw it on, grimacing as it clung to the damp parts she had missed with the towel. Barefoot, she sped down the wooden stairs.

Alissandru was in an ungovernable rage. He had flown home unexpectedly, walked into his own home and had been unceremoniously bitten by a nasty little animal he had believed to be hundreds of miles away in another country. As his mother had cooingly picked up the vicious little brute to check that he had not hurt his teeth, Alissandru had been fit to be tied but his brain had been firing on all cylinders in shock that Isla could actually be in Sicily, in his brother's house, on *his* estate.

And that startling, baffling revelation had enraged Alissandru, who liked everything spelled out in clear black-and-white predictable terms. Isla had *refused* to see him, *refused* to speak to him, refused even to take his phone calls, and yet without even giving him a warning she could take up residence in Paulu and Tania's house barely a quarter of a kilometre from him. How was he supposed to feel about that? Obviously they were going to see each other on the estate and was she planning to flaunt her hostile attitude to him here at his home? Was this why she hadn't agreed to sell the house? Had she always planned to show up in Sicily and make his life uncomfortable?

Her hand closing the lapels of the iridescent robe as it tried to slide open at her throat, Isla opened the door. 'Sorry, I was in the bath,' she began breathlessly before she saw who it was. Typically, Alissandru was sheathed in a tailored black suit that only emphasised his towering height and broad, muscular build.

In a maddening instant, Alissandru was confronted head-on by everything he had tried to forget about Isla: the triangular face dominated by huge dark blue eyes, her vivid mop of tousled curls springing back from her pale brow in a contrast that intensified the porcelain clarity of her skin. For Alissandru it was as though everyone else he met was depicted in monotone grey and only Isla was shown in full colour. Even worse, for the first time ever he was seeing her scantily clad and the idea that anyone else might have witnessed how the

thin fabric of her robe clung wantonly to her voluptuous curves incensed him. He could see her nipples,
the slenderness of her waist, the pronounced curve of
her hips, and the hardening swell of arousal at his groin
was painfully familiar.

'Alissandru...' Isla framed stiltedly, staring out at
him wide-eyed as though he had risen cloven-hooved
and fork-tailed out of the cobblestones behind him, her
heart jumping behind her breastbone in shock.

And yet she had *known* she would see Alissandru,
had known they could hardly avoid each other on his
family estate and that her arrival would infuriate him.
The golden blaze of his eyes, so bright in his lean,
darkly devastating face alerted her to his mood and
she took a cautious step back. 'I thought you'd still be
in London.'

'I always come home now at weekends if I can,'
Alissandru admitted. *'Per l'amor di Dio*...what are
you doing here?'

In receipt of that question, a little inner devil over-
powered Isla's caution. 'I have every right to be here.
This is *my* house,' she pointed out, lifting her chin.

Alissandru compressed his beautifully shaped mouth.
'It is, but you know that I wish to buy it from you.'

Daringly, Isla turned on her heel, turning her back
on him while leaving the door open because she was
determined not to politely invite him in. 'I don't owe
you any explanations about why I'm here.'

Behind her she heard the front door snapping shut.
'Did I say that you did?' Alissandru growled like a
grizzly bear.

'If I give you enough rope, you'll soon hang your-self,' Isla forecast witheringly. 'I know you don't want me here.'

'When did I ever say that?' Alissandru demanded, following her into the open-plan lounge with its sunken seated area and flashy built-in bar topped by a glittering disco ball, which was so out of place with the rest of the house.

Isla flipped round, her robe flying momentarily open to reveal a sleek stretch of pale pink inner thigh and a slender shapely knee. His mouth ran dry at the sight while he recalled the satin-soft smoothness of her skin.

Isla frowned, hating the way he was staring at her. 'You didn't need to say it after you made it clear that you didn't want anyone outside your family owning any part of this estate.'

'I won't apologise for that conviction,' Alissandru argued in frustration as he squared up to her, wide shoulders thrown back, long, powerful legs braced. 'The estate depends on the properties we own. We house our employees. Your ownership could lead to all sorts of complications. You could decide to rent it out, bring in strangers, turn it into some kind of business, argue about rights of way.'

Unimpressed by that parade of evidently dire possibilities, Isla folded her arms and stared back at him. 'I'm not planning to do any of those things... *Satisfied?*' she prompted.

'You know that's not what I'm trying to say.'

'I just want you...*gone*!' Isla surprised herself by

throwing out her arms in angry emphasis of that fervent wish.

'Couldn't you have warned me that you were intending to come here?' Alissandru demanded imperiously. 'Or would that common courtesy have crossed the line that says I have to be the bad guy in your every scenario?'

Isla gazed back at him, her attention locked to his lean, strong features and the raw tension stamped in the set angle of his jawline, the flare of his nostrils and the anger smouldering like an unquenchable fire in his stunning eyes. 'Well, you pretty much are the bad guy in every scenario…and let's not pretend that you make much effort to be anything else!' Isla slammed back at him furiously.

Alissandru froze as though she had slapped him, colour leaching from below his bronzed skin. 'You're talking about the baby, aren't you?' he prompted curtly.

Isla barely knew what she was talking about but that very personal question knocked her back on her heels and she rested disconcerted eyes on him. 'No, I'm not, I'm really not.'

'What else am I to think when you say I'm the bad guy in every situation?' Alissandru pressed between clenched teeth.

'Well, when aren't you the bad guy?' Isla demanded. 'You were certainly the bad guy as far as my sister was concerned.'

'No. Even when she made a pass at me, I kept it to myself,' Alissandru bit out with suppressed savagery.

Isla shot him an incredulous look. 'You're not serious?'

'*Che diavolo!*' Alissandru exclaimed wrathfully, swinging away from her in an angry movement that revealed that that admission had slipped out of him in temper. 'It's true that it happened but it's not something I intended to tell you about. But if you think about it, it makes perfect sense. I was rich and very much the twin Tania would have preferred to marry and until she got to know me better she saw herself as irresistible.'

Isla swallowed hard, wincing for her sister at his admission, wishing he hadn't told her that salient fact, but she could remember Tania telling her that if she put her mind to it she could get *any* man she wanted. And Alissandru would have overshadowed Paulu to such a degree that Tania had eventually succumbed to temptation, Isla gathered unhappily. Alissandru might have been Tania's brother-in-law but he was also as flawlessly beautiful as a black-haired warrior angel in a stained-glass window. Even more gilded by his great wealth, her sister had unwisely decided to make a play for him.

'Drop the subject,' Alissandru urged curtly. 'It is a distasteful one. I am sorry I spoke so freely.'

Yet in a strange way, Isla was not sorry, for she felt as though she had finally learned exactly what lay behind Alissandru's loathing for her sister and her sister's loathing for him. Alissandru would never have forgiven such disloyalty to his twin while Tania would never have forgiven or forgotten such a rejection.

'You made me into the bad guy when you lost the baby,' Alissandru breathed in a fierce undertone. 'You closed me out, ran away—'

'I did *not* run away!' Isla launched back at him in furious rebuttal. 'I just needed a change of scene. And I didn't close you out, either…you were already on the outside!'

'Because I was too honest and I admitted that I wasn't sure the child you had conceived was mine?' Alissandru fired back at her. 'I didn't realise that you were a virgin. Blame that on the passion or my concussion…whatever you like. I didn't notice anything different. Blame me for the assumptions I made concerning birth control, too.'

'Oh, I already have,' Isla said tartly.

'But in the absence of proof of whose child it was, I assumed there was room for doubt and that you could even have been pregnant before you slept with me,' Alissandru intoned grimly. 'I'm a cynic. I won't apologise for the way my mind works but I am naturally suspicious when it comes to protecting my family or myself. I tend to assume the worst and act accordingly. But I was upset too when we lost our baby.'

Isla froze. 'Don't you dare tell me a lie like that!' she flared.

Alissandru swallowed hard. 'Regardless of what you think, for you to continue holding my innate caution against me even after I have done everything possible to be supportive is unjust.'

'Is it really?' Isla flung at him thinly as he lounged back against the ugly bar, effortlessly sleek and elegant in his designer suit, utterly untouched by the maelstrom of emotions that had tormented her for weeks. 'You ran as far and as fast as you could get from me in Scotland! You hated my sister! You accused me of sleeping with your brother! How do you expect me to feel about you?'

Alissandru breathed in deep and slow like a marathon runner readying himself for a race but Isla knew he was struggling to hang on to his temper. 'I didn't *run*,' he grated.

'You couldn't handle the fact that you had spent the night with Tania's sister! You assumed I was a gold-digging slut even though I was a virgin.'

'Your behaviour…the way you were dressed…at my brother's wedding led me to make certain ill-judged assumptions about the level of your innocence,' Alissandru bit out grudgingly.

An angry flush mantled Isla's cheeks. 'I didn't have much choice about what I wore that day. Tania told me she had a dress for me and I had to wear it because I had nothing else,' she admitted stiffly. 'It didn't fit and it was far too revealing but she said I had to wear it because it matched her silver wedding gown.'

That simple explanation irritated Alissandru more than it soothed because even he could not ignore the unreasonable bias that he had evidently formed against Tania's sister the very first time he'd laid eyes on her. He waited for her to say something about her behaviour that same day, something that would explain what she had been doing in a bedroom with his cousin Fantino, but when she said nothing more, his lean, strong face hardened. He had misjudged her but she was no angel and why should she be? A woman who could make him want her even when she was clad in furry fabric was obviously more of a temptress than even he had been prepared to acknowledge.

'Time for you to go,' Isla told him feelingly, colliding momentarily with smouldering dark golden eyes that left her short of breath and almost dizzy.

He was making her remember that night in Scotland and she couldn't stand that. The feel of his mouth on hers had created a chemical explosion that raced through her entire body, the magic sensuality of his hands had utterly seduced her. She had realised instantly why she had never been tempted into bed by any other man. Nobody had ever made her feel as he had.

'I'm not leaving until we have something settled about the house,' Alissandru intoned stubbornly.

Isla cocked a delicate coppery brow. *'Seriously?'* she jibed. 'You storm in here at nine o'clock on a Friday evening, force me out of the bath and demand that we do a deal about a house that I'm not even sure I want to sell yet? Do you think that's reasonable?'

Alissandru angled his arrogant dark head back, his lean, powerful body acquiring a stunningly insolent air of relaxation. 'I'm not in a reasonable frame of mind. I'm never in a reasonable frame of mind around you,' he murmured thickly.

'And why is that?' Isla prompted dry-mouthed, her skin prickling with sudden awareness, wicked heat darting up between her thighs.

His eyes, framed by slumberous black lashes, glinted like liquid gold. 'Because every time I see you I want you and that's all I can think about.'

'You did not just say that,' Isla whispered shakily, her face burning.

'Tell the truth and shame the devil,' Alissandru challenged huskily. 'All I want to do right now is rip that robe off you and sink into you over and over again...'

Isla trembled like a leaf in a high wind, fearful of being torn loose. *'Stop it!'* she told him fiercely.

'No,' Alissandru countered softly. 'When you came here, you knew this was going to happen. Deal with the consequences.'

Isla dealt him an aghast look. 'That is absolutely untrue.'

'You want me,' Alissandru traded without hesitation. 'You may not like it but you want me every bit as much as I want you.'

'You walked away!' Isla reminded him furiously.

'I had to force myself to do it and it didn't work. You've spoiled me for other women,' Alissandru husked, shameless eyes ranging over her with a stormy sexual promise that she felt bite to the very marrow of her bones. That look made her shiver. He emanated a shocking mixture of bold challenge and assurance.

She watched like a hypnotist's victim as he uncoiled his lean, rangy body from his lounging stance and moved forward. She couldn't breathe for excitement, couldn't move for fear of breaking his dangerous spell. He reached for her, all potent male and confidence, and he lifted her right up into his arms.

'We'll talk about the house tomorrow,' he told her. 'Once this is out of the way, we'll stop fighting.'

Was that true? she wondered weakly as he carried her up the stairs with the same ease with which he might have carried a doll. One more time, she reasoned wildly, clutching at his conviction that it would free them both from temptation.

'We mustn't… We *shouldn't*!' she protested more frantically as he identified the room she was utilising and strode through the door.

'We're not hurting anyone,' Alissandru grated with finality.

And it was true, she realised. As far as she knew nobody could be hurt by them being together. In any case, who would even know? As her brain careened madly from stop to go and then back to almost panic-stricken indecision, Alissandru kissed her with searing heat, forcing her lips apart for the scorching possession of his tongue. Something clenched hard deep down inside her and she started to tremble again, her head falling back, her lips parting, and the impatient drum beat of arousal pounded through her slender body like a storm she knew she had to quench.

CHAPTER SEVEN

WHY AM I doing this? Isla asked herself as she looked up at Alissandru in the dim light filtering up from the hallway. And it was so simple she could've screamed at the answer when it slotted neatly into place inside her head. She *wanted* him, just the way he had said she did; she couldn't control the craving, couldn't drive it out of her treacherous body, either. That craving was there, simply there, and it rewrote in an instant everything she had ever thought she knew about herself.

He yanked loose the sash on the robe, spreading it open slowly as he leant over her, unwrapping her with a care that suggested she was a very precious parcel. She didn't cringe the way she had at the croft, didn't try to hide herself, either. Instead, she listened to the catch in his breath and watched his face as he looked at her breasts with fierce appreciation. His hands lifted to cup the full swells, his thumbs rubbing at the swollen pink peaks as he stole another kiss, and her hands plunged into his luxuriant hair, fingers filtering through the silky strands and then dropping to his shoulders, unsuccessfully trying to come between them to pull at his jacket.

'I know... I know,' Alissandru ground out in similar frustration, backing away to unceremoniously yank the jacket off and tug at his tie with thrilling impatience.

Isla lay there, all of a quiver with heat and desire, just watching him undress. They had made love in virtual darkness at the croft and this time she was hungry for the details and curious. He tossed condoms on the bedside table and their eyes met, his defensive, hers troubled and evasive, and he came down beside her and kissed her again then as if his whole life depended on it. Breathless, Isla squirmed at the sleek, hot, heavy weight of him and then she arched as his mouth closed over a swollen nipple, drawing on the sensitised tip until she felt as though fire raced between her breast and her pelvis, stoking the slow burn of need rising between her legs. It was an ache, a sweet, hollow ache she couldn't bear.

'Touch me,' Alissandru said urgently, carrying her hand down over his hard, flat stomach.

And for a split second she froze, unsure of herself, afraid to do it wrong, and then she connected with the hunger in his intent gaze and she jerked as if he had lit a touchpaper inside her because it was the same hunger that drove her. Her hand stroked down the length and breadth of him. He felt like satin wrapped round steel but was infinitely more responsive, arching hungrily up to her touch.

Isla pressed him flat and lowered her head, closing her lips round him as she stroked, listening with helpless feminine amusement and satisfaction to the hoarse sounds and the ragged Italian words she dragged from him. A little more and he was dragging her up to him again, driving her lips apart with the hunger of his, twining his tongue with hers and delving deeper until she writhed against him, glancing into quite deliberate friction with the hard length of him.

'I intended to go slow but I can't wait. *Madre di Dio, bella mia*…what are you doing to me?' Alissandru groaned, sliding teasingly against the tender flesh at her core.

Without even thinking about what she was doing, Isla tilted up her hips to receive him, and he began to slide home with a sinuous circling of his lean hips and then he froze and yanked himself back from her again to reach for the condoms by the bed.

'What is it about you?' he exclaimed in raw disbelief. 'I almost forgot again and I swear *never* to make that mistake again!'

For a split second, Isla froze. *That mistake*… Their baby. Of course that was how he thought about that episode, and how could she blame him? An unplanned pregnancy with a woman he'd only intended to spend one night with? A big drama and a source of stress he could naturally have done without and he would be as keen as she to ensure that that oversight was not repeated. She could not understand why that sensible fact should make her feel so unbearably sad.

'I'm so sorry,' Alissandru grated as he came back to her and captured her reddened mouth hungrily with his. 'It won't happen again.'

That sensual assault unfroze her and mercifully threw her back out of her unhappy thoughts. She could think of nothing but Alissandru as he drove into her with potent energy and an unashamed groan of satisfaction, thrusting home to the very heart of her and sending such a jolt of stark pleasure through her that she cried out, her face warming in the aftermath. Sensation gathered with his every slick invasion, the tightening bands of muscle in her pelvis increasing the waves of excitement gripping her.

'Don't stop…oh, please, don't stop!' she gasped at the height of a spasm of pure bliss when her very existence seemed to depend on his next virile lunge and her heart was thumping so hard and fast she was breathless.

She hit the heights even faster in an explosive climax that threatened to jolt the very bones from her body, so all-encompassing was the experience. Sweet paroxysms of exquisite pleasure eddied out from her exhausted body and cocooned her in melting relaxation.

Alissandru cradled her in his arms, shell-shocked in the aftermath. Just as in their very first encounter, sex with Isla was sublime but he wasn't going to think about that, wasn't going to question anything, *anything at all*, he instructed himself grimly. A kind of peace, a peace that had evaded him for long torturous weeks, enclosed him.

'I didn't even ask you if it was okay…us making love again.' Alissandru registered that omission in dismay.

Isla sighed. It was fine, nothing left to worry about.

* * *

He awoke in the early hours and for an instant could not even work out where he was, and then he looked down at Isla and began to slide out of the bed, making a real effort not to disturb her. If he woke her, she would fight with him about something and then everything would go to hell again, he thought grimly. No, he would be discreet and tactful, even if neither trait came naturally to him, but he was getting better, wasn't he? He hadn't even mentioned being bitten by the rabid midget dog, had he? He would return home before he was missed and he would send Isla flowers and possibly something sparkly, because she didn't seem to own any jewellery beyond a watch and he wanted her to know how very much he appreciated being forgiven for his past excesses and awarded a second chance.

Isla woke up in a cocoon of contentment and then turned over and found Alissandru gone. She jumped straight out of bed, checked the bathroom and downstairs and realised with an angry stab of disbelief that he had walked out on her *again*…as if she was nothing, as if she was nobody, a one-night stand he could dismiss as soon as dawn folded in!

It was a painful moment of truth for Isla.

Alissandru had used her for sex. But hadn't she used him, too? She freshened up in the shower, her body tender and sensitised beneath her fingertips, and she thought of how he had woken her somewhere in the darkness of the night and made love to her again slowly and silently, but still with that dangerous, exhilarating edge of wildness that seemed to drive his passionate nature. Afterwards he had held her close, and she had felt sleepily, unquestioningly happy and secure.

Why did he have that effect on her when he had already done more to damage her self-esteem and hurt her than any man alive? Did her brain switch off when he was around? Did she have so little pride?

In the light of day, coming to terms with what had happened between them challenged her. She had wanted him and he had wanted her and it had seemed gloriously, wonderfully simple the night before. They weren't hurting anyone else, he had pointed out, but what about how *she* was being hurt? Losing their baby had already hurt her more than enough for one lifetime. Sleeping with Alissandru again would complicate their relationship even more.

Why wasn't she dealing with the reality that she had developed more feelings for Alissandru than was safe in such a scenario? He only wanted sex. Maybe that volatile temper of his spurred his lust for her but lust didn't amount to much, did it? It wasn't feelings, it wasn't caring…

Was that what she was looking for and had hoped to find with him? When she was at the point of tearing her hair out by the roots with frustration over her distinctly confusing reactions to Alissandru, Constantia arrived at the front door with Puggle.

Isla was as wreathed in blushes as a shamefaced teenager at being confronted by Alissandru's mother the morning after the night before. She invited the older woman in for coffee, apologised profusely for the messy kitchen and grabbed a tray to carry the cups out to the pretty terrace that overlooked a rather over-grown garden at the back of the house. Once there she concentrated on practicalities and asked if there were any local charities who might welcome a donation of clothes and things. Constantia was very helpful, and she asked Isla about her friendship with Paulu, visibly relaxing over the freedom to talk about her late son.

'Your sister made my son very, very happy,' the older woman said quietly. 'At times she also made him very unhappy but I am grateful for the happiness he did find with her.'

'Did you get to know Tania well?' Isla asked curiously.

'No. I was her mother-in-law and she was wary of me, fearful that I might be the interfering type. I've never been in this house before,' Alissandru's mother confided, startling Isla. 'Your sister would never have invited me in. She guarded her privacy fiercely.'

'I didn't get to know her well at all because she wasn't the confiding type and I can hardly blame her for that when I was so much younger,' Isla conceded ruefully.

'She was very independent, possibly because she was making her own living from an early age,' Constantia remarked reflectively. 'Alissandru and Tania clashed from day one but that was inevitable with them both being such strong-willed individuals.'

'I clash with Alissandru, too,' Isla heard herself confess and then was stunned that she had spoken so freely.

'That won't do him any harm.' Constantia's smile was warm with amusement. 'Alissandru always thinks he knows best. He was the same in the nursery…bossy and bold.'

'And quick-tempered?' Isla prompted helplessly.

'Oh, yes,' Constantia agreed. 'But the flipside of that was that he was also very honest and responsible. Paulu would've lied sooner than admit he had done something wrong but Alissandru was always fearless.'

When the bell went, Isla was mulling over that conversation while she guiltily cleaned the kitchen she had ignored the night before, but only because of Alissandru's unexpected arrival, she reminded herself wryly.

She went to the door and received an exuberant arrangement of white flowers, all ready for display in a sparkling crystal vase. She didn't need to read the card in the foliage but she opened it with compressed lips, scrutinising Alissandru's initials with reluctant amusement. He was being *very* discreet because there was no message or proper signature to reveal the identity of the sender.

When the bell went a second time, she was filling bin bags with Paulu's and Tania's clothing while carefully checking pockets or bags for anything that should be retained. This time it was a man in a chauffeur-driven car who formally presented her with a gift-wrapped shallow box, clicked his heels with military precision and climbed back into the car. Once again she found an initialled gift tag and she rolled her eyes, ripping open the package with little ceremony as she stood in the kitchen, which was flooded with sunlight. A disconcerted look on her face, she flipped open the shallow jewellery case and the blinding sparkle of the diamond necklace within knocked her for six. She lifted it out, stunned by the shimmering rainbow glitter of the row of diamonds, and rage engulfed her in a flood.

Alissandru thought he could give her diamonds after spending the night with her? Some sort of pay-off—a don't-ring-me-I'll-ring-you cop-out on decent behaviour? Well, he could take a flying jump off the edge of the planet!

She leapt into the hire car, Puggle accompanying her, and drove up to the *palazzo*, powered on the fuel of fury alone. The manservant, Octavio, whom Constantia had confessed ran her son's household with the efficiency of the former soldier he had been, ushered her in and, when she requested Alissandru, escorted her at a stately pace along a corridor where he knocked on a door for her and then departed.

'Avanti!' Alissandru called.

Isla plunged over the threshold with the eagerness of a cavalry charge, stopping dead one foot in the door to press it closed behind her while glowering at Alissandru, who was seated behind a laptop at his desk.

'Isla!' he exclaimed as though she were a welcome, if unexpected, visitor.

He lunged upright, black hair untidy above startlingly bright dark golden eyes, a smile curving his sculpted mouth. He wore faded jeans and an open black shirt and was visibly in weekend relaxed mode. 'To what do I owe the honour?' he asked, feasting his attention on the vision she made in a rather shapeless grey linen shift, which should in his opinion have looked dowdy but which inexplicably merely set off her wonderfully vibrant hair and eyes and accentuated the grace of her slender limbs.

Unfortunately his dark deep voice, which was utterly seductive in the darkness of the night hours, acted on Isla like a flame thrower. 'Thank you for the flowers,' she told him curtly. 'But no thank you for the jewels!'

As she slapped the jewel case loudly back on his desk, Alissandru stiffened and frowned at her, dark brows pleating, stunning eyes narrowing beneath his curling fringe of black lashes. '*Cosa c'è che non va? What's wrong?*' he demanded, taken aback by her mood.

'If you spend the night with me, you don't pay for it with diamonds!' Isla informed him with fierce pride.

'It wasn't a payment, it was a *gift*,' Alissandru contradicted with emphasis, studying her with frowning intensity, wondering how something so simple could be interpreted as something so wrong.

'I don't want gifts *that* expensive!' Isla fired back at him. 'I won't accept them.'

'Duly noted,' Alissandru said drily. 'But does a poor choice of gift really demand this vehement a refusal?'

Isla bridled, reluctant to go into what had made her so very angry, determined not to betray herself in such a way. 'You offended me.'

'Obviously,' Alissandru conceded, marvelling that he had once believed she was a carbon copy of her infinitely more avaricious sister. 'But it was a gift, a small sign of my appreciation for the night we shared.'

Isla gritted her teeth. 'Staying around for breakfast would have been better received.'

'But that would have been indiscreet and I did promise you discretion,' he reminded her silkily. 'If I'm home before dawn, nobody notices, but a later return attracts witnesses and I wasn't sure that you would be comfortable with a more public unveiling of our intimacy.'

Hot colour washed Isla's face in a slow, burning and very uncomfortable flush, because she didn't want anyone on the Rossetti estate knowing about that 'intimacy'. 'I want last night to remain a secret,' she told him without hesitation.

'Not a problem,' Alissandru agreed carelessly, stooping down to snatch up the document case that Puggle had dug his teeth into, contriving to lift both document case and dog together into the air.

Moving forward, Isla hurriedly detached Puggle and gave him a sharp word of reproof when he growled at Alissandru. 'Give him some food and he'll stop trying to bite you.'

'What about discipline? Training?' Alissandru suggested in wonderment. 'Wouldn't that be more sensible?'

'Food is quicker and easier, but if I don't watch out he's going to get fat.' Isla sighed.

Alissandru broke up a scone lying on the untouched tray to one side of his desk and dropped a chunk of it in front of Puggle. The little dog pounced on it with glee. There was good reason for Alissandru's generosity. He didn't fancy having to evade Puggle's sneak attacks at night in Isla's house.

'Coffee?' he proffered in the awkward little silence that had fallen.

'No, not right now. I'm busy clearing the house and, since it's not something I really want to be doing, I'd sooner get it done and finished,' Isla admitted in a rush, turning away in an uncoordinated circle, wanting to escape, wondering how he had managed to turn the situation on its head so that she felt as though *she* were the unreasonable one. 'I wondered what to do about Paulu's desk and personal effects.'

'If there's nothing you want I'll send someone over to collect them and bring them back here,' Alissandru said gravely. 'His desk is probably stuffed with estate paperwork and I should have that passed over to the new manager in case there's anything of interest.'

'Of course. Well, that's something sorted.' Isla wandered over to the window, which overlooked the wooded hills to the back of the house. 'I'm planning to stay here for a few weeks.'

'There's no pressure on you to make a decision about what you're doing or how long you're staying,' Alissandru hastened to declare, recalling how haunted she had been in the aftermath of the miscarriage and wondering how much of that regret she was still carrying.

'This is sort of a holiday for me before I get back to the real world,' Isla admitted.

'And what does getting back to the real world entail?' Alissandru asked, watching her as the sunlight gilded her hair into a multicoloured bonfire of curls, the pale perfect profile, the intense wariness of her stance as if she was waiting for him to say or do something she found objectionable and use that as an excuse to escape.

He had never met a woman like Isla before and to some extent it unnerved him because she was an unknown quantity. A woman who threw diamonds back in his face, *insulted* by them, he thought, marvelling at that lack of materialism. A woman who challenged him, stood up to him, went her own way regardless, unpredictable and in some ways as volatile as he was. An explosive combination. He gritted his teeth as the silence lay, his question unanswered.

'I'll probably go back to studying,' she confided somewhat grudgingly, as if giving such personal information went beyond the bounds of their relationship.

'Studying what?' he pressed, genuinely curious.

'I'd have to pass another course first but afterwards—assuming I'm successful—I think I'd like to go to university to do a paramedics course. I want something interesting, *active*,' she admitted, turning finally to look at him, her head tilting back because he was so tall.

'It would be challenging but I think you're strong enough to do it.' Alissandru stood there, his dark head at an arrogant questioning angle, his stunning dark golden eyes welded to her with intensity and a literal flame of heat ran over her entire skin surface, warming her within and without and in places she didn't like to think about. Her reaction was so instant it was terrifying and, feeling suddenly vulnerable, she turned her head away again and headed for the door.

'Oh,' she muttered, pausing on the threshold to

glance back at him. 'A little hint if you're not too proud to take it. Your mother's ready for another dog. She adores Puggle and I think she would love a new pet.'

And with that helpful little assurance she was gone like quicksilver. Alissandru frowned even as he got on the phone to organise an employee to pack up and collect the contents of his brother's study. Isla was thoughtful, kind and intuitive. A new puppy would indeed comfort his mother, whose need for company he had failed to fulfil. Constantia had seen his brother daily and missed him the most while Alissandru had always travelled the world on business. It was true that he was home a great deal more than he used to be, but his conscience twanged that it had taken an outsider to point out a possibility that he felt he should've thought of first.

On her return to the house, Isla made a trip to two local charity shops. She was thinking about Alissandru far more than she felt comfortable with and deeply regretting her loss of temper. She had overreacted; she *always* seemed to overreact to Alissandru. She had overlooked the reality that a diamond necklace might be a *huge* gift on her terms but that it was a much lesser thing to a man of his wealth. Even so, she thought ruefully, it was better to have returned such an expensive present and to keep the difference in their circumstances out of the equation before it threatened to muddy the water and he started thinking she was a gold-digger again. Or did he still secretly think that anyway? She rolled her eyes at her meandering ruminations. She had no idea what Alissandru *thought* because to a certain extent she had already taught him to watch what he said around her.

On her return, it was a relief to see the contents of Paulu's study being packed up and removed. From those personal effects, she chose only a framed photo of the couple together on a beach somewhere, their smiling faces a good memory she wanted to conserve as her own. That and a little gold locket that had once belonged to her mother and that silly stool were the only personal items that Isla wished to keep from the house.

With Paulu's former assistant helping, Alissandru tackled a job he had long avoided, feeling almost grateful for Isla's part in virtually forcing him into the task.

'This is…er, legal,' his brother's secretary told him, passing him a folded document, complete with a notary's seal.

Alissandru frowned down at the local notary's stamp, wondering why his brother had approached another solicitor instead of Marco, the family lawyer. He opened it up and was disconcerted to discover that the document was another will and, what was more, a will drawn up and duly witnessed more recently than the one the family lawyer had had.

And that later will *altered everything*, Alissandru realised in sheer consternation. Only weeks before his death his twin had changed his mind about how he would dispose of his worldly goods, clearly having had second thoughts about leaving his home to anyone outside the family. He had left everything, house and money as well, to Alissandru, and Alissandru almost groaned out loud. Why the hell had Paulu changed his mind?

Alissandru suspected that Isla's advice had helped his brother to win his wife back and, in that first instance of reclaiming Tania, gratitude had persuaded his brother to leave his estate to his sister-in-law, should both he and his wife die first. And then perhaps Paulu, an innate worrier, had begun to think about the risk of leaving such a will in his wake and the effect it could have on Alissandru.

Alissandru gritted his perfect white teeth. It had been wrong to leave the house away from the family estate but to leave that money to Alissandru instead had been an unnecessary gesture. *He* didn't need the money, but Isla *did*.

And how was Alissandru supposed to act to redress a situation that now threatened to become a messy injustice?

He would keep quiet. He would put the new will in the safe rather than lodge it with Marco Morelli, who would kick up a ruckus and, as the family lawyer, inform Isla immediately of the new will's existence. But was suppressing the new will in such a way illegal? Alissandru breathed in deep and slow. He didn't wish to break the law and, surely, it was *his* duty as Paulu's twin to ensure that his brother's last wishes were respectfully carried out?

He would lodge the new will with Marco and tell him that he did not wish it acted upon. Assuredly, as the main legatee, he must have the right to make that decision. He wanted Isla to keep the money, he only wanted the house and he was quite happy to *buy* the house back from her.

But what if Isla decided not to sell? Or chose to sell to someone else? The new will would be his safeguard, Alissandru decided grimly, a weapon only to be utilised if he was left with no other choice.

CHAPTER EIGHT

'PLEASE JOIN US for dinner this evening,' Constantia argued, reading Isla's reluctant face with accuracy.

'It's a family do,' Isla pointed out as the older woman regarded her expectantly. 'And I'm not family.'

'Your sister was my son's wife and you will always be family,' Alissandru's mother assured her reproachfully.

'I don't really have anything suitable to wear. I'm sure you all dress up.'

'Only Grazia, Alissandru's friend, really dresses up, but then she *is* a fashion designer. A plain dress will be sufficient.'

'I'm afraid I didn't pack anything fancy.' Isla sighed, every muscle in her body tensing at the reference to Alissandru's 'friend' as she struggled to combat an overpowering urge to demand to know who Grazia was and what her relationship with Alissandru was. Secret relationships were all very well until such complications appeared, she conceded ruefully.

But liking Constantia as she did and reluctant to risk causing offence, Isla laid out her only suitable dress that evening and put it on. It was a typical little black dress that wouldn't have raised a thrill even in its fleeting glory days when she had bought it to wear at a work dinner. She went a little heavier on her make-up than she usually did, painstakingly using eye liner and more mascara than usual. Grazia? Who was Grazia? Fierce curiosity powering her, she drove up to the *palazzo* where a whole collection of cars was already parked.

Constantia made a point of introducing her to everyone and, truth to tell, although there was some very flashy jewellery on display, a lot of the women were wearing little black dresses although the majority were fancier than her own. Some of the faces were familiar from that long-ago wedding but mercifully there was no sign of Fantino the Perv, as she thought of Alissandru's cousin. Of Alissandru and his 'friend' there was as yet no sign, but then there was a burst of chatter at the foot of the huge reception room where they were gathered for drinks and Isla glanced towards the door to see their host make an entrance with a tall slender blonde garbed in a tangerine dress with giant raised shoulders and a plunging neckline. He liked blondes, she thought first, and then, he liked blondes who *clung* because his animated companion was hanging on to him so tightly it was as if she feared that he might make a break for freedom.

Isla's observations mushroomed the more she watched them. The minute anyone tried to get into conversation with Alissandru, Grazia intervened, occasionally stepping between him and someone else or hailing someone else across the room and tugging him in that direction. The blonde was very pointedly possessive. She talked constantly, demanding his attention, stroking his sleeve, at one point stopping dead to straighten his bow tie in a statement of familiarity that made Isla's teeth grit.

It was an uncomfortable show for Isla to be forced to watch when Alissandru had been in *her* bed with *her* the night before. Was she jealous? Overly possessive? she asked herself worriedly, disliking the shrewish tone of her thoughts. As for Alissandru, she could read him even better in the slight widening of his eyes when he saw her; he hadn't expected her to be present and he moved with his companion in every direction but Isla's, and by the time they all moved into dinner, Isla was angry at being ignored.

As they were passing through the big hall towards the dining room, Alissandru addressed her. 'Isla…my mother didn't tell me that you would be here.'

'It was kind of her to ask me,' Isla parried lightly, meeting Grazia's assessing dark eyes as Alissandru performed an introduction.

'So, you're Tania's little sister,' Grazia remarked. 'You don't look much like her.'

'No.' Accustomed to such comments when anyone had met Tania first, Isla merely smiled and added, 'Your dress is a wonderful colour…'

And that was all that was required to encourage Grazia to tell the tale of how she had found the material in a Moroccan silk market and imported it to make signature pieces for her most recent fashion show. They separated to find their seats and Isla was reasonably happy with the way the meeting had passed off. She hadn't scratched Grazia's eyes out. She hadn't slapped Alissandru across the face even though she was naturally wondering if he was sleeping with the beautiful blonde, as well.

Of course, she was going to wonder *that* when the woman was all over him like a rash, touching him with a level of familiarity that went beyond the usual definition of friendship. So, decidedly not just a platonic bond on Grazia's side, Isla decided, recognising that she was learning stuff about herself through Alissandru that she had never dreamt she would learn. She *was* the jealous, possessive type, she acknowledged with guilty unease. In fact, she found it very hard to look anywhere else in the room.

His mother should've warned him that Isla would be attending, Alissandru reflected impatiently, reading in Isla's stiff smiles and set little face all that he didn't want to see. Now she was furious with him, now she would be trying to throw him out of bed, her every suspicion aroused. The child they had lost had created a deeper bond between them but that extra layer both united and divided them, he conceded grimly. He cursed Isla's desire for secrecy and questioned how the hell he had strayed into so potentially chaotic an affair. In truth, he didn't know how he had ended up back in bed with Isla or why he had spent most of the day thinking about doing it again and revelling afresh in the hot, sweet welcome of her curvy body. Suddenly he was off-the-charts obsessed with sex for the first time since his adolescence and it had blinded him to every other consideration.

Isla was ridiculously unlike his previous lovers. She didn't look like them, didn't act like them, didn't think like them and was highly unlikely to respect his boundaries. Even more pertinently, those boundaries were set in stone: he didn't get attached, he didn't like strings or drama or plans for a future that stretched more than a week ahead.

'She's very jealous, isn't she?' Grazia whispered in his ear. 'She doesn't look the type to make a public scene, though.'

'What the hell have you been playing at?' Alissandru demanded grimly.

'I couldn't resist testing her out once you said she was here,' Grazia admitted. 'A woman who tosses back diamonds could be worth her weight in gold to a man like you.'

'What do you mean by a man like me?' Alissandru practically snarled back, so irate was he that Grazia was pot-stirring merely to amuse herself.

Grazia gave him a huge affectionate smile. 'Well, to be honest you've had it very easy with women. You click your fingers and they swamp you in attention, you ditch them and they still act like you're their best friend in the hope that you'll come back. And here you are having to *try* to impress a woman for the first time ever and she still won't even walk down the street in daylight with you,' she proffered. 'I think it's *precious*.'

'I shouldn't have told you about her.'

'Yes, but you didn't tell me *everything*, did you?'

Grazia said with a shrewd knowing look. 'I sense more of a back story than you're willing to share.'

'Mind your own business,' Alissandru advised her bluntly, thinking that that was one back story he would never share with anyone.

Isla stayed as long as was polite, cutting out after coffee and walking back out to her car with a sense of crashing relief that she had escaped the source of her discomfiture. Well, one lived and one learned, she reasoned with herself, and over the course of the evening Isla had learned that sex on its own wasn't enough for her. Alissandru was a womaniser and she couldn't say that she hadn't been warned, not only by Tania's gossip but also by his no-holds-barred rejection at the croft. Two people as different as she and Alissandru could only be a bad fit.

And that was *that*, she told herself as she removed her make-up and got ready for bed. She wasn't about to punish herself with regrets because it had undoubtedly been time she acquired some experience with men. And she had run through the entire range of emotions with Alissandru, from the heartbreaking loss of their child to the sheer joy she had discovered in his arms. He had been useful for that, at least, she thought ruefully. Useful for that but not for much else, she extended censoriously. A very off-putting example too, she ruminated, terrific for sex, useless in every other sphere.

The doorbell went. Isla stiffened and ignored it. It went again, shrill and sharp as if it was being jabbed by an angry hand, the noise provoking Puggle into staccato barks. Isla climbed into bed and reached for her book while wondering if she should've gone downstairs to speak to Alissandru. She just knew it was him ringing the bell. What on earth would she have said, though? Another argument would not improve matters, particularly when she would have to deal with him to sell the house. No, it was more sensible to move on and ignore him and that meant no more thinking about him, no more wondering, no more dreaming. It occurred to her that life was suddenly looking very dull indeed.

Alissandru, unhappily, had no experience of being ignored and it inflamed him. Isla blew hot and cold. He never knew what she would do next. If she wasn't shouting at him or blocking him on her phone, she was shutting him out, hugging the charmed circle of her privacy and all that made him want to do was invade it. A sensible man, however, would just go home again and leave her to stew, Alissandru reflected grimly. But Alissandru never turned his back on a challenge. He walked round to the side of the house and calculated his chances of climbing up onto the roof of the kitchen to make it into the bedroom where she had left the window open. *Go home*, logic advised, confront Isla, his volatile, stubborn nature urged. Yanking loose his bow tie to unbutton his collar, he cast his jacket over a shrub and tested a drainpipe for stability.

Isla heard a noise and looked up from her book. As she saw a hand come through the window to grasp at the sill she screamed so loud that she hurt her throat.

'*Per l'amor di Dio*...it is only I,' Alissandru drawled as he pushed the window wider and swung lithely through the gap, black hair tousled as he leant back on the ledge and stretched, long, lean black-trouser-clad legs extended.

In the blink of an eye, Isla transformed from terrified paralysis into raging-shrew mode. 'What the hell do you think you're doing? You frightened the life out of me!'

'You should've answered the doorbell,' Alissandru pointed out drily, studying her slumberously from beneath luxuriant black lashes.

'How the hell did you get up here?' Isla demanded, leaping out of the bed to peer out of the window into the darkness below. 'You climbed up? You stupid idiot! You could've been hurt!'

'But I wasn't,' Alissandru pointed out silkily, trapping her between his spread knees, big hands curving to her shapely hips. 'I don't like to boast but in my misspent youth I climbed Everest. And I'm very grateful to arrive and discover that you are not wearing anything furry...'

Isla froze, embarrassingly aware that, having taken her by surprise, Alissandru had caught her bare of make-up and wearing the shortie pyjamas she had packed for warmer nights in Sicily. Suddenly the fabric felt as though it were shrink-wrapped to her dampening skin, and she went red.

'Although you do have rather eccentric taste in lingerie,' Alissandru purred, his attention locked to the frog print on the pyjamas. 'I will buy you something much more to *my* taste.'

Isla brought her hands down abruptly to break the

spell, not to mention his hold on her hips, and she scrambled back into bed to say with as much cool as she could project, 'No, you won't be buying me anything *or* lingering to outline your fantasies. You're going to leave now…and sensibly, by the front door.'

Alissandru shook his dark head as if she had posed a question and sighed, stretching to loosen his shoulders, the front of his shirt rippling with the flexing fluidity of his muscles. Isla removed her attention from him quickly.

'What do you want?' she demanded tartly.

Alissandru dealt her a wolfish smile. 'I think you pretty much know what I want by now.'

Isla bridled. 'No. We're done.'

'Not as far as I'm concerned.'

'I didn't ask *you* how you felt about it!' Isla flung back at him in frustration.

'Why are you always angry with me?' Alissandru asked, frowning at her. 'I was your first, so I can't imagine there's a long line of bad guys who let you down in the past.'

'One of you is quite enough. Where did you stash your dinner date while you came here?'

'Grazia has gone home, probably laughing all the way,' Alissandru confided with sardonic bite. 'We've known each other from childhood as neighbours and friends. She's the sister I never had but I made the mistake of telling her about you before she arrived tonight, so she decided to play a game.'

'You told her about *me*?' Isla interrupted sharply. '*What* did you tell her about me? And since we're on a subject that *I* had no intention of raising, why does a woman you say you regard as a sister paw you like you're a cuddly toy?'

'To see if she could get a rise out of you…and drop me in it,' Alissandru told her with derision. 'She has an odd sense of humour, always did have.'

'What did you tell her about me?' Isla demanded accusingly.

'*Dio mio*… I didn't tell her anything too private… believe me,' Alissandru countered grimly. 'There are some stories you don't share and *that* tragedy is one of them.'

The worst of Isla's tension drained away and her eyes softened, acknowledging that that wounding memory was theirs alone.

'She was overdoing the flirtation so much that you should've realised that it was fake. Do you really think I would be with a woman who behaves like that with me in public?'

'I don't know. I haven't seen you in public with a woman before,' Isla pointed out woodenly, feeling foolish, feeling mortified by the explanation he was giving her and not really knowing whether to believe him or not. 'Oh, go home, Alissandru. I've had enough of you for one night.'

'But I haven't had enough of you,' Alissandru murmured huskily, beautiful eyes of pure mesmeric gold holding hers.

Perspiration broke out all over her and she swallowed hard, fighting the flush of heat uncoiling at her core with all her might.

'And tonight was a game changer,' Alissandru intoned rawly. 'If you and I were out in the open, I would've been with you tonight, *not* Grazia, so from now on—'

'No!' Isla cut in forcefully, second-guessing what he was about to say, her entire body freezing at the concept of their intimacy becoming public knowledge.

Everyone would know, she thought in horror. Everyone would think she was a slut to be sleeping with Alissandru five minutes after she arrived in Sicily and everyone would be a witness to her humiliation when it fell apart again. And what if somehow the story of the child they had lost came out? She turned cold to the bone at that fear because that memory was so very private. Her face suffused with angry colour because she knew what Alissandru was like, *knew* he didn't last longer than a couple of weeks with any woman, knew it would be foolish to imagine he would even last *that* long with her, a former waitress with no claim to fame or extraordinary beauty.

'Why not?' Alissandru asked silkily.

'I don't want people knowing,' Isla admitted without apology.

'Are you ashamed of me?' Alissandru studied her in angry fascination because he was used to women who wanted to show him off like a trophy.

Isla reddened. 'Of course not,' she muttered unconvincingly, still at war with her upbringing and the tenets that insisted sex was only really acceptable in a loving relationship. So, what did that make her? If she gave herself recklessly purely for pleasure? If she set her value so low she asked for nothing more? If other people saw those truths she would be humiliated, whereas what went on in private was strictly and literally her own affair.

'Either it's in the open or we're done here,' Alissandru delivered, rising fluidly upright, dark eyes glittering like golden blades.

Isla swallowed hard, unprepared for that direct challenge. It was an ultimatum as only Alissandru could make it. 'If we're out in the open where does that take us?' she prompted, playing for time.

'It may not take us anywhere,' Alissandru said bluntly. 'But at least it would be normal and I could share Sicily with you while you're here.'

'I'll think about it,' Isla muttered, plucking at the duvet with restive fingertips.

'Think harder, think now,' Alissandru instructed impatiently.

While you're here. A telling little comment. He didn't foresee them lasting for any appreciable length of time. But then, neither did she, so that was hardly a revelation. What did she have to lose? What did she most fear? *Losing him.* That revelation shocked her but it didn't change anything because either she chose to lose him now by choice or she faced losing him when she didn't want to in the near future. Did the baby she had lost make the idea of losing Alissandru more threatening? Was that why she felt so bonded to him? She liked that explanation. But wasn't it time she took a risk in life? Let up on the need to protect herself and broke the rules of her grandparents, who had grown up in a very different era?

'All right,' she pronounced tautly.

Alissandru shot her a wicked smile and dug out his phone, pressing a number and shooting a stream of liquid Italian into it. He tossed it aside and began to unbutton his shirt, a long riveting slice of bronzed muscular chest appearing. 'From now on, you'll let me buy you things.'

Isla cocked her bright head to one side, dark blue eyes gleaming in her flushed face. 'Alissandru? Quit while you're ahead,' she advised. 'You're supposed to be generous in victory.'

Alissandru leant down and hungrily ravished her soft pink mouth with his own, his tongue delving deep. 'No, that's when I move in for the kill, *bella mia.*'

He shed his clothes without taking his stunning eyes from her once and it made her feel as if she was the only woman on earth for him at that moment. One moment in time, she told herself, one moment to feel *that* special, was worth whatever the aftermath would cost her. This time she watched him strip without turning her gaze away in uneasy denial of her curiosity. And there he was, glorious as a Greek god, completely male, all hard contours of bone and sinew, sleek bronze skin beautifully encasing lean, powerful muscles. The prominence of his arousal made her mouth go dry and she no longer marvelled at the soreness that had taken days to ebb after their first night together.

He ripped off the frog-print pyjamas without ceremony and flung them across the room, studying her pale curves with immense appreciation, lowering his head to stroke a swollen pink nipple with his tongue. Her breath caught in her throat and she recognised the surge of slick heat at her core, her hips shifting, her body primed and ready.

'Who were you phoning?' she asked shakily.

'I was ordering breakfast for us here,' Alissandru told her, long fingers tracing the scattering of freckles across the slope of her breasts. 'I'm not sneaking out like a cat burglar before dawn in the morning.'

'*And* you'll be using the front door from now on,' she muttered breathlessly.

'As long as you answer the bell,' Alissandru qualified.

Isla sent him a glimmering smile of one-upmanship. 'Then you make sure you treat me well,' she murmured, running a possessive hand down over his flat stomach, finding him, watching him react, his lush black lashes sinking low over his vibrant eyes.

'I think I can promise that,' Alissandru husked, turning over to find the centre of her and establish his ownership with a sure expertise that made her writhe.

She found his mouth again for herself, arching up to him, needy in a way she had never allowed herself to be before, her entire body screaming for her to rush to the finishing line.

Alissandru loosed a hungry growl as she pushed against him, startled to register that he was struggling to hold on to his control because Isla's need for him set him on fire. It had never been like that for him. He was as disciplined with sex as he was with everything else in his life, but his desire for Isla was hard to quench. He flipped her over onto her knees and sank into her with a hoarse sigh of unapologetic pleasure.

Isla was so excited she didn't know which part of her was more inflamed. Her heart was thumping so crazily fast it was threatening to burst out of her chest. She was on a sensitised high of receptiveness. The throb at the tender heart of her was almost unbearable and then he was there where she most needed him to be and the intensity of that first forceful plunge sent her flying higher than the stars, her body clenching tight and exploding with scorching sensation, leaving her clutching at the metal headboard of the bed to stay in position.

But the sweltering heatwave of pulsating response only continued as he increased his tempo, grinding into her with an insistent power that drove her straight onto another high. The fierce paroxysms of pleasure blew her away until she finally collapsed under him, catching his cry of release as he hauled her to him in the aftermath, melding their hot, sweat-dampened bodies together with an intimacy that she found incredibly soothing.

'It's never been like this for me,' Alissandru breathed raggedly, burying his nose in the soft springiness of her strawberry-scented curls, feeling the slight weight of her on top of him, shaken to experience the first glimmerings of renewed arousal at the same time. 'We light up the sky.'

'You walked away from it the first time,' Isla could not resist reminding him, because she took everything he said with a large spoonful of salt, determined not to overestimate her worth in his eyes.

'We barely knew each other,' Alissandru reminded her wryly. 'And maybe I did twin you with your sister more than I should've done...'

In the darkness, Isla smiled at that grudging concession, which she had thought she would never hear.

'But nothing lasts for ever...particularly at our age,' Alissandru continued, to ensure that she didn't start thinking that their affair would be of the long-haul variety.

In silence, Isla gritted her teeth at that unnecessarily cool reminder. She didn't believe in fairy-tale happy ever afters. As a child she had continually dreamt that her mother would reclaim her and sweep her off to a more exciting life with her and Tania in London but it had never happened. In the same way as a teenager she had dreamt of the perfect man coming along and that hadn't happened, either. And then there had been the miscarriage and the loss of her first child. There had been few truly happy events in Isla's life and she was inured to disappointment. She preferred to concentrate on reaching more practical goals that would improve her life.

She would sell the house and get onto a course that would hopefully win her a place at university. As always work and effort would be what won her better prospects. With that thought in mind, she murmured drowsily, 'Relax, I'll be bored with you within a couple of weeks... You may be my "first" but you certainly won't be my last.'

The burn of hot liquid rage that flew up through Alissandru in answer to that forecast made him flinch. That was what he *wanted* to hear, he told himself decisively. It wasn't a rejection, or a criticism of his performance, it was only reality. In all likelihood he would get bored first, although he was anything but bored at that particular moment, he conceded grudgingly. There was no need to make a major production out of the discovery of great sex or imagine that it was anything more. No, the wiser approach was to make the most of any unexpected gift of pleasure and let the future take care of itself.

'I'm taking you shopping,' Alissandru announced at eight the following morning as he rifled through the wardrobe where she hung her few outfits. 'You haven't got enough clothes.'

'If you take me shopping you have to promise to keep your wallet closed,' Isla said quietly.

Alissandru ignored the proviso and tossed a plain white sundress on the bed. 'Come on, get up,' he urged impatiently. 'We're heading back to the *palazzo* for breakfast.'

'The *palazzo*? I thought you ordered breakfast to be delivered here?' Isla exclaimed in consternation, only halfway out of the bed. 'Besides, your mother's there.'

Alissandru groaned. 'My mother lives in her own entirely self-contained wing of the house and she would never dream of using the connecting door when I'm at home or I have a guest.'

Isla was unconvinced. 'But how will she know you have a...er...guest?'

'The staff will warn her.'

Isla sped into the bathroom, unnerved by the prospect of the staff that would report back to his mother, and then she scolded herself for worrying about something that was quite immaterial. Soon enough she would be leaving Sicily and only a vague memory because she was unlikely to ever return. What did it matter what anyone thought about her or her morals? Her grandparents had lived in a small tight-knit community where their reputation as a respectable family and the opinion of the neighbours had ruled their lives. Isla lived a much more anonymous life.

Alissandru noticed how Isla walked several steps away from him as if she were some chance-met stranger he had encountered on the drive and renewed irritation assailed him. He closed the gap and grabbed her hand to anchor her to his side, faint colour edging his cheekbones as she shot him a look of surprise. *Holding hands?* he derided. What the hell had he been thinking of? And how did he execute a smooth retreat?

Isla was disconcerted when Alissandru spun her close in full view of the *palazzo* and crushed her lips under his with all the enthusiasm of a man who had been held at bay for weeks. As he released her hand, she kissed him back, breathless and bubbling with sudden energy and happiness. She slid her hand shyly back into his before they headed for the front doors.

The dining room was a much smaller version of the room that had been used for entertaining the night before but, for all that, the table had been beautifully set with shining cutlery and beautiful crystal while Octavio was hovering beside a maid in charge of a large trolley.

'What do you usually eat for breakfast?' Isla asked casually.

'This morning I'm starving,' Alissandru confided with glinting amusement brightening his gaze as she coloured.

And Isla had to confess that, as soon as the silver domes were lifted on the cooked foods available, her stomach felt as though it were meeting her backbone.

Alissandru watched with satisfaction as Isla demonstrated the healthiest appetite he had ever seen in a woman and, having polished off a heaped plate, finished with a croissant and a cup of very rich hot chocolate.

'We have a busy day ahead of us,' he told her, lounging back in his chair.

'*We?*' she queried.

'It was your idea, so we're off to collect a puppy on the other side of the island where the last pug came from,' Alissandru told her. 'I could have had the dog delivered but there's a litter and I thought you should choose, being a doggy kind of person, unlike me.'

Isla's attention briefly strayed to Puggle, who was fawning at Alissandru's feet in the hope of another tit-bit. 'Are you starting to like him?'

'I'm afraid not. He's a shameless manipulator and a crawler into the bargain,' Alissandru told her in disgust.

Isla laughed. 'He doesn't care what you think as long as you feed him. He's a dog, not a human.'

The sound of her amusement animated the formal high-ceilinged room, bringing a warmer, lighter element into the atmosphere. Alissandru frowned at her as though she were a riddle he had still to solve. He could not recall a woman ever making less effort to impress him. She didn't flirt or pout to hold his attention; she was happy to disagree with him and perfectly relaxed in his company. That resistance to being impressed made her an intriguing combination and a challenge. And although he was always exasperated by women who were clingy, he was keen to see Isla make more of an effort to attract him. Was that because no woman had ever made him work so hard for approval before?

He didn't know and he didn't much care. He was content to live in the moment. Isla wouldn't be in Sicily for long and he would make the most of their time together, keeping their affair light, casual and fun until it reached its natural conclusion.

CHAPTER NINE

'So, YOUR FAMILY has always been rich and privileged,' Isla gathered without surprise, for Alissandru's awe-inspiring self-assurance was an integral part of his character. 'My background is very different. I come from a long line of poor people. My grandparents on both sides were crofters and they barely scratched a living. My father qualified as an engineer and he might have done better if an aneurysm hadn't killed him in his early thirties.'

'Why did your mother's parents raise you? Where was your mother?' Alissandru interrupted, reaching for the wine bottle to top up her glass.

'Trying to work two jobs down in London and take care of Tania at the same time. There was no way she could've coped with a baby, as well. She had poor health—she had kidney disease. There was never really any hope of the three of us reuniting as a family and living together,' she pointed out wryly, covering her wine glass with her hand. 'No more for me. In this heat too much would send me to sleep.'

'I believe I could keep you awake,' Alissandru

teased, dark golden eyes settling on her with slumberous sensuality, sending warm colour flying up into her cheeks.

The remnants of a luxury picnic lunch spread in front of them, they were sitting in a meadow that gave them a bird's-eye view of the Rossetti estate. A lush green collage of flowering orchards and vines interspersed with the silvery foliage of the olive groves stretched across the fertile rolling landscape below them. That morning Alissandru had given her a tour of the entire estate and, although Isla did not feel she had been especially active, she was now feeling ridiculously sleepy. Drenched in sunshine and warmth, she stretched her shoulders, frowning as her bra cut into her ribcage while, confined within the tight bra cups, her tender breasts ached. Had she put on weight? She supposed that was perfectly possible when they had eaten out so often. Even when they ate in at the *palazzo*, meals ran to several courses and the food was rich.

But gaining a little weight wouldn't give her sore boobs, she reasoned ruefully. She had thought that was more likely to be linked to hormones and the failure of her menstrual cycle to return to normal and stay normal after her miscarriage. But how could she possibly consult a doctor here in Sicily about something so intimate when she didn't speak the language? In the same way she had baulked at asking Alissandru to organise birth control for her. All such matters could surely safely wait until she returned to London…although by then she would no longer have any need for birth control, she conceded with innate practicality.

Ought she be doing a pregnancy test? For goodness' sake, how could she be pregnant again? Apart from that one tiny moment her first night in Sicily with Alissandru, there had been no mishaps, no oversights. And yet sore breasts and absent periods were also the most common sign of pregnancy in a woman, she reminded herself worriedly, and there and then she decided that she would be perfectly capable of identifying a pregnancy-test kit in a Sicilian pharmacy. She would do a test simply to rule out that frightening possibility.

Alissandru rested back on one elbow watching her, wondering what she was thinking about that made her look so serious. He could barely credit that she had already been in Sicily for six weeks and that he had stayed with her that long, as hooked on the pleasure she gave him now as he had been at the outset. Six weeks had to be some kind of new record for him. But then Isla was intelligent and easy company and he had enjoyed seeing Sicily through her more innocent and less critical gaze. But when would the boredom, the itch to move on to fresh fields, kick in? He had also done the bare minimum of work since her arrival, an acknowledgement that disconcerted him.

Of course, that was what living in the moment entailed, he reminded himself bracingly and, since he hadn't taken a proper break in years from his workaholic schedule, it made sense to make the most of his time with Isla because she would not be in Sicily much longer. She had already applied to join an educational course in London, which started in the autumn. He assumed that she was planning to stay the summer, but he hadn't actually asked because he didn't want to give her the wrong impression, and looking that far ahead would definitely give her the wrong impression.

Isla lay down, her drowsy gaze welded to Alissandru's flawless bronzed profile, experiencing that revealing little kick in her pelvis that made her squirm, her body lighting up as if in search of him. That she couldn't imagine life without him now terrified her. Fleeting moments of happiness had always been the norm for Isla, but the kind of effervescent happiness that Alissandru gave her was an entirely new departure for her. She had not slept alone a single night since they got together and if business or travel intervened, Alissandru was not above joining her in bed in the middle of the night or even at dawn. Either she slept in his giant carved mahogany four-poster bed or he shared her far less ostentatious double at his late brother's house.

Recovering from being part of a couple and adapting to being alone again would be difficult for her. She had never imagined that togetherness developing when their affair began. She had assumed there would be days they wouldn't see each other, arguments when they rubbed each other up the wrong way and needed a break. But she had assumed wrong because she was with Alissandru round the clock and he didn't seem bored...*yet*. In addition, they had very few rows.

Dissension usually broke out when Alissandru tried to give her some ludicrously expensive gift and took offence at her refusal. He didn't seem to grasp that she didn't need presents to feel appreciated. She was much more impressed when he took the time to drive her up into some remote mountain village and walk her along narrow cobblestone streets to a tiny restaurant he had been told offered superlative but simple food, made of the finest, freshest ingredients. Or when he had taken her to see the Greek temple ruins in the beautiful valley at Agrigento even though he was not remotely interested in antiquity.

Yes, Alissandru was just chock-full of surprises, she conceded warmly. If he hadn't told her she would never have guessed that he had originally planned to be a doctor, but that he had abandoned his studies after his father's death because his parent had made some rather risky investments and the family finances had required a steady hand. That he had put his family's needs first had shown her how much caring he was capable of, and that he missed his twin every day was also a fact that touched her heart because, quite honestly, Alissandru had had very little in common with Paulu, yet he had still managed to love and value his brother.

'Just drop me at the house. I need to go to the pharmacy for…er…sun block,' she told Alissandru as she climbed back into his sports car.

'It's a five-minute drive into San Matteo. I'll take you,' Alissandru insisted.

And Isla thought about arguing and then worried that that would only draw attention to any purchase she made. Buying a pregnancy test was ridiculous, she told herself irritably. There was no way she could've fallen pregnant again. Even so, it was wise to rule out the possibility, however unlikely it was, she reasoned.

San Matteo was a pretty little town with a charming *piazza* surrounded by several cafés that overlooked the old church and the central fountain. Alissandru parked and said he would meet her at the bar next door to the pharmacy and she sped off. Recognising a pregnancy test on the shelf was not as much of a challenge as she had feared and she dug the package deep into her capacious bag and rejoined Alissandru with a smile on her face to enjoy a cold drink.

Driving past the *palazzo*, Alissandru glanced at the sleek car parked there and suddenly braked. 'Fantino and his mother must be here for lunch. Why don't you join us?'

Isla froze. 'Your cousin…er… Fantino?'

'*Sì*, you probably met them at my brother's wedding. I'm not particularly fond of Fantino but our mothers are sisters and close,' he explained wryly.

A chill ran over Isla's skin at the mere idea of even being in the same room as the man who had taken advantage of her youth and inexperience in a manner that had taken her months to recover from. 'No, thanks. I don't like Fantino.'

'You remember him?' Alissandru's voice emerged with an instinctive chill as he recalled what he had witnessed on the day of his brother's wedding. Reminding himself that Isla had been a mere teenager at the time, he just as quickly strove to forget the memory again.

'Yes, I remember him,' Isla responded woodenly. 'Just drop me back to the house…or I could walk from here if you like.'

His black brows drew together as he studied her pale, set face. 'What's wrong?' he prompted.

Isla breathed in slow and deep and then saw no reason to withhold the truth.

'Fantino assaulted me at the wedding.'

'Say that again,' Alissandru murmured more quietly.

'You heard me the first time,' Isla retorted curtly. 'I don't want to see Fantino or have anything to do with him.'

'That's a very serious allegation,' Alissandru pointed out harshly.

'Yes, and considering that he got away scot-free with what he did at the time, I don't feel any need to justify the way I feel now. Please take me home.'

Alissandru drove her back to the house in silence, his lean, darkly handsome features clenched with tension. 'We have to talk about this.'

Isla climbed out, her face still stiff. 'It's a little late in the day to talk about it.'

'And whose fault is that?' Alissandru shot at her, snapping the key for the front door from her nerveless fingers. 'If something happened between you at the wedding, we—my mother and I—as your hosts should've been made aware of it!'

Anger gusted through Isla in a heady wave as she stalked into the house, her vibrant curls bouncing on her shoulders, her dark blue eyes outraged. 'I made Tania aware of it and she said I wasn't to tell anyone else. Believe me, it happened! And it *wasn't* "between us", either. When a man assaults a woman, it *isn't* always a shared misunderstanding!'

'Tell me exactly what happened!' Alissandru urged her as she paced uneasily round the lounge.

'Tania sent me upstairs to her bedroom to fetch her bag and your cousin followed me. He tried to kiss me and he put his hand inside the neckline of my dress and tried to touch my breast!' Isla recounted with a helpless shudder of recollection. 'He said something disgusting and when I pushed him off me, he fell over the bed, which gave me the chance to get away. Of course, he was drunk and he thought it was all very funny and he started laughing. But I was scared and I was very upset. I was only sixteen, Alissandru... I'd never been touched before and I didn't know how to handle it.'

His eyes flared as golden as flames in his lean, strong face. The mere idea of Fantino touching sixteen-year-old Isla appalled Alissandru, most particularly because he had seen Isla leave that bedroom closely followed by his cousin and he had put entirely the wrong interpretation on what he had seen. The guilt of that shocking misconception hit him hard. He had caught a glimpse of a suspicious scenario and, instead of immediately being concerned about the welfare of a very young girl, he had assumed she had either been flirting or having sex and had done and said nothing. That awareness went right to the very heart of the prejudice she had accused him of harbouring, and in that instant he knew he could no longer deny that his low opinion of Tania had automatically encompassed her kid sister as well and had coloured his reading of the situation.

'I am so sorry that happened to you, but Fantino will be even sorrier!' Alissandru swore in a raw undertone, throwing back his broad shoulders. 'But I am also sorry that I did not intervene when I might have done that day.'

'How could you have intervened?' Isla questioned without comprehension.

'I saw you coming out of that bedroom. I didn't see your face, just your back view, and then I saw Fantino coming out some seconds after you. I'm ashamed to admit that I simply assumed you had been having some sort of sexual or flirtatious encounter with him. I didn't question it.'

It was Isla's turn to stiffen and stare at him in shock. 'You thought that at sixteen I would go into a bedroom with a man and have sex in someone else's house? How could you think that of me at that age?'

'I have little justification but I *did* think that,' Alissandru admitted reluctantly. 'From the minute I saw you wearing the low-necked dress your sister put you in, I decided that you were just like her.'

Isla groaned, suddenly seeing the whole history of her relationship with Alissandru rewritten in the blink of an eye. He was finally acknowledging that that prejudice had existed, though, and that was a relief, she told herself soothingly.

'I am sickened that you suffered such an experience in my home. You should've been safe there. You were very young. In the absence of a parental figure, it was my duty to look out for your well-being…and obviously I failed,' he bit out grimly. 'On the other hand, Tania was very wrong to persuade you to keep quiet about the assault.'

'Alissandru… I didn't know any of you and I couldn't have brought myself to share that story with anyone I didn't know well. I felt humiliated and embarrassed. Tania suggested I might've encouraged him in some way while I was downstairs,' Isla told him. 'But I hadn't even spoken to him when he followed me up to that bedroom.'

'Do you want me to call the police? A sexual assault is a sexual assault, regardless of how much time has passed.'

Isla stiffened. 'No, I don't wish to make an official complaint. I've put it behind me now but I wouldn't want to meet him again or be forced to pretend that what happened didn't happen.'

Alissandru nodded gravely, his dark golden eyes glittering pale like shards of broken glass below his black lashes. He was thinking of the family jokes told about Fantino's persistent approaches to any attractive woman available. Maybe that wasn't quite so funny now that Alissandru was seeing the other side of the coin and having to question his cousin's behaviour. It had never crossed his mind to look on Fantino as a sex pest but that now seemed more accurate. That he should've dared to frighten and distress a young guest in Alissandru's home was inexcusable. He was also thinking guiltily that he too had noticed Isla's attraction that day and had dealt with it less than honestly by telling himself that she was a shameless little baggage. But he would never have acknowledged that attraction to so youthful a girl, *never* have given way to it.

'What the hell was Tania thinking of when she silenced you?' he ground out on his purposeful path back to the front door.

Wincing, Isla looked pensive and wry. 'That it would've wrecked her wedding…and it *would've* done. Imagine the atmosphere it would've created if I'd publicly accused Fantino! I was a complete stranger in a foreign country and Tania was almost as unknown to your family as I was at that stage,' she pointed out ruefully. 'Would anyone even have believed me?'

'Certainly, I hope we would have.' Alissandru breathed in deep. 'But it will be dealt with now as it should've been then.'

'Why… What are you going to do?' Isla asked worriedly.

'Deal with Fantino,' Alissandru bit out wrathfully. 'What else?'

'So, you believe me,' Isla gathered.

'Of course, I do.'

A moment later, he had gone and once the sound of his car had receded Isla paced the wooden floor, amazed at how shaken up she felt after getting that episode six years earlier off her chest. *Finally.* Her shoulders slumped and she felt relieved that that horrible secret was now out in the open. Naturally, she hadn't shared the story with her grandparents, who would've been horrified. But she had also kept quiet because she had feared that if they knew they would not let her travel alone again and back then she had still harboured the hope that the wedding invitation would lead to other invites from her sister. Of course, that hadn't happened and the sad repercussions of her encounter with Fantino had lasted a lot longer. For years she had been nervous of men, fearful of an assault coming her way without warning, fearful that something she might wear, say or do might attract such treatment. But she had moved past that eventually, survived, she reminded herself calmingly as she tripped over her bag, which she had abandoned in the hall.

Recalling the pregnancy test in her bag, she pulled it out. In the almost bare study, she lifted the dictionary of Italian words she had bought so that she could translate the directions. Fortunately, the pictorial diagrams were more easily understood and she decided to do the test immediately, rather than stress about it or be forced to attempt to do it when Alissandru was around.

He had been very much shocked by her story about Fantino, she acknowledged, but he would be a great deal more shocked, she reckoned, if she was to conceive again. It wasn't possible, she told herself as her heartbeat kicked up tempo. Her stupid hormones were still out of sync after the miscarriage and she would have to see a doctor when she got home again. Having convinced herself that the test was a simple formality to rule out an unlikely development, she went upstairs.

Fifteen minutes later, she was reeling in shock at what was undeniably a positive pregnancy test. Having returned her hire car some weeks before, she climbed into the little runaround that had once belonged to

Tania and drove back to the pharmacy to buy a second test. Just to be on the safe side, she told herself.
An hour later, she contemplated the second positive
result and felt so dizzy and sick with nerves that she
could barely breathe. After a few minutes she stood
up and went to lie down on top of the bed and think.

Pregnant...*again*! How was she supposed to deal
with the joy rising inside her and the quite opposite
effect her news would have on Alissandru? How could
it have happened when they had tried to be careful?
Yet she knew that no contraception was foolproof. Her
head swimming with confused feelings, she tried to
imagine telling Alissandru *again* and immediately
thought that maybe she *didn't* need to tell him this
time, that maybe she should wait a few months to at
least be sure she stayed pregnant.

She was, however, too sleepy to agonise for long
and, while her conscience warred against keeping any
secret from Alissandru, she couldn't help recalling
the angst she had roused with her last announcement.
Was she incredibly fertile? Was he? Would she manage
to carry her baby to term this time around? Anxiety
struck then and struck hard and she had to blank out
her worries quite firmly before she could drift off to
sleep, while telling herself that she would make decisions and worry about the consequences later.

The shrill noise of the doorbell woke her and, blinking sleepily, she scrambled up, stuffing her feet blindly
back into the shoes she had kicked off while at the
same time calling out to silence Puggle's frantic barks.
She padded hurriedly downstairs and swung open the

door on Alissandru, and that fast her cheeks burned and she ran an uneasy hand through her mussed curls.

'I have someone here who has something to say to you. It won't take long,' Alissandru murmured bracingly.

Isla spotted the car pulled up behind Alissandru's and stiffened in dismay as she spotted Fantino's weedy figure heading towards them. 'What does he want?' she hissed.

She didn't have to wait long to find out. Fantino had come to offer heartfelt apologies and regret for the distress he had caused at her sister's wedding and to insist that he would never do such a thing again. He made no excuses, offered no defence, merely concluding his awkward little speech with the assurance that he would be making a big effort to improve his behaviour. Isla studied the bruising and swelling on his thin face and swallowed hard, recognising that he had taken a beating and guessing by the granite-hard set of Alissandru's jaw that he had been the one to administer it. Jungle justice, she thought ruefully, but if it stopped Fantino in his tracks the next time he saw an attractive woman and made him think twice, she had no quarrel with the punishment.

She accepted the apology and watched Fantino jump back into his sports car with a curled lip.

'He will stay away from the estate while you're here,' Alissandru assured her.

'Did you have to beat him up?' Isla asked uncomfortably.

'I had to get the truth out of him…and I did,' Alissandru countered levelly, unable to explain even to his own satisfaction what had ignited the sheer rage that had gripped him once he'd got his hands on Fantino. The concept of anyone laying a single finger on Isla without her permission had incensed him. The awareness that she might not be his cousin's only victim had made him even angrier and determined to keep a watch on Fantino to ensure that he kept his promises to reform.

'I didn't want any violence, and your mother must've been very upset by all this,' she muttered ruefully.

'A generation back, a man could've been killed for any action that could damage a woman's reputation. Community disapproval controlled bad behaviour. My mother is only upset that you did not feel you could trust us with the story of what happened to you that day,' Alissandru explained grittily. 'Now, if you are in agreement, let us bury this matter.'

Isla nodded vigorously. 'Yes.'

'I have a fundraiser for a children's hospice that I support to attend this evening,' Alissandru told her. 'Will you accompany me?'

'If it's black tie, I have nothing to wear.'

'Grazia has already offered to provide you with a suitable dress,' Alissandru cut in. 'She'll be present tonight and would like to see you again. She is probably planning to ask you at least a hundred nosy questions.'

Isla looked up into his lean, darkly handsome face and tried to face telling him what she knew she had to tell him and she lost colour and dropped her head.

'Thank her for her offer. It's a very generous gesture, but I'm afraid I'd prefer to spend a quiet evening here.'

'You've had a distressing afternoon,' Alissandru conceded reluctantly, studying her with his shrewd gaze, picking up on her pallor and the shadows of strain below her eyes, wishing he could give her thoughts a more positive turn, wishing that Fantino's sleazy behaviour hadn't cast a pall over their day, for there was no denying that it had with Isla looking so drawn and fragile.

'A quiet evening and a good sleep will do me good,' Isla declared with a forced and brittle smile.

'How important is it that you sleep alone?' Alissandru asked bluntly, a long forefinger tracing the ripe curve of her lower lip. 'Because I don't sleep so well without you...'

Her dark blue eyes flew wide, her heart thumping at the smouldering appraisal he was giving her. It sent wicked little tingles coasting through her, started up a hot, needy throb at her core. *Because I don't sleep so well without you...* That was a statement that threw her heart wide open, filling her with dangerous warmth and an almost overpowering desire to throw herself into his arms. He was going out without her but he still wanted to spend the night with her.

Alissandru bent his dark head and kissed her, savouring the softness of her lips and the sweetness of her instant response, fierce arousal threatening his self-control and just as quickly unnerving him. You can go *one* night without her, he told himself irritably. You're *not* an addict. Why was everything with Isla so blasted complicated? He thought of Paulu's second will, which he had lodged with Marco, and suppressed a heavy sigh. He had felt foolish when Marco had erupted in approval of that discovery on the family's behalf when he knew he had no intention of having the contents of that second will actioned. Should he already have explained that decision to the family lawyer? But admitting that he was in a relationship with Isla had struck him as too private a revelation to make to one of his employees. If further explanation was required in the future, he would deal with it then, he thought in exasperation.

'I'll call you tomorrow,' he told her abruptly, releasing her to stride back to his car.

Isla stood there a few seconds longer, wondering what had happened, wondering why he had changed his mind about joining her after the fundraiser. She wandered back indoors, feeling strangely unsettled by her recollection of the sudden detachment that had momentarily frozen Alissandru's lean dark face, banishing his usual smile. Maybe he was getting tired of her, maybe he was only just beginning to realise that, she reasoned.

And how did that make her feel? As if the roof was about to fall in, she acknowledged guiltily, taken aback by the awful hollow sensation that filled her when she thought of Alissandru walking away from her. She had got attached, hadn't she? Seriously attached in spite of all the signs that he was not in the market for any kind of commitment. And even worse, now she was pregnant and that fact was more important than her feelings or his.

Isla walked around the house, busying herself with tidying up while she pondered her dilemma. There was really no avoiding the obvious. Alissandru had always been honest with her and she owed him the same honesty. A couple of hours later, her nerves nibbling at her in painful bites, she showered and changed and drove up to the *palazzo*, trying not to ask herself how it would feel when she saw angry resentment and regret in Alissandru's face when she told him she had once again conceived. As ever impervious to mood, Puggle danced at her heels, eager to see Constantia or Alissandru, both of whom could be depended on to feed him.

As she mounted the steps, a thickset older man emerged and hesitated. 'You must be Tania's sister, Isla,' he guessed as he extended his hand. 'I'm Marco Morelli, the Rossetti family lawyer.'

Isla tensed at the explanation. 'I suppose you'll be getting together some papers for me to sign,' she remarked, thinking of the legalities of selling the house back to Alissandru. She had already nominally agreed to sell the house back to him but the sticking point was that she was only willing to accept market value while Alissandru seemed to think that it was somehow his duty to pay very generously for it.

The older man frowned and shook his head in grave dismissal. 'No...there's nothing. A mistake that none of us could know *was* a mistake is already being rectified. Now that the new will has been lodged, it is merely a question of sorting out the tangle Paulu left behind him. I am sorry you have had this experience.'

Isla had fallen very still. '*New* will?' she queried breathlessly.

'Alissandru said that he would explain it all to you.' Marco Morelli checked his watch and sighed. 'Unfortunately, I have another call to make and I can't go into the complexities of a more recent will turning up and reversing the original right now, but if you have any questions, I would be happy to answer them for you at my office. Perhaps tomorrow...or the next day?' he prompted helpfully.

'So, there's nothing for me to sign,' Isla managed to gather, striving to act normally rather than betraying the reality that she had been dealt a body blow.

'No, once you return the inheritance the matter is fully concluded,' he assured her cheerfully. 'I know Alissandru wishes to compensate you for this most regrettable confusion but, to be frank, he owes you nothing because he was no more aware of the second will's existence than anyone else. I persuaded him that he had to have the will lodged legally with the courts if he wanted to avoid further complications.'

The older man bid her good day and hurried back to his car, leaving Isla standing there like a stone statue.

Slowly, very slowly as if her very bones ached, she retraced her steps to Tania's car, Puggle lagging behind her. She knew she couldn't face Alissandru at that moment. She had to gather herself, work out what to do next...aside from repaying what she owed. It was as if her life were a deck of cards that someone had tYhrown up into the air and now everything had changed radically.

Her independence, her plans, everything she had depended on was being torn away. Just her bad luck, as the lawyer had said. From somewhere, Alissandru had obtained another will and, within it, Paulu had presumably left his worldly goods to his brother instead. Isla was shattered. She remembered the contents of Paulu's desk being taken away and surmised that that was most likely where the second will had been found. Even she knew that a more recently dated will would take precedence over an earlier one. But Alissandru had seemingly learned about that will *weeks* ago!

Yet he still hadn't told her. The house was already his yet he was even now determined to *buy* it from her. Why? Because he *pitied* her. Her self-esteem squirmed as though it had come into contact with something very nasty and hurtful. And she was hurt, seriously hurt that he had not told her about that second will as soon as he became aware of its existence.

Knowing that Alissandru had seen her sister as avaricious, she had made a big effort to keep Alissandru's wealth out of their relationship. Pride had demanded that she stand on her own feet and Paulu's legacy had made it possible for her to do that. But now that financial security had vanished. And, even worse, it left her broke and in debt to Alissandru because everything she had spent in recent months, after being given access to Paulu's money, had not been *her* money to spend. How was she ever going to repay that money?

Thank goodness she hadn't spent like a lottery

winner, she thought heavily. Her native caution with money had meant that she was careful, but she had spent a fair bit of money simply travelling to Sicily and had been living off it ever since. How could he not have told her about the second will?

It had been a lie of omission. Feeling sorry for her, Alissandru had kept quiet. He had planned to virtually pay her off by paying for a house he already owned and he would never have told her the truth because he would've let her walk away with his brother's money. And now she was pregnant and she was going to cost Alissandru even *more* money. She would be the financial liability he had never wanted.

Hot tears of mortification burning the backs of her eyes, she entered the house that was no longer hers and went upstairs to pack. She would return to London. What else could she do? She had to find herself some way of making a living again, at least until the baby was born. But no way was she about to tell Alissandru about the baby now face-to-face, not with this horrible financial bombshell engulfing her at the same time. She felt devastated and humiliated and taking herself quietly away seemed like her only dignified option.

She would write Alissandru a letter. That way, he could curse and storm when he found out that there was to be another baby. He wouldn't be forced to be polite; he wouldn't be forced to hide his true feelings. Once the dust had settled on that revelation, she would get in touch with him again.

She went online to see how soon she could get a flight to London but ran into difficulties when it came to travelling with Puggle. Travelling with a dog across Europe could not be done without foresight and planning. Puggle had to receive an injection several days prior to travel and she would need to arrange that first. Constantia would take him, Isla thought ruefully, but when would she ever be able to return to Sicily to reclaim him? Furthermore, leaving her dog with Alissandru's mother would entail making explanations she had no desire to have to make.

Writing a letter to Alissandru took Isla hours. After several failed attempts, she decided to keep it simple. She admitted that she had found out about the second will and that she had no alternative other than to vacate the house. She made no promises of repayment because, with neither a home nor employment awaiting her in London when she finally got there, there was little point in talking about what she couldn't deliver. She wrote about the baby in bald terms and assured him that she would get in touch once she was settled again.

Hearts didn't really break, she told herself firmly as she walked out of the house with Puggle confined in his carrier. She would recover…*eventually*. Alissandru had not encouraged her to fall in love with him. He had been quite clear from the outset that they were simply having a casual affair. Now she needed to concentrate on finding a local veterinary surgeon and somewhere she could stay with a dog in tow.

CHAPTER TEN

ALISSANDRU DROVE HOME from the fundraiser and the whole way he assured himself that he was giving Isla a night of unbroken sleep. But his foot hovered over the brake as he reached the *palazzo* and failed to connect, ensuring he drove on in the direction of his twin's former home. Isla had had an upsetting day and it was natural that he would want to check on her to ensure that she was all right, he reasoned ruefully.

The house was in darkness, which he hadn't expected because it wasn't late. Anxious now, he banged on the door, wondering if she had fallen asleep, and, when even that failed to rouse her, he dug out the key he had always had but neglected to mention and stuck it in the door. He called out her name, switched on lights, frowned and took the stairs two at a time, striding into her bedroom to find it empty. Where was she? The dog was missing, as well.

Obviously she had gone out. Was she with his mother? Since his mother had got the puppy, she had been communicating regularly with Isla about dog training. As if Isla could tell anyone anything about dog training, Alissandru reflected wryly. He called his mother to ask if she had company and, while she was telling him that she had not, he finally noticed the letter lying on the bed with his name printed on it.

As he read the first paragraph, which mentioned her unexpected meeting with Marco, he froze and he cursed. When she referred to her having left, he wrenched open the wardrobe door so roughly it almost fell off its hinges. It was empty. *Per l'amor di Dio*... Isla had *left* him. Alissandru was stunned into momentary paralysis. He hovered in the centre of the room and tried to entertain the concept of Isla being gone. No, he wasn't addicted to her, maybe a little obsessed...occasionally. Isla *gone*.

The shock of that knowledge made him sit down on the side of the bed because his legs turned weirdly weak. He returned to the letter with renewed interest and then reached the section about the baby on the way again and suddenly, in the midst of his turmoil, Alissandru was smiling. What was it about them? They got together and five minutes later...hey, no complaints, Alissandru reflected abstractedly, enthusiasm at the prospect leaping through him. Isla was going to have *his* baby. Obviously they were meant to be. It wouldn't have happened again, he reasoned, if the fates hadn't intended it so.

Alissandru smiled, temporarily in a world of his own, and then he unfroze. Isla had walked out on him when she *needed* him. He couldn't live with that awareness. In fact, it filled him with panic. Where was she? How was he to track her down? Could she have flown out of Sicily already? Should he go to the airport first?

His mobile buzzed, and he snatched it up.

It was Grazia and he only answered it because, if he didn't, Grazia would simply keep on ringing and ringing.

'Alissandru…' he breathed harshly.

'Have you lost anything? Or should I say anyone?'

'How do you *know* that?' Alissandru demanded rawly.

'Because I've found what you lost by the side of the road, complete with a yappy little dog.'

'By the side of the road?' Alissandru exclaimed, leaping upright in consternation.

'The getaway car broke down,' Grazia said succinctly. 'I drove past them on the way home, had to practically force Isla into my car. What have you been doing, Alissandru?'

'I screwed up,' Alissandru bit out in a roughened undertone.

'Well, they're at my house and I'm off to my parents' for the night. Keys in the usual place. Admit it… I'm the best friend you've ever had.'

'You're the best friend I've ever had,' Alissandru recited breathlessly as he practically ran down the stairs, slammed through the door, flung himself into his car.

'Now stop right there and *think*,' Grazia urged as he fired the engine. 'You don't go in cold and without knowing what you're going to say.'

'I know. I know exactly,' Alissandru told her boldly, and he did know, just the same way as his twin had once told him he knew, only it had taken an awful lot longer for the truth to hit Alissandru.

But the truth had hit him at remarkable speed when he'd walked through that empty house and the prospect of spending even one night without Isla had hung over him like a thunderclap of doom.

Emotionally speaking, Isla was all over the place. She had had the strength to walk away and then Tania's car had broken down halfway between the estate and San Matteo. That was when the floods of tears had engulfed her. That was when everything going wrong had just combined into one giant heavy rock grinding her down, squeezing the life out of her. But above all had been the screaming sense of having left part of herself behind, as well.

She *loved* Alissandru Rossetti. She hated him for feeling sorry for her and neglecting to tell her about the will, but he was still the father of her baby and the man she loved. When Grazia had stopped and initially offered her a lift into town, Isla had had no choice but to accept the offer, and when she had asked if Grazia knew anywhere she could get a room for the night with a dog, Grazia had informed her that there was only one place. And she hadn't explained until she'd pulled up outside a beautiful, newish-looking, modern detached house outside town that the only place that would take a dog for the night was *her* house.

Practically pushing Isla through the front door, Grazia had then shown her up to an en-suite bedroom, urging her to get into something comfortable while telling her that the kitchen was full of food and to make herself at home.

Puggle had required no such encouragement. He had curled up in a basket in the kitchen with Grazia's elegant little grey whippet, Primo, and gone straight to sleep, the trauma of being pushed into his transport carrier gratefully left behind him.

Isla had showered and put on her pyjamas. She wasn't hungry and she wasn't sleepy either and the prospect of watching Italian television when she couldn't speak the language had little appeal. When she heard the front door opening, she assumed it was Grazia returning from wherever she had rushed off to, and she stood up. The sight of Alissandru walking through the door was a total shock and her eyes flew wide.

'How did you know I was here?' she gasped.

'Grazia. She knew I'd want to know. I owe her a massive thank you,' Alissandru bit out harshly. 'How could you just run off like that? What on earth possessed you?'

'What else could I do in the circumstances?' Isla hurled back. 'How did you think I'd feel when I found out about the second will? Where was it anyway?'

'Paulu's assistant found it in the contents of his desk... Look, sit down. You shouldn't be getting all riled up,' Alissandru framed jerkily, shaken to look at her and appreciate that she was carrying his child again, even more shaken by how that made him feel. It made him feel better; it made him feel that he had a future again.

'Why shouldn't I be getting all riled up?' Isla asked combatively. 'You withheld vital information from me. Information that I had a right to know.'

Alissandru yanked loose his bow tie and undid his collar while expelling his breath slowly. He didn't look as knife-sharp elegant and self-contained as he usually did. His black hair was untidy and lines of strain bracketed his mouth. He stared at her with glittering golden eyes. 'Where were you going when the car broke down?'

'I was hoping to find a hotel that would take Puggle but Grazia said there wasn't one that she knew of and brought me here. Then she just disappeared.'

'She's gone to her parents' for the night,' Alissandru explained and he stalked round the room, stopped to shrug and then looked at her again. 'How was I supposed to tell you about the second will? I knew it would wreck all your plans. I knew it would make you leave Sicily and that you wouldn't accept my financial help. I didn't *want* you to leave.'

'I'm leaving,' Isla told him, dry-mouthed. 'I have to deal with this situation and get on with my life. I may be pregnant but I'm not living off you unless I'm forced to.'

'*Expect* to be forced,' Alissandru muttered half under his breath while scooping up Puggle and ruffling his curly head with a wry apology for not having a treat for him. 'You see, if you're Puggle, life is simple. He trusts and likes the people who feed him.'

'I don't need you to feed me, Alissandru,' Isla said drily, while watching in surprise as he stroked her dog. 'When did you start liking him?'

He set the dog down. 'I wouldn't go as far as saying I like him yet, but he's yours and that makes a difference. He accepts me, I accept him.' He glanced at her through the tangle of his long black lashes, golden eyes bright as sunlight. 'I *want* this baby… I really, really *want* this baby. By the time I warmed up to the idea of the first baby, it was gone.'

'I didn't know you'd warmed up,' Isla whispered shakily, thoroughly disconcerted by what he had declared.

'You didn't give me the chance to tell you,' he reminded her. 'You just shut me out after the…miscarriage. I didn't think you'd believe me if I told you how I felt or that I was grieving, too. It was a loss to me, as well. I'd started looking forward to becoming a father, seeing the whole situation in a very positive light. But what restricted me back then doesn't restrict me now.'

Her brow furrowed as she tried to accept that he had felt much more than she had given him credit for when she'd miscarried. But she could not doubt the sincerity in his eyes or the husky emotion lacing his words. 'What restricted you?'

'I still had you all tangled up with Tania inside my head back then. I didn't trust you, didn't really know you. That's all changed,' he pointed out.

'Yes. But after the miscarriage, you said that it wasn't meant to be, and that really upset me,' she admitted unevenly. 'I assumed you meant that people like you and me, from such different backgrounds, don't have children together.'

His ebony brows pleated. 'Of course, I didn't mean that. I'm not a snob. I don't rate people by how much money they have.'

'You did me,' she reminded him helplessly.

'Tania cast a long shadow,' he said ruefully in his own defence. 'And I received a bad first impression of you. I didn't want to make the same mistake Paulu had and get involved with the wrong woman. That's why I left the croft so fast that morning. I wanted to stay longer. I wanted to spend time with you and that shocked me. I thought I'd soon get over it but after you, I didn't want other women. You spoiled me for them. I've only been with you since that first night.'

Genuine joy unfurled inside Isla at that unexpected assurance. She had wondered, of course she'd wondered whether he had been with anyone else before she came to Sicily. The discovery that he had only been with her made her feel much more secure. That he wanted their baby as well and was willing to openly acknowledge the fact warmed her down deep inside.

'When I stood in that empty house tonight, I was devastated that you were gone and I knew then that I loved you and that nothing but marriage would satisfy me this time around.'

It was quite a speech and it shook Isla where she stood. She blinked and swallowed hard and when she looked again he was still studying her as if she was the only woman in the world for him. 'You love me? You want to marry me?'

'You once said you wouldn't marry me if I was the last man alive. I hope I've risen a little higher in your estimation since then,' he confided with entirely surprising humility as, to her shock, he got down on one knee.

'Marry me, Isla,' he urged. 'I do love you, more than

I ever thought I could love any woman. Unfortunately you came into my life when I wasn't expecting you but having you in my life means everything to me and I don't want to lose you.'

Absolutely gobsmacked, Isla stared down at him without words, in such shock that she was reeling. 'You really love me?'

'I started falling for you the first night but I didn't realise why I couldn't forget you. So, will you marry me? I'm starting to feel like a bit of an idiot down here!' he told her drily.

'Of course, I'm going to marry you,' Isla informed him with newly learned confidence as she hauled him up to her with greedy hands. 'You love me, you want me, you want our baby…that's the biggest surprise of all!'

'A piece of you, a piece of me, maybe even a dash of my brother or even Tania,' Alissandru pointed out with only the faintest flinch at that final possibility. 'How could I not want my child? It took me a long time to get here, Isla, but now you've got me, you're not going to get rid of me again.'

Isla stood in the strong circle of his arms, trying to compute how life could travel from being totally horrendous to totally wonderful in the space of minutes, and not doing very well. 'I don't want rid of you,' she mumbled shakily, and then the tears were coming, cascading from her eyes as though she had taps behind them.

And Alissandru grabbed her up in a panic and sank down on the sofa holding her. 'What's wrong?'

'I'm j-just s-so h-happy!' Isla stammered apologetically through her tears.

'But you're crying,' Alissandru said gently as though she might not have noticed.

Isla gave an inelegant sniff. 'I think it's my hormones. I think it's being pregnant.'

Alissandru was bewildered. 'So…you're happy? You're *definitely* going to marry me?'

'Obviously.' She gulped. 'You're not usually this stupid.'

'I've never been in love before. Never been with a woman who would dare to call me stupid, either,' Alissandru admitted with a spontaneous laugh.

'Well, of course, you're going to be stupid sometimes,' Isla told him briskly, having finally mastered the tears dripping down her face. 'But, you know, you're not the only one who fell in love this spring. I love you too, but this time I thought we were only having an affair because you kept on hinting that we weren't going to last for ever.'

'That was the last dying strands of the single guy trying to stay free,' Alissandru told her with wry amusement in his gaze. 'Paulu told me once I didn't know what love was and he was right. I would forgive you just about anything…but now don't take that as an invitation,' he added with his usual caution.

'Are you really happy about the baby? How do you think it happened?'

'I haven't got a clue and don't care. I'm just delighted that it has,' Alissandru confided with warmth glowing in his level dark golden eyes.

'I'm scared that something will go wrong again,' Isla confided in a rush.

'We both are, but at least we're together now and *together* we can handle anything,' Alissandru said with confidence. 'I've got you and a whole future with you waiting for me…and I've never been happier in my whole life than I feel at this moment.'

That was quite a declaration from the once cynical love of her life and Isla rested her head back against his shoulder, struggling to accept that such wondrous happiness could finally be hers. 'I love you,' she whispered, stroking a fingertip along his shapely upper lip. 'And we're going to be incredibly good together.'

Alissandru smiled down at her with such tenderness in his beautiful eyes that her heart squeezed tight as the hold she had on him. This man with all his emotion would love strong and true, she sensed, thinking of his care for his own family. They had travelled a rocky road to their happy ending but they had both learned a lot on the journey. Her whole life was now opening up into a new dimension and the knowledge that she was no longer alone was a great source of joy to her. Alissandru and a baby too, she thought blissfully…

Almost four years later, Isla presided over a Christmas spent in London in their town house, which was filled to capacity with dogs and children. Indeed, Alissandru was talking about looking for a larger house as a London base.

'I just don't know how you've managed to acquire

four of them so fast,' Grazia pronounced, eying the
four children surrounding Constantia with astonish-
ment. 'Thank heaven, I'm only having one,' she added,
patting the swell of her stomach beneath her highly
trendy mint-green dress.

'Two sets of twins adds to the count,' Isla pointed
out with amusement sparkling in her eyes, for Grazia,
who had become a dear friend, had only married the
year before and motherhood was entirely new to her.
Entering an environment cluttered with the parapher-
nalia of *four* young children was more than a little
daunting for her.

Gerlanda and Cettina had been born first—identi-
cal twins, dark haired and blue-eyed, two very lively
little girls now three years old. Luciu and Grazzianu
were non-identical boys and still babies, one noisy and
demanding like his father but with red hair, the other
quieter and more contented and dark. They had truly
planned their third pregnancy although they hadn't
planned on a second set of twins.

Isla's favourite photograph of their wedding sat near
the fire, ring-fenced by a guard to protect the children. It showed her gorgeous traditional wedding dress,
which had been nowhere near as trendy as poor Grazia
had wanted to make it but had been everything that
Isla had dreamt of, which was exactly as it *should* be,
Grazia had said of a bride's gown. Her uncle had given
her away at their beautiful Sicilian summer wedding
and it had been a wonderful family day, her relatives
as welcome as the Rossetti clan could make them.

It was hard for Isla to credit that she had been married to Alissandru for almost four years. While she was pregnant with the girls she had done the London course she had wanted to do to complete her education to her own satisfaction. That achieved, she had discovered that she was happy to be a stay-at-home mother with a bunch of kids and dogs because she liked to be available when Alissandru was at home. He didn't travel as much as he once had and he was always home at weekends and holidays, she thought fondly, watching Alissandru lift his youngest son in his arms and talk with apparent confidence about his feeding schedule. As if *he* had anything to do with it, Isla ruminated with amusement. They had a nanny to help and Alissandru got more involved with the fun side of parenting like bathtime and bedtime and buying toys. My goodness, could that man buy toys!

That had possibly been the biggest surprise of their marriage, Isla conceded with a tender smile. Alissandru adored kids, adored her being pregnant and wanted more. And she had told him no, four was *enough* and he would just have to content himself with four.

They spent most of their time now in Sicily and Isla could speak the language, although she made a fair number of mistakes, which she could depend on Alissandru to always correct. Sometimes, she thought ruefully, he was the most annoying man and yet if anything, after four years, he owned even more of her heart than he had at the outset of their marriage. He treated her as if she were as fragile as glass and tried to protect her from anything that he deemed prejudicial to her state of mind.

He strode over to her, clutching Grazzianu to his chest like a well-wrapped parcel. 'He's ready for his nap.'

As he bent his dark head down to her she saw the devilment in his gaze and knew that the only person ready for a nap was Alissandru and it *wasn't* a nap he meant. She collected Luciu from his adoring grandmother and they took the babies upstairs to the nursery to settle them into their cots.

'I... I just wanted to give you this,' Alissandru confessed, surprising her as he loved to do, wrapping a diamond necklace round her throat like a choker and fixing the clasp before she could object. 'You thought I meant sex,' he said piously, as if such an idea would never have occurred to him.

'It's not even Christmas Day yet!' Isla exclaimed, ignoring that crack.

'I love buying you stuff. I love that you can't say no now, *mia bella*,' Alissandru confided, tugging her close to his lean, powerful frame.

'I have more diamonds than I know what to do with,' she muttered repressively, thinking of the king's ransom in jewellery he had given her and the shelves and shelves of glorious handmade silk and lace lingerie, which she was willing to admit that she enjoyed wearing. 'But thank you very, very much,' she whispered, because she knew it was his way of showing how much he loved her and that she couldn't change him and wouldn't have changed him even if she could have done.

'But you're the most precious diamond of all,' Alissandru intoned huskily. 'I just adore you.'

And Isla smiled with the tremendous warmth that had attracted him from the very first time he saw that smile, he acknowledged thankfully. She was the centre of his world and all the sunshine in it, and the idea that he might have walked on by and missed out on what he had found with her still terrified him in retrospect.

'And you know you're loved…or you ought to,' Isla informed him, kissing that smoothly shaven jaw line, which was as far up as she could reach, thinking how different he felt unshaven as he had been at dawn and as hot and rampant as only Alissandru could be and making her equally so.

'I like to be told occasionally,' Alissandru countered, taking a stand.

'Why don't I *show* you instead?' Isla whispered, watching those stunning eyes of his light up with alacrity and smiling even more.

* * * * *

THE
BILLIONAIRE'S
CHRISTMAS
CINDERELLA

CAROL MARINELLI

Dear Sam.

With love, always. xxxx

PROLOGUE

'I KNOW THAT this is a very difficult time for the Devereux family. However—'

'That may be the case but it has no bearing on this discussion.'

Abe Devereux interrupted the Sheikh when few people would. It was an online meeting, with Abe in his stunning high-rise New York City office and Sheikh Prince Khalid in Al-Kazan, but Abe would have responded in the same terse manner had they met face to face.

The Devereux family was extending its empire into the Middle East. The first hotel was under construction in Dubai and the site for the next had recently been sourced in Al-Kazan.

Except the landowners, Khalid had just informed Abe, had added several million to their previous asking price. To refuse jeopardised not only the Al-Kazan project—the knock-on effect would be huge. If the Devereuxes didn't agree to the new asking price, then construction in Dubai might cease.

Abe refused to be bullied.

Khalid was very possibly relying on the fact that he was a personal friend of Abe's younger brother, Ethan.

Or perhaps he had hoped for a rare moment of weakness or distraction, given that Jobe Devereux, the head of the Devereux empire, was gravely ill.

But there would be no weakness or distraction from Abe.

Khalid would soon come to understand that he was dealing with the most ruthless of the Devereuxes.

Abe would never be swayed by emotion.

This was business, and nothing ever got in the way of that.

'Whose side are you on, Khalid?' Abe asked the question few would dare. 'We are supposed to be in this venture together.'

'I am on the side of progress,' Khalid answered smoothly. 'And for the sake of a relatively small sum we risk thwarting the inroads that have been made.'

'If Al-Kazan is not ready for such progress then we shall look for another site.'

'Have you discussed this with Ethan?' Khalid checked.

Ethan was supposed to be here but he hadn't made it in, which was perhaps just as well, given that he was friends with the Sheikh.

Abe wasn't particularly friendly with anyone but, even had he been, it wouldn't have swayed him.

'Ethan and I are both in full agreement,' Abe lied smoothly, for he had not had a chance to speak with his brother. 'The price remains as originally decided or we look elsewhere.'

'If we could perhaps discuss it with Ethan present?' Supremely polite, still Khalid pushed his agenda. 'He was here recently and understands the sensitivities.'

'There's nothing more to discuss.'

'But if we can't come to a satisfactory resolution, even a temporary one, construction in Dubai may well cease.'

'In that case...' Abe shrugged '...no one gets paid. Now, if you'll excuse me, I really do have to go.'

'Of course.' Khalid nodded graciously, though it was clear he was displeased. 'Would you pass on my best wishes to your father?'

It was only when Abe was satisfied that they had been disconnected and Khalid's face had disappeared from the screen that he let out a curse that indicated the gravity of the situation. If the Dubai construction ceased, for even a few days, the knock-on effect would be dire.

Abe was quite sure that Khalid was relying on that fact.

For a couple of million, Abe could resolve this. It was small change in the scheme of things and he was certain that Ethan would be willing to pay up rather than jeopardise the project at this tender stage.

But Abe refused to be bullied.

And threats, however silkily delivered, would not change his stance.

Abe got up from his desk and, from his impressive vantage point, looked out over a cold and snowy Manhattan and beyond. It was a stunning view towards the East River and he drank it in for a moment, barely turning his head when his brother's PA knocked and explained the reason for his absence from this morning's meeting.

'Ethan's been at the hospital with Merida since last night. Apparently, she's in labour.'

'Thank you.'

Abe didn't ask for details.

He already knew more than enough.

Ethan had married Merida a few months ago, though only because she was pregnant. Abe had, along with his father, signed off on the contract that would ensure that the new Mrs Devereux and her infant would be well provided for when they eventually divorced.

But as clinical as a contract sounded, it had its merits—Abe hoped to God it ensured that the baby would be treated better than he and Ethan had been.

He could not think of that now.

Abe closed his eyes on the glorious December view.

It wasn't even nine a.m. and it was already proving to be a long day.

He had Sheikh Khalid testing his limits and the Middle East contract on the brink of collapse.

As well as that, in the hospital a few streets away from this very building he had his brother's wife giving birth in one wing…

And his father dying in the other.

No.

He corrected himself—his father was fighting for his life in the other.

His mother, Elizabeth Devereux, had died when Abe was nine. She hadn't been in the least bit maternal and Jobe had been far from a hands-on father. In fact, a fleet of nannies had raised the Devereux boys—but Abe greatly admired his father and was not ready to let him go.

Not that he showed it, of course.

For a second so brief it was barely there Abe considered discussing the Middle East issue with him. Jobe Devereux was the founder and the cleverest man Abe knew. Yet Abe quickly decided he could not stress his father while he was fighting just to survive.

Only that wasn't the real reason that Abe didn't head to the hospital now—Jobe had never shied from giving his view after all.

It was more that Abe had never asked for help in his life.

And he wasn't about to start now.

But before he could tackle the work waiting, his private phone rang and Abe saw that it was his brother.

'A little girl,' Ethan said, sounding both tired and elated at the same time.

'Congratulations.'

'Merida was amazing!'

Abe made no comment to that. The fact that Merida had just had a baby did not suddenly make him a fan of hers. 'Have you told Dad?'

'I'm heading over to tell him now,' Ethan said.

Usually they called their father Jobe, as it helped with the business side of things, but this, Abe was fast realising, wasn't business.

Oh, there might be a watertight contract in place and the marriage might all be a charade, but a little girl had been born this morning. And that moved him. He thought of his father, about to hear the news that he was a grandfather.

'Will you be coming in to meet your niece?' Ethan asked.

'Of course.' Abe glanced at the time. 'Though not until later in the afternoon.'

'Merida's friend, Naomi, is getting in at midday. We were supposed to be there to meet her.'

'Do you want me to organise a driver to pick her up?'

There was a brief stretch of silence before Ethan responded. Neither of the brothers liked asking for help, even from the other. 'Abe, is there any chance of you going? She's Merida's best friend.'

'I thought she was the nanny?' Abe frowned. He only knew that because a full-time live-in nanny had been a part of the terms agreed to.

'Naomi's both.'

'Give me her details,' Abe sighed, and pulled out a pen.

'Naomi Hamilton.' Ethan gave her flight details. 'If she can come to the hospital before being taken to the house, that would be good.'

'All sorted,' Abe said, and glanced again at the time. 'I really do have to go. Congratulations.'

'Thanks.'

Luckily Ethan was too muddled to ask how this morning's meeting with Khalid had gone and certainly Abe did not volunteer the information.

Cool heads were needed for dealing with this situation and currently the only Devereux who had one was Abe.

He buzzed through to his own PA. 'Jessica, could you organise a gift for me to take to the hospital this afternoon?'

'For your father?' she checked.

'No, the baby's here.'

There was a little squeal that had Abe pulling the phone back from his ear; then came the inevitable questions. 'What did Merida have?'

'A girl.'

'Does she have a name yet? Do you know how much she weighs?'

'I don't know any more than that,' Abe responded. He really hadn't thought to ask. 'I also need you to sort out a driver to do an airport run from JFK to the hospital.' He gave the flight details. 'She gets in at midday. The name's Naomi Hamilton.'

Despite his brother's request, Abe would *not* be playing chauffeur.

As well as Khalid to contend with, he had the first-of-the-month board meeting to attend. Before that he was meeting with Maurice, the head of PR, to discuss the annual Devereux Christmas Eve Charity Ball.

It was a highlight on the social calendar, but, for the first time since its inception, Jobe Devereux would not be attending.

Tabled on this morning's agenda was discussion of contingency plans should Jobe die close to, or on, that date.

Not pleasant.

But a necessary task, given that people travelled from far and wide and paid an awful lot of money to attend.

Emotion had to be put aside and unpalatable scenarios played out and usually Abe was very good at that.

Abe wasn't just cool…he was considered cold.

And not just in the boardroom. His reputation with women was devastating, though that had calmed in recent years. But his aloofness extended also to family.

He had stopped trusting others by the age of four, looking out for his brother and doing his best to ensure that he came to no harm.

Abe kept his emotions in check.

Yet, unusually, this morning he was struggling to do that.

His schedule was always daunting but he thrived on the pressure and handled it with ease. Yet the auto-pilot he usually ran on felt, this morning, as if it had disengaged.

The news of the baby had punched a hole in the wall he carefully erected between himself and others.

He put a finger and thumb to the bridge of his nose and squeezed hard, then took a long cleansing breath. Pushing all the drama out of his mind, he'd get on with holding down the Devereux fort.

Someone had to.

CHAPTER ONE

'A New York Christmas…'

Naomi smiled as her very chatty fellow passenger told her what a magical time she would soon be having.

'There's nothing better.'

'I'm sure there isn't,' Naomi agreed.

It was easier to.

Privately she cared little for the festive season. Well, she made sure it all went smoothly for whatever family she was with but it was just another day for Naomi.

Actually, no. It was a very lonely day for Naomi—it always had been and no doubt always would be.

But she wasn't going to bore the woman in the next seat with that.

They had got on well.

Naomi was a little on the large side and had tucked her elbows in and tried to make herself very small on take-off. But by the time they came into land, neither had slept and they were chatting away like old friends. Still, there were things even old friends didn't need to know.

Born on Christmas Eve, from the little Naomi knew her first weeks of life had been spent on a maternity ward before the first of many foster-care placements.

Now a maternity nanny, she looked after newborns and ensured better for her tiny charges. Her job was to look after the mother and infant during this very precious, tumultuous time before the permanent nanny took over.

She wasn't a part of the family, though.

On a day such as Christmas, her role was to make it as seamless and as stress-free for the new mother as possible. And Naomi usually ate in her room alone.

This year, though, would be different as it was her best friend whose baby she would be taking care of.

Merida, an actress, had come to New York City with Broadway on her mind and, sure enough, had landed a part in a new production called *Night Forest*.

She had never made it to opening night, though.

Pregnant by Ethan Devereux, she had said goodbye to her acting career and entered into a marriage of convenience.

Although, inconveniently for Merida, she was head over heels in love with her husband.

Naomi had had reservations about accepting the job.

Ethan and Merida had insisted that she be paid, and though they were probably just trying to be nice, it would have been easier on Naomi to have been asked to stay as a friend.

But she was concerned for Merida and that was why she had agreed to take the post.

As the cabin lights were dimmed for landing, Naomi looked out of the small, moisture-streaked window. There wasn't much to see, just snow-laden clouds, but then her breath caught as jutting up in the distance she saw the iconic skyline rising out from gunmetal-grey water and it sent a frisson of excitement through Naomi.

She was here—actually here. And for someone who had never been out of the United Kingdom it was an exciting moment indeed.

The plane banked for its final approach but that first glimpse of the city left a smile on Naomi's face.

Naomi had freshened up as best she could after breakfast had been served but she took out her compact and checked her reflection. She was excited to see Merida but her reflection showed tiredness. Her dark chocolate curls were limp and beneath her deep blue eyes were dark smudges. Her very pale complexion had turned to pure white.

A sleep would fix that, she told herself.

Naomi was determined to beat jet lag at its own game and stay awake for the entire day.

It was beyond exciting to be here and she wore her smile through baggage collection, though she felt it wane a touch at customs.

All the paperwork had been arranged but still she felt very nervous when she told them that, yes, she was here to work.

'A nanny?' the border security official checked, and took the folder containing all of Naomi's paperwork and had a through read through of it. 'For the Devereuxes?'

'Yes, there's a letter from Mr Ethan Devereux and if there are any problems...'

'There's no problem.'

Her passport was stamped and she was on her way.

The ground staff were lively and funny, blowing into their hands and telling her it was bitterly cold as she awaited her baggage.

'You'll need a coat, Miss,' one said as she passed.

'I'm getting one!' Naomi called back. 'I'm headed straight to the shops.'

She had, a few days previously, left her good coat on a train and had been about to buy one for her trip when it had dawned on her she was heading to the shopping capital of the world. Naomi had decided her first stop would be the city's most famous department store.

For now she had to make do with a rather flimsy jacket and a thick scarf that she would put over her long dark hair before heading outside.

Naomi had a lot of luggage.

Well, two cases and her hand luggage.

It was, though, her entire world that she carried in those bags.

She lived wherever work took her. In between jobs she aimed to take a brief holiday, but Naomi didn't have a home as such. She had shared a flat with Merida for a couple of years, which had been brilliant, but since then she had lived with the families she'd cared for. Generally, she arrived two weeks before the baby's due date and stayed between six and eight weeks after the baby was born.

And she was tired of it.

Not so much her work, as exhausting as it was.

Naomi was just tired of living out of suitcases.

As she stepped into the arrivals lounge Naomi scanned the crowd for a glimpse of Merida, who was generally unmissable with her shock of red hair, although, given how cold it was, she may well be wearing a hat. Or, given that the baby was due on December the fourteenth, she may well have not made it to the airport. As she wheeled her trolley Merida saw a sign with her name on it held by an older man in a black suit.

'I'm Naomi Hamilton,' she said.

'Guest of?' the gentleman asked.

Clearly security was tight around the family, Naomi thought as her status was double checked. 'Merida Devereux.'

'Then come this way.' He smiled. 'Here, let me help you with that...' He took over the trolley. 'Where's your coat?'

Naomi told him her plan to get one as they walked and it really was freezing outside.

'Jump in,' he told her when they reached the car. Naomi didn't need to be asked twice and sat in the back, watching the world go by as her cases were loaded.

'Are we headed to the house?' Naomi asked as they drove off.

'No.' He gave her a smile in the rear-view mirror. 'I'm to take you to the hospital. More than that, I don't know.'

How exciting!

Naomi was very aware, though, that the next few weeks were not going to be plain sailing. Merida was completely in love with Ethan, who had only married her to give the child his name, and the plan was they would divorce after a year. Naomi was worried for Merida. Also, the patriarch of the family, Jobe Devereux, was seriously ill.

Even if Merida hadn't been her friend, Naomi would have been aware of that fact. The Devereuxes were a hugely powerful family and Jobe's health woes had reached the press in England.

Naomi just wanted to make these precious first weeks as peaceful and as calm as she could for the new mother and baby, and would do whatever she could to ensure that.

The car was warm and despite the stop-start traffic it was lulling, and as they drove through a long tunnel Naomi resisted the urge to rest her head on the window and close her eyes. But, given she'd had to be at Heathrow so early, she hadn't slept last night, neither had she slept on the plane, and as the traffic backed up Naomi found that her eyelids grew heavy and finally she gave in.

'Miss…'

Naomi startled and opened her eyes, taking a second to gather where she was. In fact, the driver had to orientate her.

'We're at the hospital.'

So they were.

The private wing was incredibly warm and as she passed a couple of rooms and saw empty beds Naomi thought about how she would love to claim one and stretch out and sleep; but as she stepped into Merida's room jet lag was completely forgotten.

'Naomi!' Merida was sitting up in bed, looking a mixture of exhausted and happy and clearly delighted by the arrival of her friend.

'Merida! How are you?'

'So happy. We had a girl.'

Ethan was holding the precious bundle. 'I'm sorry I couldn't get there to meet you,' he said, giving her a kiss on the cheek, and was rather more friendly than Naomi had expected.

'Well, you were rather busy…' Naomi smiled.

'Is Abe with you?' he asked.

'Abe?' Naomi frowned for a second then remembered that was Abe was the elder Devereux brother. 'No, the driver brought me. Bernard, I think...' She was distracted then as the blanket fell back and she caught a proper glimpse of the baby. 'Oh, my, she is gorgeous.'

Naomi, in her line of work, saw a lot of new babies, and they were all very precious, though for Naomi there had never been one more precious than this little girl. With no relatives of her own, Merida and her very new daughter were the closest thing to family that Naomi had known.

When Ethan handed her to Naomi she found that her eyes filled up with tears as she held the new life.

'Does she have a name?'

'Ava,' Merida said. 'We just decided.'

'Oh, but it suits her. She's completely stunning.' Little Ava really was, with a shock of dark hair like her father, and huge dark blue eyes and a sweet little rosebud mouth. 'How was the birth?'

'It was actually wonderful.'

When Ethan headed off to make some calls, Merida elaborated a touch. 'Ethan was right there the whole time. Naomi, we're okay now,' Merida said, her eyes shining. 'Ethan told me he loves me and that we're going to make this marriage work.'

Naomi rather thought it might be the emotion of the birth that had Ethan showing devotion, but of course she didn't say that to her friend as she popped the now sleeping baby into her little crib.

'How long do you think you'll be in for?' Naomi asked.

'A couple of days. I feel terrible that you'll have to find your own way around.'

'I'm quite sure I can manage. I'll head off soon and

get in some sleep and tomorrow I might do a bit of sight-seeing *and* buy a decent coat.'

'I can't believe you're actually here.' Merida beamed. 'Naomi, I've got so much to tell you.'

But it would all have to wait.

Ethan returned at that moment and a short while later Jobe, the grandfather of little Ava, came down in a wheelchair, escorted by a nurse. And then came the photos, though not just the family kind—a professional photographer had been brought in for the occasion.

It was clear that Jobe was very ill indeed, yet he had refused to have the baby brought up to visit him and had made a supreme effort to be a part of such an important day.

As the photographer snapped away, even though Jobe had a nurse with him, Naomi helped too, positioning little Ava in his arms and making sure that as soon as he tired she took the baby with a smile.

'Thank you,' Jobe said, noting how she had hovered discreetly. 'You're Merida's friend?'

'Yes.' Naomi nodded. 'And also little Ava's nanny for the next few weeks.'

'Well, any friend of Merida's is a friend of the family. It's good to have you here, Naomi.'

It was such a little thing. She had expected to be daunted by this powerful man, but instead they clicked on sight and he made Naomi feel very welcome and a part of it all. She was used to being the nanny and hovering in the background, but today, on her first day in New York, she'd had her picture taken while holding a tiny little baby who was new to all of this too!

'Has Abe been in?' Jobe asked, as Naomi held little Ava, who was close to falling asleep in her arms.

Naomi might look as if she wasn't listening, but her ears were on elastic. She knew Abe was a force to be reckoned with and wanted to get a feel for things and work out the dynamics so that she could help Merida as best she could in the weeks ahead.

'Not as yet,' Ethan said, and Naomi heard the edge to his voice. 'I specifically asked him to pick up Naomi, but instead he sent a car.'

'Well, he must have got caught up,' Jobe suggested.

With little Ava asleep and Merida looking like she needed the same, Naomi decided it was time to head off. 'I'm going to go,' she said, and gave Merida a hug and a kiss. 'Jet lag is starting to creep in and I want that well behind me by the time you bring your little lady home.'

'We're staying at Dad's place for now,' Ethan explained, 'while we have some renovations done.'

'Merida told me.' Naomi nodded. 'It's fine.'

Famous last words.

'Dad's place' was a huge, grey stone mansion on Fifth Avenue, overlooking Central Park. Naomi had to pinch herself to believe that she was really here. Oh, thanks to her job she had stayed in some amazing residences, but nowhere had been nearly as grand as this.

One of the heavy double doors was opened by a gentleman who said that they had been expecting her, and as Naomi stepped into the foyer an elderly woman came rushing over.

'Naomi!' She gave her a welcoming smile. 'I'm Barb, Head of Housekeeping.'

'It's lovely to meet you, Barb.'

The house was even more stunning inside.

The huge foyer with marble floors and archways

was impressive, as was the large curved staircase, but it was all made a little less daunting because the first thing that greeted Naomi was the delicious scent of pine.

There in the corner was a Christmas tree, bigger than any she had ever seen.

An undressed tree.

'We were waiting to find out what Merida had,' Barb explained. 'Have you ever seen a tree decorated pink?'

'No.' Naomi laughed.

'Well, you soon will.'

And even with a soon-to-be-pink tree it was sheer New York elegance and this was only the entrance. Naomi could only imagine what lay behind the high doors.

'Have you seen the baby?' Barb asked.

'Yes, she's very beautiful. She's got black hair and a lot of it…'

'Oh, how precious.'

Naomi didn't reveal her name, or show the photos she had taken with her phone, as she wasn't sure it was her place to. Not that Barb asked, she was far too busy chatting. 'It's fantastic that you've arrived on such a good news day. We were just having a little celebration,' she added. 'I'll show you around.'

'That can wait.' Naomi shook her head. 'A bath and bed is all I need right now. Just show me where I'm sleeping and you can get back to celebrating the baby's arrival. Though if you can show me the alarm system, that would be great. I don't want to set it off if I get up in the night.'

Barb did so and as they walked up a huge staircase, lined with family photos Naomi told her about the time she'd had to call an ambulance on her first night at a job for the mother of one of her charges. 'When I let the paramedics in I set the whole house off. It just added to the chaos.'

'What a fright you must have had,' Barb said as she huffed up the stairs. 'Now, don't turn left here or you'll end up in Abe's wing.'

'Does he live here?' Naomi asked, because she hadn't been expecting that, but Barb shook her head.

'No, he's half an hour away, but if he's been visiting his father late into the night, sometimes he comes home.' She gave a little laugh. 'Well, to the family home. Now, this is you.'

She opened a heavy door, and behind it wasn't the bedroom that Naomi had been expecting to see. Instead, it was more of an apartment, with a lounge, its own bathroom, a small kitchen as well as a bedroom. 'And the baby has a room, of course...' Barb said, opening the door onto a small nursery. It wasn't the main one—this nursery was, Naomi rightly guessed, for the times the nanny had the baby overnight. Not that Merida was intending for that to happen, she had made it clear she wanted the baby with her, but it gave Naomi a glimpse of how things had once worked in the Devereux home.

'I have to say, I never thought I'd see the day when we had a nanny here again,' Barb admitted. 'I got on well with the last one.'

'How long ago was that?'

'Let me see, Abe must be nearly thirty-five and Ethan's thirty. They had nannies till they went off to boarding school, so Ethan's last one must have been some twenty years ago. They had their work cut out, let me tell you...' Barb's flow of words halted.

'Did the boys run wild?' Naomi pried, but Barb changed the subject.

'Now, Merida made it very clear that you're a guest as well as the baby's nanny, so you're to use the main entrance, as well as having access to a driver, and you've got full freedom of the house. Still, it might be nice for you to have your own space.'

Naomi nodded.

She guessed that Barb had stopped talking so freely when she'd remembered that Naomi wasn't just staff but also a guest.

'I'll bring you up some dinner, or you're more than welcome to join us. We're just having some nibbles...'

'Don't worry about dinner for me.' Naomi shook her head. 'I ate on the plane. All I want now is a bath and then bed.'

'Well, you make sure to let me know if you wake up hungry.'

'If I do, I'll call out for something,' Naomi said. She was very used to staying in new places. 'You go and celebrate and don't worry about me.'

Once Barb had gone Naomi explored a little. Her bedroom was gorgeous, dressed in lemon and cream with a splash of willow green, and Naomi couldn't wait to crawl into the plump bed, but first she unpacked and then had a long bath. She had intended it to be a quick one but she dozed off in the middle. She really was very tired so pulled on some pyjamas and crawled into bed. It was delicious to stretch out but sleep wasn't as forthcoming as she'd hoped it would be, and she lay there with her mind whirring.

A little girl.

Ava.

Oh, she was so thrilled for Merida but, despite her friend's assurances that everything was fine now, Naomi was very aware that that might just be the high of giving birth and Ethan making promises he might not keep.

Yes, he'd seemed friendly and happy but the Devereuxes were not exactly famous for their devotion to their marriage vows.

Naomi was also worried about the dark times ahead because, having seen Jobe, it was clear to her that he was nearing the end.

It was certainly going to be an emotional time and Naomi was glad that she would be here for her friend.

Ava hadn't been due for another two weeks. Naomi's loose plan had been to get over jet lag, as well as the exhaustion of her previous job—usually she would have allowed for more time between jobs but for Merida she had made an exception.

Really, she didn't consider Merida work, though they had insisted on paying her handsomely.

It still didn't sit quite right with Naomi, but she tried not to think of that now.

Her plan had been to catch up on her sleep and get her bearings, and to do some sightseeing at the start of her trip. With Ava's slightly early arrival all her plans had changed.

Tomorrow, she decided, she would go through the nursery and check if there was anything needed and then she'd call the hospital. And then she'd cram in as much sightseeing as possible. Before she could do that, though, she had to buy a coat.

It was on that thought that she fell asleep and then awoke, Naomi had no idea how much time later, to the unsettling feeling she generally had during her first couple of days in a new home.

There was an eerie silence.

Soon she would wake knowing where she was and recognising the shadows on the walls, Naomi told herself as she lay there, but for now it was all unfamiliar.

One feeling she did recognise, though, was the fact that she was starving.

Usually she would have emergency supplies for nights such as this, but there was nothing in her luggage, and anyway a snack wasn't going to fix this hunger.

Naomi pulled on her robe and drew back the drapes, then understood the odd silence for there was a blanket of snow outside and it was still falling heavily.

Even though the house was warm, the sight made her shiver and she did up the ties on her robe.

It was coming up for midnight and, Naomi decided, there was just one thing she wanted more than anything in the world on her first night in New York.

Pizza.

A big pepperoni pizza, but she wondered if they'd deliver.

No problem!

Naomi ordered online and just fifteen minutes later tracked her pizza working its way along Fifth Avenue!

She padded down the stairs and was just about to sort the alarm when she startled as the front doors opened. A dark-coated man walked through them, bringing with him a blast of cold air and, to Naomi, the warmest of glows.

Perhaps he floated through them, Naomi thought, for he was almost too beautiful to be mortal.

He was *more*.

It was the only word she could come up with as she stood in the grand entrance, yet it was an apt one.

He was a smidge taller than Ethan and his jet-black hair was worn a touch longer, and was currently flecked with snow. And he was more sullen in appearance than his brother had been, with almost accusing black eyes narrowing as they met hers.

And he was, to Naomi, a whole lot sexier.

Yes, he was *more*.

He made her heart quicken and she was suddenly terribly aware of her night attire and tangle of hair, because he was just so groomed and glossy and more beautiful than anyone she had ever seen.

'I thought not,' Naomi said by way of greeting.

And Abe frowned because not only did he have no idea what she meant, he also had no idea who this voluptuous dark-haired beauty, dressed in her nightwear, was.

Then she walked past him and he watched as she took delivery of a large pizza box and now he better understood her odd greeting.

No, Abe Devereux was definitely not the pizza delivery man!

CHAPTER TWO

'I'M NAOMI,' SHE offered by way of introduction as she closed the front door. 'Merida's friend and the baby's nanny.'

'Abe,' he said, but didn't elaborate. It was his father's home after all and he was also in no mood to engage in small talk.

But she persisted.

'Have you seen her?' Naomi asked. 'The baby.'

'Yes.'

He said no more than that. Abe Devereux did not offer his thoughts or his opinions. There was no 'Yes, isn't she gorgeous!' No 'I can't believe I'm an uncle,' and it was clear to Naomi that he did not want to speak.

It didn't offend her.

Naomi was *very* used to being the paid staff.

He removed an elegant grey woollen coat and beneath that was a suit, cut to perfection, enhancing his tall, lean frame.

Abe glanced briefly around, no doubt, Naomi thought, expecting someone to come and take his coat, but when no one appeared, neither did Naomi hold out her hand. With that lack of a gesture she drew a very important line. She might be staff, but she was Ava's nanny, and *not* his maid.

He tossed the coat over an occasional chair as Naomi opened the lid of her pizza box and peered into it. 'I'll say goodnight...' She was momentarily distracted from his utter, imposing beauty by the sight that greeted her. 'Just how big is this thing?' Naomi asked.

The pizza was massive.

Seriously so.

It smelt utterly divine.

And, she remembered, she was not just the nanny but Merida's friend, and so she persisted with the conversation when perhaps usually she would not.

'Would you like some?' she offered, but Abe didn't even bother to reply so she took her cue and headed up the stairs.

There were pictures lining the walls of the stunning Devereux family over the years. The two brothers, as babies and then children. Their stunning mother who, Naomi knew, was dead. She wondered if they missed her on a day like today.

Yes, Naomi often wondered about things like this, especially with not having a family of her own.

And then she heard his voice.

'I would.'

She turned on the stairs, a little unsure what he meant. Did Abe Devereux actually want to share in her midnight feast, or had she got things completely wrong and he was about to tell her he would like staff to refrain from wandering at night, or something?

But, no, she hadn't got things wrong.

'A slice of pizza sounds good,' Abe confirmed.

He himself was surprised that he had taken her up on her offer. And it wasn't the normality of it that had had him say yes, for it was far from normal—Abe didn't do pizza. And, more pointedly, a woman in pale pink pyjamas with a big robe on top wasn't the norm either. Silk or skin was the usual sight that greeted him at this time of night.

He had just come from the hospital, though not the maternity section for he had visited his brother and wife earlier in the day.

Instead, he had spent the evening and half the night with his father.

Jobe had put everything into staying alive for the baby's birth and visiting the little family today, and Abe had this terrible, awful feeling that now it was done he'd just fade.

He had sat there, watching his father sleep and the snow floating past the window, and though warm in the hospital room he had felt chilled to the bone.

They might not be particularly close but Abe admired his father more than anyone in the world.

Ethan had grown up never knowing what a cruel woman their mother had been.

Four years older than his brother, Abe had known.

Elizabeth Devereux's death when he was nine had come as a shock, but all these years later Abe already grieved for his father.

Not that he showed it.

Abe had long since closed off his heart and far from hiding his emotions, he *chose* not to feel them.

Yet choice had been unavailable to him tonight.

'Why couldn't you come to me, Abe?' his father

had asked, when his medication had been given for the night.

'It will sort itself out,' Abe had said. 'Khalid is just posturing.'

'I'm not talking about Khalid,' Jobe had snapped, and then, defeated by the drugs, had closed his eyes to sleep.

Yet where was the peace? Abe thought, for despite the good news of the day, despite Jobe's goal to see his grandchild being met, still his face was lined and there was tension visible even in his drug-induced sleep.

There had been a long moment when his father's breathing had seemed to cease and he'd called urgently for the nurse.

It was normal, he'd been told, with so much morphine for respirations to decrease and also, he'd been further told, albeit gently, things slowed down near the end of life.

But no matter how gently said, it had hit him like a fist to the gut.

His father was dying.

Oh, he had known for months, of course he had, but he had fully realised it then. Abe had glimpsed the utter finality of what was to come and, rather than do what instinct told him to and shake his father awake and demand that he not die, Abe had held it in and headed out into the snowy night.

He had sent his driver home ages ago, and had stood for a moment looking up at the snow falling so quietly from the sky.

Instead of calling for his driver, or even hailing a cab, he had crossed the wide street and headed over to Central Park.

There he had cleared snow from a bench and sat by the reservoir, too numb, and grateful for that fact, to feel the cold.

Here had been the park of his childhood, though it had never been a playground.

Abe had never played.

Instead, on the occasional times his mother would take them, unaccompanied by a nanny, it would be he who would look out for Ethan, making sure he didn't get too close to the water.

And that had been on a good day.

The park closed at one a.m. and, rather than being locked in for the night, Abe had stood with no intention of heading home.

There were plenty he could call upon for the usual balm of sex. As disengaged as he was with his lovers, Abe did generally at least manage some conversation, but even that brief overture before the mind-numbing act felt like too much effort tonight.

And so he had walked from the park to his father's residence, which was far closer to the hospital than his Greenwich Village home. He had decided to sleep there tonight.

Just in case.

And now, for reasons he didn't care to examine, conversation felt welcome.

Necessary even.

He walked through to the drawing room and she, Naomi, Merida's friend, followed him in and took a seat on the pale blue sofa as he lit the fire that had been made up and then checked his phone.

Again, just in case.

'The snow's getting heavy,' he said. 'I thought it might be wise to stay nearer to the hospital tonight.'

'How is your father?'

'Today took a lot out of him. Are you a nurse?' he asked, because he had no real idea of the qualifications required to be a nanny. Perhaps that was why he had pursued conversation, Abe thought—so that he could pick her brains.

But she shook her head.

'No,' Naomi said. 'I'd always wanted to be a paediatric nurse but...' She gave an uncomfortable shrug. 'It didn't work out.'

'Why not?'

'I didn't do too well at school.'

She opened up the box again and tore off one of the large slices but the topping slid off as she attempted to raise it to her mouth. 'How on earth do you eat this?'

'Not like that,' he said, and he showed her how to fold the huge triangle.

'I haven't had pizza from a box in years...' Abe mused as he took his slice. 'Or rather decades. Jobe used to take Ethan and me over to Brooklyn when we were small. We'd sit on the pier...' His voice trailed off and he was incredibly grateful that she didn't fill the silence that followed so he could just sit and hold the memory for a moment as they ate quietly. 'This pizza's good,' he commented.

'It's better than good, it's incredible.' And made more so when he went and poured two generous drinks from a decanter.

'Cognac?' he offered.

She had never tasted it before and, given for once she

wasn't working, Naomi took the glass when he handed it to her.

'Wow,' she said, because it burnt as it went down. 'I doubt I'll have much trouble getting back to sleep after that.'

'That's the aim,' Abe said. 'You can rely on my father to have the good stuff on tap.'

'What did you think of the baby?' Naomi asked as he sat down. Not on the sofa but on the floor, leaning against it.

'It's very loud,' Abe said, and she laughed.

'She's gorgeous. What are you getting her as a gift?'

'Already done.' Abe yawned before continuing. 'My PA dealt with it and got her some silver teddy.'

'I did all the shopping before I came,' Naomi said, 'though now I know it's a girl I'm sure there'll be more. Are you excited to be an uncle?'

He raised his eyes, somewhat disarmed by her question.

Abe really hadn't given being an uncle much thought. Since he'd heard that his brother had got Merida pregnant it had been the legalities that he'd focussed on— making sure the baby was a US citizen and ensuring Merida couldn't get her hands on any more of the Devereux fortune than the baby assured her.

Only, lately, Merida seemed less and less like the woman Abe had been so certain she was.

In fact, Ethan looked happy.

He didn't say any of that, of course.

But if you are going to do pizza by the fire on a snowy December night, you do need to do your share of talking, and so he asked her a question. 'Do you have any nieces or nephews?'

'No.' Naomi shook her head and then let out a dreamy sigh. 'I actually can't think of anything nicer than to be an aunt.'

'Do you have any brothers or sisters who might one day oblige you?'

She shook her head.

'So you're an only child?' he casually assumed, and then watched as for the first time colour came to her pale cheeks.

'I don't have any family.'

He saw the slight tremble of her fingers as she put down the crust of her pizza.

'None?' he checked.

'I count Merida as family,' she admitted, 'but, no.'

Yes, she and Merida were close, but Naomi was very aware that though they were best friends, Merida was far more of Naomi's world than the other way around.

And that said nothing against Merida. But she had parents, albeit awful ones, and a half-brother and half-sister, and cousins and grandparents.

Naomi had...

Merida.

Her birth mother had wanted nothing whatsoever to do with her and Naomi had no clue who her father was. There had been a foster mum when she'd been a teenager that had been amazing but she'd taken a well-earned retirement in Spain, though they still corresponded. And there was another foster family that she still sent a Christmas card to.

And of course, there were friends she had made along life's way, but there was no family.

None.

Zip.

'My mother gave me up for adoption,' Naomi said, 'but it never happened.'

She tensed as she awaited the inevitable 'Why?' that even virtual strangers felt compelled to ask.

It just made her feel worse.

There were millions of families who wanted babies, surely?

Or, 'What about your grandparents, didn't they want you?'

It was hell having to explain that, no, her mother hadn't fully relinquished her rights for a few years, which had held Naomi in the foster system. And, no, her grandparents hadn't wanted to clear up their daughter's mess.

And that, no, there would be no tender reunion between mother and daughter.

At the age of eighteen Naomi had tried.

But her mother had remarried and wanted no reminder of her rebellious past.

Thankfully, though, Abe didn't ask.

Instead, he watched her pinched face and two lines deepen between her dark blue eyes like a castle gate drawing up in defence. He thought of his own loud, brash family and the dramas and fights at times. He even thought back to his mother, and while there were no warm memories there, still there was history.

He couldn't fathom having no one.

Yet he did not pry.

And she seemed incredibly grateful for that.

He watched as she visibly shook off dark thoughts and pushed out a smile.

'So what sort of an uncle do you want to be?' Naomi asked.

Given what she'd just told him, he didn't dust off the notion, instead he told her the truth. 'I really haven't given it much thought.' Now he did. 'I don't know,' he admitted. 'I can't imagine that she'd want for anything...' He'd made very sure of that. But as he'd combed through the contract and ensured decent chunks of access for his brother, there had been no thought of where he himself might fit in.

'I'd like to be...' Who examined it? Abe wondered. Who actually gave consideration to the type of uncle they wanted to be?

She had made him do just that.

He could hear the spit and crackle of the fire as he gazed into it. Maybe he was feeling maudlin. It would be his father's funeral soon after all, but on this cold December night, the most guarded and closed off of all the Devereuxes paused a while and thought of the uncle he would like to be.

'I could take her for pizza now and then,' he said.

'And show her how to eat it?'

'Yes,' he agreed, but then shook his head. 'I can't think of anything else.'

'That's plenty to be going on with.' Naomi smiled and when he tore off another slice, it seemed easier, rather than have him hand it to her, to join him on the floor. It simply did. And they sat side by side and spoke, not a lot but enough.

'So,' he asked, 'you're going to be looking after Ava?'

'For a little while.' She saw his frown. 'I'm a maternity nanny.'

'What does that mean?'

'I generally stay between six and eight weeks with

a new family before the permanent nanny takes over. I try to allocate four weeks between jobs, but it never really works out. Babies come early, as we saw today.'

'Do you go home between jobs?'

'No, I generally have a holiday. Sometimes if there's a decent gap I might house-sit.'

'Where's home?'

'The next job.'

'So you're a nomadic nanny.'

'I guess.' That made her laugh, she'd never really thought of describing it like that. 'Yes.'

'And you only look after newborns?'

She nodded.

'That sounds like constant hard work.'

'Oh, it is,' Naomi agreed. 'But I completely love it.' Or she had.

Naomi didn't share that with him, of course. She didn't tell him that she was tired in a way she'd never been before. Not just from lack of sleep but from the constant motion of her lifestyle.

There was one slice of pizza left and both their hands reached for it at the same time.

'Go ahead,' Abe said.

'No, we'll share it.'

And when he tore it and there was one half a bit bigger, instead of not noticing, she looked at him until he tore a piece off the bigger half. 'That's fair now,' Abe said.

'Hmm.'

She was so full it shouldn't matter, but she had never, ever tasted something so delicious, Naomi thought. Or was it the open fire keeping them warm as the snow fluttered outside the window, or was it adult company in the middle of the night that made it all so nice?

'Do you ever have,' Abe asked, 'er, *issues* with the fathers?'

'Gosh no.' Naomi laughed. 'I dress like this for work. I don't think the mothers have anything to worry about.'

He begged to differ.

Scantily dressed Naomi wasn't, but for Ethan there was no doubting her sensuality. It wasn't just her curves or the very full mouth or ripple of dark hair and how it fell in her eyes, it was more subtle than that. Little things, like the way she covered herself when her robe gaped, and how she closed her eyes after each and every sip of cognac as she held it on her tongue for a moment, and the lick of her lips when she'd first glimpsed the pizza.

Yet, he mused, the mothers wouldn't have anything to worry about.

She was nice.

Moral.

The sort you would trust your baby to.

And for Abe she had made this hellish night so much better.

'Do you ever get asked to stay on?' Abe asked.

'All the time.' Naomi nodded and then took the last bit of her pizza and he waited, watching the column of her pale throat as she swallowed, before asking another question.

'And do you ever consider it?'

'Never.'

'Ever?' he checked, for she sounded so adamant.

'Never, ever.'

'Why not?'

She looked into the fire and wondered how to answer him. Naomi never told her employers her real reason for declining.

She would never even consider staying on. In fact, it was stipulated in the terms of her employment that a permanent nanny be signed to take over before Naomi commenced her role. And should that fall through, it was specified that an agency be used, for she would not be extending her contract.

No matter how wonderful the terms or the family.

Actually, because of just that.

'Why don't you stay in one place?' he asked again, and now he did probe, because suddenly Abe really wanted to know some more about her.

'I guess because I've never stayed in one place for very long. We do what we're used to, I suppose. Revert to type...'

But he shook his head at her excuses.

Abe wasn't buying it.

'Why?' he asked again.

He was brilliant at maths, but she didn't add up.

Abe wasn't one for sitting talking by a fire, but she'd made him feel at ease, she made the place feel like a home, yet she chose not to have one for herself.

'You want to know why?' She looked at him then, blue eyes on black as they held the other's gaze.

'Yes.'

'Because I'd fall in love with the family,' Naomi said. 'And then one day it would be time for me to leave.'

Her blue eyes were serious, and there was no trace of tears, which told him this was no revelation, she had known this about herself for a very long while.

Naomi twisted his heart in a way no one else could, and a hell of a lot had tried.

She twisted a heart that Abe hadn't even known he had.

He wanted to reach for her.

It was as instinctive as that.

And he wanted to chase her loneliness away in the only way he knew how.

Abe looked down at her full lips, all shiny from the food they had shared, and he wondered about her pepperoni kisses and just laying her down and taking her by the fire.

He wouldn't.

Not just because he had a conscience.

Abe had long thought his conscience had been severed along with the umbilical cord.

No, he wouldn't make a move because there was something so rare about tonight.

Something he didn't want to jeopardise.

And there was *nothing* he wanted her to regret.

Naomi felt the burn of his gaze and she felt the shift in the atmosphere.

The way he first held her eyes and then the lowering of them as they took in her mouth had her body prickling with sudden awareness.

Naomi had never encountered a moment such as this.

Just for a second, when rational thought was suspended, she wanted to know the feel of his mouth, and there was a sense of certainty that if he leant forward a fraction, then so too would she.

There was silence, save for the hiss and occasional spit from the fire and the tick of a clock on the mantel, yet she could hear the roar of blood in her ears and she almost closed her eyes in anticipation of bliss.

But Abe did not move forward. Instead, she watched as he looked away and reached for his drink, and so inexperienced was she that Naomi was certain she'd misread things.

Jet lag, cognac, and an absolute dearth of knowledge about men told Naomi that she'd been imagining things, and had come very close to looking a fool. She blushed as she pictured herself sitting, eyes closed, and waiting for a kiss that would never come. Embarrassed, she told herself that if she was having fantasies about a playboy wanting her, then it really was time for bed.

'I ought to get some sleep,' Naomi said. 'I've got a load of sightseeing planned for tomorrow.'

She stood and re-fastened the tie on her robe then reached for the box. 'Leave it,' he said, because if she bent down to retrieve it, he might just pull her in.

''Night, Abe.'

''Night.'

She made her way up the staircase and found her door, holding it together until in she was in the bedroom. But once there she sat on the bed and, head in hands, Naomi moaned.

Not because she'd foolishly thought he'd been about to kiss her. She could easily talk herself down from that—he was surely one of New York's most eligible bachelors, and there was no way he'd be interested in her.

No, it was because of how *she* felt.

In the space of an hour Naomi knew she had developed a king-sized crush on Abe and that was something she didn't want or need. Not just because she was here to work and nothing must get in the way of that, but because she was scared of being hurt.

Naomi guarded her heart with the same ferocity that she guarded her tiny charges.

There had been no dates, no romance in her life.

Her career took care of that, and she was grateful for it, especially on a night such as this.

She simply refused to open herself up to potential hurt.

CHAPTER THREE

ABE.

Naomi knew *exactly* where she was the very second that she awoke, and her first thought was about last night.

It was as if, in the hours since they had said goodnight, Abe Devereux had not left her mind.

Of course, she had surely left his.

She had overslept and it was after nine. No doubt he was at work now and not even thinking of their lazy fireside conversation on her very first night in New York.

Naomi was, though.

She'd heard of the Devereuxes before Merida had met Ethan. She had worked with a prominent family in London who'd had dealings with them. Now that she thought on it, Abe's name had been bandied about at the time. And not fondly. He was the gatekeeper to the Devereuxes. The one you had to get past if you wanted a deal to go through.

And when it came to women, his reputation had been equally formidable.

That was all she knew.

When she'd been trying to work out the dynamics

of family, in order to best help her friend, Naomi had tended to skim past the articles on Abe.

Still, she recalled enough to know that that it wasn't just a case of lock up your daughters when Abe Devereux was around.

Lock up your wife too.

And possibly the nanny!

He had no scruples, that much she knew.

Determined not to dwell on him, Naomi reached for her phone and looked at the weather forecast.

Snow, with more snow to come.

It would have been so much easier to lie under the covers for a while longer but Naomi was very used to forcing herself out of bed and did so today. Her hair she left down and didn't worry about make-up. She rarely did. There wasn't much point when working with babies. She decided on black jeans and a huge silver-grey jumper as well as black boots, which she pulled on while sitting on her bed. Naomi topped it all off with her less-than-substantial jacket. Before heading out she would add a woolly hat along with her scarf, but for now she carried them down the stairs and headed into the kitchen.

And then nearly dropped them when she saw Abe sitting on a breakfast stool, drinking coffee and reading on his tablet.

'Morning.' Barb smiled. 'How did you sleep?'

'Very well,' Naomi said. 'In fact, I overslept.'

'You're not the only one,' Barb said, and she glanced over at Abe, who didn't look up. 'You got a pizza in the night, I see. You could have called me for something to eat if you were hungry. Come and sit down and have some breakfast...' And then she must have remembered that Naomi was actually a guest. 'Or take a seat in the dining room and—'

'I don't eat breakfast,' Naomi said quickly.

That was a complete lie.

Naomi loved breakfast and the first café she saw she was finding a bagel, but she was a touch flustered by Abe's presence and trying not to show it. She hadn't expected to see him, and certainly, if he'd still been here, she hadn't expected him to be sitting in the kitchen. 'I'm actually heading out.'

She kept reminding herself there was nothing to be flustered about.

Except, far from relaxed, as she had been last night, the sight and scent of him, freshly showered, with damp hair and all clean shaven, was doing the oddest thing to her heart rate. She felt like a teenager.

An awkward one at that.

And Barb would not let her go.

'You're not leaving this house without a coffee at least,' Barb said, as she poured her one from the pot. 'Cream?'

'Just black, please.'

As Barb poured she chatted to Abe and it became clear he'd been updating her on Jobe. 'Is there anything I can make for him?'

'I don't think so,' he said, only glancing up from his tablet. 'I'll let you know, but really he's not eating much.'

'Ginger's good for nausea,' Barb said, and then turned her attention to Naomi. 'So, what are your plans for today? I sure hope you're not going out in just that jacket.'

'I'm buying a coat,' Naomi *again* explained. 'I'm heading to a department store first.'

'I'll call Bernard to drive you.'

'There's no need.' Naomi shook her head. 'I really want to walk. The baby may well be home tomorrow or the day after that so I want to see as much as I can today. I can give you a hand tonight with the tree, though…'

'A hand?' Barb checked. 'I shan't be decorating it…' She laughed at the very thought. 'We'll leave that to the experts. You just enjoy your day and don't worry about us.'

Abe carried on reading as Barb and Naomi chatted and it would seem she had rather high expectations of all she could cram in today.

Especially on foot.

'I want to see the tree at the Rockefeller Center, and I want to see the window displays…' She reeled things off as Abe sat there, reading. 'I really wanted to see feed the squirrels in Central Park but they'll be hibernating—oh, and I want to walk over Brooklyn Bridge.'

'Today?' Barb checked.

'Well, not *all* of it today,' Naomi said. 'I'll have to get a map and plot it out. I'm useless at following directions on my phone.'

'I've got one somewhere.'

As Barb bustled off to find it she was left with Abe, and Naomi had to remind herself there was nothing to feel awkward about.

She just did.

The air felt a little warmer, so much so that as she pulled on her hat she decided the scarf could wait until she was at the front door.

And then, without looking up, Abe spoke.

'Squirrels don't hibernate.'

It took a moment to register he was commenting on her conversation with Barb.

'I think you'll find that they do,' Naomi said, and now he looked up, those gorgeous black eyes meeting hers.

'And I'm certain you'll find that they don't.'

There was a small stand-off.

Abe watched her lips open to argue, but he was more than sure he was right. 'You can apologise to me tonight once you've found out I'm right.'

Two things in that statement surprised Abe.

That he could be bothered to debate the hibernation habits of squirrels.

And that he was already thinking about tonight.

Especially when she gave up arguing and a smile spread over her lips.

'So I *can* feed them?' Naomi checked, nerves forgotten now, for he made conversation so easy and despite his officious tone he simply made her smile.

'Yes.'

'What should I get?'

'Get?'

'For them to eat?'

'You can buy nuts there.'

'Oh.'

'Hot ones. Fit for human consumption.'

'Yum,' Naomi said. 'But first I need to head to Macy's for my coat.'

'There are stores other than Macy's.'

'No, it has to be that one.'

'Why?'

'So that when I'm asked where I got my gorgeous coat, I won't sound pretentious by saying New York. I'll just say Macy's, but they'll know.'

'I see.' He didn't. 'If you can wait five minutes, I'm leaving. I can have my driver drop you there.'

'But I want to walk.'

She had no idea the size of the place, Abe thought. 'Walk once you have a coat.'

Naomi knew she should say no to his offer, just as she had with Barb.

And that she should keep as much distance as possible between them and remind herself to shield her heart, because this crush on Abe was blowing up in her chest like a bouncy castle inflating. And, yes, away from him she was wary, but when they spoke, when he looked right at her all the warnings tumbled away and she just fell into conversation with him, forgot that she was usually awkward around men, and she forgot too to feel big and clumsy.

The rules Naomi generally lived by did not seem to apply when she was *with* Abe.

'Okay,' she conceded with a smile. 'While you're there, you could get something for Ava.'

'I've already given the baby a present and...' He halted. Abe had been about to point out that his driver would be taking her to Macy's *after* he'd been dropped off at work, but now that he thought about it a couple of hours off sounded appealing. Khalid was expecting him to call and, Abe decided, a well-timed unexplained absence might be in order to remind the Sheikh who was boss!

He drained his coffee. 'Come on, then.'

As they were driven, it was nice to take a familiar route with someone who was so excited by *everything*. Even tiny things like overhead traffic lights got a mention. 'It looks just like I'd imagined it but better,' Naomi said.

'It looks just like it always does,' Abe said, but he did pull his eyes away from his tablet and stopped scrolling through the mountain of emails that had accumulated overnight and stared out at the city he loved.

The horses and carriages were all lined up, and the streets were bustling.

'I fell asleep on the way from the airport,' Naomi explained, 'so I didn't see anything yesterday.'

And now he regretted not going yesterday to meet her and sending a car instead.

Abe didn't do regret, yet for a second there he did. Not that she let him linger in it—Naomi had far too many questions.

'Have you done your Christmas shopping?' she asked.

'I don't do all that.'

'What, you do it online?'

'No, I don't do it online. I just don't do Christmas. Well, there's the Christmas Eve ball and I give Jessica, my PA, a weekend away, but that's about it.'

She was appalled. 'What about your father? Surely you get him a present?'

'What could he possibly need?' Abe asked, but as she opened her mouth he got there first. 'I'll think of something.'

'Good.'

'What do you want for Christmas?' Naomi asked.

'Peace and quiet,' Abe said, and, to her credit, she laughed. 'We're here.'

So they were.

'You couldn't have walked it,' he pointed out as they pulled up at the iconic store.

'I could have,' Naomi insisted as she got out of the car. 'I'll walk back instead.' She stood and looked up at the magnificent building, dressed for Christmas with red and green bows. People were already crowded at the windows, looking at the displays. 'Oh, my goodness. I can't believe I'm really here.'

'Your coat awaits.'

Abe had on his own coat.

It was a long black woollen one worn over his suit, but once they had agreed where to meet and Naomi had wandered off, Abe saw that he was being noticed and decided that a wool hat of his own might be in order. He didn't want to be constantly recognised all day, or for his sightseeing trip to be captured on someone's phone just to be sold to the papers and all the palaver that would cause.

And, yes, he was taking the day off, and called Jessica as he took the escalator.

'What should I say to Khalid?' Jessica responded, clearly perplexed, because there was not a single Devereux in the office today, and that hadn't happened in all the time she'd been there.

'That I'm unavailable,' Abe clipped.

'Felicia and her entourage are here for you,' Jessica said. 'To measure you for next season as well as the Devereux Ball.'

Abe wasn't listening. For the first time in what felt like for ever his mind wasn't on work. In fact, his eyes were drawn to the most ridiculous, huge, pink bear with big black eyes, as black as Ava's would undoubtedly be someday.

'Sort it,' Abe said, and rang off.

He thought of what Naomi had said, about the type of uncle he wanted to be. It had never entered his mind he might be the uncle-bearing-teddy-bears type. But if you couldn't buy a giant pink bear for your one-day-old niece, who could you buy one for?

And that was how she next saw him.

Naomi was wearing the most gorgeous new red coat and held a large bag containing things pink. Pink sleepsuits, a pink blanket and also a little sleepsuit in a bright cherry red, the same shade as her coat. She was standing happily watching the world go by as she mentally planned the rest of her day, but then she saw Abe, standing on the escalator, wearing a black hat and holding a huge pink bear. He wasn't smiling. Instead, he looked moody and scowling, and on seeing him her first thought was, *Help!*

Help! Naomi thought again, as he caught sight of her and smiled and walked over.

Please get on with being the utter bastard I've been warned that you are.

But help wasn't arriving.

'Nice coat,' he said, which in itself wasn't a problem.

More it was the approval in his eyes and the flurry it set off in her chest.

They loaded the bear into his car but, instead of saying goodbye to her, the driver was sent on his way, and it took a moment for Naomi to register that Abe was going to be her tour guide for the day.

'To make up for not picking you up at the airport,' he offered by way of explanation.

'Really?'

'Ethan asked me to, but I had a lot of meetings yesterday.'

'And you don't today?'

'Nope,' he said. 'Well, I should go in, but there are a few issues and it might serve me better...' He hesitated, because certainly he shared business matters with no one. 'I forgot you were friends with Merida for a moment there.'

'Oh, not you too,' Naomi huffed. 'I've got Barb backing off because I'm not real "staff" and now you...'

'Really?' he said, genuinely intrigued. 'What would Barb tell you if you weren't a friend of Merida's?'

'The gossip.' Naomi smiled.

And on a slushy, wet street they faced each other.

'Well, I don't have gossip as such,' Abe said. 'Just a headache developing in the Middle East. One that I don't want my brother to know about just yet.'

'My lips are sealed.'

He wished they weren't.

As he looked down at them, Abe rather wished he was prising them open with his tongue, and possibly she was thinking the same thing because she pressed them together in response to the sudden scrutiny.

'So,' Abe said, rather than do something very un-Abe-like and kiss her in the middle of the street, 'I've got a clear day, so if you want company...'

'I'd love it.'

And he was wonderful, wonderful company.

Naomi did her share of sightseeing on her days off, wherever she went, but always alone.

On this cold, cold day, she was embraced by his company as they first took in the breath-taking Christmas window displays filled with enchanting scenes.

Abe didn't hover at the back or subtly nudge in, he moved straight to the front and took her with him. Every window told a story. There were fairies waving their wands and trains made of candy and the sounds of delighted children's laughter and music playing brought tears to her eyes.

For the first time it was starting to feel like Christmas should, Naomi thought.

She could gaze at the displays for ever but it seemed they had a schedule to adhere to! 'Ready?' Abe said.

'For what?'

The Empire State Building was what!

And, because it was December, they didn't have to line up and soon they were on the top of the world, or rather, Naomi corrected herself, the top of New York City. 'But it feels like the top of the world.'

'Actually, my office is higher.'

'I don't believe you.' Naomi smiled, stamping her feet against the cold and digging her hands into the pockets of her coat. She had never felt so cold, or so exhilarated and happy, all at the same time.

He pointed out landmarks and the bridges and the snow had thinned enough that she could see the Statue of Liberty.

'I'm going to do one of the river cruises on my day off,' Naomi said.

'You'll freeze.'

'I don't care.' Naomi laughed.

From up high she did her best to get her bearings in a snow-blanketed city. 'So, you live that way?' She pointed.

'No,' Abe corrected, 'my father lives there and...' he guided her by the elbow to the other side '... I live there at Greenwich Village. See the green?' She followed to where he pointed. 'That's Washington Square Park and the view from my bedroom window.'

'Oh, I'd love to see it…' Naomi said, but it came out wrong. 'I meant Greenwich Village is on my to-do list…' *Not* the view from his bedroom window.

'I know what you meant.'

He gave her a smile and it felt as if the snow stopped and even the wind eased as he corrected her little faux pas. Except it didn't feel like one, it felt more like a Freudian slip.

From the giddy heights of the Empire State Building they moved on to the Rockefeller Center and the gigantic tree, and, yes, he took her photo in front of it. As he finished, a German tourist asked if they'd like one together, and would he mind taking theirs, *bitte*?

It was easier to just say yes, or *ja*, than to explain to a stranger that they weren't, in fact, a couple.

And as they stood side by side, and the German tourist waved them to move closer and he put an arm around her, Naomi found her smile a touch stilted for the very first time that day.

It was all just so amazing, so wonderful that Naomi knew, just knew, she'd be looking at this photo for a very long time to come.

CHAPTER FOUR

IT WAS HER PERFECT DAY.

In every way.

There was so much to see and do and they crammed in all they could.

'I should have bought some gloves,' Naomi said, blowing into her hands as they wandered down Madison Avenue, but Abe had a trick for that and bought them huge pretzels, hot from the cart, and they warmed their hands very nicely.

'My dad taught me that,' Abe said. 'Though I think it was more that he loved to eat them.'

'You did some nice things with your dad.'

'We did,' he admitted, and stole a look at her and wondered why this amazing woman had no one. And how come she had no family?

And so he pried, only it didn't feel that way to him. He just had to know.

'Do you, did you...?' He watched as she braced herself, no doubt used to the question, so he rephrased it. 'Do you have any memories at all of your family?'

'Not good ones,' Naomi said, and she peeled off some warm dough but didn't put it in her mouth. Instead, she told him the truth. 'I've never seen my mother. I tried contacting her when I was old enough to, but she didn't want to know.'

'Then she missed out,' Abe said, but it sounded like a trite response and he knew it so he tried again. 'Maybe it was for the best.'

'I doubt it.'

'Some people shouldn't be parents,' Abe said, and he shared with her something he had never, ever shared with anyone. Not with his father, not with Ethan. Oh, they knew it, of course, but he'd never said it out loud. 'My mother was one of them.'

Naomi knew that she was hearing the truth, rather than being placated. And she knew, too, that he was sharing a very private part of his rather public life.

'And,' Abe added, only this time, given what he'd just shared, it didn't sound trite, 'she *did* miss out—I can't imagine anything nicer than a day spent with you.'

It was possibly the nicest thing he could have said to her.

They stood on a busy street but it might just as well have been empty because it felt as if it was just the two of them. Then, not used to too much disclosure, he peeled off some dough and popped it into his mouth. 'Come on,' he said. 'Lots to see...'

He fought not to take her hand and Naomi had to ball hers into a fist so as not to reach for his.

And so, rather than make herself look a fool, she peered into a very well-dressed window. 'Now, *that's* a coat!'

It was long and the deepest shade of violet, perhaps more of a velvet cape than a coat.

It was absolutely exquisite.

'I'm supposed to be get measured up,' Abe said,

thinking of the fitter he had blown off today and deciding that while they were here to just get it over and done with. 'Let's go in.'

Naomi would never, in a million years, have entered such a place and neither would she have been greeted as warmly. But as she was with Abe the blonde and groomed sales associate was very amenable.

'Mr Devereux!'

'Felicia.' Abe's return greeting was less effusive, but it didn't matter. Of course, he was told, it wasn't a problem that he'd missed the private appointment that had been scheduled to take place in his office earlier today.

'I was just speaking with Jessica,' Felicia said with a smile, 'and trying to arrange another time. Let's get you measured. Will your, er...' She glanced at Naomi and clearly didn't know how to place her, but she gave it a go. 'Will your assistant be coming through?'

It was the only awkward moment.

Well, it was for Naomi.

Of course, they would never think she might simply be *with* him and merely assumed that she was one of his staff.

'I'll just look around,' Naomi said, declining the offer of refreshments and looking at the stunning outfits that were completely beyond her reach, though it was heaven to gaze. Still, she did wonder how long it took to be measured when, half an hour later, she was still looking around.

'It shouldn't be too much longer,' Felicia said.

As it turned out, Mr Devereux wasn't just selecting a tux for the ball. There were swatches and buttons and collars and cuffs for suits that would see him to summer.

'How long have you worked for the Devereuxes?' Felicia asked as they chatted.

'Oh, I don't work for them,' Naomi corrected her. 'We're just...' she didn't really know what to say, so possibly she took a slight leap in her description '... friends.'

Well, they were acquaintances perhaps.

Two people who had one person, Merida, who connected them. Still, she wasn't about to explain all that to Felicia.

But in that moment *everything* changed.

The slightly casual air to their conversation disappeared and suddenly, now she was no longer mere staff, Felicia was on higher alert. 'You like the wrap?' she asked, when Naomi's hands lingered on a length of fabric so soft it felt like mercury running through her hand.

'I love it,' Naomi said.

'There's a dress,' Felicia said. 'It would go with your colouring.'

'Oh, I doubt that it comes in my size.'

Felicia was actually very skilled at her job. So much so that twenty minutes later Naomi stood in high heels with the gorgeous floor-length dress on, and, lo, it did come in her size.

'You look,' Felicia said, 'stunning.'

'Ah, but you're paid to say that.'

'No.' Felicia shook her head. 'I don't want anyone wearing something from our range if they don't suit it and absolutely you do.'

Did she?

It was nice to dream. It was just dress-up and fun, and, no, not for Abe's eyes, but she came out of the dressing room smiling.

In contrast, Abe was scowling.

'I didn't think it would take that long.' He rolled his eyes as they headed out. 'Just how many shades of black are there?'

Naomi laughed.

Her happiness remained, even heightened as the sun sank lower and Naomi found out that, yes, there were still squirrels in winter in Central Park.

At first there was just one that she could see as Abe headed off and bought some nuts.

'They're for the squirrels,' Abe reminded her, when Naomi had a taste.

'There aren't any.'

Except then she saw one, sitting upright in the snow.

She tossed him a nut and very boldly he came and took it and then scuttled off.

'There's one,' Abe said, and he took some nuts and threw them, and then there was another.

And another.

They came very close, right up onto the benches, and Naomi laughed as she fed them nuts and some even took them from her fingers.

Abe took some photos on her phone.

'This is like a dream come true.' Naomi was beside herself. There were squirrels coming from everywhere.

She looked like Snow White, Abe thought, but of course didn't say so. 'Was I right?' Abe checked. 'Or was I right?'

'You were right, Abe,' Naomi teased. 'Squirrels don't hibernate and I apologise for ever doubting you.' And she took them back to their conversation and neither could believe it had been just this morning, because after a day spent together it felt like a long time ago.

'You missed that one,' Abe said, pointing out a little black little squirrel who held back from the others.

'He won't come...' Naomi said, because she'd already noticed the little creature, who shook and startled but clearly wanted to join in. Finally, with coaxing, he came over and had his share of the little packet of nuts.

'Do you want to get some more?' Abe offered.

'Another time,' Naomi said. 'I can't feel my feet.'

It was growing dark and it was utterly freezing so some real food and serious warming up was called for. 'Do you want to go for a drink?' he offered as he handed her back her phone and they walked towards the park's exit. 'Or perhaps an early dinner? We could go over to the Plaza?'

He nodded in the direction of the gorgeous building and it was an invitation she could scarcely comprehend.

'I'm hardly dressed for the Plaza,' Naomi pointed out. Her coat might be gorgeous but beneath that she wore jeans and the bottoms of them were drenched.

'It doesn't matter.'

And it wouldn't matter, Naomi knew.

She could be dressed in sackcloth and ashes and they would make the exception for him. But it mattered to Naomi—she knew she must look a fright. It was better to leave things here, Naomi decided, to simply end their perfect day. And she had the perfect excuse too... 'I promised Merida I'd be in to visit this evening.'

Perhaps it was for the best, Abe thought.

He too was supposed to be at the hospital.

In the space of a day he'd gone from wearing a hat so he wasn't recognised to offering to step out together in the Plaza.

It could only cause trouble.

On *so* many levels.

'I'm going to go back to the house and get changed,' Naomi said, 'and then head to the hospital.'

'Well, I'll call my driver.' Abe took out his phone and did just that. 'I'll head to the hospital now and drop you home on the way.'

'Sounds good,' Naomi agreed. 'Abe, thank you for the most wonderful day. I wouldn't have seen half as much if you hadn't been with me.' Though it was more than the sights she had seen that had made it so special. 'It's been amazing,' she said.

'It has,' he agreed.

'How's your Middle East headache now?' she asked.

'Gone!' he said. 'Though probably not for long. I bet Ethan's found out.'

'Found out what?'

He smiled at her persistence. 'Khalid and Ethan are friends. They went to college together. I warned Ethan not to mix business and friendship.'

'It can work.'

'Not in my book.' He shook his head. 'Khalid has helped pave our way into expanding into the Middle East, I admit that, but it's a business agreement and one he'll benefit from enormously. I refuse to be beholden to him. He's got feet in both camps.'

'I don't understand.'

'Well, he's a partner in our Middle Eastern branch, but he's also Prince of the country where we're looking to extend.'

'So he's got both your interests at heart.'

He gave a wry laugh. 'It makes better business sense to view him as screwing us out of millions than looking out for his people.'

'Perhaps,' Naomi said. 'It's nicer to think of it the other way around, though.'

'I don't play nice.'

'You did today,' Naomi said.

'Today was an exception.'

Or rather today had for Abe been exceptional.

He felt as if he'd been born fighting. Keeping one eye out for Ethan and another on his mother. And later there had been no halcyon days to his youth. Just the weight of the Devereux name and the depraved reputation he upheld.

Today, in the midst of the darkest times, it had felt as if the world as he knew it had been put on hold.

He stopped walking, they both did, and turned and faced each other. Naomi looked down as he took her hands in his.

Finally.

Oh, they'd been blown on and thrust deep into pockets, and wrapped around hot pretzels and bags of nuts, and all day they had resisted this. So many times he had wanted to reach for hers, and all day her hands had felt as if they had secretly sought his.

Now they met and she watched his fingers wrap around hers and felt the warmth that came not just from his skin but from the surge in her heart.

She was here in New York to work, and usually Naomi did not do foolish things such as get involved with family, and she always guarded her heart, but all that faded when she met his eyes.

There was gentle snow and there *were* squirrels and there was a hush that descended over a noisy city as his mouth neared hers. His scent was close, not quite familiar yet, and she imprinted on her mind the heady notes as she breathed him in.

The first intimate touch sent a slight tremor through Naomi, but then came a flutter of relief as their mouths met, for it felt as if she had waited for ever to know this bliss.

She had.

Abe Devereux's was her very first kiss, and the first time she had lowered the gates to her heart.

He sensed it.

Abe felt her slight jolt at the first contact, and then her untutored return to the caress of his mouth. And he fathomed only then that this kiss was her first. The magnitude of that had him hold back a fraction, his approach now more tender, lest he startle her again.

Kissing was usually a means to an end to Abe.

A mere precursor to bed.

He did not hold hands in public, let alone kiss in a park, yet there was no thought to his surroundings at that moment. Just that her lips were cold so he must warm them. He felt her hesitancy mingled with shivering want, and she reminded him of that little squirrel, nervous and cautious yet yearning.

Abe made her yearn.

The pressure of his lips was sublime. He dropped her hands and wrapped his arms around her, and winter disappeared as he pulled her closer into his strength and warmth and she was cradled in the arms of bliss. Her lips parted without thought, lost to his kiss, but then came the next shock, the feel of his tongue, which had her head pulling back, but his hand was exerting slight pressure there, and after a second she sank into the stupor of his deepening kiss and the feather-light strokes that stirred her inside.

Naomi gave in to the sweet and sensual pleasure of mouths mingling, tasting and exploring each other, and she savoured each sensation, from the surprising softness of his mouth to the slight scratch of his lightly stubbled jaw, which increased as he kissed her harder, their mouths more insistent, and she knew what to do now.

As pleasure and want merged, she moaned and he swallowed it, guiding her generous hips into his with the palm of his hand, and then held her in a sensual embrace.

She felt a new hunger, one she had never known before, unfurl inside her. And when he had kissed her so hard that she was breathless, when he had taken her from hesitant to urgent with the stroke of his tongue, he pulled back.

Abe had no choice but to do that for the feel of her in his arms dictated a need for more, and the strength of their kiss had to be severed, for decency's sake.

Their foreheads rested against each other's, and he could feel her breasts against his chest as her breathing refused to calm, and the shock of how good a kiss could be was Abe's now.

'I've been wanting to do that since last night,' Abe said, their lips still almost touching, and she let out a small laugh.

'I've been hoping you would,' Naomi admitted, relieved that she hadn't been imagining things after all. That this knowing, sensual man had been feeling the same way she had.

His arms held her steady and Naomi looked up at

him and, quite simply, if he took her hand now, and if somehow there could be a magical bed, then he could lead her to it.

For Naomi, it was a revelation.

Till now she had never been kissed, never been close enough to another to touch them intimately, let alone consider sharing a man's bed.

And when he released her, when the world rushed in, so too did doubt.

He could hurt her, her mind warned.

Hush, her heart said.

He pulled out his phone and read a text informing him the car was here. 'We'll speak tonight,' Abe told her.

They sat apart in the car, and not just because of the giant teddy commanding its own seat, but because it was just all too new and too complicated to fathom, let alone share with the world.

But she was floating, and wondering how to deal with Merida and Ethan and, gosh, how to tell this suave man that she'd never slept with anyone before.

Yes, she was certain that this was where it was leading.

'Thank you,' Naomi said, as she got out of the car.

It felt a little paltry to offer such bland thanks for giving her the very best day but she kept things polite and smiled at Barb as she was let into the house.

'How was your day, exploring?' Barb asked.

'Marvellous.'

'Was that Abe's driver that dropped you off?'

'Yes,' Naomi answered as casually as she could. 'He said to let him know when I was finished sightseeing, and that he'd give me a ride back...' Then she stopped having to think up excuses as she was suddenly blind-sided by the tree. 'Oh, my...'

It was pink.

Yet it was still elegant.

There were pale pink snowflakes that looked like blossoms dotted on the branches, and pale pink baubles that were so delicate that they looked like they might pop like bubbles if she so much as breathed.

'It's heavenly,' Naomi said, but there really wasn't time to dwell too long. 'I really have to get changed and then head to the hospital. I'll get a cab...'

'No need, Bernard will take you.'

Before she changed, Naomi sat on the bed for a moment and tried to steady herself, because when she was away from him she felt fat and uncertain and it all felt impossible.

You're here to work, she told herself.

But she had a life too.

One that had been devoid of men.

Devoid of passion.

Devoid of love.

And it was too soon to be even thinking that, but every part of this was new to Naomi.

So instead of panicking about the impossibility of it all she pulled on dry jeans and a black jumper, and as she did so she recalled his kiss.

And while she tried to reel herself in, her heart felt as if it was rolling out and she ran down the stairs on a cloud of excitement about all the night might hold.

Bernard, as it turned out, was Barb's husband and had been Jobe's driver. 'I've driven him for close to twenty-five years,' he told Naomi as he drove her to the hospital. 'Barb started working for him after Mrs

Devereux passed and then he took me on as his driver. We were going to stay for two years,' he told her as he pulled up at the hospital. 'That was the plan.'

Naomi was about to laugh and say something about the best-laid plans, but it died on her lips when she saw his strained face and remembered that tonight not everyone felt as happy as she did. He must be so terribly sad about Jobe, and perhaps worried about his and Barb's future.

'It's such a difficult time,' Naomi said, and Bernard nodded.

'It's great news about the baby, though.'

'It is,' Naomi agreed.

'I'll wait for you here.'

'Thank you.'

Naomi headed into the private wing and, having shown her ID, was let through to see Merida, who was rather more flustered than yesterday.

'How are you?' Naomi asked.

'Fine, but she's not feeding and they said she needs to go under the lights. That she's got jaundice.'

It was all completely normal, but for Merida completely overwhelming, and Naomi took her time to reassure her that all was well, but Merida was worried about Naomi too. 'I feel terrible that you're here and rattling around the house on your own.'

'Don't be daft,' Naomi said. 'Barb and Bernard have been lovely and I've been out sightseeing today.' She had already decided not to mention that her day had been spent with Abe.

In fact, she would have to work out when, or even if, she would tell Merida.

For now, though, she focussed on the baby, who was

crying and hungry. 'Try and relax,' Naomi said as she positioned her to feed. 'Maybe try talking to me while you feed her.'

And it worked, because as Merida chatted about all that had been going on between her and Ethan, she relaxed and so too did little Ava.

'I know you've been so worried about our marriage, and in truth so have I, but things are going really well. I know you must be thinking it's just in the rush of Ava being born, but it was before that. We talked, I mean, we really talked. I think this is a new start for us.'

'I'm so happy for you.'

'We *both* want this marriage to work.'

She looked down at her baby. 'I'm so glad that Jobe got to see her. Ethan and he are finally talking…'

'But they work together,' Naomi pointed out.

'I mean, they're finally close. There's some stuff with the mother that I found out…' She didn't elaborate and Naomi didn't push—in fact, her eyes came to rest on the huge teddy bear.

'Abe brought that in for Ava this evening,' Merida said when she saw where Naomi was looking. 'Hard to believe. There must be a heart in there somewhere…'

'Everybody's nice if you give them a chance.'

Merida shook her head 'Not Abe. He's an island. And a hostile, uninhabitable one at that.'

And Naomi had no choice but to listen as Merida spoke on.

'Honestly, the way he works his way through women… I don't know how Candice puts up with him.'

'Candice?' Naomi checked. She'd heard that name, or rather she was sure that she had read it somewhere as she'd skimmed articles on Abe during her research into the Devereux family. She had only really been trying to find out about Ethan, so she could help her friend.

So, who was Candice?

Merida soon answered. 'Abe's partner.'

Thankfully Merida was looking down at Ava so she didn't see the look of horror wash over Naomi's face.

'His partner?' Naomi echoed, struggling to keep her voice even.

'Yes, they've been together for a couple of years.'

'They're *still* together?'

Merida frowned at either the sudden inflection or the sudden interest in Abe Devereux's love life and Naomi had to think quickly. 'It's just I thought I'd read somewhere that they'd broken up.'

'You probably did.' Merida nodded. 'They're always breaking up—he constantly cheats and she always ends up taking him back, but, no, they're definitely together. She came in to visit with him tonight.' Merida looked up. 'Believe me when I say he's an utter bastard.'

Oh, Naomi believed her.

She had just found that out for herself.

CHAPTER FIVE

ABE HAD A PARTNER!

Merida's words had left Naomi reeling but she'd had to remain calm and dig deep to smile her way through the rest of the visit.

That didn't end at visiting time, though, when she wished she could walk home from the hospital, if only to gather her thoughts. Instead, after a visit spent reassuring Merida, and with her own head spinning, Naomi stepped out of the hospital to the car waiting for her.

She wanted to cry but she refused to.

More than that she wanted to erase the day. Her wonderful, beautiful day, she simply wanted it gone, and to never, ever have known how it felt to be held and kissed by Abe, and to be utterly fooled by those dark eyes.

So she chatted away to Bernard on the drive back and then the door opened and there was Barb, anxious for news about mother and baby.

'How's Merida?' she asked as Naomi took off her coat.

'She's doing well.'

'And little Ava?' Barb checked, taking the coat and clearly anxious for a more detailed update.

'Gorgeous.'

'Will they be home tomorrow?'

Her mind felt as if it was wading through mud just to formulate a response. 'I think it might be a couple more days,' Naomi said, and then she saw Abe, coming out of the drawing room. His jacket and tie were off and he was holding a glass. He looked exquisite. She quickly jerked her eyes away, refusing to even allow herself that thought.

'I've got dinner ready for you...' Barb said, and her voice seemed to be coming from a long way away. She could feel Abe's eyes on her.

'That's lovely, but I'm really tired. I've walked for miles today and I think jet lag has finally caught up with me.'

She knew.

Instantly, Abe was certain that she had found out about Candice. He could tell from her pinched expression and the way she turned away from him.

Damn!

Candice had met him at the hospital, as had previously been arranged, except he'd forgotten. His driver had dropped him off, and there, beside the elevators to the private wing, had been Candice.

'What the hell is that?' she had asked when she'd seen the bear.

'It's for my niece.'

'Well, it would hardly be for me.'

As arranged, they had gone in to visit together.

He had spent years fashioning his life, and only Candice, himself and Abe's private attorney knew of the deal they had agreed to.

He had admitted to Ethan the truth of their status, but that had been on the night he had told him that

Merida was pregnant and Abe had attempted to show his brother that there were other ways to deal with the situation than marriage, but they had never discussed it since.

Abe's seeming relationship with Candice was a business arrangement. Her stability and presence appeased the board, but they hadn't slept together in years.

Their arrangement allowed a veneer of respectability to put a layer of gloss over his rather debauched life.

He housed her in an Upper East Side apartment and paid her a generous monthly allowance and, in return, she seemingly stood by his side.

Certainly, it was not something he shared with someone he'd had one kiss with.

It was not something he'd ever intended to share with anyone.

He waited till Barb had taken her coat and had headed off before he attempted to speak to her.

'Naomi…'

She ignored him and headed up the stairs.

Possibly not the most adult way of dealing with things but, hell, Naomi just wanted to process what she'd found out alone, and work out how she felt about it all, before having to deal with him.

'Naomi!' He called her name more sharply and came to the bottom of the stairs, and she had the feeling he wouldn't hesitate to follow her up.

'Yes?' She turned and attempted to look composed, but she looked past Abe's shoulder at the gorgeous tree rather than at him.

'Come through to the drawing room,' he said. 'It's more private in there.'

'We have nothing *private* to discuss,' Naomi answered. She didn't want to hear his excuses and lies, but more than that she wanted to be alone with her own thoughts and to assemble them into some sort of order before she discussed this with him.

But Abe was persistent. 'We need to talk.'

'I think we already did quite enough of that,' Naomi said. 'In fact, we spoke most of last night and all of today, and during all that time you refrained from telling me the one thing I should have known.'

'Can we not do this on the stairs?' Abe suggested.

'Can we simply not do this?' Naomi implored.

She loathed any sort of confrontation and, though she would never, ever admit it, despite her devastation, Naomi was just the tiniest bit relieved.

Yes, relieved that the feeling he evoked, the hope that had been gathering, could now safely lead…nowhere.

That she could reel in her heart right now, before it was too late.

She had learnt, long ago, how it felt to be discarded, to put down tentative roots and then be plucked up and moved along. Not so much in romance, she had no experience there. But in love, in family, at school and with friends, and she never wanted to revisit those feelings again.

And with that thought she was able to look him in the eye and dismiss the magical time they had shared. 'It was a day out. It was a kiss. Probably small change to you and I was tired from flying and…' She shrugged. 'Abe, I'm here to work and to be a friend to Merida. Can we please just forget it happened?'

'Naomi…'

But she had already walked off.

To Abe's discredit, he was just a touch relieved by her dismissal.

It had been a day out that had ended with a kiss, nothing more.

Certainly, it was nothing worth rocking the boat over.

God knew, there was enough else going on.

Abe was absent from the kitchen the next morning and again that night.

And he was absent in the two weeks that followed.

His name came up in various conversations, some Naomi was a part of, though most she was not.

'Abe's staying over at the hospital tonight,' she'd heard Ethan tell Barb on the day Ava had come home.

And when Ava was two weeks old, and Naomi and Merida were about to head over to the park, Ethan rang to say that Khalid was flying to NYC to sort out, face to face, the land sale issue.

'Don't ask,' Merida said, and rolled her eyes.

Naomi definitely didn't.

She was doing her level best to put the elder Devereux brother out of her mind.

And there was more than enough to be getting on with.

Merida was still struggling to feed Ava herself, and the baby was hungry and difficult to settle and liked to sleep the morning away and stay up all night.

Mid-afternoon, rather than have Merida give in and feed her again, they bundled her up in blankets and a hat and she lay screaming in her new pram.

'Isn't it too cold?' Merida checked.

'She's as warm as toast,' Naomi said. 'And they like the motion of the pram.'

Ava did.

She didn't sleep, but she did hush as they walked the paths. The snow had let up and it was a crisp, sunny day as Merida told her just how difficult Naomi had been theh previous night.

'I don't want to take her into bed with me, but she takes the tiniest feed and then falls asleep. The second I put her down, she starts to cry.'

'Why don't you let me have her for the night?' Naomi suggested. 'I could bring her in four-hourly for feeds.'

'I want her with me.'

Abe, damn him, was right.

Business and friendships were best kept apart.

Oh, Naomi didn't consider her work as business as such, but she was professional in her role.

Usually her employers wanted a nanny.

Merida didn't.

She wanted her baby with her at night and though she was completely lovely, the fact was most new mothers didn't want their close friend around twenty-four seven as they stumbled through the first weeks of parenthood.

Had she not been paid to be there, Naomi might have suggested that she check into a hotel, or even just come for a week or two.

Not two months!

They came to the lake and sat down on the bench but almost as soon as they had, the lack of motion set Ava off.

'Let's walk,' Naomi suggested when she saw that Merida was close to tears.

'No, let's head back.'

Poor Merida was so exhausted that she took Naomi's

suggestion that, rather than feed her, she head off for a sleep. 'I'll wake you at six,' Naomi said.

'I can't leave her crying till then.'

'She won't be,' Naomi said, rather hoping that was true.

Ava did her level best.

'Is she hungry?' Barb asked a couple of hours later when Naomi came into the kitchen with a screaming Ava over her shoulder.

'She wants to use her mum as a dummy,' Naomi said, then corrected herself so that Barb would understand. 'A pacifier. I'm hoping that if Merida can have a proper sleep and I can calm Ava down, they might get a good feed. I'll give her a bath soon and hopefully that will calm her.'

'Doesn't her crying bother you?' Barb asked.

'A bit,' Naomi admitted, 'but nowhere near as much it upsets Merida—she has the keys straight to her mother's heartstrings.'

But held upright and lulled by the conversation, Ava started to calm. 'What are you making?' Naomi asked Barb.

'Chicken soup, the proper way. For Jobe.'

Naomi smiled and decided to watch and see how chicken soup was made the *proper* way. There was a whole chicken simmering in the pot, along with vegetables and herbs, and the kitchen smelt divine—it must have because, though awake, little Ava had stopped crying and was resting on Naomi's shoulder.

'Bernard will take it in later,' Barb said. 'And some for Abe too.'

'He's there a lot, is he?' Naomi couldn't help but check.

'He goes in after work and I think he's staying till late at night. I wish that he'd stop here afterwards, but he seems to have stopped doing that.'

Naomi swallowed. She really hoped that what had happened between Abe and her wasn't affecting his decisions. She doubted it, though. Of course she had looked him up online more thoroughly and it would seem a kiss in a park was extremely chaste compared to his other well-reported shenanigans over the years.

She doubted he had given it a second thought.

Whereas she thought about him all the time.

All the time.

Yet how could she not?

There were photos lining the walls and his name was dropped into the conversation numerous times. And each night she'd lain there, with ears on elastic, wondering if he might have decided to stay after he had visited the hospital.

It would seem that he hadn't.

'You came just after Mrs Devereux died...' Naomi said.

'Yes.' Barb rolled her eyes. 'We'd have lasted five minutes otherwise. She went through staff like a dose of salts.' Barb had started to chat more easily with Naomi now and had admitted that all the staff had no idea, apart from what they read, how serious Jobe's illness was. 'Twenty-five years we've been here now. Bernard's worried that we won't get another live-in job if...' She paused. 'Well, there's nothing to be gained stressing about that.'

It was clear to Naomi that she was stressing, though.

Naomi's little ploy to keep Ava awake and Merida asleep seemed to have worked. After a bath and dressed in her little sleepsuit, Ava was more than ready to feed and Merida seemed a lot more relaxed.

'What time will Ethan be back?' Naomi asked as Ava fed.

'He just called, he's going to come and have some dinner and then head over to the hospital. They're meeting with Jobe and his specialist. He's not doing so well. The treatment he's having just drains him. It's tough. Especially as Ethan and he have just started talking. I mean really talking.'

'You said they'd just started to get on. Weren't they close before?'

'No.' Merida shook her head. 'Oh, they worked together and were polite and everything but Ethan grew up thinking that his father had had an affair with his nanny and that was the reason that their mother had left...' Merida took a breath. 'This is just between us?'

'Of course.'

'Their mother was absolutely awful. Everything in the press has her painted as a saint and Jobe let Ethan think that. Over the months I've been piecing things together but finally Jobe confirmed it—she was cruel. The reason Elizabeth left was because Jobe had found out what was going on. She painted herself as the perfect mother but she just ignored the boys. More than that, she neglected them. She left Ethan in a car once, in the height of summer. If Abe hadn't told the nanny his brother was still in the car...' She shook her head. 'Abe nearly drowned in the bath. If the nanny hadn't come in when she had...'

Naomi shuddered.

'Apparently the nanny that everyone thinks Jobe had an affair with was actually the person who stood up for the boys. She told Jobe all that was going on. He'd always been too busy with work but as soon as he knew he confronted Elizabeth. She headed off to the Caribbean, insinuating she'd found out that Jobe was sleeping with the nanny. When she had her accident Jobe's name was mud, but he never revealed the truth, not even to Ethan, until the night Ava was born.'

'What about Abe?' Naomi asked. 'Did he think his father had cheated?'

'No.' Merida shook her head. 'Apparently he always knew that the mother was awful. He always looked out for Ethan. Hard to believe, really, when he never gives Ava a glance. But who knows what he went through? Perhaps that's why he's so dark. He was never under the illusion that his mother was perfect, far from it. Jobe put up with a lot from the press and, sure, he's had his fair share of wives and drama, but he's done his best as a father.'

'Do you think he'll make it till Christmas?'

'I don't know,' Merida said. 'There's the big ball on Christmas Eve and Jobe insists that it goes ahead. I can't imagine going.'

'It's still a couple of weeks away.'

'It's ten days away.' Merida grimaced. 'I haven't a hope of getting into a dress. I'm rather hoping that Abe and Candice can fly the Devereux flag without us.'

Naomi felt her cheeks go warm from the sting of Merida's words, but thankfully her friend carried on chatting away and didn't notice. 'Khalid's flying in on Friday and Ethan's meeting him for dinner and things. It's all business as usual, except we all know that it's not...'

Naomi wondered if she should tell Merida that the

staff were worried too but decided against it. She certainly didn't want to add to Merida's stress, especially when finally both mother and baby looked more relaxed.

'She's asleep.' Merida smiled.

'And she took a good feed.'

'I don't know how I'd have done this without you,' Merida admitted.

'I've hardly done anything. You've had her in with you at night.'

'Honestly, you've been amazing, Naomi. I was all set to put her on the bottle this morning.'

'She's a fussy little thing.' Naomi smiled. 'I think if you can stretch her out again, especially with Ethan being out tonight, then you might get her into a bit more of a routine. Let me have her and I'll bring her up to you again at ten and then again at two.'

'You'll be exhausted.'

'That's what you're paying me to be,' Naomi pointed out, but that didn't work with Merida, so she changed tack. 'I can sleep tomorrow,' Naomi said with a smile. 'This is like a holiday for me, Merida. Usually I have the baby, or babies, twenty-four seven and just take them in to the mother for feeding and cuddles and such.'

'Well, it's great that you're here.' She looked down at her now contented baby.

'Then use me.'

Merida looked up. 'Ethan wanted me to go for dinner with Khalid on Friday. He's hoping to soothe the feathers that Abe's ruffled.'

'Is there still no agreement?'

'None. Abe refuses to budge.'

'Why don't you go?' Naomi suggested. 'Dinner

sounds far less daunting than a ball and you know that I'll babysit.'

'I don't really want to go,' Merida said. 'And I don't need you to babysit. I thought might go to the hotel and take Ava. Just have a nice night away…'

'Sounds perfect,' Naomi said. 'And even better if we can get her sleeping between feeds.'

'Would you be okay, though?'

'I'm sure I can find something to do,' Naomi teased—they were in New York after all. 'Go!'

It was a plan, and all the more reason to get little Ava settled, so for this night at least Naomi assumed more of a nanny role. When Ava woke up half an hour later, again Naomi walked the floor and did the same thing at ten. 'I'll take her downstairs,' Naomi said, because her little cries wafted from Naomi's floor right up to Merida's. 'And I'll bring her back for another feed at two. She is sleeping more in between, Merida,' Naomi assured the new mother. 'And she's taking much bigger feeds now.'

And so at midnight Naomi sat in the drawing room, holding a still wakeful Ava, although she wasn't crying now. Just alert and awake and utterly gorgeous.

'You *are* going to sleep after the next feed,' Naomi told her. 'And you're going to be good for your mummy on Friday night…' Her one-sided chatter stilled as the door opened. Ava must have picked up on Naomi's sudden tension because she started to cry.

And Naomi was tense because almost two weeks after she'd seen him last, Abe was finally here. Until now she had only seen him in a suit or coat, but tonight he wore black jeans and a thin black jumper, his immaculate hair needed a cut and he was unshaven. He looked like he could be on a wanted poster, Naomi thought.

He most certainly was.

Wanted.

Not that she dared to show it.

'Hey.' He gave her a grim smile as he came into the drawing room. 'I wasn't expecting anyone to be up.'

'I was just about to take Ava upstairs.'

'No need, I'm heading up myself.'

'Then I'll stay down here,' Naomi said, and then, worried he'd think she meant she was avoiding him, added, 'I mean, I'm trying to get her into a routine, she'd only disturb you.'

'I don't think anything would disturb me tonight. Do you want one…?' he offered as he poured himself a drink.

'No, thank you.'

As he poured, Naomi sneaked a look and what she saw concerned her. He'd lost weight—his trousers hung lower on his hips and he looked utterly exhausted. There were dark smudges under his eyes, and the fan of lines looked deeper than they had just a short while ago.

'How's Jobe?'

Abe didn't answer at first but not because he was ignoring her. It was more that he had to dig deep to find a steady voice.

'He's just made the decision to stop all treatments.' It was the first time he'd said it out loud. So badly had he wanted to dissuade his father, to suggest he try to stay for Christmas, or make it to the New Year. Yet he'd known deep down he was being selfish. He was used to making decisions and it was terribly hard to accept that this one wasn't his.

'I'm so sorry.'

Abe took a belt of his drink and let out a long-held breath. 'He says he wants to enjoy the time he has left, and the meds are making him tired and nauseous. He used to love his food.'

'He might again,' Naomi offered.

'That's what he's hoping.' Abe nodded. 'Ethan's staying there tonight. I was going to go home but then I remembered I'm minus a driver.'

'How come?'

'He's moving to Florida.'

'Oh.'

'The snow's really piling up. I don't want to be too far away just in case.'

'Abe…' Naomi knew, even if it was awkward, that she had to broach things. Jobe's health trumped a moment spent blushing. 'I would hate to think you might be staying away because of me…'

'Of course not.'

He had been, though.

It had been one day, he kept telling himself.

No big deal.

Yet it had been the nicest day he had known.

And her company still was.

So much so that despite his intention to head straight up to bed, instead he sat down and looked over at little Ava. 'How is she?'

'Being difficult in the way two-week-old babies generally are. Don't catch her eyes. She's looking for attention when she should be sleeping. We're trying to get her into a routine.'

'Maybe she's like her uncle and loathes routine.'

'Well, she's certainly been burning the candle at both ends.'

Instantly Naomi regretted her words for they seeped the indignation she felt and they told him, if he listened closely, that she'd been reading up on his rather wild ways.

But there was no retrieving them so she just screwed her eyes closed for a second and then prised them open and stared into the fire and offered an apology.

'That sounded…' She didn't know what to say. 'No wonder you've been avoiding home. All I need is a rolling pin and to be standing at the door.'

He gave a low laugh, taken aback by her honesty, so he returned it.

'I *have* been avoiding coming here,' he admitted. 'Not because I didn't want to see you, more because I did.'

Her eyes filled with tears, and she felt her face redden—or was it the glow of the fire?—but in that midnight hour it felt as if there was space to be honest, and admit to the hurt she'd felt. 'I know it was just a kiss to you, Abe, but it was my first.'

She didn't look at his reaction, didn't want to see the surprise on his face. Yet there wasn't any. At some level, he'd known that the mouth that had met his had been an inexperienced one, that the woman he had held in his arm had not flown into them easily, and the hurt he had caused gnawed at his gut.

'You shouldn't have wasted it on me,' Abe said in a deep, low voice that both scalded and soothed her soul.

'It wasn't wasted.'

There wasn't silence between them, just little noises from Ava as she tried to catch an adult's eye in the hope of staying awake awhile. And it was Abe who gave in to her, taking one of her little hands and watching as the tiny fingers coiled around his.

Naomi didn't halt him, or warn him that he was messing up a routine. Some things were important and to see him care for his niece, to reach out and get to know her, felt as if a small battle had been won.

And he wanted to warn Naomi, to tell her to stay the hell away, yet he moved closer, not physically but sitting beside her felt so right it reminded him of just how wrong the world could be.

'When Ethan was born, we had a family photo taken,' Abe said, 'sitting on this sofa. And then Jobe and I headed up to the terrace garden for some father-son shots. It was for a magazine.'

'How old were you?'

'Four,' Abe said, 'nearly five.'

And she smiled because on that glorious day they'd shared, he'd told her things about his father. About pizzas and pretzels, and precious times spent.

'I came back down. I think I'd forgotten something and I found Ethan lying face down on the sofa…'

The smile drained from her face.

'Like one of the cushions. Elaine, the nanny, came in and I remember her turning him over and he was purple. She was shouting at me for not picking him up, for not doing something…'

'Where was your mother?'

'She'd gone for a lie down. Just dropped him like a doll once the photo was over. I never let him out of my sight after that. I used to dread coming home from school, wondering if he'd be safe. It's hard to believe that he's now a father himself.'

'And a very good one.'

'Yes.'

He didn't know if Naomi knew about the contract between him and Merida. It seemed irrelevant now. Abe could see how happy his brother and Merida were and, like every new father, Ethan came in every day with tales about his new baby.

And his wife.

Despite the contract and Abe's gloomy predictions, it would seem they were very much in love.

It made his relationship with Candice, or rather the lack of it, so hollow.

So shallow.

Or rather, more simply, low.

And as Abe looked down at the fingers so tightly holding his, he knew that the woman who held this baby deserved to know that her first kiss hadn't been entirely wasted on a cheat.

Even if it broke the terms of a contract he himself was bound to.

'Naomi, I can't really go into details but I am sorry that I wasn't upfront with you about Candice.'

'It doesn't matter.' She shook her head, loath to confront things.

'I think that it does.'

Naomi swallowed. She just looked at down at Ava, who lay blowing bubbles and utterly content and oblivious to a sometimes cruel world.

'This can't go any further,' Abe said.

'She's two weeks old.' Naomi deliberately misinterpreted, deflecting with a tease, but then she was serious. 'If you mean me, you don't have to worry, I'd never breathe a word.'

'I know that.' Intrinsically he did. 'The truth is that Candice and I have an arrangement—as far as the press and the board are concerned, we're in a relationship. We're not, though.'

Naomi frowned, she simply didn't understand. 'But she came to the hospital to visit Ava, you're going to the Devereux ball together...' she pointed out, recalling Merida's words.

'It's for appearances' sake,' Abe said. 'The ball is just work and I have to take someone.'

'So it's just an act?'

He nodded, but that wasn't enough for Naomi.

'Are you saying that you've never been in a relationship and that you've never slept with her?'

'No. We were together for a while. What I'm saying is that lately we haven't been. We don't...'

'And she doesn't have feelings for you?' Naomi did look at him then, and she watched his jaw clamp down. 'If you offered her more, she wouldn't take it?'

'It's not like that,' he insisted. 'We have an agreement.'

But Naomi had heard enough. 'Abe,' she said, 'can we not do this?'

'But I want to tell you how it is.'

'Well, I really don't want to hear it.'

'Naomi...'

'Please, Abe, we're both very different. Thank you for trying to explain things to me, and I'm glad that you don't think you were cheating.'

'I wasn't.'

Her eyes told him she believed otherwise.

'Look, I believe you when you say that you have arrangements in place and all sorts, but it sounds like a recipe for hurt to me. And I would never knowingly hurt someone. It's a promise I made to myself a long time ago.' She looked right at him. 'I could have so easily gone the other way, Abe.' She never did the woe is me with her childhood, but she opened a tiny window on it then.

'I was moved from pillar to post and some of those pillars and posts weren't very nice. I was so close to sticking my fingers up at the world. I was so close to going off the rails but instead of being nasty, I chose to be kind. And, as much as I want to, I can't really believe that Candice is okay with it all.'

'Naomi, she is. I pay for her apartment and—'

'Abe, I don't want to hear it. We had a wonderful day out and we shared a kiss at the end...' She tried to downplay it, to somehow neatly file it away. 'Let's not make it any more complicated than that.'

'It doesn't have to be.' His voice dropped to huskiness and his eyes were as black and as enticing as treacle. A personal preference perhaps, but treacle was up there with her favourite things. Yet more dangerous than a sugar hit was the pull of Abe, and how she had to fight not to lean into him.

To forgive and forget, or at least pretend to.

Thank goodness for Ava, Naomi thought, for without her she might just have given in, but instead she gave a slight shake of her head, as if to clear the spell. 'Please, Abe.' She just came out and said it. 'It might be completely straightforward to you but it's all just too sordid for me.'

He just sat there as, without malice, she gave her verdict.

She was close to tears and didn't want him to see

them, or to resume this conversation, so she chose to make a rapid escape. 'Could you hold Ava for me, please?'

'Sorry?' Abe said, his mind miles away.

Her words had been like a punch to the gut, but he didn't show that, of course.

'I need the loo and if I put her down now she'll just start crying.'

He hadn't held Ava.

Not once.

He held out his arms and when Naomi handed her over, she was so tiny and light that it felt as if he was catching air.

And Naomi disappeared and left him, literally, holding the baby.

Such a new baby.

And he knew that Ava would be okay.

Abe had spent his early years looking out for his brother, and the later years protecting Ethan's false image of his mother.

He must have got something right, Abe decided, for it would seem Ethan was far more capable of love than he.

Naomi's summing up hung in the air.

Sordid.

Abe had never looked at his life from the outside before and until then he had never really cared what others thought.

Yet he found himself caring what Naomi thought.

If she'd just let him explain…

He and Candice had come to an arrangement a long time ago, when they had first broken up.

Or rather when he had ended things.

He thought back to Candice's pleading and pointing out the anger emanating from the board about his reckless ways. It had been Candice who had suggested that they lie and pretend that they were back together. If she could appear to have forgiven him, then surely the rest would follow?

It had worked.

For eighteen months there had been a veneer of respectability.

Sure, he had been *caught* at times, but with each passing affair Candice had provided an air of stability.

Yes, despite his attempts to justify things, Abe looked down at his niece and thought about Naomi's question on the night she'd been born.

What sort of uncle do you want to be?

Not this one.

And as Abe searched the depths of his soul, Naomi looked into the bathroom mirror and asked a similar question of herself, about the type of woman she was.

Oh, she wanted to believe Abe—that it was all neat and straightforward and that there was really nothing untoward about the kiss they had shared. Yes, Naomi wanted to believe him because, quite simply, she would like more time in his arms.

She would like to go back in there now and say that she had the night off on Friday. That perhaps they could go and see the Christmas lights. That they could possibly continue from where they had left off.

But she'd meant what she'd said—his arrangement with Candice was too sordid for her.

So she splashed water on her face and then dried off and blew out a long breath before heading back to the drawing room, where she paused at the door. Little Ava was finally asleep in Abe's arms and when she approached, Abe looked up, gave a small smile and with his free hand put a finger to his lips.

'You got her to sleep.'

'Isn't that what babies do?' Abe asked.

'Not this one. I thought she'd be awake till two. I might even get an hour's sleep.'

'Are you taking her up to Merida?'

'No, Ava's in with me tonight.' She held out her arms but as Abe went to pass her across little Ava's little face frowned at the intrusion.

'I'll carry her up.'

They headed up the stairs and into Naomi's suite, where there was a crib set up for little Ava. He placed her in it very tenderly and pulled the little sheet over her with great care.

And then he turned and faced Naomi.

She wanted to fall into his arms. It felt as if there was an iron bar attempting to unbuckle her knees so she might just topple onto him.

And if she did, he would catch her.

He would hold her and he would kiss her and it wasn't some sense of professionalism that stopped her, for he would take her from here and lead her to the bedroom.

They wanted each other.

As inexperienced as she was, that much she knew.

And it wasn't just the thought of Candice that held her back.

He melted her with his eyes, he turned her world and spun it gold, and she could not fathom untangling herself from him.

There could be no dusting herself off and carrying on when he inevitably ended things.

And it would be he who ended them, Naomi was

sure. And if his internet history was anything to go by, she'd be nursing a broken heart this side of the New Year, and she was supposed to be in New York until the end of January.

Oh, get out now, she told herself.

With one kiss, she was already in way too deep.

And so, instead of leaning into him, as her body instructed, she gave him a smile.

'Thanks,' she said in an upbeat voice, as if he was Barb and had just popped into her room and dropped off a pile of Ava's washing.

'No problem,' he said, as if he'd done the same. ''Night, then.'

''Night, Abe.'

It was better this way.

Surely?

CHAPTER SIX

THERE WERE NO further sightings of Abe.

Ava woke at two, and she could see the light coming from a room down the hall.

When she woke at six and she carried little Ava toward the stairs, Naomi caught a hit of his cologne, the clear, sharp scent of bergamot, and she knew, simply knew, he had showered and left.

And she knew, just knew, he would not be staying tonight.

She should be relieved, Naomi told herself, yet she felt anything but as she lay the next night, awaiting a creak on the stairs that might indicate he'd come home.

It never came.

Friday dawned.

Her official day off, and when she came down to the kitchen Barb told her she should have stayed in bed. 'I was going to bring you up breakfast. I used to do it in the old days on the nanny's day off.'

'I don't eat breakfast,' Naomi reminded Barb, at the very same time that she selected a pastry and they shared a smile. They both knew she'd lied.

'You can have breakfast in bed for your birthday,'

Barb said, refusing to be put off. 'Merida said it's coming up. I'll make you my special.'

'What's your special?' Naomi asked, licking her lips. 'I am dying to try lox.'

'Do you value your kidneys?' Barb checked, and Naomi laughed.

'I love salt.'

'Hmm.' Barb wasn't so sure. 'You'll have to get yourself dinner tonight, given it's the staff Christmas party. You should come,' Barb pushed, for she'd asked her before. 'It's at Barnaby's. Jobe takes his household staff there every year. Usually he's with us, of course.' She cast an anxious look at Naomi. 'Have you heard how he is?'

'Not really,' Naomi fudged, and she truly felt torn. Abe had told her that Jobe had stopped all treatment, though that had been a very personal conversation. It was one of the reasons she had declined the offer to go tonight. She knew they might press her for more information and she didn't think it was her place to share information. 'I know he's been off his food.'

'We all know that!' Uncharacteristically Barb snapped. 'I'm sorry,' she said quickly. 'It's just hell, not knowing. I pick up snatches of conversation but, of course, no one thinks to tell us.'

Merida came in then, her red hair freshly washed and looking a whole lot more like her old self. Barb snapped back into housekeeper mode, asking what time their luggage would be ready to take to the hotel.

'Ethan's going to meet me at the hotel,' Merida said. 'I should be ready to leave by five. Does that give you time to get ready for your party?'

'Of course.' Barb nodded but, Naomi noted, she didn't ask Merida if there was any news on Jobe.

It was a lovely day, cold and brisk. They bundled Ava up and headed out to a café and had spiced Christmas coffees, just two friends sharing a gorgeous day out.

'I thought you wanted to do the river cruise on your day off,' Merida checked.

'I'm going to do it after Christmas,' Naomi said, slathering butter on a slab of warm gingerbread. 'Are you looking forward to going away tonight?'

'I am.' Merida grinned. 'Though I'm not so sure that Ethan is, given that he's got to deal with the daggers flying between Abe and Khalid.'

'Oh, is Abe going?' Naomi asked, oh, so casually.

'Apparently. They're meeting at the office before-hand and then heading from there to dinner. I'm so glad that I'm not expected to join them. Ava and I shall be watching the movie channel.'

Naomi laughed.

From all Naomi could glean, Abe had stood firm and refused to give in to demands, although construction had not ceased, as had been threatened by Khalid.

'You *can* leave her with me,' Naomi reminded Merida, while mentally crossing her fingers that Merida wouldn't because, determined not to dwell on Abe, she had made plans for tonight. Still, she would cancel her plans if need be, but thankfully Merida declined.

'I know you'll have her, but I really want to see how I go without back-up,' Merida said with a smile. 'You're welcome to come. Ethan can book you a room…'

'I am *not* coming on your date night,' Naomi said.

'It's hardly a date night. I just hope Ethan can smooth

things over with Khalid. Abe's just about jeopardised
the whole project,' Merida said. 'He should have discussed this with Ethan at the time rather than shutting
down talks.'

'Oh, so he should have popped his head around the
door while you were giving birth?' Naomi didn't really
have a clue what the issues were but she couldn't help
but jump to Abe's defence.

'I guess.' Merida rolled her eyes. 'You won't come?'

'No.'

'So, what are you going to do tonight? You'll have
the place to yourself as it's the staff Christmas dinner.'

'I know...' Naomi hesitated, wondering if she should
broach the subject of just how worried the staff all were
about Jobe, but she knew it didn't come down to Merida to tell them, and so she carried on chatting instead.
'Barb asked if I wanted to go with them, but I thought
I might take in a Broadway show.'

'Do you know what you want to see? I can sort out
tickets...'

As an actress *and* a Devereux, no doubt Merida
wouldn't have a problem securing plum seats even this
close to Christmas, but Naomi had already sorted it
out, though she was hesitant to admit it, worried that it
might upset Merida. 'I've already got a ticket.'

'For what?' Merida asked, then must have seen Naomi
blush. 'You're going to see *Night Forest*, aren't you?'

'Yes, it's just I've heard so much from you about it
that I wanted to see it for myself. I didn't think I had a
hope of getting a ticket, but it would seem one ticket is
easier to get at the last minute. You're not upset?' Naomi
checked, because she knew it had broken Merida's heart
to step away from playing Belladonna.

'I would have been upset a short while ago,' Merida admitted. 'Not that you were going, more at the very mention of its name. But not now.' She did up the last of the poppers on Ava's outfit and scooped her up for a kiss. 'Ava more than makes up for it. And, anyway, it doesn't have to spell the end of my career. Ethan and I have spoken and I'm going to see if I can go back when Ava's a little bit older. Maybe as an understudy.'

'Part time?'

Merida nodded. 'It's far too soon to be thinking of it now, but it's nice that Ethan's been so encouraging.'

It was odd, but it was at moments like this that Naomi felt lonely.

And it wasn't about Merida and Ethan being happy, or pining for Abe—in fact, it had nothing to do with coupledom. It was about families, and having support and someone completely in your corner.

It was all the things that Naomi had missed.

Not that she showed it, or said anything. Instead, it was Merida who spoke. 'I'm actually pleased that you're going to see it. Sabine, my old understudy, is now Belladonna. I'd love to hear what you think. Ethan has been twice and so far only gotten to see one half of it...' The first time Ethan had gone had been opening night when, thanks to her absence on stage, he had found out that Merida was pregnant.

The second time had been when he'd taken Merida and she had gone into labour.

'Well,' Naomi said, 'I intend to see the whole thing and I'll let you know what I think tomorrow.'

The day passed in a blur and if Naomi had been in any doubt as to the status of Ethan and Merida's relationship when she'd first arrived, it was completely put to rest when Ethan unexpectedly arrived home to take his wife and daughter on their first night out.

He was so gorgeous to both Merida and little Ava that it made Naomi's heart twist to see the little family so happy as they headed off for their first trip away.

Even though Naomi wasn't a new mother, she ran on the same timeline as one. Worse, because she'd spent most of the afternoon helping Merida get ready, there was little time to do the same for herself. So by the time Merida had gone there wasn't time for Naomi to wash her hair so she just had a quick shower and then tackled her limited wardrobe.

For the most part her clothes were practical for work and, given the transitory nature of her work, there wasn't much going out at night. She had two nice dresses. One that she usually wore for christenings and things but it was far too summery. The other was black and gorgeous but she had put on even more weight since she'd last worn it and her cleavage spilled out.

It would just have to do, she decided. She'd be wearing her new red coat there and for inside the theatre she had a lovely silver scarf.

Naomi applied her make-up carefully, put on her not so little black dress and told herself to smile when she looked in the mirror. After all, on her night off she was going to see *Night Forest* on Broadway!

And, of course, she was excited.

Well, not really.

But she didn't want, even to herself, to admit that.

There had been a dull ache, or rather a space in her chest, since the other night. A space that Naomi did not want to examine because if she did she might break down and cry.

It was just a kiss.

She kept saying that like a mantra.

But Abe's was the only kiss she had ever known, and worse, far worse, was the feeling she had let both of them down the other night. He'd tried to talk but she'd felt unable to listen.

As she headed downstairs the staff were all getting ready to pile into the cars lined up in the drive for them.

'You look wonderful,' Naomi said to Barb.

'I could say the same for you. It feels odd to be heading to the party without Jobe. Maybe next year.'

Naomi said nothing.

It was hell sometimes, having a foot both upstairs and down, but surely the staff ought to know?

When they had gone, Naomi went to order a car of her own. The staff phone was ringing in the kitchen but she ignored it. After all, it couldn't be for her.

As she went to get her coat from the cloakroom, it reminded her so much of her day with Abe that she just buried her face in it for a long moment. There was the faintest scent of him, she was sure. Naomi didn't wear perfume and there was a sharp, clean note of bergamot on the collar. And she recognised another, wood sage, she was sure. It was the scent she had breathed in when they had kissed. The same scent that had met her in the hallway the morning he had left before dawn.

Then the phone rang again and she suddenly thought of Jobe and how sick he was and decided she ought to pick it up.

'Devereux household.'

'Naomi?'

She closed her eyes at the sound of Abe's voice.

Not for a second did she think it might be Ethan, even if they spoke with the same accent, even if their voices were both deep and low. It was as if Abe's were etched like a signature on her heart.

'Yes.'

'Is Barb there?'

'It's the staff dinner tonight,' Naomi reminded him. 'Everybody's out.'

'Of course.' He let out a sigh. 'It doesn't matter.'

'Is everything okay?' she couldn't help but ask. 'Is Jobe—?'

'He's good,' Abe said quickly, as he hadn't intended to alarm her. 'Well, when I say good, now that he's off a lot of the meds he's suddenly hungry and eating.' He spoke so easily with her. 'As well as that he's talking. A lot. Reminiscing, I guess.'

'I thought…' She hesitated. As far as she knew, Abe was supposed to be out with Ethan and Khalid tonight, but it would seem he'd chosen to spend the time with his father. It wasn't her place to pry.

'There's a photo he wants. I was going to ask Barb if she could take it down and have Bernard bring it over…'

'I can do that.'

'Would you?'

'Of course. Where's the photo?'

'It's on the main staircase,' Abe said, and he could hear the clip of her heels as she walked on the marble floor of the entrance. 'Are you on your way out?'

'Why?'

'I can hear heels.'

'Yes, I'm on my way out.' Naomi offered no more information than that.

'Where are you going?'

'Why?'

'I'm just curious.'

He could remain so, Naomi decided. 'I'm at the stairs.'

'Okay, about a third of the way up there's a photo of Ethan and me eating pizza…'

'There's one of the two of you on a yacht, and there's one of you…'

She was looking through his youth.

There were load of formal shots and then she saw the one he had referred to the other night. Ethan was a tiny baby and Abe was sitting on his father's knee, wearing a smile. Elizabeth was looking adoringly at the newborn she held.

And this was one picture, Naomi thought, that didn't paint a thousand words—instead it lied.

Only not quite, because now that she knew Abe she could see the fixed smile and that it did not meet his eyes.

'It's halfway up the stairs,' Abe said, trying to direct her, and Naomi dragged her eyes away and located the correct photo.

'Got it.'

It was gorgeous. Abe was looking very serious but more relaxed than in the others, and Ethan was holding a huge slice of pizza. Jobe was squinting against the sun that shone in his eyes.

'I'll bring it over now,' Naomi said.

'Are you sure you don't mind? I can wait outside if there's somewhere you need to be…' he fished shamelessly. 'I mean if you have a reservation or you're meeting someone.'

'It's really no problem,' Naomi said, and carried on

being evasive. She wasn't bitchy in the least but she did manage a rather satisfied smile when she ended the call, because he clearly wanted to know what she was up to tonight.

Well, Abe Devereux could keep right on guessing.

Naomi was actually well ahead of time as she left the house. She'd allowed ages for the snow but, of course, New York was considerably more geared up for heavy snowfall than London, and her ride soon arrived.

As she climbed into the car, though, instead of asking to be taken to the private wing of the hospital, Naomi thought of what Abe had said about his father eating and him being rarely hungry, and she made a decision.

'Could we take a little detour on the way to the hospital?' Naomi asked. 'I want to get a pretzel.'

'From?' the driver asked.

'The first cart we see.'

It didn't take long to find one and before long she arrived at Jobe's door. For Abe it was like a breath of fresh air had swept in. Hospital visits, even the better ones, were hard going at times and she just breezed in wearing her red coat and her hair glossy, and for the first time he saw her made up. But it was her smile and her effortless way with his father that knocked him sideways.

'Hi, there, Jobe.' Naomi smiled and went straight over. 'It's Naomi, Ava's nanny and Merida's friend...' He gave a nod of recognition. 'It's so good to see you again.'

'Am I already in heaven?' he asked. 'What's that smell?'

'I brought in a pretzel.'

And whether he could eat it or not, it didn't matter. The scent alone made him smile.

'Where are you off to?' Jobe asked.

'It's a secret,' Abe answered for her. 'We're not allowed to ask.'

And then he looked at Naomi as her face broke into a smile. They had been teasing and flirting, even if she refused to admit it.

'Jobe can know,' Naomi said. 'I'm going to see *Night Forest*. The production your daughter-in-law—'

'I've seen it,' Jobe said. 'You're in for a magical night. Who's the lucky fellow?'

'Jobe, I've barely been in the country for three weeks! And,' she added, 'I'm working.'

'Not tonight you're not,' Jobe said, taking in her heels and make-up. 'Where are Ethan and Merida?'

'They're out with Khalid,' Abe said. 'I chose to give it a miss, though I can feel my ears burning.'

'You took a risk,' Jobe scolded.

'Someone had to.' Abe shrugged.

'Well, you should have spoken to me about it,' Jobe insisted. 'Not that he's ever come to me for advice,' he added, rolling his eyes for Naomi's benefit, and that made her giggle. And that made Jobe smile. 'You know, while you're here you should go to the Devereux Christmas Eve Ball. It's the best night of the year.'

'I'm working.'

'Pah!' Jobe said. 'I thought Merida said that she didn't want a nanny.' Jobe looked at his son. 'You could take her. Ethan will be there with Merida…'

'Stop interfering.' Abe's voice was harsh, and it was Naomi's first glimpse of it, not that it seemed to bother Jobe.

'Just saying.'

'Well, don't.'

Naomi looked at Abe's gritted jaw and gave a tight smile. She didn't blame Jobe, of course, he was a little confused and was just being nice, but it made an already awkward situation worse.

'I have to go, Jobe,' Naomi said. 'You look after yourself.'

And when she had safely gone, confused or not, Abe waved a finger at his father. 'Don't even go there.'

'What?'

'Suggesting I take someone to the ball.'

'She's only here for a few weeks, she deserves a big night out…'

'I've never asked for your permission or help with my love life, and I shan't start now.'

'I never said anything about love,' Jobe said. 'I was just saying take the girl to the ball. She's nice.'

Abe said nothing.

'Remember how I used to buy you one of these to warm your hands?' Jobe said.

'Sure.'

'Even back then, you never told me what was on your mind.' He wasn't confused now, just bewildered that Abe hadn't been able to come to him. That he'd had to hear from the nanny what was going on in his own home. 'You could have told me, Abe…'

'I know now.'

'Why didn't you?' Jobe said, and then he gave a wry laugh. 'I know, even back then you trusted no one.'

He stayed a few hours, doing work when his father dozed then making small talk when he woke up.

And then it moved from small talk to more serious matters as Jobe tried to tie the loose ends in his life. 'I don't like this business with Candice.'

'Don't worry about that now.'

'But I do.'

'Well, you don't have to. I ended it this afternoon.'

'How did she take it?'

He should possibly soothe his father and assure him everything was fine, but that would make him a liar. 'Not very well.'

'I don't trust her, Abe.'

'You're a Devereux and, as you just pointed out, we don't trust anyone,' Abe quipped. 'Don't worry about it.'

And Jobe stopped worrying about Candice and lay back on his pillows and saw the foil from his pretzel and he was back to the days of his sons' childhoods again and reminiscing.

'Nice girl,' Jobe said, just before he dozed off again.

'Yes, she is,' he admitted this time.

And for Abe, that was the problem.

She was so nice that now he would never be able to eat a pretzel again without thinking of not just long-ago times with his father but the day he and Naomi had spent, and now the gift she had given him and his father tonight...

The memories both evoked and made.

CHAPTER SEVEN

THAT *NICE GIRL* sat feeling blue and alone in a packed theatre.

Well, not alone. The seat had been available because, after all, few people go to the theatre alone, so Naomi found herself on the end seat beside one huge, happy family, and Naomi listened to their plans for Christmas and New Year. And, yes, this one she'd be spending with her dear friend and the person she was closest to in the world.

Yet it was Merida and Ethan's first family Christmas and Ava's first.

Naomi knew that, no matter how kind and welcoming they were, she'd feel a bit of a spare part.

Oh, Merida would do her best to make sure that Naomi was included but tonight that was how Naomi felt—like a spare part in a two by two, loved-up world.

It was a relief when the lights finally dimmed and she could lose herself in another world.

The production was breath-taking, so much so that Naomi forgot that the birds were actors, but when Belladonna came on, Naomi knew this had been Merida's part. When she heard Sabine singing and realised the complexity of the role it hit home just how talented and accomplished Merida truly was.

And she was so proud of Merida, but tonight, as she stood next to the very large family for the standing ovation and applauded the cast, Naomi felt very small.

Well, *not*-small Naomi was well aware that she could lose the equivalent weight of three Avas and still have more to go, but tonight she felt insignificant and more than a little alone in this world.

It took for ever to get a cab, and Naomi had to walk for ages until the theatre crowd thinned out. It was cold with an icy wind, which didn't help matters much, and she wasn't assertive enough with her flagging, but finally she was sitting in the back of a warm cab and would soon be home.

The Christmas lights were amazing and the drive was a night-time version of the walk she had taken with Abe.

But this time as they passed the Rockefeller Center she was alone.

And the sight of the lights in the stores along Fifth Avenue reminded her of teardrops and suddenly Naomi let her own fall.

Oh, she loathed feeling sorry for herself, but tonight she did.

It was her own fault, Naomi knew.

She could have been with Abe tonight.

Naomi knew it in her heart.

The right thing to do really was the hardest thing.

But then the nicest thing happened. Whoever had warned her about New York cabbies clearly hadn't met this one, because he was so kind that he handed her a wad of kitchen roll to wipe her eyes.

'Christmas makes it that much harder...' he said.

'It does,' Naomi agreed, and his insight just made her cry some more.

Then he told her about his wife, and how much he missed her, so much so that he chose to work through the nights. He was the nicest cab driver in the world.

'You work for the Devereuxes?' he commented, as they pulled up at the huge grey house.

'I do.' Naomi nodded.

No, it wasn't really home.

Tomorrow she'd put her game face on again.

Just not tonight.

She turned the key and stepped into the entrance and had to think for a moment to remember the code, but then she stood rigid as Abe came up beside her and she watched as his long fingers punched it in.

'You've been crying.'

It sounded more like an accusation. 'No, I'm just cold.'

'It must be the night for it,' Abe said. 'Barb just said the same thing, but in your case I don't believe it has anything to do with the wind chill factor.'

Naomi didn't even bother to take off her coat, she would do that upstairs. She just brushed past him and had made it halfway to the stairs when he spoke.

'I'm sorry,' Abe said. And even though it was his first apology in all his years on this earth, it didn't go down well.

'Sorry for what?' Naomi said, and then spun around.

'Upsetting you,' Abe said. 'For not telling you about Candice.'

'You!' Naomi shouted. 'It's not all about you, Abe.' She was furious, not just with him but with herself, because of course he was there at the bottom of the well she was crying from, not that she'd let him know that. 'You're so arrogant. Doesn't it even enter your head that I might have other things to be crying about?'

Abe just stood there, which was a feat in itself. Usually he turned his back on hysterics or drama, especially when they were of the female kind.

'Christmas is *hard* for some people. Not that you even celebrate it. And, no, Barb wasn't crying because of the wind…' She stopped herself, because it wasn't right to break Barb's confidence in the heat of the moment.

So she collected herself.

'Believe it or not, I wasn't crying about you.' She shot him a look that confirmed it and didn't even bother to say goodnight, just headed up the stairs and closed her door in relief.

Damn Abe for seeing her cry.

She took off her coat and then held in a choice word when there was a knock at the door.

'Naomi?'

'Go away,' she called out.

'I can't do that,' he replied. 'Not without seeing for myself that you're okay.'

The door opened and she stood in her dress and shoes, her face tear-streaked but angry. 'Well, you can see that I am.' Then she looked down at the bottle of champagne and two glasses he was holding. 'I'm not in the mood for celebrating.'

'That's okay,' he said. 'Neither am I.'

Yet he made no move to go.

'Why should I talk to you?' Naomi said.

'Because there's a lot to talk about.'

'I don't want to hear your excuses.'

'Good,' Abe replied, 'because I don't make them.'

He made her smile, albeit it was a watery one. And she did want to hear what he had to say, so she pulled open the door and let him in and they headed through to her small lounge.

Naomi sat on the sofa and watched as he expertly poured two glasses and handed her one. He looked at her shaking hand as she took it, and then at the slight pull of her face as she took a sip and the way she moved away a touch when he sat down on the sofa.

He knew not to dive in too deep straight away so he asked something that had been troubling him since he'd spoken to Barb.

'What's wrong with Barb?'

Naomi swallowed. 'I shouldn't have said anything.'

'Too late for that.'

'Barb's worried, they all are. They really don't know what's happening. And they're sad too, as well as hopeful. She said to me tonight that she hoped Jobe would be able to come with them next year. I know they're just staff to you, but—'

'Firstly,' Abe said, 'they're my father's staff.'

'I know.'

'When Jobe went into the hospital it was for further treatment. It's only been a few days since he's accepted that it's terminal.' Abe was silent for a moment. 'I haven't.'

Naomi swallowed and suddenly felt terribly small.

Well, not thin and interesting, but she'd just shrunk inside at her own insensitivity.

'I'm starting to, though,' Abe admitted. 'I want him to fight.'

'It must be so hard to let him go.'

Abe nodded. 'I always thought we'd have more time to sort things out...' He didn't elaborate, didn't feel the need to, because it felt as if she understood. He dragged his mind back to what the conversation was about. 'I will speak to them,' Abe said. 'Stupidly, I thought it might be better to wait until after Christmas...'

'I'm sorry,' Naomi said. 'I shouldn't have said anything.'

'No, I'm very glad that you did. Leave that with me.'

She nodded, rather hoping that their little talk was over. 'Thanks,' she said, and stupidly went to stand.

To see him out.

To say goodbye.

But he took he wrist and pulled her back down onto the couch. 'Why were you crying?'

'I already told you,' she said, and pulled back her arm.

'No...' He dismissed her excuse. 'I think it was a bit more than Bernard and Barb, and you've made it very clear your tears have nothing to do with me. So why were you crying?'

'Why do you care?'

'I'm not sure,' he admitted. 'But I do.'

And so she answered in part. 'Because I'll never be on Broadway.'

'Not you as well,' he groaned. 'I thought that was Merida's beef.'

'No.' Even in the midst of her tears he still made her smile. 'It's more that I could never be. The only real talent that I've got is putting babies to sleep.'

'There are an awful lot of new mothers who would kill for your skills, although, for what it's worth, I think there's an awful lot more to you than that.'

'There really isn't.'

'How about that you go into people's homes at presumably a tumultuous time and make everyone's lives that much better? You certainly have here.'

'Thank you.' She didn't know what to say now. 'I think I'm just tired.'

'Of course you are,' Abe said. 'Getting up to other people's babies every damn night.'

'It's my job to do so, and I happen to love my work, though it has been a busy year,' Naomi admitted. 'I took on an extra client in the summer when I should have taken time off, but it was her second child and I'd been there for the first. And then there were twins before Ava, but the mother delivered early. I just haven't had a break. I'm sure that I'll be fine in a few weeks. I'm taking a decent slice of time off after this,' Naomi said.

'How long?'

'I actually haven't lined up another job. Deliberately.' She had told no one her plans. In fact, 'plans' sounded a rather too grand a word for the tentative ideas that had been taking shape, but he was such bliss to speak to. He just topped up her glass and it felt as if he stopped the clocks too, for time ceased to matter when Abe was around. 'I think it's time to find somewhere more permanent to live. And, when I do, maybe work more locally...' She shook her head. 'I'm not sure. I just want...' She didn't finish or she'd start crying again, but both knew she just wanted a home. 'I don't know where to start looking, though,' Naomi admitted. 'I've lived in so many places.'

'You'll know it when you see it,' Abe said. 'I had an apartment, not far from here. In fact...' He hesitated. It was actually the apartment Candice was in now, but they had never lived there together and it truly wasn't relevant here. 'I still have it, it's on Madison.'

'Nice,' Merida said.

'Perhaps, but it also happens to be ten minutes from my father's and about five minutes from work...' He didn't know how best to explain how confined he'd felt by the exclusive address and the old money vibe of the Upper East Side. 'I just wanted away. I came across this old brownstone in Greenwich Village and I knew straight away that it was where I wanted to live, though when Jobe got wind of it you'd have thought I was moving out to the slums.'

Naomi laughed.

'I just needed a space that wasn't linked to the Devereux name. And a place that was mine. It's more laid back compared to here,' he explained. 'Jobe said I was buying a pile of trouble and admittedly the renovations took a while...'

'You did them?'

'Hell, no, but when I walk in that door I know I'm home. You need that.'

She nodded.

And they weren't talking about fancy addresses, there was no need to clarify that.

'I go to buy something,' Naomi said, 'and I have to think if it will fit in my case, or if I'll have to put it in storage.'

'No more,' he said, and she nodded, relieved to have voiced it, and relieved that she had finally voiced her other thoughts.

'How did you meet Merida?' Abe asked. 'Was it when you shared a flat?'

'No, we were at the same school for a year,' Naomi

said. 'I was moved on, but we kept in touch. She wanted to be an actress and I wanted to be a paediatric nurse but the teacher said we were both dreaming.'

'Why?' He frowned. 'I get they might say that about acting…'

'I was very behind at school,' Naomi said. 'I was never going to make the grades to get into nursing.'

'It doesn't sound as if you had the most stable schooling.'

'You make me sound like a horse.' She aimed for a smile but he refused to allow her to joke her way out of it.

'Listen.' He took her face in his hands and his thumbs brushed at the tears but they kept spilling again. It felt to her as if he had tapped a river, it felt as if all the hurt she held inside he *allowed* to come out. And where most ran from raw emotion, he fostered it. 'I'm sure that if a nurse is what you want to be then you could do it.'

Still held by his hands, she shook her head, because she didn't want to be a nurse any more.

'I don't know what I want,' Naomi admitted.

Except that wasn't quite true, because right here, right now she wanted his kiss.

Was it him she wanted, Naomi briefly wondered, or just contact?

And when she met his eyes the answer was simple. Him.

Yet even when it was held by his hands she shook her head and he knew that she was thinking about Candice.

'We broke up.'

'Abe?' Naomi wanted to believe him, and to her shame she was so hollowed out with want that she almost didn't care, yet she needed more if she was to believe him.

'It's over,' he said. 'I told her yesterday and my father tonight.'

And it was enough clarification, enough that she bent her own rules.

He first kissed her cheek and she closed her eyes at the bliss of contact. His mouth was soft and the room felt very still as he held her so steady. Then she tasted her own tears on his lips as his mouth softly brushed them. It was a kiss that made things better, even if in the morning it might just have made things a whole lot worse.

His tongue slipped in and was met by hers as they toyed with each other. It was a kiss that made her burn and a kiss that somehow soothed. She felt a connection like she never could have envisaged. His scent was faint-inducing, and there was the bergamot, and the wood sage, and now she inhaled a juniper note, and she felt she knew him more now.

His hands left her face but the contact remained as his mouth dizzied her. She felt the cool of the air on her back and it registered that he had pulled down her zip, then she felt the warmth of his palm on her back.

Abe wanted her in bed, yet he made no move to stand because he wanted to kiss her some more.

For Abe, nights necking on a sofa had never happened, let alone were long gone, but he was pulling her dress down over her arms, desperate just to feel her.

'Abe…' She wasn't protesting, but before his kiss toppled her she wanted access to skin and she was pleasingly un-shy and unabashed as he undid her bra, for she was too busy working on the buttons of his shirt.

The crush of him against her chest was delicious. The force of his kiss was denied to her mouth and Naomi closed her eyes as his mouth tasted her breast, wetting and teasing one nipple and then blowing it cold, and when she ached for more of this pleasure he came back to her mouth.

She never let herself get out of hand, but she let him take her to that place now. His kiss pressed her back onto the sofa and the weight of him atop her was sublime.

He looked down at her, and he wanted her stripped beneath him, but he could not resist one more taste so he kissed her again, a deep, sexy kiss as his hips pressed in.

Her hand pushed at his shirt, and finally he shrugged it off, and he felt the dig of her fingers in his back then the flat of her palms exploring him.

It was their second kiss, yet their mouths were adoring each other's and they were locked in the same urgent tune. He could feel the passion beneath and he pressed in hard. They were a tangle of legs and hot, dirty kisses, and what she lacked in experience was made up for by the instinct that pressed them on.

She felt his hand on her legs, pushing the skirt of her dress up, and she didn't care—in fact, she wanted the same.

Then that same hand moved between them, slipping between their melded bodies, and he lifted his hips and unbuckled his belt.

'Abe...'

That word reminded him she was a virgin for, God knew, his body had forgotten. And then he felt her hand there, at first to halt him, but then she just felt him for a moment, hot and hard beneath her palm.

'Oh...' Her word came out in a shudder and she held

him some more, feeling the velvety smooth skin and the strength beneath.

She was on the edge of somewhere she had never been, so Abe got back to kissing her, deep, urgent kisses, so that she did not lose her pace.

And he wasn't taking her, she was half-dressed and panties on, but he was pressing into her and she was lifting into him.

He'd never so urgently pursued another's pleasure, but he demanded it now.

Abe took her hands and held them over her head and he kissed her hard and felt her resisting almost the pleasure she was on the very edge of. And she rued being a virgin for a second, only because had she not been, she knew he would have taken her then.

Abe would have taken her hard and fast on the sofa and she would have let him, and with that thought, with Abe pressing into her, she shattered. He felt her tense and the heat of her face on his cheek and the exquisite moan, and he held on for dear life not to join her, just kissing her red face and smoothing her damp hair, now plastered to her cheeks, and telling himself the wait would be worth it.

'Come on,' he told her, and she heard his voice breathless, and he stood, tucking himself in. 'Come to my—'

'Abe...'

She was a little stunned as she sat up to find that the lights were on, for locked with him it had felt as if the world had gone the most decadent shade of black.

It was supposed to have been a kiss, except she'd been lost in the moment and drunk in the heat that they'd made together. It surprised her how normal the room looked. The glasses on the table were upright, the lights were on, and everything was in place, except a thoroughly rumpled Naomi, who he now wanted in his bed.

Except she wasn't ready for that and in truth wasn't sure that she'd ever be.

Naomi came with a heart attached.

She pulled her dress up over her breasts, just a little embarrassed to be half-naked now.

His shirt was on the floor, and though his trousers were done up again, she could see how aroused he was; more, she could feel that energy still in the room. She wanted to take his hand, she wanted to be led to his bed, but she did not want the pain that would surely follow in the days or weeks to come.

'I can't, Abe,' Naomi said. 'I can't just be a distraction.'

'Where did that come from?'

'Because I am one,' Naomi hotly responded. Abe was hurting tonight, she knew. He was raw about his father and breaking up with Candice and she was a safe bet because in a few weeks she'd be gone.

And when she had, Abe Devereux would be someone she'd hear about in passing through her friend, or maybe see on the rare occasion that she was here.

And he'd forget her, of course he would.

Whereas she'd be left with a broken heart.

'Abe, I've never been a relationship. Until you I hadn't kissed anyone, let alone slept with anyone.'

Clearly it didn't daunt him. 'Isn't it time to change that?'

Ah, but though she might be innocent Naomi wasn't

a fool so she pressed him a little. 'I doubt we're talking relationships.'

He gave a half-laugh. 'Naomi, I'm terrible at them.'

'So you mean sex?'

It sounded clinical and it might even have felt it, except he didn't answer from a distance. Instead, he came and sat down beside her and did the nicest thing. He helped as she wrangled her arms back into her dress.

'How about,' Abe said, and for her he raised his game, 'when you're done here, I take you away?'

'Away?'

'To Cabo.'

She frowned, never having heard of it.

'Cabo San Lucas,' he said, and he told her about his Mexican hideaway and private stretch of white beach, and it was everything, he decided, that she deserved. 'The weather will be beautiful,' he told her, 'the sea like glass...' He was persuading her yet warming to the idea himself, and so used was he to getting his own way with women that it took a moment to realise she was shaking her head.

'And we'll sleep together?' Naomi checked.

'No,' he said immediately, his voice dripping with sarcasm. 'We'll have separate rooms and play charades at night. Of *course* we'll sleep together.'

There was a part of her that wanted to shoot her hand up, and shout, *Me, please*, but there was a deep scar that ran through her heart, a birth trauma almost, except it hadn't faded with time.

And it ached its warning now.

It throbbed in her chest and it reminded her of the hurt she'd endured and warned her there could be so much more to come.

'Then the answer's no.'

He didn't get it, he just didn't. 'I've told you, I'm no good at relationships.'

'Then you're no good for me.'

It was the hardest thing she had ever said. *The* hardest thing, but sex to Abe was as easy as flicking on the light on the way in.

She, on the other hand, would be left carrying that light—a torch named Abe.

And, no, Abe didn't get it. One minute she'd been hot in his arms, the next he was practically offering her a honeymoon vacation, yet still she'd pulled back. 'You'll be telling me soon that you're saving yourself for marriage.'

She'd never really thought of it like that, but that was what Abe did—he made her explore who she was. 'I suppose I am.'

He looked suitably aghast.

'I don't know if it will ever happen for me, Abe, but, yes, I guess I am waiting for that. The simple fact is that I can't just loan out my heart in return for a fortnight in Cabo San... Cabo San Wherever.'

Even if she'd love to.

Even if every inch of her body felt as if it were screaming in silent protest as her decision was made. 'I don't expect you to understand.'

He didn't.

Because the worst part of no was that both their bodies screamed yes.

There was the scent of sex in the air and her nipples were thick beneath her dress and her eyes were still glassy from her climax.

His weren't!

'I'm sorry if I...' she attempted as she saw him to the door.

'Stop apologising,' he snapped.

'Very well.'

''Night, Naomi,' Abe said for the second time in her quarters, but he wouldn't be leaving with his tail between his legs.

This time he kissed her goodnight.

It would seem that that was allowed in her virgin world.

A deep, hot, passionate kiss and he prised her mouth open with his tongue, and when her hands shot to his head as she kissed him back, he removed one and moved it, unresisting, down and held it over his thick length.

Now he pulled his mouth away.

And, yes, he left her wanting.

As was his intention.

And by the time he'd made it to his bedroom for the first time Abe did have a wish list—Naomi Hamilton in his bed by Christmas.

Pleading!

CHAPTER EIGHT

Bergamot, wood sage, juniper *and* vanilla.

His delectable scent was in the hall and still on the stairs as she made her way downstairs the next morning.

Naomi had deliberately come down late in the hope of avoiding him.

It would seem that she hadn't.

Naomi felt like a sniffer dog picking up scent as she headed to the kitchen. She wanted to scuttle back up the stairs but pressed on, determined to keep to her usual routine and not appear to be avoiding him, but when she got there, unusually, *thankfully*, Naomi found that the door was closed.

She could hear Abe's low voice coming from behind it, and she quickly realised it was closed for a reason.

Abe must be speaking to Barb about Jobe.

She headed back upstairs, made coffee in her little kitchen and found a muesli bar lurking at the bottom of her bag, and decided that would just have to do.

It didn't.

And she couldn't hide in this room, avoiding him.

Merida wasn't due back for ages and would hardly demand that she be here, waiting for her, so Naomi decided to head out.

She walked over to the park and once there she re-played last night over and over in her mind.

It had been breath-taking.

Literally.

Even now, she stopped walking, simply recalling last night.

Naomi had always just pushed down that side of her. She had shied away from boys and later men, yet she was herself with Abe. Despite his fierce reputation, de-spite his bad name. Not once, for even a second, did she feel anything other than safe around him.

Safe enough to be herself around him. To discover herself even.

She was quite sure she should be feeling embarrassed and awkward, but she wasn't. She felt sad, about the conversation taking place in the house, and sad for her-self that she had gone and fallen for a man who would give her more than she had ever had, and who would leave her with nothing.

Abe didn't even offer hope.

Had he said they could try, maybe see if they worked, then Naomi doubted even wild horses could drag her from his bed.

So rather than keep looking back at the house, she walked on. Better that than run back to the house and tell him she'd changed her mind and, yes, please, take her to San…wherever it was and make love to her over and over.

She walked for a good hour, till she stood in the very place where they had first kissed, and she wished, how she wished, that she'd had the courage to say yes to him. Wished she could have had the courage to throw caution to the wind and just said yes to one wild, crazy night.

But she hadn't.

So rather than wishing for the impossible, and one night in his arms, she went and bought a hot dog instead.

For once, it didn't help.

'There you are.' Barb smiled when Naomi returned. 'I was just saying to Merida I thought you might be doing the harbour cruise.'

'No, I just went for a walk,' Naomi said, and looked at Barb's face for signs she'd been crying, or any sign really that *the conversation* had taken place, but she looked, well, just like Barb. 'Is everything okay?'

'Everything's fine,' Barb said. 'We had such a lovely night.'

Naomi headed up the stairs and met Merida coming down them.

'Where's Ava?' Naomi asked.

'Asleep.' She was carrying a bag from the hotel, which she handed to Naomi once they were in her little living room.

'What's this?'

'A robe from the hotel's gift shop.'

It was gorgeous, the fabric was very thick and soft, and it was so heavy that for a second Naomi's mind flitted to her luggage, but then she reminded herself that she didn't have to think like that now.

She might need excess luggage this time, but she would soon have a home. Things might not have worked out between herself and Abe, but she hoped that she would get to tell him just how much he had helped her last night.

'How was *Night Forest*?' Merida asked, oh, so casually.

'Wonderful!'

'And Sabine?'

'Terrible,' Naomi said dutifully, and they both laughed. 'No, she was amazing, but I just know that you would have been too. How was Ava?'

'She was cranky,' Merida admitted. 'But we got there. Khalid came up to the suite for a drink before dinner and met her, and she was perfectly behaved then.'

'Was it tense?'

'Not at all! Can you believe that Abe backed down?'

'Really?'

Merida nodded. 'He didn't even come to dinner. He told Ethan that right now he's got more to worry about than placating a sheikh…' She let out a hoot of laughter. 'I gather that Candice finally saw sense and dumped him. Good for her.'

Naomi wondered what Merida's reaction would be if walls could speak!

'So it's all sorted?' Naomi checked. 'The Middle East stuff?'

Merida nodded. 'It seems to be. Khalid's even staying on for the Devereux ball. Mind you, as nice as it was to have a night away, it made me realise I don't want to go. I am not black-tie-ball ready. Either physical or mentally. It's really catty, apparently, and anyway it's your birthday. I'm not leaving you on your own. We can have cocktails and watch the red carpet on live-stream—'

'Merida,' Naomi interrupted, 'you know I don't like a fuss on my birthday. Don't make excuses, it's fine not to want to leave Ava. She'll only be three weeks old.'

'That's just it. And it's not just the night, it's getting ready and all that it entails. I just want to stay home with my baby. I hope that Jobe understands.'

So too did Abe.

He left the office at lunchtime and a short while later walked into his father's hospital suite and saw him resting back on his pillows and looking out of the window to the reservoir. Abe wondered what his father was thinking and he just stood there for a moment, taking it in—the precious time left where he still had a father he could turn to.

If only he would allow himself.

'Jobe...' Abe watched as his father snapped out of his trance and then turned and gave him a tired smile. 'Do you think you might be able to stick around for a while longer?'

Jobe gave a tired laugh. 'Why's that, then?'

'Because I need your advice.'

'Well, they say if you live long enough you see everything once...' Jobe responded. 'What is it you want?'

Abe could tell that Jobe didn't really believe that he needed his father's take on whatever was on his mind, but Abe wasn't placating his father. 'I really could use some guidance. I think you're right and that I should take Naomi to the ball—she deserves an amazing night.'

'Then what's stopping you?'

'I'm not at all sure that she'll agree to go.' He didn't say why. 'But even if she did I'm rather certain that Ethan and Merida would talk her out of it. They'll need her to babysit.' There was an edge to his voice at the final part, and inside Jobe smiled.

'Well, Ethan was just in and said that Merida's not up to a black-tie ball.' He gave his son a wink. 'I'll tell them it's my idea, they're not going to argue with me.' He patted his son's hand. 'I'm sure we can come up with a plan.'

They did, and it took a few days to thrash it all out, deciding it best not to tell Ethan and Merida until the eve of the ball.

And certainly not to let on to Naomi.

Naomi, with time to think about it, would work out a million reasons why she couldn't go.

It had to be a surprise.

'Just avoid her,' Jobe said, 'until the day of the ball.'

Abe tried.

There were places to be and people to see, and what's more there was suddenly more life in Jobe. From having little to do with the details of the ball this year so far, suddenly he wanted everything run past him.

It was a very busy few days.

And not all of them pleasant.

Candice had not taken the break-up well and there were a lot of meetings between Abe and his attorney.

He stood in his office looking out at a cold grey winters day and refused to be screwed over. 'We weren't married,' Abe pointed out. 'It was a contracted agreement.'

'And one that you're breaking.'

'That's covered,' Abe pointed out. 'There are get-out clauses…' And then he stopped, because that's what he did of late.

Since Naomi had come into his life, more and more he was trying to do the right thing—with Khalid, with his father, but, goodness, Candice took every bit of goodwill and milked it for gold.

'She can have the apartment for a further six months.'

Candice wanted twelve.

Abe stormed out of his office, slamming the door

behind him, and was pulling on his coat, ready to head down in the elevator and cool off, when he saw her.

Or rather them.

There was Merida, Ava in her pram, and their very awkward-looking nanny.

'Hi, Abe.' Merida gave him a tight smile. 'We just came in to show off Ava…'

He just stalked past them, and Naomi closed her eyes and asked herself how, *how*, she could be so crazy about the kind of man who didn't even stop and say hi to his niece.

But then he halted and looked into the pram and said, of all things, 'Good morning,' to a three-week-old, and then he gave a curt nod to Merida.

And he offered *nothing* to her.

It had almost killed her that since that night she hadn't seen him and now that she had, Naomi hurt even more.

And that hurt was compounded on the eve of her birthday.

There was a rather mad rush on as Jobe had asked that Ethan bring Merida and Ava to see him that night. 'He wants us all to watch the montage we've put together for the ball. Abe too,' Ethan explained to Merida as Naomi dressed Ava.

'Abe will see it tomorrow.'

'I guess…' Ethan agreed, changing his tie. 'I guess he just wants us to see it together.'

'Has Jobe seen it?' Merida asked.

'Not yet.'

They chatted away, as couples did, and then, halfway up the poppers on Ava's little cherry-red suit, came the conversation Naomi had been dreading.

'Who's Abe taking?'

'His latest.'

Naomi messed up the poppers and had to undo the top half and start again.

'Who?'

'I can't keep up with the names.'

It was just a throw-away comment. Such a little thing so that neither noticed Naomi's pale face as she handed Ava over.

'I don't know how long we'll be,' Merida said as she gave Naomi a quick kiss. 'It depends on Jobe.'

'Don't rush back for me,' Naomi said. 'I think I might just head off to bed.'

Which she did.

Naomi peeled off her jeans and top and sat on the bed in her knickers and bra and did her damnedest not to cry.

Abe had moved on.

She'd expected no less.

Of course he would take someone else to the ball.

'No way,' Jobe said.

He was holding Ava as he watched the montage that had been painstakingly put together. Merida was sitting in the chair beside them as his sons stood, awaiting his verdict. 'It looks like I'm already dead. Use that one next year and put up some clips of me dancing.'

'The ball's tomorrow,' Ethan pointed out.

'Then you'd better crack on,' Jobe retorted. 'But first...'

He *told* them what would be happening.

'No way.' It was Ethan's turn to say it. He gave a curt shake of his head as Merida cast him an urgent glance.

Abe had expected nothing less from his brother, who, now married, had made himself the moral majority.

'Absolutely not.' Ethan looked straight at Abe. 'You can't have him take Naomi to the ball.'

Oh, there wasn't an argument bedside, but the Devereuxes were not the type to let a little thing like death get in the way of a heated discussion.

'But why not?' Jobe frowned. 'You two aren't going and Abe has to take someone and Naomi's a lovely young lady. As well as that, tomorrow's her birthday. Why shouldn't she be treated to a glitzy night out?'

'It's the company she'll be keeping that concerns me,' Ethan said, and again shook his head. 'No.'

'So you're the type of boss,' Abe checked, 'who dictates what his staff does on their night off. Assuming she gets a night off on her birthday.'

That derisive note was back to Abe's voice. He did *not* like the fact that Naomi was employed by his brother. And it wasn't just snobbery, more he could not stand that he had to go to his younger brother to even take Naomi out. However, he acknowledged that for tomorrow to work, he did indeed need their help.

'Of course I don't dictate what she does in her free time,' Ethan snapped. 'I just wouldn't encourage her to be spending it with you.'

'Well, I think a night out on the town is just what she needs.' Jobe smiled. 'There are a few of the nurses from here going. I'll tell them to look out for her if Abe gets waylaid. I want this, boys...' he told them.

'Boys?' Ethan checked.

'How about,' Abe suggested, 'we leave it for Naomi to decide?'

'Jobe.' Merida found her voice then. She'd been so

taken aback at the thought of her shy friend on Abe's arm at the rather daunting ball that she'd been stunned into silence. 'While it's a lovely idea, women spend months preparing for this night. Dress fittings, spa trips, you can't just spring something like this in on her the day before the event.'

'I agree,' Jobe said. 'I think it better that you tell her tomorrow.'

CHAPTER NINE

'HAPPY BIRTHDAY TO YOU...'

Barb, as she did for all staff on their birthdays, carried a huge tray into the bedroom as she sang a tuneless rendition of 'Happy Birthday'.

'Breakfast in bed!' Naomi sat up. She had completely forgotten about the promise of breakfast. 'How lovely.'

'Not just any breakfast,' Barb said. 'All my best dishes are there.'

There were scrambled eggs with lox, but when Naomi took a taste of the briny smoked salmon she reached for water. And there was *bialys*, round bread with the dent filled in with caramelised onions, and a serving, too, of breakfast potatoes, and it was all topped with bacon crisped to near extinction.

'Take your time,' Barb said.

For someone who loved their food, it was the best, and as she ate, Naomi stuffed down the hurt and planned her day off, *determined* to make the most of it.

She would go on the river cruise, Naomi decided, and then she'd do some last-minute shopping.

And that took care of today, but she could not bear to think of tonight.

Merida's suggestion that they have cocktails together

and watch the live-stream of guests arriving sounded like a form of slow torture to Naomi.

She'd have to wriggle out of it, Naomi decided as she dressed, though she had no idea how.

As Naomi came down the stairs with her tray, Bernard was kneeling beneath the Christmas tree, adding presents to the pile, and he smiled when he saw her.

'Happy birthday, Naomi.'

'Thank you.'

'Once you've dropped that in the kitchen, can you go and give Merida a hand with Ava? They're putting up stockings in the drawing room.'

'Sure,' Naomi said. 'I didn't hear them up…'

She pushed open the drawing-room door and there were Ethan, Merida, Ava and Barb all standing by a table, and on it there was gorgeous birthday cake and for the second time that morning she was greeted with song.

'You know I don't like a fuss,' Naomi pleaded.

'This year you're getting one,' Merida said.

Barb had bought her a huge scarf and from Ava there were long silver earrings.

'She has very good taste.' Naomi smiled, privately wondering where on earth she'd ever wear them—a baby's little fingers tangled up in one would have her earlobe off.

'This is from Ethan and me,' Merida said, and handed her a pale gold envelope. The paper was thick and heavy and as she took out the card inside Naomi frowned as she read it.

'A spa day?' She couldn't keep the question from her voice, and for a moment she wondered if Merida had gone completely mad. Naomi was the last person to go to a spa day, especially one in New York.

God, the women would all be hovering around the hundred-pound mark!

'Thank you,' Naomi duly said. 'I'll look forward to that.'

'You don't have to wait.' Merida smiled. 'It's for today.'

'Today?'

'Yes. You are not to do anything other than be thoroughly pampered...'

'Merida, no...' Oh, she hated saying it, but thanks to Abe she was becoming quite proficient in its use. 'It's a lovely idea and everything, but it's Christmas tomorrow, I've got far too many things that I need to do today.'

'You *have* to go to the spa today because tonight,' Merida said, and then went a little pink, 'you're going to the Devereux ball.'

'No.' Naomi immediately shook her head. 'I can't.'

'You can. It's Jobe's gift to you.'

Naomi felt sick.

Oh, it might not sound a big deal to some, but Naomi so rarely went out.

And certainly not to black-tie balls.

And while it was the most wonderful thought and a gorgeous invitation, she simply could not face it. 'Merida, I shan't know anyone.'

'Jobe's thought of that.' Ethan spoke then, and she caught a tiny look that flashed between him and Merida. 'Abe's going to take you.'

She would wake up soon, Naomi decided, because it was like being stuck in a nightmare.

Yes, any minute now Barb would come singing through her door.

Except everyone stood smiling at her.

She thought of Abe's gritted jaw when Jobe had suggested it, and his utter dismissal of her when they had stopped by the office.

Then she thought of his embarrassment at having her on his arm on this most prominent night.

Oh, he fancied her, she knew that.

But it was a between-the-sheets thing, Naomi was sure.

And while he might be prepared to have sex with her on a private beach, he would not, Naomi was positive, want her by his side at such a high-profile event.

'Merida, please put your magic wand away. I don't want to be foisted on Abe and I do not want to go to the ball.'

'Naomi…' Merida saw her friend was struggling but she just made it worse. 'Abe will be working the room all night. Khalid will be there and, I promise, Ethan has asked him to look out for you. He's an utter gentleman. And Jobe has two of his favourite nurses going with their husbands…'

'What about Abe, what does he have to say about this?'

'He wants what his father wants,' Merida said.

And she must remember those words, Naomi thought to herself.

He'd been dragged into it by Jobe, possibly not screaming as she doubted Abe had the emotional capacity towards her for that, but still he was doing this to please Jobe. But that meant tonight Abe would be punching above his weight, and not in the usual sense.

Naomi was not being self-effacing but she was not his usual type and she knew it.

It was Merida who calmed her down.

She waved Ethan and everybody off and then sat on the couch with Naomi, who was still clutching the card from the spa. 'Abe will be working the room. You'll hardly have to see him. Just one duty dance and then you can drink Manhattans all night long.'

She'd wished for this, Naomi realised.

Standing in Central Park, she'd wished for one more night in his arms.

And she felt a jumble of things.

Nervous.

Reluctant.

Yet also incredibly, terribly excited.

This was a real black-tie ball and it was the only time she would ever get to attend one.

And she'd dance with Abe.

Even one duty dance from him she would take.

Naomi knew, absolutely, that she must not get ahead of herself. It wasn't a date. This family did this sort of thing all of time and clearly Jobe had been angling for it.

She felt sick.

A little dizzy.

But she was starting to get excited now.

'Bernard's going to take you to the spa now, and don't be shy when you're there,' Merida warned.

'No.'

'Naomi, I mean it. I had a hell of a time when I first got here. I had this stylist, Howard, and he talked down to me all the time. Don't let them.' She held her friend's hands. 'Be yourself and just enjoy it.'

'I have to get some presents…'

'I can get something for you for Barb. Who else?'

'Jobe.'

'I'll think of something. Anyone else?'

Naomi shook her head. She certainly wasn't going to let on to Merida that she'd wanted to get something for Abe.

It was too late for that now.

Naomi would not be intimated at the spa.

Hell, that part came later when she stood with Abe alongside Manhattan's finest.

And so she walked into the spa with her head held high.

Blushing, but her head high.

'Ah, yes.' The receptionist didn't really smile when Naomi gave her name. 'Jobe asked that we squeeze you in. Come this way.'

It was impossible to relax as she sat down in the chair and was eyed up by the colourist and the skin technician.

Together they looked at her hair, her nails, her bone structure. The only thing they didn't do was pull back her gums and check her teeth.

'So, you're one of the nurses?' the skin technician said, and made her a charity case straight away. 'Jobe is so-o-o generous.'

'Actually, no, I'm…' Naomi chose not admit to being the nanny. 'I'm a friend of the family.'

Ms Skin Technician did not raise her eyebrows, Naomi wasn't sure she'd be able to, but her glance to her colleague said it all.

'And do you have a date tonight?' the colourist asked.

'I do,' Naomi said. 'Abe.' There was a not-so-tiny pause and Naomi found out she wasn't such a nice person after all as she suppressed a self-satisfied smile, and just for a moment she lived the dream.

'Abe Devereux?' they both simultaneously checked.

'Yes.' Naomi nodded. 'Abe's taking me to the ball tonight.'

Now they got out their wands because, at the dropping of his name Naomi went from squeezed-in charity case to seriously spoiled.

First oil was placed in her hair and she was sent to relax in a small pool with an eye mask on.

Then another pool.

And then she was massaged from head to toe with rough salt and after their that she was rinsed off and then pummelled and plucked and trimmed in places even Abe, despite their tryst on the couch, had never seen.

It was, though, the best gift she'd ever been given and despite feeling so shy at first, it turned out to be an amazing day.

As she lay having her shoulders rubbed, there was an oil they used that was so utterly fresh and relaxing she asked if she could buy some.

There was actually a very exclusive gift shop and, wrapped in a dark robe, waiting to be made up, Naomi browsed, deciding to purchase a bottle of the oil and a vaporiser.

For Jobe.

For Barb she got the biggest bottle of bath oil and some scented candles and at the last minute she added a pretty tin of extraordinarily expensive mints to her pile.

'They'll fit nicely in my purse,' Naomi said to the sales assistant.

But, yes, it was in case he kissed her.

'Tell us about your dress,' she was asked as she moved to the final chair.

'It's black,' Naomi said, because it was the only one she had.

'By whom?'

And she would not admit to having bought it online so she fudged instead and gave the name of a designer she knew Merida had worn.

'What look are you aiming for tonight, Naomi?'

And she looked in the mirror and didn't know how to answer that for a moment.

She didn't know how to be beautiful and she didn't think she could ever look as if she belonged.

'Do you want to leave it to us?' the senior clinician checked. 'We're very good.'

They were.

Naomi had never known her hair could be so smooth and glossy and it was gently pinned up, so that some curls fell at the front.

It was a look she had tried several times herself and failed to achieve.

Then the make-up artist set to work.

Her skin was incredibly pale, and they left it at that, just smoothed her complexion out. Her make-up was, in fact, very subtle, with neutral colours and soft lips, the only exception to that being her eyes. Though initially delicately shaded, the look was finished off with lashings of eyeliner, and when Naomi declined false lashes, they went to town with the mascara.

It was odd looking back at her reflection, but there was no big reveal because time was running out.

Instead, she put on a robe and was bundled into the

car, like a child in pyjamas being taken home from her parents' night out.

Only Naomi's night was just starting.

Merida was waiting for her and it would seem the countdown had started because she practically raced her up the stairs.

'Happy birthday,' Merida said, once they were in Naomi's rooms and she handed her another parcel.

'You already got me a present.'

'Well, I got you another one,' Merida said.

They were silver knickers and the most amazing lacy silver bra.

'Abe is not to see them,' Merida warned, and Naomi laughed. 'I mean it, Naomi. You look stunning, even in a robe. And I know he's devastatingly handsome, but trust me when I say he's wrong for you.'

'I've already worked that out, Merida.'

'No, I know I've told you but you have to listen to me—'

'Merida,' Naomi interrupted. 'Leave it, please.'

'Naomi?'

And Naomi had seen it more times than most—the utter fog a new mother descended into, and the frown that formed when they first came blinking out of it and found that the world as they had once known it had completely changed.

'What am I missing here?' Merida asked.

'Not much,' Naomi said, and she tried not to cry on her new eyelashes as she held her friend's hands. 'But I know his reputation, and I also know why women fall so easily for him. He can be wonderful. So wonderful that you could choose not to believe the warnings and very easily believe you were the only girl in the world. I *know* all that.'

'Oh, Naomi. I'd never have agreed to this if I'd known. I—'

'No,' Naomi interrupted. She'd had the whole day to think about it. 'I'm so happy we get tonight and for a minute I can dance with him, and…' Well, she didn't go into detail but she wanted this night. Even if Abe had been put up to it by his father, even if she was a bit of a charity case, Naomi wanted a night on and in his arms. 'I want to go the ball.'

'Then you shall.' Merida smiled and held open the bedroom door. 'And I don't get fairy godmother status for this. It was Abe…'

On her bed was the very dress she had tried on that day while he'd been fitted for his suits, and Naomi offered silent thanks to Felicia, who must have remembered her size.

'Oh, my…'

She had never owned anything so heavenly before and then she checked herself. 'Is it on loan?'

'No,' Merida said. 'It's yours.'

And where would she keep it? Naomi thought as she held up the decadent garment. The top was boned so it would fill up half a case, but she'd pay excess luggage for the rest of her life rather than ever let it go.

Merida left Naomi to get dressed but, once alone, Naomi stood staring at the gorgeous dress. Beside it were shoes and a bag. Every detail had been taken care of and she had never felt so looked after before.

The deep violet of the dress and the stunning make-up brought out the blue of her eyes and her porcelain skin, and her new silver earrings gleamed at her throat.

'My bust looks huge,' Naomi said, and if there was one detail she could change, she wished the dress had straps because she felt as if her breasts might fall out.

'It looks amazing,' Merida assured her. 'You look amazing.'

'I need a wrap...'

'I've got a black one that will go beautifully,' Merida said. 'Oh, Naomi, you look completely stunning.'

'Honestly?'

'Absolutely. Abe's not going to know what's hit him.'

On the contrary.

Abe had always known she was a beauty and when she came to the top of the stairs and he saw her, it was simply confirmed.

From her hair to the paleness of her arms and the spill of creamy cleavage, he drank in the view.

She lifted the skirt of her dress and on unfamiliar heels walked down and then paused. Not from nerves, more that she too could take in his absolute splendour.

The wanted-poster look might be gone—his black glossy hair had been cut to perfection and he was cutthroat-razor shaved—but she had never wanted someone more in her life.

His suit was divine, and he stood tall and elegant and utterly still except for the glint of desire in his eyes.

And when it was just them, when he looked at her like that, all self-doubt ceased.

That he wanted her, still.

That he always had, made her feel beautiful.

And when she came to the foot of the stairs and inhaled his cologne, Naomi had to dig her newly neutral, manicured nails into her palms so as not to lift her hand to feel his smooth jaw.

And then she looked down and over his left arm was draped violet velvet. Abe had taken care of every detail tonight. 'Happy birthday,' he said, and wrapped her in the cape she had not dared to try on that day.

The lining was silk and she felt its coolness as he draped it around her and then the weight of the velvet

Naomi found out then how it truly felt be taken care of.

With this single moment he made up tenfold for the million lonely moments she had known in her life.

And even as she warned herself not to go there, it was way too late.

Naomi knew then that she was in love.

'Ready?' Abe checked.

And she hesitated, because the private realisation of the depth of her feelings was confronting, but there was no real time to examine it. Merida was dashing down the stairs with the wrap she no longer needed and Ethan had come out from the drawing room to see them off.

'Bernard's waiting...' Ethan told them.

'I can't wait to hear how it all went.' Merida smiled. 'If Ava's up when you get in...'

And her words incensed Abe.

How dared they wait up.

They were carrying on as if she were a lamb being led off to slaughter, and having seen Naomi into the waiting car he marched back up the steps to where his brother and sister-in-law stood.

'Do you insist that your staff be back at a certain time?' Abe demanded.

'Of course not,' Merida gritted. 'But Naomi's a friend.'

'And yet you give her one night off in seven and then dictate how she spends it.'

Yes, he was still a bastard.

'Abe,' Ethan warned. 'Don't take it out on Merida. With your reputation, she has every right to be concerned.'

'And yours is so lily white?' Abe checked, and he looked at them both. Hell, he loved them but he would be dictated to by no one, especially in this. 'Butt out!'

He turned and walked briskly down the steps and he could see Naomi's anxious face peering out of the car, making sure that everything, everyone was all right.

And she just stopped him in his tracks, for how could he be angry at two people who were looking out for Naomi?

Abe knew his own reputation after all.

He turned on the steps and, swallowing his pride, he walked back up them.

'You have nothing to worry about,' he told them. 'I'll take perfect care of her.'

Abe fully intended to.

CHAPTER TEN

IT SHOULD HAVE been a gorgeous drive to the hotel.

The snow was falling lightly over a snow-capped Central Park and had he held her hand it would have been utterly perfect, except he silent drummed his fingers on a long, suited thigh.

'Do you have to greet everyone?' Naomi asked.

'God, I hope not,' Abe said. 'Don't worry, there'll just be loads of air-kissing for you. You don't have to remember anyone's name.'

He was trying to put her at ease, but she could feel his tension.

Perhaps, now they were near, he was rueing the fact he'd agreed to take her, Naomi thought, because while he'd been lovely at the house, he was on edge now.

Naomi went into her bag and prised open her tin of mints, more for something to do than because she wanted one.

Except they weren't mints!

It took a second to register they were mint-flavoured condoms.

Oh, God, Naomi thought, stuffing them back in her bag, terribly glad she hadn't offered him one!

And then, as she stepped out of the car, she suddenly

thought how she'd, oh, so casually added them to her purchase, explaining how they'd fit in her purse. Maybe it was nerves but she suddenly stifled a laugh and arrived smiling on the red carpet.

It was Abe who was tense.

She felt as if she had stepped into Christmas when they entered the hotel.

There was a huge scarlet Christmas tree centrepiece in the main foyer that looked as if it were made of velvet. But as her cape was removed and she was handed a single red rose, Naomi saw that the tree itself was made entirely of the most exquisite red roses, each bloom perfect.

'It's beautiful.' Naomi would have loved to linger and just take it all in, but there wasn't time to as Abe was quietly informed her that they were to go straight through.

She held onto Abe's arm as lightly as she could, and tried to slow down her heart rate as they entered the ballroom. It was stunning. The chandeliers dripped Icelandic-looking crystals and despite the warm air she felt as if her breath should blow white. It was so breathtaking that for a moment Naomi simply drank it all in and tried to forgot her nerves.

But as guests arrived, heads turned in her direction.

Naomi tried to tell herself that they were all looking at Abe. After all, a lot of the women here tonight had eyes only for him, yet she could not fail to see the slight surprised reactions at his choice of date for the night.

When she had been introduced to, shaken hands with and been air-kissed by more people than she could possibly remember, Abe told her he had to go and speak to someone. 'I'll leave you in Khalid's safe hands.'

Oh, please, don't, Naomi thought, because she didn't know if her nerves could take it—Khalid was a sheikh prince.

Except he was completely charming.

Dressed in a long gold robe, he looked both exotic and formidable, yet he was delightful.

'It is a pleasure to meet you, Naomi.' His smile was warm and unexpected. 'I have heard a lot about you.'

'I'm a good friend of Merida's,' she replied, assuming that Merida, or perhaps Ethan, must have mentioned her when they were talking about Ava.

'Merida?' he checked. 'Of course. Abe did say you were from England. Ah, so that is how you and Abe met.'

Naomi nodded.

'I have to thank you,' he added.

'Me?'

'For pouring oil on trouble waters. I never thought Abe would agree, but—here we are.'

Naomi assumed he had mixed her up with someone, or that she had lost the thread of the conversation, given how hard it was to concentrate. She could feel eyes on her and sometimes she caught the raised hands as people spoke behind them and asked each other who she was.

The women were absolutely stunning and must have taken rather more than a day to prepare for tonight. They reminded Naomi of tiny hummingbirds, and not just because of their elegant clothes and glittering jewels, but from the dainty sips of their drinks.

Naomi realised she had already drained her glass.

Khalid gestured for another.

'I'd better not,' Naomi said.

'Relax,' Khalid said. 'Enjoy yourself. You look wonderful.'

'I'm not used to wearing...' She didn't want to go into detail, but the bones of her gorgeous dress were digging in just a little and she kept reaching for a strap that wasn't there, and wanting to check her cleavage was behaving, but then Khalid made her laugh.

'I too feel awkward,' he told her. 'Usually in New York I wear a suit, not a robe of gold. But it is a national holiday in my country and so it is appropriate that I represent it.'

Naomi doubted he knew what it was to feel awkward, even for a moment, but it was so nice of him to try and put her at ease that Naomi found she did relax and speak more easily. And it was a blessed relief because she did not want to look as if she needed rescuing. The last thing she wanted was to be a drag on Abe tonight.

She certainly wasn't.

Naomi soon recognised the nurse who had brought Jobe down for the photos with Ava on the day she had arrived in New York, and they chatted.

And then a second before the speeches came a lovely surprise.

'I knew you'd look stunning...'

'Felicia!' Naomi's smile was genuine and wide, thrilled to see another familiar face. 'How lovely to see you.'

'It's even lovelier to see you. I wouldn't be here otherwise.'

Naomi frowned but Felicia explained.

'Abe called and said he wanted to surprise you and could I sort out your dress. I told him about the dress you'd liked and he mentioned how much you'd adored the coat. For my efforts, I got invited to the Devereux ball. Cheers!'

'Thank you so much.' Naomi beamed. 'I can't believe you managed to sort out my clothes and get ready yourself all in a day.'

'A day?' Felicia frowned. 'I've—'

But whatever she was about to say would have to wait because the speeches started at that moment.

And there were many, but they were all very thoughtful and emotional, pointing out Jobe's absence tonight and the equipment the funds from the ball had provided for the children's wing of the hospital where Jobe was a patient.

There was a small montage of footage from the ball over the years, and as she looked at the footage Naomi saw a much younger Jobe, dancing with Elizabeth, his late wife.

And as Naomi looked around some of the women were reaching for handkerchieves and there were murmurs of 'how beautiful' she had been.

And she had been, Naomi thought.

On the outside.

Naomi found her gaze falling on Abe. He stood there, his expression unreadable as he looked at the screen, and she wondered about the thoughts behind his impassive facade.

Yet she knew them a little.

That he had told her some of his past felt like a great privilege. That in this room packed with his acquaintances, colleagues and friends there was a shard of him he had shared with her that so few knew.

Oh, their time together was so precious to her that even if it was fleeting, she treasured each second and would never forget this night when she felt so special and a part of this world.

And then came the final speech, and Naomi found she held her breath as Abe took the microphone.

She wanted to capture in her mind his beauty and the way he held the room, she wanted to embed his features so deeply in her brain that when she closed her eyes in the nights and years to come she would remember even the tiny details.

The darkness of his eyes and his exquisite cheek-bones.

And the deepness of his voice.

How he barely smiled as he thanked the room, yet there was no surly note to his tone.

It was just that he rarely smiled.

How he did not waste words as he thanked those present, and he did not repeat all that had been said.

Instead, he shared something new with them all.

'The roses were Jobe's idea. He wanted each woman to have a flower from him tonight. He was aware that some of you will have received roses from him person-ally over the years…' It was a slight allusion to Jobe's philandering tendencies, but it was said in the kind-est way. 'He would like you to accept one more, with his love and thanks.' There was a pause and, Naomi guessed, there might be some women in this room who would be pressing the bloom they held in their hands between pages tonight. She would be, for his was a life to remember, as was this night.

Abe spoke on, and to conclude he said how his fa-ther wished he could be there but, though not present, he had insisted that every detail of the night had been run by him.

'I hope,' he said, 'to make him proud.'

And then he looked over at Naomi, and he met her eyes and he smiled.

It was unexpected, and she felt eyes on her as she returned his rare smile, but then forgot about everyone else. Abe had the skill of making you forget there were even others in the room.

So much so that she almost forgot to clap at the end of the speeches.

And when he came over to her and the music started, it was without embarrassment or thought that she took his hand.

Naomi had never been kissed until Abe.

And she had never danced with anyone until tonight.

As he led her onto the dance floor, she didn't care if it was a duty dance if for one dance in her life she was held by him.

But when he held her, when he pulled her into his arms and his hand took hers while the other held her waist, Naomi knew she lied. As she rested her head on his chest, her eyes drifted to the band, and silently pleaded that this dance never end.

He felt the warmth of her skin through the fabric and his palm resisted the urge to drift a fraction lower.

It was Abe who, for the first time, had to focus on his breathing. Who had to stare beyond the fragrant curls and out into the corporate world and remember his vow to himself to be a perfect gentleman tonight.

Then she moved in his arms and her heavy breasts squashed into his chest, and he recalled them naked against his skin on the night she had denied him.

And she felt her heartbeat quicken at the heat from

his palm and desire took hold and she closed her eyes in an attempt to resist it.

'Naomi?'

'Yes?'

'I'm going to have to do the rounds soon…'

She nodded and reminded herself that this was work to him. 'That's fine,' she said, and pulled her head back and looked up.

A dangerous mistake.

One only ever read about Abe's scandals.

For all the trysts he'd been caught up in there had never been as much as one single public display of affection.

That ended tonight.

His mouth found hers so easily and both took their fill.

And the band must have read her earlier plea for they played on as the whispers chased each other around the room.

Abe Devereux and *that* woman.

Who no one knew by name.

One thing was certain, though, and both tongues and cameras were clicking tonight.

This kiss may have started on the dance floor but it would end in bed.

Tonight.

CHAPTER ELEVEN

I⫟ was Naomi's night of nights and, quite simply, she wished it would never end.

Even when they left the dance floor as Abe had to go and work the room Naomi felt as if she floated from his arms. She spoke with Felicia, with Khalid and even with strangers, and every now and then he would look over, checking that she was okay.

Naomi felt shielded from the whispers and stares that had plagued her since she had walked in, and in that ballroom indeed she was. There was Abe looking out for her, Khalid and, unbeknown to her, Felicia was too.

The night was starting to wind down and couples were starting to leave, the women still clutching their rose. 'I might nip to the loo,' Naomi said, and Felicia frowned. 'The restroom,' she clarified.

'Good idea.' Felicia nodded. 'I might come with you, there'll be a rush on soon.'

But as they picked their way through the ballroom, Felicia turned to the sound of her name.

'Felicia?'

Naomi also turned at the sound of the voice and saw a very handsome man walking towards them, a curious look on his face. 'It *is* you,' he said.

'Leander...'

Naomi watched as the confident and assertive Felicia, stood, looking stunned, but then she attempted to gather herself. 'Leander, this is Naomi.'

'Naomi,' he said.

Except, as he said it, his eyes never left Felicia's face, and Naomi, who had played a part, perhaps more than most, knew it was time to leave.

No matter.

Naomi wasn't one for moving in a pack and was more than capable of going to the restroom alone.

The possibility that Abe might have asked Felicia to keep a close eye on her never even entered her head.

And with good reason.

Naomi, with her new and fragile confidence emerging, truly had no idea of the snake pit lurking beneath the well-dressed tables or the daggers that were being thrown from behind frozen smiles.

She assumed everyone was as happy tonight as she was.

Naomi washed her hands and as she went into her purse for her lipstick she saw the little tin that *didn't* contain mints and her final gift was sorted out.

She *would* be with Abe tonight.

And not hesitantly.

A short-lived affair she could live with far more than she could live a life without it.

Naomi did not need San Cabo, or wherever it was, to be with him, or promises he could never keep to be with him.

She heard the band strike up a Christmas song that had always made her cry.

It wouldn't any more, for it would remind him of this night for ever.

In a few moments it would be Christmas, Naomi thought, and she crammed her *mints* back into her purse, ready to head out there for the chance of one last dance, when she heard her name.

'Naomi?'

Naomi turned and smiled at a petite blonde woman in a stunning high-necked red dress.

'You're Naomi, right?'

'Yes?' There was a question in her voice, wondering if she ought to know the woman, or if they'd been introduced for, yes, she looked a little familiar. And then Naomi found out why. She had seen her in photos, of course.

'I'm Candice,' she confirmed.

'Oh.' Naomi really didn't know what else to say and felt the little colour she had leach from her face and she swallowed nervously.

'Please…' Candice smiled and put out her hand and gave Naomi's arm a reassuring squeeze '…don't feel awkward, I'm very used to all of this.'

Only Naomi *wasn't* reassured and she *did* feel awkward.

'I really ought to get back out there,' Naomi said hurriedly. She knew she was being an utter wimp, but a less than friendly chat with Abe's very recent ex felt uncomfortable, to say the least.

But Candice wasn't letting her go just yet.

'It really is fine.' She gave Naomi another smile, only one that was almost sympathetic. 'I've long accepted Abe's affairs.'

'We're not…' Naomi blew out a breath. She really

didn't know what she and Abe were. It was hardly an affair. And at every level Naomi knew too that whatever they had briefly found couldn't last. She knew too that she was just his plus one tonight. But all she wanted was this perfect night and she didn't want Candice getting in the way of that. 'We're not together, as such,' Naomi said, and made to leave.

'Of course you are,' Candice said. 'Abe was just saying to me this afternoon that he was bringing you tonight.'

That stopped Naomi in her tracks and slowly she turned. 'This afternoon?'

'When he came by our apartment.'

Naomi felt sweat trickling between her breasts. 'I thought the two of you...' She halted herself, refusing to be drawn in, but Candice used her small opening wisely.

'You thought we were finished. Is that what he told you?'

Naomi's jaw gritted.

'I guess Abe would say that, but of course we're not finished.'

Naomi found her fire then, just for a second. 'I know that he pays you...'

It was futile, of course.

'Of course he does.' Candice shrugged. 'Abe likes me to look good *all* the time. In fact, I just signed a contract for another year.' She took out her phone and pulled up a document.

'I don't need to see that.'

'Oh, I'd suggest that you take a good look,' Candice said, 'because you really do seem rather clueless as to how this all works. There's reams of it...'

And there was, and even if she tried not to look, she

saw the Madison Avenue address and, yes, it was all too sordid for her.

Not that Candice had finished marking her territory and warning Naomi off. 'In a nutshell I just accepted his terms again. I'll turn the other cheek and be back by his side in the new year and back in his bed.'

'Abe said that you don't sleep together.' Naomi was trying her hardest to keep it together, and she wasn't being a bitch in her response, more trying to explain she would never be involved with Abe if she thought he was with someone.

'And you believed him when he said that?' Candice let out a tinkle of laughter. 'As I said, I accept his affairs, although I have to say…' she looked down at Naomi's full figure '…he's scraping the barrel right now. Maybe he's having a fat phase. Then again, as my friend just said when she saw the two of you dancing, it's always so much harder to get the vehicle serviced when it's snowing.'

As Candice walked off, Naomi felt sick.

She felt embarrassed.

And guilty too.

Because even if nothing much had happened between herself and Abe, deep down Naomi had been hoping that tonight it would.

She admitted it to herself then.

The pampering and preening had all been in the hope of being made love to tonight by him.

Naomi had even accepted that for Abe it could only ever be a fling.

She had lowered her standards over and over to be met by him, all the way down to a one-night stand, but she would never have agreed to tonight had she known that he was still with Candice.

Naomi gripped the sink and tried to hold in the tears, but they had already started to come.

Big fat tears that took with them the lashings of mascara and slid down her cheeks in oily black streaks, and her nose went from white to red with the speed of a supercar's engine.

And that red nose ran too.

She tried to blot the tears with one of the little fluffy hand towels and she tried to hold in the great shuddering sobs, but they were building and women were coming in, and looking at her sideways. And she thought about what Candice's friend had said, about her size and how it was hard to get serviced when it was snowing, and for Naomi it was just all too much.

They were *all* laughing at her, Naomi was sure.

And she was heaping loathing on herself for daring to dream that things could be different, even for one night.

Naomi walked away from the stares in the restroom to the stares in the gorgeous foyer, crowded with people collecting their coats, and it felt as if they turned *en masse* to look at her.

She could not face collecting her gorgeous coat, and she could not imagine going back into the ballroom to find Abe.

There was no point anyway because at the entrance doors to the ballroom she saw the flash of red of Candice's dress. She was talking to Abe and running a hand along the lapel of his jacket and all Naomi could think in that second was how stunning they looked together.

And she did the only thing instinct told her to, and she fled.

Past the gorgeous people all effortlessly chatting.

And past the doorman, who called her back.

'Do you have a coat, madam…?'

It was like her first day in the city but without all the excitement, without all the hope, because all hope had gone.

She just fled down the stairs and out into the freezing night, losing not just a shoe but her hairstyle too, because her carefully pinned hair all came tumbling down.

And Abe saw her leave.

He had been standing at the doors, shaking hands with a guest while looking out for Naomi, when he'd seen Felicia. 'Where's Naomi?'

'I was just…' Felicia had clearly lost track of her. 'She went to the restroom.'

It was then that he saw Candice making a beeline for him.

She wasn't on the guest list but, of course, he didn't keep the party planners in the loop as to the status of his love life, and this late at night, things must have slacked off. It would seem that Candice had slipped in.

Of course she had. He had been a fool to think she would go quietly.

'Hey.' She smiled and came over.

'What are you doing here, Candice?' he clipped.

'I come every year,' she pointed out. 'Well, I have for the last three. You're looking very smart…' She ran a possessive hand down his jacket and looked right into his eyes.

He should never have attempted to play this nice. The one time he'd tried to the right thing it had backfired spectacularly because as he looked out of the ballroom it was just in time to see Naomi running off.

'What the hell did…?' He didn't even bother asking the rest of the question, he didn't need to hear from Candice what had been said. All he knew was that Naomi was hurting. He pushed past the crowds and the doorman didn't see him coming because he'd gone after Naomi and was retrieving her shoe and trying to call her back, but Naomi had continued to run.

'She's distressed, sir,' he said as Abe approached.

He could see that.

And she was cold.

Freezing, in fact.

And the cars were all a blur as she crossed the road.

'Naomi!' She heard him shouting and she cared not if she was making a scene, she just wanted to get as far away from Abe Devereux as her legs would allow.

Somewhere private where she could cry out loud, as she hadn't been able to on the day she'd first found out what an utter pig he was.

She made it to the edge of the park before he caught up.

'Leave me alone!' she shouted.

'Come back inside.'

'Never! I'm not going back there. They're all—'

'I've booked us a suite,' he interrupted, but his attempt to soothe only served to incense her.

'Was I such a sure thing?'

Of course she was—Naomi knew that.

He reached for her arm but she shook him off. Naomi was trying to remember if she had money in her bag to get a cab, except with one bare foot and bare arms on a freezing night she was struggling to think. The frigid air delivered more than a cold slap. It was like the pain of stubbing her toe, except it ran the length of her body and did not abate, and she wrapped her arms around herself in a futile attempt to get warm.

'Here...' He held out his jacket but she declined it.

'I want nothing from you.'

'So you're going to freeze to death to prove a point?'

And she very possibly might, because her teeth were chattering and her hair was going stiff, and she was no Cinderella as he pushed her down onto a bench and put his jacket round her shoulders and then pushed her less-than-dainty foot into the shoe.

And he was no Prince Charming because he was telling her off.

'You just can't run off in this weather,' he snapped, making sure her foot was in the shoe 'What the hell were you thinking? If you're going to be with me, you'd better get used to being talked about and not always nicely, and not run off crying every time someone makes a disparaging comment about me.'

'With you,' Naomi sobbed. 'I want to be as far away from you as possible, Abe. Did you sign another contract with her, with Candice?'

'Not now,' he said, and stood, but Naomi wanted answers.

'Were you with her today?'

He didn't respond. In fact, he didn't breathe because the air didn't blow white as he declined to comment.

'I'll take that as a yes,' Naomi answered for him. 'Are you *keeping* her for another year? Agh!' She revolted loudly at the end, for she hated that word, and hated that she'd been reduced to asking him, but that was what this man did—he kept women.

'I was trying to be nice.'

'Nice? You wouldn't know nice...' she attempted, but she couldn't get the rest out. Naomi, who would never hurt anyone, had risen to her feet, and the only reason she didn't pummel his chest was because she knew she might end up sobbing on it.

'Let's not do this here,' Abe suggested.

And she should respond, *Let's not do this at all*, as she had the first time he'd broken her heart, but all she wanted was to get back to the house, pull the covers over her head, and for this horrible birthday to be finished with.

For Christmas to be over and done.

To conclude this.

And so she let him lead her, but she threw off his arm and walked alone.

He called his driver to come over and as they waited, she watched all the beautiful people spilling out of the hotel, and heard shouts of *Merry Christmas* as they climbed into the waiting cars.

It certainly wasn't a merry one for her.

Abe said nothing. He just looked ahead, unable to believe how his meticulously planned night had panned out.

Where are we going?' she asked as they sailed past his father's home.

'To my place,' Abe said. 'I don't particularly want your fan club policing this.'

'My fan club?'

'Merida, Ethan, Barb, Bernard... You've got a lot of people in your corner, you know, my father included.'

And while she was grateful to have them, Naomi looked over at the one she wanted more than anyone in the world.

It was a pointless want.

He might as well be a poster on a teenager's bedroom wall or a film star on the screen he was so unattainable, but for a while there she'd let herself think that she might belong, even for a night, in his world.

His world was stunning, Naomi thought as she stared out of the car window. The streets were wider here and the trees were sparkling with fairy lights. There really was a village feel to the shops, with shutters open, revealing gorgeous displays and Christmas wares. Closed cafés that by day would beckon you in for catch-ups and brunch and she could see why Abe loved it here so much.

'We're here.'

They had turned into a gorgeous tree-lined street and the car pulled up outside a huge brownstone house. She climbed out of the car and, rather than hold his arm, she held onto the rail as she climbed the stoop and then stood as he opened the door to his home.

As she stepped inside, it was luxurious, yes, but it was certainly a home.

The hallway was long, with archways, and there was one staircase leading up and one leading down.

'Come through,' he said, but she did not know where so she followed him down the long hallway, the dark wooden floors softened with a Persian rug that her heels sank into. Beyond the hall she could see a large kitchen and she could almost picture him sitting on one of the stools, sipping coffee. Beyond, Naomi glimpsed a softly lit garden, and it was cruel to be in his home, for now she would picture him here for ever.

Abe pushed open a door and as she stepped through it the delicious scent of pine hit her, and even though

t was officially Christmas Day, the sight of a tree gor-
;eously decorated and beneath it presents added an-
•ther layer to his lies.

Naomi stood clutching her bag and shivering in his
acket as he lit the fire. He was drenched from melted
now and his hair was as wet as if he'd just come out
•f the shower.

He'd lit a fire on the night they had met, Naomi re-
alled. It felt such a long time ago. Then she'd sat, at
irst innocent to his charms.

She wasn't now.

He'd snaked into her heart that night, Naomi thought.

So much so that when she'd found out about Candice,
he'd chosen to believe him when he'd said it was over.

Those dark eyes, that kiss had melted her inhibitions
way. She looked at way the shirt clung to his back, re-
•alling her hands sliding over his naked torso as he'd
•rought her to her first orgasm.

And for him she'd broken all her own rules because
he'd been hoping for more tonight.

Instead she stood there dripping wet, and the night
uined, by his fire.

On Christmas morning.

She looked at the ornaments on the mantelpiece, and
he tree in the corner with presents beneath and she un-
•arthed another of his lies. 'I thought you didn't bother
vith Christmas.'

'I don't usually,' Abe said, and with the fire starting
ie stood. Her absolute lack of faith didn't perturb him,
ie got why she had none. 'Naomi, how many times do
have to tell you that Candice and I are through?'

'And I'm supposed to believe you? She told me—'

'Why would you listen to her?' Abe demanded.

'Who else would I listen to? You?' Naomi retorted 'You haven't spoken to me in a week. You couldn't even look at me when I came to your office...'

'I've been cleaning up my life,' Abe said. 'I've been trying to right an awful lot of wrongs. Naomi, I saw Candice this afternoon, yes. And she finally signed a contract that means for another twelve months she can live in the flat, but that's it. I thought I'd sorted it, but I hadn't. I'm sorry for what you went through tonight but the fact is you're going to have to start trusting me.'

'Trusting you?' The man with the reputation, the man who should come with a warning sign attached the man she still wanted, even *now*. 'You!' Her purse clattered to floor as she jabbed a finger into his chest 'I wouldn't trust you if you were the last man...'

Except he was the *first* man.

The first man to really make time for her. The first man she had wanted and her very first love, and she was terrified that he really was her last, because she couldn't envisage ever feeling this way again.

'Naomi...' He took her angry hand that was jabbing at him and gripped it between their bodies. 'I was going to talk to you when we were alone. I'd booked a suite for after the ball.'

His assumption incensed her. 'You were you so sure that I'd come up?'

'Yes,' he shouted, because he had been sure, and more so on the dance floor, and even more so as she went to pull away the hand he was tightly holding, but she took his with it. He could feel the softness of a heavy breast and the rise and fall of her chest and when her hand released his, Abe's remained. His fingers were like ice on her skin but she did not flinch, and he looked right into her eyes as she looked into his face.

'Well, I wouldn't have come,' Naomi insisted, except her voice was all breathless.

'Liar,' he told her, and then proved that she was with his kiss.

It was rough and demanding but, then, so was she, her tongue duelling with his, and she was pushing him away but only to get to the buttons of his damp shirt.

She barely knew herself.

All the hurt was placed on hold as all her anger morphed into the want she had suppressed for so long. For she would give anything to be bold enough, to dare enough to give in to the desire that screamed in her veins.

'You would have,' he insisted between hot kisses, his hands rough and delicious on her body, roaming her curves and pulling her into to his primed body.

'I would have,' she whimpered, as his mouth located her neck and he kissed her deeply there.

Yes, yes, she would have. She didn't need Cabo San... Oh, why couldn't she remember its name? But, yes, she would have gone up to the suite, Naomi knew, recalling the certainty before Candice had ruined their night. And she thought of what was in her purse, and while she still had a shred of common sense she dropped to her knees to retrieve it.

And down on the floor she heard his voice and for a second froze.

'Oh, Naomi...'

There was this gravelly note to his voice, and his hand came to her hair and it took a moment for her to register he wasn't asking why she was down there.

Did Abe really think…?

She was at eye level with his crotch and simply couldn't *not* touch, and she looked at her unfamiliar, manicured hand, so pale against the black of his trousers as she felt him through the fabric. And Abe made it so easy not to think, to just completely misbehave, because his gorgeous long fingers were making light work of his zip and Naomi felt a little dizzy as he undid his trousers, revealing just how turned on he was.

'I was getting protection,' she attempted, except her voice was all thick and she had to clear her throat before continuing, but before she could he spoke.

'I know you were.'

'You know?'

'I saw them in the car…'

And, of course, a man like Abe wouldn't mistake them for a tin of mints.

'The thought of us has been driving me wild all night,' he told her.

And now didn't seem the time to tell him it had been a complete accident because, right now, she didn't want to be anywhere else. She looked at his thick length, darker than the rest of him yet pale against the black of his suit, and it looked both delicious and crude jutting out, yet she felt her heat tighten with the desire and the ache of needing to see more of him, but Abe had other ideas.

'Taste me,' he said.

She could feel him warm at her cheek and the male scent of him was enticing but she told him her truth. 'I don't know how.'

'Try.'

He sounded breathless. He sounded tense, but not

in a way that she'd ever heard, and she pulled back her head and looked up at him.

Oh, this was so not what he'd planned, Abe thought, but in the very nicest of ways.

She must have had too much champagne, Naomi decided, because she kept missing with her mouth, yet she'd only had two glasses.

Then she held him with her hand, and she broached with tentative lips and tasted the tip slowly with her tongue, and his moan was her reward.

His hand came to her cheek and he brushed her hair back and she felt the caresses of his gaze as she kissed down the sides, growing accustomed to the feel of him as he grew to her palm, and then she took him a little way into her mouth.

He tasted soapy and his scent had always driven her wild. His fingers were in her hair, pulling out all the pins that had been so carefully placed there. He was so tall that she was up on her knees, and holding onto his thighs now to steady herself. Abe's hands guided her deeper than she would ever have dared go herself and his ragged breathing brought intense pleasure that had her wanting to sink back on her knees, except she knelt higher and took him deeper. She could feel his restraint, even as he started to thrust.

Naomi could feel her breast spilling out of her gown, and though she'd dreaded it happening all night, it was freeing now.

She felt him swell and his hand push her head down, and it didn't daunt her, it thrilled her, and when he climaxed, the real shock for Naomi was the desire-filled, intimate beats of her own, the pleasure so mutual that it made her feel giddy as she knelt breathless, topless and his.

Always his.

How did he look so immaculate? she wondered as he tucked himself in and, holding out his hand, brought her to stand.

Abe pulled up her dress and tucked her in too, as if he was readying her for church, rather than about to carry her upstairs, but even if she loved him, Naomi did not know this man.

He went and poured two drinks but he drained his in one draught.

'As I said…'

And she frowned as he handed her a drink and then continued the conversation where they'd left it an indecent while ago.

'The press are going to be merciless, and there will be exes selling their stories, but if you're going to be my wife then you're going to have to start trusting me.'

She heard the first bit.

And the last bit.

But there was too much roaring in her ears when she tried to replay the middle.

Did Abe just say she was going to be his wife?

CHAPTER TWELVE

WIFE?' NAOMI CROAKED.

She really couldn't believe what she was hearing.

Even when he retrieved his jacket, which had long since dropped to the floor.

As he went into a pocket and took out a box, Naomi kept waiting for the punchline, for a mocking flash mob to appear, for this to be some sort of terrible, elaborate joke, for she just did not know love.

'Naomi,' he said. 'That came out wrong…'

He was nervous, Naomi realised as he spoke on.

'I had flowers and champagne and everything planned, but as long as you say yes, I wouldn't change a thing. Will you marry me?'

Naomi stared down at an exquisite marquise-cut diamond set in delicate rose gold and could not quite comprehend it.

'So that I'll sleep with you?'

'In part…' He smiled, but it faded when he looked at a woman who had never known love yet would have been brave enough to risk her heart to him, and he took that very seriously indeed. 'Naomi, when you told me that you wouldn't sleep with me until we were married, I didn't take it that well.' He looked at her. 'I didn't tell

Jobe that I was going to ask you to marry me, but
asked for his help to get you to agree to come the ball

'Jobe was in on it?'

Abe nodded. 'I needed his help to get Ethan an
Merida on side. I knew they wouldn't want me takin
you to the ball and, in fairness, I can see why. And
had Khalid looking out for you, and Felicia.' He rolle
his eyes. 'She was so good sorting out your dress tha
I asked her to the ball on the condition she shadow yo
all night. I know how poisonous that lot can be. A fa
lot of good she did.'

Naomi giggled, but then it died in her throat as th
magnitude of it all caught up with her. Abe hadn't bee
ignoring her, instead he had been paving the way fo
her to be in his life. And then he told her why. 'Naom
I'm asking you to marry me because I love you.'

And to hear Abe Devereux saying *I love you* felt a
if molten gold was being poured into her heart, and sh
started to believe this was real.

'Do I have to ask you again?' Abe checked, whe
still she hadn't replied.

'No,' Naomi said, because he did not have to as
her twice. 'I mean yes, oh, yes, Abe, I would love t
marry you.'

'Well, that's all right, then.' He slipped the ring ont
her newly manicured fingers and when she looked dow
she didn't even recognise her own hand, let alone th
world he was inviting her into.

And when she looked up into those black eyes Naom
knew it would take for ever to know him, but they ha
for ever now.

'I love you,' she told him, and, for Naomi, it wa
the ultimate luxury to share those words with anothe

'I know you do.'

'Take me to bed,' Naomi said, and he obliged, taking her by the hand and leading her up the stairs, presumably to paradise.

Except paradise was a lot more like a guest room than the master lair she'd been expecting it to be.

'You've got your own bathroom…' he said.

'Abe?'

'You wanted to wait until we were married,' he pointed out. 'We've come this far…'

'Oh, no! You can't just leave me like this,' Naomi pleaded. She was in love and in lust, turned on and turned inside out by all that had happened tonight.

And a sated Abe was heading off to bed!

'Hell, isn't it?' Abe said as he gave her a light kiss and wished her goodnight.

'Abe, please…' she said, but the door was closed.

His Christmas wish had come true.

Naomi Hamilton in, okay, a guest bed, rather than his own.

But she *was* pleading.

'Happy Christmas.'

Those were the words she woke to on the best Christmas Day yet.

There was snow on the window and there was the sound of carols being sung outside somewhere, and there was a ring on her finger.

No bells on her toes, but she was quite sure, if she asked, Abe would oblige.

Then again? 'Are you still on a sex strike?' Naomi smiled, and stretching luxuriously realised she'd slept in for the first time ever on Christmas morn.

'I am,' he told her. 'You don't have to be, though, I'm more than willing to repeat last night.'

'Two can play at that game,' Naomi said, even if she was blushing to her roots as she said it.

He sat on the bed and he looked at her, all panda-eyed with mascara and smiling as she examined her ring, and at that moment he knew what true happiness was. 'We'd better get married quickly, Miss Hamilton,' he said, squeezing her thigh through the sheet.

'I agree, Mr Devereux.'

She smiled and then he was serious for a tiny moment. 'I meant what I said, if you marry me there will be more to come. If I don't give the press scandal, I don't doubt they'll make it up, or drag in an ex to sell her story. There are going to be a lot of people hoping that this marriage fails...'

'It shan't.'

She said it with such confidence and assertion because she knew it to be true.

The morning, of course, ran away with them. His present to her was a key to the door.

'Your home,' he told her.

And her present to him... Well, Naomi weakened, and suddenly it was edging too close to nine to even think of stopping at his father's for a change of clothes. Abe was all right, of course, but Naomi really had nothing apart from last night's clothes to wear.

'You're going to have to the do the walk of shame,' Abe said.

His driver had Christmas off, so Abe drove them and she looked out at the beautiful streets she was fast coming to love and it dawned on her that this amazing city would be her home.

'I spoke to Barb,' he told her as they drove alongside Central Park on Christmas morning, and Naomi still felt as if she was in a dream. 'I've spoken to all the staff, and they'll all be taken care of. But Barb and Bernard...'

She turned and looked at him.

'They're going to work for me. Us,' he corrected. 'Dad's place is getting too big for her, and I've had renovations done downstairs.'

'The basement?'

'It's stunning. It's got its own entrance and garden—I don't do things by halves...'

No, he didn't.

'But not yet,' he said, 'hopefully not for ages...' Because they all still need Jobe to be here.

'Abe, once I've finished work we can—'

'You're not working for my brother any more.' He glanced over. 'Absolutely not.' And, yes, he was being a snob, but what the hell? 'The only babies you're getting up for from now on are ours.'

'I can't just leave them in the lurch.'

'Oh, please,' he dismissed. 'They can get a proper nanny if they need one, and you can get on with being Ava's aunt.'

'We're here,' he added, before she could argue.

Only how could she possibly argue with that?

He was talking babies already and she had gone from having no one to being a fiancée and soon-to-be aunt...

There wasn't time to dwell on it, though, as they were at the hospital and the press were waiting.

Of course they were, they'd been taking photos on the day his mother had died, so why not now?

Only they weren't just here for Jobe.

They got their shot of Abe Devereux in black jeans

and jumper and the mystery woman in a velvet dress and his jacket from last night.

The same woman he'd been chasing with a shoe he'd retrieved, and who was now wearing a sparkly ring!

'Merry Christmas, Abe,' they called. 'And to the mystery lady…'

Abe made no comment, but then relented. 'Merry Christmas,' he said.

But then the true spirit of Christmas shone, for the cameras went down and their next words were heartfelt. 'Give our very best to Jobe.'

Abe nodded. 'Thanks.'

They walked along the hallway and came to a stony-faced Ethan, who was clearly looking out for them. He was holding tiny Ava, who was wearing a little elf suit and was thankfully sound asleep in her father's arms. 'Where the hell have you two—?' Ethan snarled, and then stopped himself asking the obvious because, still in last night's dress and with slightly tangled hair, it was seemingly clear.

'Go and say hi,' Abe suggested to Naomi, who was thankful to duck into Jobe's room.

'You'll take perfect care of her?' Ethan sneered, as cries of 'Happy Christmas' started up in his father's room. 'The one time I ask you…' And then his voice halted again because there weren't just Christmas greetings being exchanged, there was a cry of delight from Merida, and he heard Jobe actually bark out a cheer.

'Absolutely, I shall be taking perfect care of her,' Abe said to his younger brother. 'Naomi has agreed to become my wife.'

'You and Naomi?' Ethan was sideswiped, sure he'd

heard wrongly, but Abe nodded. 'When did this happen—last night?'

'No, it started on the day this little angel was born,'
Abe said, stroking Ava's cheek, and then he looked at
his brother. 'Would you mind if I borrowed your nanny
on New Year's Eve?' Abe checked. Not only was it the
hardest night of the year to find a babysitter, there was
more bad news to come. 'Oh, and I shan't be returning her.'

It was a *true* family Christmas.

Naomi's first.

And a true family Christmas meant happy bits,
amazing bits and more sadness than you dared to show,
because grief and its journey was the price of love.

But a life well lived garnered wisdom, and there was
plenty still to be shared.

Between the celebrations, congratulations and fes-
tivities was a man they all loved, who watched quietly
as they chatted about the upcoming nuptials that were
now scheduled for New Year's Eve.

Or rather he watched Naomi.

She didn't want a church, and she didn't want anyone other than her and Abe present, even when he suggested they get married here at the hospital.

Ethan would be best man, Ava a flower baby, Merida the matron of honour...

But no.

'We'll get married quietly.' Naomi shook her head
as she smiled. 'Just us, and then we can have a drink
back here.'

And that suited some. It worked for Ethan but...

'Can I speak to Naomi?' Jobe said. 'Alone.'

'Are you kicking us out?' Abe checked.

He was.

'Why no fuss?' he asked when everyone was gone. 'Is it because of me?'

'I don't need a big wedding.' Tears were pooling in her eyes and she did not want to spoil the happiest day of her life, but he had such wise eyes and they had clicked on that very first day, so she told him the truth. 'Jobe, there's no one to give me away.'

'Could I?' Jobe asked, and he looked at the kindest, sweetest woman who had come into their lives and changed them all. 'Because nothing would make me prouder.'

It wasn't such a tiny wedding.

There were an awful lot of nurses and doctors all helping them to achieve this day and there was Bernard in a suit and Barb in a hat and even a sheikh prince, but today he wore a suit.

And as for the bride, she wore white, because she deserved to.

'It's a myth that people with pale skin can't wear white,' Felicia had told her. She had been forgiven for losing Naomi at the ball.

Just as Abe had moaned about the many shades of black, Naomi had, with Felicia's help, pored over whites and found the perfect one. A snow white that was as pure as the love that had saved them, in the softest silk faille.

The dress hugged her curves and silhouetted her fuller figure, and a Bardot neckline revealed her creamy décolletage to perfection.

She wore her dark hair down and it fell in shiny

coils, with only minimal make-up. There was no point in wearing more as she knew she'd cry.

Merida looked gorgeous in a lavender dress and she had taken care of the flowers herself. Purple lilacs for first love, lavender roses for love at first sight, and white heather for protection. 'It also means wishes that come true,' Merida said.

'They're beautiful,' Naomi said, taking her wedding bouquet with shaking hands.

And less than a month after she'd met Abe Devereux, Naomi took the walk to become his wife.

The walk through the hospital was happy one, with smiles and encouragement every step of the way as doctors, patients and relatives alike first stood back to let them pass, and then followed the entourage to steal a peek of this most unexpected wedding.

The music came from a speaker, but was beautiful to all ears as Naomi walked into Jobe's room and saw Abe, standing by his father's bed, smiling *for* her, encouraging her, as he always would.

He wore a charcoal-grey suit, as did Ethan.

Two brothers, who had both known privilege and hell, smiled when the bride arrived, but when he saw she was struggling Abe came over and held out his hand for her to take so he could walk his bride down their makeshift aisle.

It was then Naomi started to cry because, twenty-five years later than most, Naomi found herself loved.

And, thirty-four years later than most, Abe *let* himself be loved.

They kissed before the service.

This backward love they'd found, which was both

instant and savoured and would be confirmed at a time of their choosing.

When her nerves had calmed somewhat, he released her from his embrace and walked her to the bedside, and Naomi found another hand waiting to hold hers.

Jobe.

He was in bed but wearing a silk dressing gown, and pinned to it was a lilac rose. He looked so happy and proud and gave her hand a squeeze.

'You look wonderful,' he told her.

'Thank you,' Naomi said, and squeezed his frail hand back.

'Today,' the officiant said, 'we celebrate the union of Abe and Naomi…' And then she smiled. 'I have to ask if anyone has an objection.'

There were none.

'Who gives this woman to be wedded to this man?'

'I do,' Jobe said in a strong, clear voice that told how much this day meant to him. He gave one more squeeze of her hand, and then let her go to his son and closed his eyes and savoured their vows.

'I will love and protect you,' Abe said, and he meant it with every beat of his heart.

He pushed the ring onto her finger and there could be nothing more valuable to Naomi than that simple band of gold, for she belonged to another at last and in the nicest of ways.

'You may now kiss your bride.'

He cupped her cheeks with his palms and he looked deep into her eyes, and he would not be rushed, for they had waited for this moment, neither having really expected it to arrive.

Bergamot, wood sage, juniper…and another scent

she could not decipher yet it would always and for ever be his.

He kissed her lips and it was hard and *just* thorough enough that she could feel its hum on her lips as she sipped champagne.

And they did not dance and make a fuss because today Jobe was tired, and that was okay, he had given enough...

Naomi to Abe.

'Welcome to the family,' he said as she kissed him goodbye.

And as the stand-in father of the bride he had words for Abe. 'Take care of her.'

'Always.'

Cars tooted as they drove past Central Park and love was in the cold air as they approached the hotel.

Abe led her up the very steps that a few nights ago she had run down, crying.

'Mr and Mrs Devereux...' The door was held open and his grip was tight on her hand as they stepped inside.

The foyer was as beautiful as she remembered. More so, for all the roses on the tree had opened and their fragrance was splendid, only this time she didn't linger.

His hand was in the small of her back and she was terribly conscious of it in the most pleasant of ways.

And he remained the perfect gentleman as the elevator carried them to the top floor.

They stepped into the suite and gold drapes were drawn and the lights were dim and they were finally together, alone.

She was both nervous and shy enough to blush at

his seductive gaze but she tried to be bold and reached
for him.

'I've got this,' Abe said.

He kissed her then, but not her mouth. He kissed th
eyes that had met him at the door on a night when he'
run out of places to hide.

He kissed plump cheeks that blushed so readily an
moved to the shell of an ear that had chosen to listen.

Then he kissed slowly down a neck that enticed an
he felt the little tremble she gave when her nerves lef
and the passion they made arrived.

She was shaking, not visibly, but she tremored insid
to his skilful caress, and when he slid down her dres
and he stood for a moment, just drinking the sight o
her in, she knew why she loved him, for with Abe sh
never had to try and make herself small.

Not physically, they were way past that.

He adored her before he saw her, she knew that.

And she *adored* all she had not seen too.

'I love this,' Naomi said, running her fingers ove
his flat stomach. His chest she had kissed, and then he
hand moved lower.

'Gently,' he warned, when she cupped him to
tightly, but they had fun working that out and then h
took her to near heaven with his mouth.

'Abe…' she was pleading, but in a way she neve
had before. He had teased and cajoled with soft, slov
sucks and a probing tongue that made deliciously sur
she was ready for him.

He moved up her then, kissed her so deeply an
weighted her to the bed.

The first nudge of him had her brave, and the sec
ond had her unsure.

Her nails dug into his shoulders and Naomi didn't feel so brave now, but this was the first and last time he would willingly hurt her. He could hold back no more and tore in and made her his.

She felt every searing inch and there was no space even to draw breath and scream, as for a second it felt as if the lights went out.

Yet darkness never lasted.

With each slow thrust pain peaked, yet her body welcomed him and he drove in until any discomfort dispersed, building toward an intimacy neither had ever known as she released his shoulders and there was no holding back.

They moved beyond pain, and he thrust in deep, and when he felt her tense beneath him, and the grip and throb of her intimate flesh, only then did he give in.

Abe climbed out of bed and she watched as he moved the champagne bucket by their bed, opened the bottle and poured them both a drink.

'Are you going to kick me out again?' he asked, remembering the last bottle of champagne they'd shared in her room.

'Not this time.' Naomi smiled.

He removed the silver cloche and there was a feast of delicacies to sate both appetites, but before coming back to bed he pulled back the drapes.

'There're lights,' Naomi murmured, still high from their lovemaking, but then she realised there must be a party going on in the park.

'It's New Year's Eve,' Abe reminded her.

'So it is.' Naomi smiled, choosing from the delicacies to eat. But then came the very inappropriate buzz of his phone.

'You are *not* checking your phone on our wedding night,' Naomi warned.

Not that he listened.

Abe had planned this night down to the last detail.

'It's for us,' he told her.

'Us?'

Naomi still wasn't used to hearing that, and frowned when she took his phone.

And he watched as that frown was replaced with a smile.

'It's from Merida and Ethan. Happy New Year, Mr and Mrs Devereux, from your brother-in-law, sister-in-law and your still awake niece.'

And he watched as tears filled in her eyes as another pinged in.

Happy New Year. Dad.

This was family.

There were fireworks lighting up a New York sky and she was in bed with her husband, the person she most loved, but there were others out there, loving them too.

'Happy New Year,' Abe said, and he kissed her tears and he kissed her eyes and he held her close enough to hear his heart.

It truly was.

* * * * *